WHAT THE NANNY SAW

WHAT
THE
NANNY
SAW

Fiona Neill

RIVERHEAD BOOKS

a member of Penguin Group (USA) Inc.

New York   2012

RIVERHEAD BOOKS
Published by the Penguin Group

Penguin Group (USA) Inc., 375 Hudson Street, New York, New York 10014, USA • Penguin Group
(Canada), 90 Eglinton Avenue East, Suite 700, Toronto, Ontario M4P 2Y3, Canada (a division of Pearson
Penguin Canada Inc.) • Penguin Books Ltd, 80 Strand, London WC2R 0RL, England • Penguin Ireland,
25 St Stephen's Green, Dublin 2, Ireland (a division of Penguin Books Ltd) • Penguin Group (Australia),
250 Camberwell Road, Camberwell, Victoria 3124, Australia (a division of Pearson Australia Group Pty
Ltd) • Penguin Books India Pvt Ltd, 11 Community Centre, Panchsheel Park, New Delhi–110 017,
India • Penguin Group (NZ), 67 Apollo Drive, Rosedale, North Shore 0632, New Zealand
(a division of Pearson New Zealand Ltd) • Penguin Books (South Africa) (Pty) Ltd,
24 Sturdee Avenue, Rosebank, Johannesburg 2196, South Africa

Penguin Books Ltd, Registered Offices: 80 Strand, London WC2R 0RL, England

Library of Congress Cataloging-in-Publication Data

Neill, Fiona.
What the nanny saw / Fiona Neill.
p.   cm.
ISBN 978-1-59448-716-3
1. Families—England—London—Fiction.   2. Nannies—Fiction.
3. Family secrets—Fiction.   I. Title.
PR6114.E55W47   2012   2012009900
823'.92—dc23

Printed in the United States of America
1   3   5   7   9   10   8   6   4   2

Book design by Lovedog Studio

ALWAYS LEARNING   PEARSON

For John and Mags

It is better to be roughly right than precisely wrong.

—*John Maynard Keynes*

WHAT THE NANNY SAW

PART
ONE

1

July 2008

"When did you first notice something was wrong?"

Ali Sparrow sighed. Everyone asked her the same question. And she was always careful to give the same answer. But somehow she had expected greater originality from Foy Chesterton, a man who had recently sung every verse of "American Pie" at his seventieth-birthday party and organized a signed copy of his self-published autobiography for the three hundred guests as a going-home present. Although, of course, now the happy ending looked a little premature.

Ali had come into the room hoping for solitude and an excuse to examine the objects on the circular mahogany dining table in her own time before the antiques dealer arrived. As had Foy, actually. But by the time she noticed the familiar tousle of wiry gray hair emerging from an armchair by the fireplace it was too late for either of them to retreat without having it look as though they were trying to avoid each other.

"You must have seen things, overheard conversations . . ." His voice trailed off as he peered around the side of the chair to fix her with his blue eyes. "Nannies always have the bird's-eye view, Ali. People forget you're in the room. You melt into the scenery. Like wallpaper. *N'est-ce-pas?*" The tone of his voice was molten, as though every word contained hidden intent. He smoothed down the front of his mustard-colored corduroy trousers with one hand and patted the seat of a stiff upright dining chair with the other, indicating that she should come and sit down beside him.

"You can help us. Help Bryony. She's been good to you, hasn't she? We're all trying to understand what has happened. Nick's act of folly . . ."

"Acts of folly," Ali wanted to correct him. Instead she stared at the chair until its red and green silk stripes started to dance before her eyes. This room had always intimidated her. It was less the imposing furniture, the hard bronze statues by Caffieri that straddled the fireplace, or the armchairs in ghostly colors with feathery fringes around their edges. After more than two years, she was accustomed to its bitonal formality. It was more what went on here. This was the room where everyone was called to account, and she was no exception. She walked toward Foy, aware that her role had imperceptibly altered over the past month and she no longer needed to humor him, but unsure how little she could indulge him.

Ali was vaguely aware of him looking down at her bare feet. Apart from Foy, no one wore shoes in the drawing room unless there was a party. It was one of Bryony's rules. Ali enjoyed the way the pile was so thick you could feel it like grass between your toes and trace your tracks back across the room. But there was something vulnerable about bare feet, especially when the rest of your body was covered and you were standing before someone who had an innate ability to make you feel exposed. Instinctively, she curled her toes into the pile, but it was too late. He had already absorbed the gold ring on her index toe and the small tattoo across the instep.

"It's just decorative," said Ali, anticipating his next question. "Like wallpaper." She remained standing, knowing that if she sat down she might never get up. The urge to unburden herself might prove irresistible, and then she would write herself out of her role in this drama. Besides, she was due to meet Felix Naylor in less than two hours for what he described as a "preliminary chat," and he had given her firm instructions to talk to no one but him because no one else could be trusted.

"Stellar trajectory. PPE at Oxford, Harvard MBA, analyst, associate, vice president, director, M.D. by thirty-five. Visionary investment banker," muttered Foy, picking out phrases from the newspaper and arguing with himself. "Well, he didn't see this one coming, did he?"

Ali ignored him.

"So when did you?" Foy persisted. He started to close the newspaper in his lap. It was *The Guardian.* He folded it in half, smoothed the surface so many times that the palm of his hand blackened, and then into quarters, as though engaged in an origami project. Until the scandal broke two weeks ago, Ali had never seen Foy read a paper that wasn't *The Telegraph*, and she tried to think of an appropriate witticism to highlight this unlikely change of political allegiance. Even now, shattered as he was by events of the past couple of weeks, Foy was still someone people liked to please. Then Ali saw he was reading another story about Bryony and Nick, and decided to change tack.

"Nothing ever feels quite right when you move in with someone else's family," Ali responded, pleased to note that the nervousness she betrayed the first time someone had posed the question had been replaced by something approaching quiet confidence.

It was her first line of defense and as close to the truth as she dared go for the moment. She half turned toward Foy and began rattling off a few carefully inconsequential examples that best illustrated her outsider status at 97 Holland Park Crescent, hoping it would distract him from what was surely another blistering piece about his daughter and son-in-law. What was the point in reading everything that was written about them? Ali wondered. It didn't change anything. It just made everyone feel even gloomier.

"The dog still growls at me when I come into the room, I'm the only one without a nickname, and people sound disappointed when I answer the phone," she said, muddling up her list of responses so they sounded less rehearsed. Over the past couple of weeks she had discovered that the most persistent inquisitor, even Bryony's younger sister, Hester, was generally satisfied by a variation on this response.

"Come on, Ali, you can do better than that," said Foy wearily. It was one of his stock phrases. One of the few he used in English—*"Alea jacta est"* and *"Carpe diem"* being his firm favorites. Although it struck Ali that the idea that the die was cast was totally at odds with the concept of seizing the day. Especially now. This brought to mind an even more appropriate and as yet untapped example of Ali's outsider status: The expressions invented by Foy and adopted by his extended family when they wanted to pass comment on people without anyone else understanding what they meant. Chesteranto, he called it.

Nick, for example, was currently assumed to be "at forties and fifties." This was code for depression, although "depressed" seemed an understatement for what Nick must be going through. It didn't sound monumental enough; Bryony was constantly "in the breakers," snapping at anyone who crossed her path at the wrong moment; and seventeen-year-old Izzy described a journalist who buttonholed Ali at the end of the road the other day as "menacing," which meant he was dangerously attractive. Ali had never used any of these expressions. Neither had Nick, which seemed significant now. Although through the prism of the scandal, everything seemed imbued with significance.

"I know you feel more at home here than anywhere you have ever lived," said Foy, noisily folding the newspaper into an even smaller shape, as though this might somehow diminish the contents of the story on the inside page. He was trying to ensnare her in conversation. Still, Ali winced at the incontrovertible truth of this statement. She hadn't wanted to become one of those employees who live their life through someone else's family. She'd seen enough examples of that in the time she had worked here. They attracted that kind. But moving in with the Skinners was like relocating to an exotic country and finding the prospect of going back to live in your own impossible.

Life was simply more exciting with them than without them. Especially now.

Ali winced mostly because Foy's comment was a guilty reminder that she hadn't returned any calls from her parents for more than a week. There were six saved messages on her mobile phone that needed dealing with. Four from them. One from Felix Naylor and one from Mira, a Ukrainian nanny friend.

For the first time since she had moved in, her parents had left a couple on the Skinners' answering machine. Bryony dutifully played both to her yesterday. They were sandwiched between a bland message from one of Bryony's colleagues hoping she was weathering the storm and wondering what to tell her clients and a more urgent request to call Sophia Wilbraham, a parent at the children's school who lived just down the road. The same Sophia Wilbraham, Ali recalled, who came home after her travel plans were canceled, to find her husband in bed with their nanny of five years. At the time, it seemed there could be no greater scandal than that.

Ali's messages were banal by comparison. The first and most embarrassing was from her mother, asking whether she was all right and suggesting she might like to come home for a while until things had blown over. It wasn't the note of anxiety in her mother's voice that annoyed Ali, it was the treachery implicit in the idea that she would leave the Skinners just when they needed her most. The second, from her father, said calmly that they didn't believe everything they read in the papers, and it would be nice to hear Ali's version of events. As he said good-bye, her mother interrupted to say that the neighbors were asking questions that she couldn't answer.

"Sounds hideous," Bryony said, raising an eyebrow. "You'd better phone them. Before the alliums bow their heads in shame."

Naturalistic planting schemes hadn't reached Cromer, Ali had wanted to point out. It was still all sweet peas and nasturtiums. But she wasn't even sure that Bryony recognized this description of her own carefully landscaped garden. Instead she had tried to reassure

Bryony that their neighbors in Cromer were the kind of people who thought it was rude to hang their underwear to dry on the washing line and the idea that they were pressing her parents for details was ludicrous. Bryony, however, had stopped listening.

"Ali, you're ignoring me," Foy whined. She was suddenly aware that he was speaking to her again. She resolved to call her parents that evening, knowing that by then her good intentions would inevitably be eclipsed by further drama today. Bryony's colleague was wrong to describe this crisis as a storm. A storm had a beginning and an end. A storm passed. This was something you couldn't shelter from, and although Ali could see how it might have begun, she had no idea how it would end.

"What I'm trying to say is that you fit in," Foy said benevolently. "In a way that none of the others did." He pointed at Ali with a pair of scissors for emphasis and then unfolded *The Guardian* and began cutting out the story. Since the crisis, Foy spent most of the day in the drawing room at Holland Park Crescent, going through newspapers and trawling the Internet for pieces about Nick and Bryony. He consumed everything he could on the banking crisis and the credit crunch. Ali didn't have the heart to point out to him that a fat package of photocopied stories arrived from a press-cuttings agency every morning and was read by Bryony almost as soon as it landed on the doormat at six-thirty.

He smiled warmly up at her. It was a rare occurrence these days. Foy was diminished by events. His eyes were watery with regret. They looked for sympathy but mostly found none. Tita, his wife of forty-nine years, seemed to blame him for what had happened. His youngest daughter, Hester, appeared a couple of times a week and was overly solicitous, fetching him cushions and making him unwanted cups of tea. It was her way of silently highlighting the fact that Bryony, the child she perceived as her father's favorite, not only had finally come unstuck but also was in some way precipitating his decline.

"Don't try and flatter me into submission." Ali smiled despite herself.

"So you do know more than you're revealing," said Foy.

"Save the analysis for later," said Ali, quoting back one of Foy's favorite phrases to him.

"There might not be any later for me," said Foy, only half joking. "My body is giving up on me."

"Don't be so maudlin," said Ali.

"Do you know that last night I had a dream that I was young again?" Foy said. "It's the first time that's happened for years. I think it's a sign I'm about to pop it."

He dropped the newspaper cutting onto a pile on the floor, inhaled deeply, and carefully put a hand on each armrest. He splayed his fingers as wide as they could go and dug them into the expensive upholstery to gain purchase. Then he tried to push himself up out of the chair. His arms trembled with the effort, and for a few seconds his hips hovered above the seat. Within seconds he slumped back down, looking forlorn.

"Damn legs," he muttered.

Ali turned away from him toward the table, knowing that he wouldn't want her to see the humiliation in his eyes. She heard him grunt as he tried to catch his breath.

"I was at a party and all my friends were there," Foy wheezed, ignoring what had just occurred. "They had aged, but I looked exactly as I did in my early thirties. People kept coming up to me and telling me how well I looked. Julian Peterson, do you remember him? He's Bryony's godfather. He told me in great detail about all his problems with his prostate and how he had to get up four or five times in the night to pee but his stream was reduced to a trickle. He said the doctor was the first person to stick his finger up his arse in twenty-five years."

"I can't imagine Mr. Peterson speaking like that," said Ali in disbelief. She recalled the polite, quiet man who came for lunch at the family home in Corfu at least a couple of times in the summer.

"Well, it was a dream," acknowledged Foy, grateful at last to have Ali's full attention. "I couldn't believe it, either, because he's only marginally less buttoned up than Eleanor, and they've been married for fifty years and I just couldn't imagine her doing that to him."

"Absolutely," agreed Ali, wondering whether bemusement or shock was the quickest way of derailing this unexpected outburst.

"Then I realized it was all just an excuse to overwhelm me with his superior medical knowledge," continued Foy. "He started talking about partial prostatectomy and how the doctor stuck a resectoscope up his penis."

"But Mr. Peterson isn't a doctor, is he?" asked Ali.

"Quite right," agreed Foy. "He was deputy director general of the BBC. But Julian always likes to remind me of his superior intellect and the fact that I never went to university."

"Does he?" said Ali, reminded of her own lack of qualifications.

"Then he said that it had made him impotent," said Foy. "And I felt this huge sense of gratification, a tsunami of satisfaction, pour over my body. Because it's the loss of desire that makes you feel old, not the fact that you can't remember someone's name, and I felt at that moment as though I had won a significant battle."

"So what did you say then?" asked Ali.

"I walked off, because I had seen Eleanor on the other side of the room," explained Foy dreamily. "From behind. She looked gorgeous. Her back was bare. She was wearing a lemon-colored dress that I hadn't seen for half a century, one of those fifties numbers with a wide skirt. I ran my fingers down her back and felt her lean toward me. She had a young person's back, if you know what I mean. Her skin tone was even, there were no loose folds or ugly moles. I whispered in her ear that we should go upstairs and get away from all these old fogies."

"Gosh," said Ali.

"We had a thing for a couple of years when we were on holiday together. Ages ago," Foy explained quickly, hoping to preempt any further interruptions. He didn't wait for Ali to register any response, assuming correctly that his philandering was widely known. "But when she turned round, her face was old and wizened like everyone else in the room apart from me. I realized that having propositioned her, I was going to have to go through with it."

He stopped for a moment, and Ali realized he was trying to get out of the chair again. He closed his eyes to focus his energy, took a deep breath, and then pushed down again on the armrests. This time he succeeded and began slowly to shuffle toward the table, where Ali was standing.

"What do you think?" he asked.

"So did you?" asked Ali. "Did you go through with it?"

"What do you think it all means?" asked Foy.

"I think Nick's therapist would have something to say about it all." Ali smiled tentatively. This was not the kind of conversation she could have ever imagined having with Bryony's father. But the rules of engagement had evolved beyond recognition since that first visit two weeks ago from Felix Naylor, warning Bryony that there were rumors about Nick sweeping the City. There was something about disasters that made people reveal more of themselves than they might have thought prudent in normal circumstances.

"Ha," said Foy triumphantly. "Ha, ha! I knew I'd learn something significant from you. The question is, does Bryony know?" Ali immediately realized her mistake and held up her arms in defeat.

"He saw her a couple of times at most," she said reluctantly, trying to calculate how much information would satisfy Foy and what exactly he could do with it. "Toward the end, when everything had started to unravel. I don't think Bryony knew."

"Why was he seeing a therapist?" asked Foy.

"Lots of people see therapists," Ali said with a shrug. "Especially rich people. One of Bryony's friends even took her therapist skiing last year. She couldn't manage a week without him."

"Not investment bankers," muttered Foy. "Especially not one of the rainmakers." He had now edged his way forward until he was standing right next to Ali. She could see a small patch of gray bristles on the side of his face that his razor had missed. It reminded Ali of a shave you might get in the hospital or in an old people's home. It made him look old and vulnerable. His rib cage rose and fell a little too quickly as he struggled to catch his breath now that he was standing. Ali realized that his sense of victory had been quickly eclipsed by doubts over how this piece of information could be used in Bryony's favor. "Nick is a significant figure. It would be seen as a sign of weakness. His judgment would have been called into question. There's no place for emotional incontinence in the boardroom. It's all about appearing confident. You don't want to hand millions of pounds over to a weak-minded ditherer."

"He didn't know that I knew," Ali lied.

"A spy within our midst?" questioned Foy.

"Someone else told me," said Ali.

"A friend?" Foy pressed for more details.

"Something like that," conceded Ali.

"I can't believe Nick was seeing a shrink." Foy shook his head in disbelief. "He was always so vociferously opposed to anything alternative. God, he wouldn't even drink herbal tea in case people thought it made him look soft."

"Was the story of your dream true?" asked Ali. Foy nodded.

"What happened next?" Ali asked.

"I woke up because I needed to pee," Foy said, and laughed. "Then the phone rang, and it was Julian telling me that there was nothing he could do to help me control the stories coming out about Nick and Bryony. He said he didn't know anyone in management at the BBC, even though his son works there, and that the best thing we can do is to batten down the hatches and hope something bad happens in Afghanistan to take us off the front pages. So it was another night of insomnia."

They stood in companionable silence and surveyed the scene on the table before them. It reminded Ali of an elaborate tombola. Except that there was nothing random about any of the items, and instead of cheap soaps in pastel colors and bubble bath that made your skin go red, there was expensive-looking jewelry and silverware that Ali had never seen before. There was a diamond teardrop-shaped pin with a handwritten label attached that said "Cartier, 1920s," and a Franck Muller watch.

"Quite a spread," said Foy, frowning. "It will keep the wolves from the door, at least. They've frozen their bank accounts. Did Bryony tell you?"

"I read it in the paper," said Ali.

"They've got to live off three hundred fifty pounds a week." Foy snorted.

It was, Ali agreed, a ludicrous proposition. She noticed that Foy's forehead had developed an intricate network of horizontal and vertical lines. It was a hard-fought battle between anger and self-pity, thought Ali, before turning her attention to the table again. A thin shard of sunlight seeped through the window and highlighted a gold bangle with two green enamel frogs on either end. The frogs had emerald eyes and tiny diamond warts encrusted on their backs. Beside them sat a pair of matching earrings. Ali was puzzled. Bryony would never wear something so gaudy, and Nick was too cautious to buy something so exotic for his wife without her blessing. Not that *cautious* was an adjective many people would attach to Nick Skinner right now.

Ali glanced over at the windows to check that the curtains were closed. Then she picked up the bracelet and closed it around her wrist, running a finger across the diamond warts. It made her shiver in the same way that it did when the twins ground their teeth at night or Izzy picked at the skin around her fingernails until it bled. She held the bracelet up to the light and slowly turned her wrist from one side to another, wondering when anyone would wear something so ugly.

"Take it, Ali. You deserve it," Foy said gruffly. Ali wondered what he was talking about and then realized that she had wandered to the other side of the table with the bracelet still on her wrist. "I got it for Bryony when she got engaged, but she never wore it. It's a David Webb animal suite. The sort of thing that was popular in the seventies. I thought the frog was a good symbol of my first success persuading a British supermarket to stock smoked salmon." Ali looked confused.

"Well, it's an aquatic animal," Foy continued, misinterpreting Ali's silence. "If they'd done a diamond-encrusted salmon I would have bought that. It was symbolic." He didn't understand. It was the ego-centricity of the present that amazed her, the fact that even at the beginning of Nick and Bryony's relationship it had been all about him rather than them.

"It's probably worth about fifteen thousand pounds, and I can't see how you'll get paid for the next six months. Take it in lieu of salary," Foy insisted, "or as a wedding present when you finally get hitched."

"I don't have a boyfriend," Ali said primly.

"You don't have a boyfriend?" repeated Foy in mock horror.

"The job wasn't conducive to relationships," Ali explained, noting that she was talking about it in the past tense, "and the bracelet isn't really yours to give away."

"I bought it," said Foy petulantly.

"It was a present," Ali insisted.

"That's the problem with you, Ali," Foy said, and sighed. "You're incorruptible."

"What are you trying to give away, Dad?" Bryony had come into the room. She was breaking her own rules and padding across the car-pet in a pair of Ugg boots, leaving a thin trail of mud that would insinuate itself into the thick pile. Her hair was pulled off her face and tied into a rough ponytail at her nape. A few strands had already escaped. She had a kind of bruised beauty. Anxiety had taken away Bryony's appetite, and she had lost weight. Her green eyes over-whelmed her face. Her jeans and cashmere sweater hung off her frame. Without makeup she looked even more fragile. It was difficult to be-lieve she was forty-six years old.

Bryony was no longer wearing work clothes, although she still got up earlier than anyone else to check her e-mails and pound the tread-mill before sitting down to breakfast with her children. She stressed to Ali the importance of sticking to routines, pointing out that throughout World War II, Winston Churchill rose at exactly the same time every morning, had the same breakfast, and read the newspapers in the same order before disappearing into his bunker.

"I'm concerning myself with Ali's welfare in case she gets lost between the cracks," said Foy. Ali immediately removed the bracelet and placed it carefully beside the earrings. "Why don't you sell this table?"

Bryony didn't answer.

"You should sell this table," said Foy more insistently. "It's a Jupe, isn't it? It must be worth something."

"Nick bought it for our tenth wedding anniversary," said Bryony, protectively patting its shiny surface. "There's only a couple this size in Europe."

"I don't think you'll be a popular dinner party destination for the next couple of years," said Foy. "If you sold this table you could free up enough cash to pay the mortgage for the next six months, and then you'd have one less thing to worry about."

"Stop interfering, Dad," said Bryony

"I'm just trying to be practical," said Foy, turning round to calculate the distance that now stood between him and the armchair.

"The table stays," said Bryony firmly. "I want to keep it for when Nick comes home."

"What about the mirrors?" He pointed to a pair of eighteenth-century Italian silver gilt mirrors that hung on either side of the fireplace. "You'd get a good price for those."

There had been heated debate the previous evening about the table, although it was its location, not its value, that was up for discussion. Bryony had suggested that it was essential the antiques dealer view the objects under natural daylight, and it should therefore be shifted to the other side of the room, parallel to the floor-to-ceiling windows that looked out onto Holland Park Crescent.

Her sister Hester vehemently argued against moving it closer to the prying lenses of the photographers who periodically congregated with their stepladders on the other side of the crescent. Even such a minor change could provide them with a useful new angle for their story, especially if their telephoto lenses could pick out exactly what was on the table. They had all waited for her to finish. Hester's point of view might have sounded more coherent, but it wasn't necessarily completely objective. In the following breath she told everyone that the problem with owning the biggest house on one of the most expensive streets in London, apart from the obvious public relations problem that it now presented, was that its location at the center of the arc of the crescent provided fantastic breadth of vision for photographers.

"Of course, if you were a teacher and lived in my street in Stoke Newington, it would all be much easier," Hester had said, venting one of her longer-term resentments.

"If I was a teacher in Stoke Newington, there wouldn't be photographers outside the house," said Bryony dryly. Foy had laughed, signaling victory to Bryony.

"What do you think, Ali?" Foy had asked. One of the few merits of the current crisis was that people sought Ali's opinion. At the outset she assumed this was a tactic to ensure that she didn't run out on them like Malea, the Philippine housekeeper who read the runes and defected on day three to a family from the twins' school. Then she thought it was because she was an impartial observer to the crisis being played out before her and that her opinion was valuable. It was only yesterday after the argument over the table that she realized that her presence meant they could avoid discussion about the one subject really worth debating. Was what the papers were saying about Nick true?

After a few minutes Ali had concurred with Bryony. Not because it was easier—disagreeing with Hester was far more difficult—but because it was right. She pointed out that most of the snatch shots were taken by photographers after midday, when the sun no longer blinded their vision. Then she offered to make absolutely sure that the curtains were kept closed, to prevent anyone from seeing what was going to take place in the dining room the following morning.

This meant primarily preventing the seven-year-old twins, Hector and Alfie, from opening the curtains. Since the scandal had broken two weeks earlier, the twins had longed to be photographed so that their picture would appear in the paper and they could show their friends at school how famous they had become. Ali didn't have the heart to tell them that it was a futile exercise because they probably wouldn't be going back to their school in Kensington in September and they had dropped to the bottom division in the playdate league.

Foy, on the other hand, actively encouraged their plan. He helped them draw up elaborate strategies for sneaking into the dining room and hiding under furniture until the room was empty and they could stand in full view of the windows. He bought them World War II Commando comic strips and showed them *The Great Escape* for inspiration. He encouraged them to stockpile supplies around the house.

So Ali would find rotting apple cores and biscuit wrappers underneath the walnut tallboy and empty cartons of orange juice stuffed down the sides of chairs. Bryony didn't care. Beyond meetings with an interior decorator when a room needed overhauling, Bryony never had more than a functional interest in her surroundings. And although Ali played the role of the enemy in the twins' game, she was more like a double agent, because it cheered her to see them happily distracted from the crisis. It compensated for the fact that most nights they crept into her bed at the top of the house, and some mornings she woke up to find the sheets sopping wet.

The two older children were more complicated. Initially, Izzy's phone had buzzed with interest. Her excitement at being the center of attention had rapidly diminished as she absorbed the implications of what was happening around her. Quite often Ali would find her sitting at the kitchen table, reading newspaper stories about her parents. She soon stopped returning text messages. Ali encouraged her to go out and meet friends, but Izzy dreaded running the gauntlet of photographers outside the front door, in case they took a picture of her.

Jake was a different proposition. Since he had come home from university, he came and went as he pleased. Apart from Ali, no one seemed to notice what he was up to. He had stopped referring to his father from the moment the first stories appeared in the newspaper. Once, as she was getting up with the twins, she had bumped into Jake coming up the stairs on his way to bed. He was standing unsteadily in the middle of the landing.

"He did it, Ali," Jake said, gripping her arm so tightly that she could see the blood drain where his fingers were wound round her wrist. Ali peeled his hand away.

"We don't know anything for sure," she tried to reassure him.

"He was never honest," Jake insisted. "You know that."

"He was always good to me," said Ali.

"You're as deluded as the rest of them," whispered Jake.

How would she keep the twins occupied today? Ali wondered. She needed to get them out of the house. The next-door neighbors had initially seemed willing to allow them safe passage over the garden fence, through their basement, and out the front door, where they could escape incognito to Holland Park. But a few days ago the ladder mysteriously disappeared from their side of the fence.

Bryony now suspected the Darkes were behind an anonymous neighborhood flyer that had appeared through letterboxes this week, demanding the Skinners retreat with their "media circus" to their country home. The idea that she could control the press had made Bryony laugh. "Clients pay me hundreds of thousands of pounds to do just that," she had told Ali yesterday, "and I have known some of the people writing these stories for almost twenty years. But I can't control what they say about my own family. Don't you think that's ironic?" Ali didn't have the heart to point out that even after a year of renovations, the house in Oxfordshire was still unfit to live in.

"Ali, any ideas on how they got hold of this?" Ali was aware that Bryony was talking to her again. She jumped as Bryony slid a newspaper across the table toward her. It landed on the floor.

"You should complain. Your picture credit is so small you can hardly read your name," she said. Ali picked up the paper from the floor. It took her a moment to recognize the photograph, because she had taken the original in color and this was reprinted in black-and-white: it was of the entire family in Corfu during the summer.

"Absolutely no idea," Ali said. She looked over toward a table to the left of the dining room door and saw a space where the picture used to stand.

"Someone must have stolen it," said Foy, shrugging his shoulders in disbelief. "This is my Conrad Black moment"—he laughed so hard that he started to wheeze—"except I'm dressed as a Greek peasant woman, not Cardinal Richelieu."

The picture was part of an elaborate joke conceived by Foy after a long lunch one afternoon during their summer holiday in Greece. He had recently purchased a twenty-acre olive grove adjacent to his estate in Corfu to celebrate his retirement, joking that he was becoming a gentleman farmer. The olive trees produced enough oil for about a hundred one-liter bottles, and Foy wanted to have a photograph of everyone dressed up as a Corfiote peasant family to print on the label on the front because it would amuse his friends.

At the time it had seemed an inspired idea. He had borrowed a long black skirt, apron, and scarf from the Greek cook. Ali persuaded the twins to dress up in traditional Greek costume, no small feat, given this involved short pleated skirts and long white tights. The rest of them wore black trousers and shirts.

Foy had one arm around Tita, who stood unsmilingly beside him, and the other around Hester. Her husband, Rick, was nowhere to be seen. The twins sat at their feet, holding a jar that contained a couple of dead crickets. At the end of the line, beside Jake and Izzy, stood Bryony and Nick. Nick was pulling Bryony toward him, away from the rest of her family, toward a couple of chickens that had wandered into the scene. Poor Nick, thought Ali. He never stood a chance. Beside the photograph was a picture of a bottle of Foy's olive oil. And beside that a photo of Foy's boat, *The Menace*, moored at the rocky beach at the foot of the estate.

"Classic Chesterton Family Extra-Virgin Olive Oil," the label on the bottle read. Underneath, in smaller lettering, it said: "Superior-category olive oil, obtained directly from olives and solely by mechanical means. Acidity 0.1–0.8%."

"With all this publicity I could sell the olive oil on eBay for a fortune, don't you think, Ali?" Foy demanded. "Our current notoriety probably lends it a certain cachet."

"Stop worrying about money, Dad," Bryony chastised. "Nick will take care of it all."

"If what they're saying about him is true, then he could go to prison," said Foy.

"He's got a good lawyer," said Bryony, "and the FSA has a bad track record on prosecutions. Don't believe everything you read."

"If he didn't do it, then why has he done this disappearing act?" asked Foy.

"He's not in his right mind," said Bryony, fixing Foy with a steely gaze that made her look just like her father. "And he thinks that they'll go away if he's not around."

Her hand pointed toward the window and the other side of Holland Park Crescent, where the posse of journalists and paparazzi congregated almost every morning.

"When did you last hear from him?" Foy asked.

"A couple of days ago," replied Bryony vaguely.

"Do you know where he is?" Foy asked. Bryony shrugged her shoulders.

"His disappearance has become the story," said Foy, echoing exactly what Ali was thinking.

"I want to listen to the news," said Bryony, ignoring her father. She switched on a television that had been brought into the dining room from the kitchen after Malea had left. Bloomberg News immediately appeared on screen. A business reporter who had come to their last Christmas party was talking about the bank where Nick worked. Bryony and Foy moved closer to the screen. Bryony turned up the volume, warning Foy and Ali to stay quiet.

"Liquidity crisis . . . Shares slump twelve percent . . . jittery investors . . . exposure to subprime . . ." Ali had overheard enough conversations under the Skinners' roof over the past year to know none of this was good and that somehow it related to Nick.

"What's she talking about?" Foy questioned Bryony, pointing at the television screen.

"There's rumors that PIMCO has stopped trading with Lehman's," Bryony said.

"Who?" said Foy.

"The world's biggest bond company won't touch Lehman's," said Bryony flatly.

"What does it mean?" Foy asked.

"It means they're fucked," said Bryony.

Ali moved closer to Bryony and Foy. This was surely the moment where the glassy-eyed reporter would finally reveal to them exactly what Nick was meant to have done. But by the time Ali reached Foy's elbow the reporter had moved on to talk about some improbably named American mortgage companies that were running out of capital. Freddie Mac and Fannie Mae. They sound like a couple of porn stars, thought Ali.

"This could be good," said Foy hopefully. "It could divert attention from Nick."

"Or put him in the eye of the storm," said Bryony. "Remember, he still works for Lehman's."

"Did you know the word 'credit' comes from the Latin for 'to believe'?" Foy suddenly said. "I wonder if Nick knew that."

2

Felix Naylor was waiting at a table in the corner of the café. He was early, which Ali saw as a sign of aggression rather than politeness. He wanted to get the upper hand. He looked up as Ali approached and gave a quick smile, putting his newspaper down on the floor and pulling out the seat beside him. There was music playing. Noah and the Whale.

The café was full of students. It was a good choice, thought Ali. She knew from experience that there was no more self-absorbed group than a bunch of undergraduates. No one would have any interest in them. And with his T-shirt, jeans, and artfully scruffy hair, Felix blended in with everyone else in a way that would have been impossible for someone like Nick.

Ali sat down and glanced around her. The person opposite was examining a text message and asking his friend whether the fact the girl had signed off with a couple of kisses meant more than if she had used just one. And was it significant that the kisses were in uppercase. The friend was indifferent. He didn't want to get involved in a plotline that had obviously been discussed too many times before.

At the next table a couple were earnestly discussing whether Robinson Crusoe was a symbol of individualism that led to the rise of capitalism. "Did you know that in his book of travels around Britain,

Daniel Defoe wrote about how two hundred ships sailing from Great Yarmouth sank in the Devil's Mouth?" she wanted to ask. "And that Robinson Crusoe was wrecked off the coast of East Anglia on his first voyage? It could have been his inspiration."

A couple of years earlier she would have unself-consciously joined in this discussion. Now it felt incredible that she could ever have been part of it. She put out a hand on the table to steady herself, grateful for the heavy oak surface that spoke of steadiness and longevity, both attributes missing in her own life at the moment.

It was difficult leaving the house, because as long as she was inside, Ali felt there were incontrovertible truths about her life. She was both loved and in love. She was indispensable. She was witness to an event of historic importance, or at least she was unwittingly immersed in a news story that had captured the national mood. And yet as soon as she set foot outside the front door this was replaced by a sense of vertiginous uncertainty, because she could just walk away from it all and no one would follow her or even notice her absence.

"Did anyone tail you?" Felix asked, sensing her agitation but mistaking its cause.

"I'm just the loyal nanny," Ali said, and shrugged. "They're not really interested in me." Then, as an afterthought, she added, "Thankfully," in case it sounded as though she was resentful about the lack of attention. In fact, an enterprising tabloid reporter had walked down the street with her, pressing her for information about what was going on behind the closed doors of Holland Park Crescent. But she had followed Bryony's instructions and kept her head down and her mouth shut, and eventually he had given up.

Felix hadn't said anything on the phone about why he wanted to see her. Ali assumed his agenda was self-serving. He was a journalist. She was a source. She even suspected that he might have been responsible for removing the photograph that had appeared in today's paper. She had read enough tabloids over the past month to know that anyone associated with the Skinners was potentially corruptible.

The personal trainer who had come to the house every day for the past two years had sold a story about Bryony's beauty and health rituals, including quarterly coffee enemas and chemical peels. Malea had been interviewed in a piece about the life and style of bankers' wives that failed to mention that Bryony had a successful career of her own. Instead it focused on the weekly deliveries from Net-a-Porter, the decorator who arrived each month to paint over finger marks on the walls coated in un-child-friendly shades of off-white, and the fact that Bryony had spent more than a thousand pounds in the Portland Hospital on a photograph album of the twins just after they were born. Thankfully the unnamed live-in nanny who acted as the children's tutor warranted just a sentence at the end.

Then there was a feature in a weekend magazine that quoted "a family friend" describing the Skinners as "an accident waiting to happen." All families were an accident waiting to happen, Ali had thought, as she skim-read the piece. There were insinuating anecdotes about parties attended by Jake and Izzy where there was underage sex and conspicuous drug consumption. There was a photo of Izzy at her thinnest, and yet again the one of Jake smoking dope in the garden of his Oxford college. The alleged "family friend" also suggested that Nick had an eye for younger women. In the next sentence it mentioned how one of his closest friends had an affair with the twenty-seven-year-old nanny who looked after his children. Foy was described as a "party animal," which was a euphemism for a multitude of sins.

"How's Bryony?" Felix inquired.

"She's okay."

"And the children?"

"It's obviously difficult, but they are fine."

"You know that Bryony is an old friend of mine?"

"I know that you went out with her before she met Nick." A waitress came over and brought Ali a cup of tea.

"I introduced her to Nick."

"I think I knew that."

"I want to talk with you openly, Ali," said Felix, looking serious. "I'm not for sale."

"What do you think I want from you?"

"I think you want to pump me for information that you can use to sell more copies of your newspaper," said Ali. "I think you want to use your relationship with the Skinners to further your own interests and make a fast buck along the way. Or you're going to try to persuade me to sell my side of the story to the highest bidder."

"I'm not Max Clifford," Felix protested, stirring his own tea so vigorously that it slopped over the side into the saucer and splattered the front of his T-shirt. He didn't seem to notice. "I don't do those kind of stories. I cover financial news, the economy, business, the stock market. I work for a broadsheet, not a tabloid."

"It was your newspaper that had the photograph of them dressed up in Greek costumes that I took in Corfu," said Ali accusingly. "You're all the same."

"I didn't steal that photograph," said Felix. "Lots of newspapers had it."

"Then how do you know it's missing?" Ali accused him.

"Because Bryony told me," he said. "Look, I know it's difficult to know who to trust at the moment, and I'm not asking you to trust me. What I want to know is if I can trust you."

Ali looked up and frowned at him. He had one of those perennially youthful faces where it looked as though a toddler had etched in the wrinkles as a jokey afterthought. His cheeks were ruddy, alcohol rather than fresh air, Ali thought, and he had an almost girlish bow mouth the same shade as his cheeks. His face was embarrassingly open, as though he retained a childlike innocence that made it impossible to conceive of him doing anything duplicitous. It was as if he had been designed to be as unthreatening as possible. As someone used to being the keeper of other people's secrets, Ali recognized a kindred spirit.

"This isn't a ploy. I'm not that complicated. If I was more Machiavellian I might have ended up marrying Bryony," he said, reading her mind. "It's because I still care about her that I've asked you to meet me."

"I'm not sure how I can help."

"Do you understand what is going on? Do you understand the nature of the accusations against Nick?"

"I think he's been accused of corruption and his finances are being investigated by the Financial Services Authority, and it all has something to do with what's going on with all those banks at the moment."

"A good summary." He paused. "Do you know that there are all sorts of rumors about Bryony and Nick swirling around London? There are people digging around for stories. Looking for corpses."

"What sort of stories?"

"They're trying to build a picture of how all this could have happened. Do you have any theories? What could have led a man to make such a catastrophic series of judgments that were so contrary to his essentially cautious nature? Did you notice anything was wrong? Did he seem imbalanced in any way?" Ali rested her elbow on the table, hand on chin, adopting her most thoughtful pose.

"Nothing ever feels quite right when you move in with someone else's family," she began. Felix put up his hand.

"That sounds like a well-rehearsed response. If you can't give me more than that, then I might as well leave now. Do you understand how serious this all is?"

"Look, sometimes you think things are odd for the wrong reasons. What I mean is that your instincts are right but your conclusions are wrong. Also, you have to remember that I come from a very different world, so the things that I found strange might be perfectly logical to someone from their background."

"I want to be completely candid with you, Ali, because you are the only person in a position to help here." The furrows in Felix's face deepened until he looked so anxious that Ali thought he might be about to cry.

"What's wrong?" Ali asked.

"They're saying that Nick wasn't acting alone."

He stared at her intently, and Ali realized that he was looking for answers to his question in her expression.

"What do you mean?"

"The initial investigation has thrown up some interesting leads suggesting that Bryony must have been involved, too. Nick had access to information that only Bryony could have known. Do you understand what this means?"

"Not really."

"It means that Bryony will become a suspect. If she is found guilty then she could also go to prison." He leaned forward and gripped her arm. "I don't believe she would have done anything so reckless."

"I'm not sure how I can help."

"Tell me everything, Ali. Tell me everything that you observed living with the Skinners. Even details that you think might be insignificant. I'll try and piece it together, and perhaps even if Nick goes down, then Bryony at least will be saved. We can meet up a couple of times a week and you can give me your side of the story." He paused again to allow her to absorb his request. "There's one other thing that you should know. There are people suggesting that you and Nick were involved. That you clouded his judgment, that she helped him as a last-ditch attempt to salvage their marriage."

Ali opened her mouth to speak, but it was as though his words had winded her. She moved her lips, but no noise came out.

"You don't need to justify yourself to me. I just want you to know that you need to watch out. You're no longer seen as the innocent bystander. You're fair game, and I'm one of the few people who can protect you."

He got out a notebook and a tape recorder from his pocket.

"Shall we start now?"

3

········
········

August 2006

The job was advertised in the back of *The Spectator*. Hidden among
the classifieds. Discreet typeface. Possibly Times New Roman. No
elaborate borders.

> Modern-day Mary Poppins required to take care of needs of
> busy professional London family. Must have university degree.
> Clean driving license. Desire to travel. Experience working
> with children desirable. Loyalty, discretion essential.

Ali Sparrow sat at the dining room table of the Skinners' London
home, rereading a photocopy of the advertisement that Bryony had
left there, trying to find meaning in the order of the list of requisites.
As she read, she twisted her hair into knots, preoccupied that there
might be hidden clues she might have missed. She shifted awkwardly,
crossing and uncrossing her legs, aware that the gray wool skirt she
had borrowed for the interview from her much shorter flatmate was
riding toward her thighs, causing the backs of her legs to stick uncomfortably to the leather surface of the chair. Trying to imagine what
attributes the Skinners didn't want in a nanny, she pulled the hem
back down to her knees, glanced down at her black shirt, and did up
the top button. "No bunny boilers. No cleavage. No anorexics."

She pulled a mirror out of her canvas handbag and checked her face. She had dyed her hair chestnut a couple of days earlier, and she hardly recognized herself. Her eyebrows now looked too pale by comparison. She licked a finger and smoothed them down in an effort to darken them a couple of shades. Dying your hair before an interview might make you look as though you had something to hide, Ali decided. In general, however, she liked what she saw. The hair matched her almond-shaped brown eyes and contrasted well with her windburned skin.

She thought of her friends' advice late last night as they shared a cheap bottle of wine around the table of their flat in the center of Norwich. Rosa was still trying to persuade her to join Sugar Daddies. She had shown Ali the website, hoping to convince her that sleeping with a successful middle-aged man for £500 every couple of months was somehow less demeaning than working as a nanny.

"Sometimes they just want to take you out to dinner," Rosa said. "Of course, they're old enough to be your father, but generally they're generous and kind. If you don't find them attractive, you don't have to go through with it. You're in total control of the situation."

They had a fierce, wine-fueled argument about whether selling your body for sex was an acceptable postfeminist solution to the problem of tuition fees. Rosa, who had dated two men the previous year, believed it was.

"One day we'll be those forty-something women who are married to these men," Ali had said. "Imagine if you discovered your dad on that website."

"It's a simple transaction," said Rosa.

"It's a form of prostitution," said Ali. For a moment Rosa looked taken aback.

"Well, just turn down the job if the father seems remotely leery," said Rosa cheerfully.

Maia, ever pragmatic, said to make sure there was a cleaning lady, otherwise Ali would end up scrubbing toilets as well as looking after four children. Tom suggested that she look ambivalent, whatever salary they offered her. Rosa, whose family used to have money, then advised that she should avoid falling in love with her employer and talked about nannies developing Stockholm syndrome and being unable to leave even the most awful families. Although she didn't expand, it was obvious that she was talking about her own, because their nanny still lived with them. At two o'clock in the morning Ali told them resolutely that she was going to bed, because she had to be in London for her interview in eight hours' time.

Ali considered the wording of the advertisement again. The university degree and driving license were common professional qualifications, of course. Boxes that could be either ticked or left blank. The rest was what really mattered. But was there any significance in the fact that discretion was mentioned last, when it was obviously a more important characteristic than the desire to travel? Weren't loyalty and discretion the same thing, anyway? Why didn't they ask for a non-smoker? She patted her pocket and felt the comforting bulk of a packet of Silk Cut. And why Mary Poppins and not Jane Eyre?

Actually, none of it really mattered, because Ali fell at the first fence: she hadn't graduated from university. Yet. Although surely if that was a deal breaker, she wouldn't have got through the first two rounds of interviews. She could see a letter to that effect tucked in a transparent plastic folder marked "Ali Sparrow No 5." It sat on top of a pile of papers beside the briefcase that Bryony had left open when she got up from the table two minutes after the interview started to take a phone call, mouthing, "Sorry, I've got to sort this out," as she backed out of the room.

"The journalist got the valuation right, so I'm not sure that Merrill Lynch has got much recourse," Bryony had said into the phone. "What I'm less clear about is who gave the numbers to Felix Naylor. You know how leaky Goldman's is."

As she reached the door, Bryony glanced between Ali and the open briefcase, making a quick assessment of Ali's trustworthiness. Then she closed the door firmly after her. "I'll call Felix and try and damp it down. He can quote me as a source familiar with the situation."

All very cloak-and-dagger. Ali was flattered rather than insulted that Bryony wanted her out of earshot. It made her feel significant. As though she really might overhear something of importance and actually understand what she was talking about. Privacy was an alien concept to students, thought Ali. The only time she left a room for a phone call was if her parents called about her sister, because even though the news was always the same (Jo had either left home or come back again), Ali's mother didn't want anyone to overhear their conversation.

Ali was intrigued by the way Bryony's whole demeanor had changed as she answered the phone. She stoc̣   ̣able, pulled back her shoulders several times, and j   ̣̣ ̣her chin as though trying to shed a layer of skin, all the time speaking. Her pale skin didn't color, and her wavy hair bobbed compliantly. "Listen to me carefully," she said quietly into the phone, "I'll give him something better on one of my Russians and he might agree to drop it." Her eyes narrowed slightly, making her lids look heavy, and she pursed her lips. Ali admired the way she gracefully backed out of the door in her expensive-looking high-heeled shoes. This was the first time that she had met a woman who wielded so much power.

It occurred to Ali that she had never asked the woman who conducted the first two interviews exactly what the Skinners did. She sensed it would be a mark against her, but such was her ambivalence about the job that she hadn't really been interested. Now it was apparent that not only Bryony's husband but also Bryony had a significant career, and that fact somehow inflated the importance of the job. She wouldn't be playing under-mummy for a spoiled City wife, as one of her friends had suggested, she would be the linchpin of the family, helping support the career of one of those women whom Ali usually encountered only on the pages of glossy magazines. For the first time since she had sent her CV and letter of application to the concierge agency charged with searching for a new nanny for the Skinners, Ali decided she actually might want the job.

Glancing around the empty room, she impulsively leaned over the table, carefully lifted the plastic folder from the briefcase, and began reading its contents. It might give her some advantage over the competition. She didn't know whether to be gratified or alarmed by the wodge of carefully stapled papers inside. Ali found it surprising that there was so much to say about her.

The first document was a letter on headed paper from her tutor at the University of East Anglia English department, confirming that Ali was taking a year out "to secure her financial situation" and would then, he hoped, be returning to complete her degree. Professor Will MacDonald had testified to her good character, underlining the fact that she was a model student who produced work of a consistently high standard. Other phrases caught her eye. She was "willing to please," "loyal and adaptable," "motivated," and "methodical and articulate." He mentioned that Ali was the babysitter of choice for his three children and that he and his wife were very fond of her. Ali stopped reading at this point. His words made her want to cry. It was mawkish and self-indulgent reading a character reference, because of course the person you asked to write it was going to be kind.

Instead she turned to the copy of her driving license attached to this letter. It was spotless. Testament to the fact that she had barely been behind the wheel of a car since she passed her test a couple of years earlier. Living in Norwich, there was no need to drive anywhere, and her parents had only one car, which they didn't like to lend out in case there was any trouble with Jo.

Beneath that was a three-page letter from the concierge agency retained by the Skinners for a hefty monthly fee to resolve any administrative issues ranging from contracting a new nanny to sourcing tickets for a sold-out Coldplay concert. It was signed by the woman who had conducted the first two interviews with Ali. It mentioned that a criminal check had come up clear and that although she was in debt, a £5,000 overdraft had been approved by the bank where her account was held in Cromer. Her debt was related to living expenses as a student. Her biggest expenditures, apart from her rent on the three-bedroom house she shared with friends in an insalubrious area of Norwich, were cigarettes and clothes from Topshop. She had never defaulted on her rent or utility bills.

Ali momentarily wondered how they had gathered this information, because surely it was confidential. But she was gripped by the account of her background that followed in the next document. It was the first time she had seen her life laid bare. The detail on the first page was fairly innocuous. It covered her education at local schools. It mentioned that she had been chosen for the gifted and talented program at primary school, was in the top class at secondary school, and had been a responsible and motivated student despite her older sister's problems. Because of her older sister's problems, Ali corrected the notes. There was even a photocopy of her last school report.

It then gave a brief picture of her parents. Her father was a fisherman and her mother worked part-time at the council. It mentioned the A-level results that had won her a place at the University of East Anglia. Then there was a brief, cold description of Cromer: "A small town whose depressed economy is dependent on seasonal tourism and the crab industry. At one time Cromer had the highest rate of registered heroin addicts in East Anglia. It used to be a fashionable destination for Victorian travelers."

Outrageous, thought Ali. How could they describe Cromer without mentioning the sea? She was affronted. It was as though they had missed a crucial part of her personality. Her parents' house on the front was so close to the water that during a storm the spray would lash against her bedroom window. This defined her more than any school report. At night she would sometimes open her window to listen to the voice of the sea, trying to gauge its mood, without being able to see its surface. In a storm it was always angry, but occasionally the anger was tempered with a mournful wail that made her feel almost sorry for its lack of self-control. In the summer, it sometimes turned a luminous turquoise color. People were tempted into its embrace, and most were released. But every August someone, usually an intrepid child, was dragged out into the waters by the fierce crosscurrents.

Cromer might be a backwater, but Ali was certain its rhythms were controlled by primitive higher forces. Ali's father made his peace with the sea through rituals and routines, listening to the forecast a couple of times a day, and learning to adapt to changes in wind direction like someone who switches effortlessly between two languages. But Ali never fully trusted the melodic tones of those who read the shipping forecast, nor the irrational store her father set by his self-imposed set of rules. On a clear day, from her bedroom window Ali could see as far as the lost village of Shipton, consumed by the water two hundred years earlier.

For Ali the sea was a beguiling friend who could never quite be trusted. Much like the Skinners, as it would transpire. But at that moment, waiting in their dining room, Ali couldn't know this. And if she had, would it have made any difference? So she kept reading and licked the skin around her mouth, missing the taste of salt on her tongue. She remembered learning at school that salt is as essential to human beings as water, and feeling as though that was as close as she was ever going to get to anything approaching a belief system.

It said there was no mention of Ali or her parents in any local newspapers apart from an article that appeared in the *Eastern Daily Press* ten years ago, when her father caught a six-pound crab. To Ali's embarrassment there was a color photocopy of this piece, with her father dressed in his yellow fisherman's trousers, holding the crab. It even mentioned that a distant relative in Great Yarmouth had invented these trousers. Ali had her father's smile, everyone told her. But this was the first time that she could see it herself. "A life without consequence," she said out loud as she skimmed down the page reading notes about herself.

Unlike the people who lived here. Ali had stood outside the house in disbelief when she arrived. It was an imposing Regency-style building with stucco moldings and a glass portico that stretched from the wrought-iron gate at the end of the front path up the eight steps to the front door. Because it stood in the center of the concave arc of the crescent and was the only double-fronted building on the street, it appeared as though the other houses were leaning deferentially toward it. Everything here spoke of consequence, from the blue plaque on the façade announcing that a famous scientist had once lived under this roof, to the Francis Bacon hanging above the fireplace.

A self-important pile of newspapers sat at the opposite end of the dining room table. The headlines were all about yesterday's foiled plot to blow up planes on transatlantic flights. Ali smiled as she remembered her mother phoning to suggest it was too dangerous to live in London.

Ali heard a noise outside the dining room and quickly turned to the next page in the plastic file. Her time was surely running out. It must have been at least ten minutes since Bryony had left the room. This bit was easier to absorb because whole sentences were highlighted in yellow pen. The first said that Ali had recently finished a relationship with another student. Someone had put an exclamation mark beside this point. The second said that Ali had an older sister with "mental-health issues." Beside this, in tiny black writing, someone had written "interesting!" She stood up abruptly and angrily put the file back where she had found it. She was incensed, less by the fact that they had unearthed all this information about her than the casual use of exclamation marks.

Ali stood up and smoothed down her short dark hair and the skirt. She would leave the house without anyone noticing and call the woman at the concierge agency to let her know that something else had come up. As she pulled on her jacket and headed swiftly toward the dining room door, she heard a low guttural growl.

"Come on, show your face," she said. The growling stopped, and Ali stepped decisively toward the door again, but as she touched the handle, the dog started up again. This time it gave a single bark. It stood up, and Ali could see it was a small, sandy-colored pug. Its teeth were bared and its hackles raised. It wasn't the sort of dog that Ali would have matched to Bryony. She would have suited something smooth-coated and long-legged.

"You're all talk," said Ali, stretching out her hand toward its collar to find out its name and then abruptly pulling away as the pug lurched toward her and snapped at her fingers. She stepped back and the dog reverted to growling. Ali decided to wait a moment for the pug to calm down and then make her escape.

On a delicate half-moon table on the other side of the door she found a pile of hardcover books, one written by a former cabinet minister. She looked inside it and saw that there was a handwritten dedication from the author to his "very dear friends, Nick and Bryony Skinner." If they were such dear friends, then why did he bother with their surname? Behind these was an orderly battalion of photos. There is a direct relationship between people's wealth and the number of photos they display of themselves in their home, thought Ali. And generally, the more professional-looking the photos, the more dysfunctional the household. That's what Rosa always said, anyway. These pictures were all encased in expensive-looking silver frames.

Center stage was a large photograph of a group of eight people gathered around a dinner table in the middle of a meal. The cutlery was still two rows deep, and there was an equal number of wineglasses. There were no women. Ali guessed the middle-aged man tipping his untouched glass of champagne toward the photographer was Nick Skinner. He stared at the camera with a benevolent smile as though bestowing the photographer with an enormous favor. His other arm was crossed tightly over his chest, making his pose a curious juxtaposition of freedom and restraint. He had the air of someone who was accustomed to such attention.

The man on his right was gripping his forearm. Ali recognized this face but couldn't put a name to it. When she took up residence a month later, one of the children told her that it was someone very important from the Bank of England, and asked if Ali agreed that he looked like a character from *The Wind in the Willows*. For the moment Ali turned her attention back to Nick. His teeth were unnaturally white, she thought, but perhaps it was the contrast with the black dinner jacket. He had dark hair, cut short, sleek as an otter. For a middle-aged man, he was still in good shape. Ali observed the full glass of wine and half-eaten plate of food in front of him and the empty glasses and plates in front of his fellow diners. He was someone who watched what he ate and drank, and felt irritated if he glanced down at another man's stomach and compared it unfavorably with his own.

Beside this was a wedding photo. Ali immediately recognized Bryony. She was engulfed by the two physically imposing men on either side of her. The taller one was Nick. The other, Ali guessed, was her father. Each had an arm around Bryony, but she somehow seemed separate from them both, as though she was stepping away from them toward the camera. Bryony was wearing the kind of wedding dress that Ali would choose if she ever got married. Handmade by Vera Wang, she would soon discover. On the end, slightly apart from the group, was a disheveled figure with wild, dark hair, tipping a glass of champagne toward the camera. He was an impostor, decided Ali. Later she discovered from the children that his name was Felix Naylor and he had once been in love with Bryony. "Still in love," Izzy corrected the twins.

The door suddenly opened, and Ali was unnerved to find herself still holding the wedding photo and staring at an older version of Nick Skinner. His hairline had receded and there were a few wrinkles around his eyes, but otherwise he was unchanged. These changes were good, decided Ali, because they bestowed a gravitas that wasn't present in the wedding photo.

"God, I've missed the interview, haven't I?" he said, holding out a hand, and delivering a winning smile. "Bryony will kill me."

It was said in a way that suggested that Bryony was probably so used to such shortcomings that she would barely flinch. Ali clumsily put the photograph back on the table and tried to explain, as she awkwardly shook hands, that the dog wouldn't let her leave the room.

"Leicester was an anniversary present from Bryony's parents," he said, scratching the dog between the ears. "He most definitely wasn't on our wish list. He's so inbred that he's developed a sort of canine dementia that means he lets people in the house but won't let them leave. Really he should be dead."

"Is there anything you can do?" Ali politely inquired.

"Well, I suppose we could accelerate the inevitable," said Nick, curling his fingers into a gun shape and pulling the trigger at Leicester's head. "We should have done it years ago, but Bryony said it would send the wrong message to her father."

"I meant for the psychological problems," Ali stammered.

"You're not going to believe this, but actually, a couple of years ago, Leicester did have his very own head shrinker." Nick laughed. Ali echoed him with a nervous laugh of her own.

"It was one of Bryony's wilder ideas. Leicester had developed a very scatological response to situations that he couldn't control. He was seen by an animal psychologist for almost a year. He went to the canine equivalent of The Priory for three months and came out completely cured," explained Nick, as though relieved to find something to talk about. "Although he's been on antianxiety drugs and a special diet ever since."

"What did he do?" Ali asked.

"Every time Bryony's father came to visit, he mounted a dirty protest," Nick said, and laughed. "There was some suspicion by the dog psychologist that I'd trained him to do this. But no evidence was ever uncovered to substantiate those claims." He laughed again. "He was particularly fond of shitting in my father-in-law's shoes. The more expensive, the better."

"Why did he do it?" Ali asked, her curiosity overcoming her reticence.

"The therapist blamed it on us," said Nick, "as his parents. He even wanted us to do family therapy with the dog. That's when we opted for residential care."

Ali half wondered whether he would be having this conversation

with her if he didn't know about her sister's history. She quickly decided she was being paranoid and that Nick Skinner was simply trying
to put her at ease.

"It looks like a beautiful wedding," Ali spluttered, pointing at the
photograph she had just put down.

"We got married in Greece," Nick explained. "Bryony's father
bought a house in Corfu years ago. We go every summer. Have you
been to Greece?"

"No," said Ali.

"Well, you will when you start the job," said Nick. Then he fell
silent, as though unsure what to do next. "How did the interview
go?"

"It hasn't really happened yet," said Ali.

"I read your file," said Nick awkwardly. "Very impressive. Did
Bryony tell you what we're looking for?"

"We didn't really get that far," said Ali. He signaled toward the
table, and Ali followed him back. She noticed that her cigarettes had
fallen on the floor beside her chair.

"I'm a smoker," confessed Ali.

"So is Bryony," Nick said, smiling, "but she won't admit it to you.
She thinks that I don't know." He sat down opposite her, removed
his tie, and opened up the top two buttons of his shirt. Then he slowly
turned his head to each side a couple of times to stretch his neck.
There was something vulnerable about seeing him slowly expose himself in this way. The clavicle where the shoulder bones met just
below his throat, a fine down of chest hair, and the remnants of a summer tan slowly revealed themselves to her. Ali was used to boys in
T-shirts and jeans. Her tutor at university occasionally wore a shirt but
never a tie.

"You don't mind, do you?" Nick asked when he realized Ali was
staring at him. Ali felt herself flush with embarrassment.

"I thought I should de-suit to look less formal," said Nick good-
naturedly. "But I'll put the tie back on if it's too unnerving."

She was relieved when Bryony came back into the room and

seemed unsurprised to find Nick sitting at the table opposite Ali. She shook her BlackBerry triumphantly in the air.

"Good news?" Nick inquired.

"Nothing I can talk about," said Bryony firmly. "Let's just say I've done a good trade. Closed down one story, and they've taken the bait on another about a Russian oligarch who's on the lookout for a football team. You must be a lucky charm, Ali Sparrow." Bryony smiled warmly. She was carrying a plate of scrambled eggs that Ali assumed qualified as breakfast, but instead of heading back to the table she put them down beside the dog.

"He loves the way Malea cooks them," she said, ruffling the dog's fur. "Leicester is one of life's true eccentrics. Do you like dogs? We just assume that people will fall for him immediately."

"Mostly," said Ali, as Leicester jumped down from his silk throne and, with one eye still on Ali, consumed the scrambled eggs.

Bryony sat down beside Nick. She pulled out a couple of hair ties, and her fox-red hair fell around her face, semi-obscuring her dark, brooding husband. Ali half shut her eyes. It was like looking at the sun coming out from behind a cloud. Bryony glanced down at her watch, a gesture that convinced Ali that she was going through with the rest of the interview only out of politeness. Then her phone rang again. This time Bryony ignored the call. Instead she rapidly began to describe their four children.

"Jake is almost eighteen. He's in his last year at Westminster. He's lazy. But with the right attention he could do very well. He needs to be pushed." She made a fist with her hand to underline this point. "He's strong-willed and articulate, so we need someone capable of organizing him. More stick than carrot, if you know what I mean." Ali didn't. She did a quick calculation in her head and worked out she was only four years older than Jake. She was about to point out that this might inhibit her authority over him, but Bryony had already moved on to his younger sister, Izzy.

"Even though she's three years younger, Izzy is very focused," she said with approval. "She'll ask you to test her on stuff and let you know if she needs help, but she's fairly self-disciplined. You need to watch the biscuits. She's at that age where you don't want to lay down any excess fat. She's a very talented cellist, and you'll need to help encourage a good schedule for practice. She needs an hour a day. She plays in a quartet at school." Bryony paused to catch her breath, and Nick smiled encouragingly at Ali from the other side of the table. He showed little inclination to add anything to the conversation.

"The twins are five. They've spent a lot of time with each other, and I want to try and encourage them to live life a little more separately. They're identical and a bit too codependent. They'll be going to school five days a week from September. You'll need to take them, pick them up, and then get them to all their activities. You'll organize playdates, help them refine their pencil grip, and monitor piano practice."

"Their pencil grip?" Ali repeated inanely.

"Handwriting, spelling, that sort of stuff," said Bryony, waving her hand as if to bat away the question. She leaned forward toward Ali. "I believe that every moment of the day represents a learning opportunity for them. When you're in the car, put on Radio Four or Classic FM, read quality literature to them at night, write any words they don't understand on the blackboard in their bedroom. And I'd like you to do twenty minutes of maths with each of them every evening. It's essential to maintain a regular schedule."

Bryony continued to talk about the twins without referring to them by name. She said that they had developed a tendency to start and finish each other's sentences, that they were obsessed with Thomas the Tank Engine in a non-autistic way, and that they showed some skill on the football pitch. She wanted them to develop their own friendships and go separately to friends' houses.

The objectivity of Bryony's appraisal struck Ali. She tried to imagine her own mother giving such a detached assessment of her own children.

"Jo has a low threshold for boredom and sometimes self-medicates with drugs, which causes severe mood swings. Jo has a very short-term approach to life, which makes it difficult for her to plan for the future. Jo is a risk taker who finds it difficult to accept the consequences of her actions. There is an inverse correlation between Jo's behavior and that of her younger sister, Ali. Ali has suffered from the disproportionate amount of attention paid to Jo. Ali feels an excessive sense of responsibility toward her sister and would benefit from a period of separation from her family, to find herself."

Her mother would never be capable of such dispassionate analysis. She would get bogged down in anecdote or diverted by the swell of emotion that now accompanied most conversations about Jo.

Bryony's version of motherhood appealed to Ali because it was less emotive. Bryony represented the possibility of having children without totally losing yourself in the process. It was not a version that was familiar to Ali.

"I can see that you got eleven GCSEs and top grades in your A-levels," said Bryony, pushing a piece of paper toward Nick, who glanced down the page and gave an appreciative whistle of approval. "So you'd obviously be able to help the children with schoolwork. We both work long hours, so this is a priority."

"Absolutely," said Ali.

"Latin?" questioned Bryony. Ali nodded.

"Apart from babysitting, do you have any experience with children?" Bryony asked.

Ali started to explain how, as part of a program to reduce teenage pregnancy, girls at her school had all been given a fake baby to look after for a day. The doll was programmed to cry if it wasn't fed or its nappy wasn't regularly changed. She had proven to be totally responsible.

"What about the other girls in your class?" asked Nick.

"One of them dropped the doll off the end of the pier by mistake, and another was already pregnant and it made her lactate," said Ali, pleased to find a verb that was suitably scientific.

Nick and Bryony stared at her in silence for a moment. "We're not familiar with this program," Nick said finally, and smiled. Bryony looked nonplussed.

"We'd also expect you to help organize our domestic life for us," Bryony said, trying to pull the interview back to familiar territory. "Anything from birthday parties to collecting dry cleaning, getting the car serviced, and buying clothes for the children. Would you be happy to do that?"

"Sure," said Ali enthusiastically.

"Do you have any questions for us?" Bryony suddenly asked. Ali muttered something about driving in London being a very different prospect from driving in Cromer.

"You can use Addison Lee," said Bryony.

"Is he your chauffeur?" Ali asked. Nick and Bryony laughed, and Ali felt herself blush again.

"It's the name of a taxi company," Nick explained. "We have an account with them."

This was what she remembered of the interview years later. There were no questions about how to recognize the symptoms of meningitis or what to do if a child was choking. Both were questions Rosa said her mother always asked a new nanny.

Instead there had been more talk about Ali's ability to schedule the lives of four children and of the hours she would be expected to work. She compared it to revision timetables for exams and they reveled again in her academic qualifications. The Skinners liked the facts that she would be able to help the children with schoolwork and that she was a strong swimmer. They agreed that it was unfortunate that she didn't ski, but then neither did three of the other applicants for the job. Ali pointed out that cooking might be a problem, and they explained that they had a Philippine housekeeper, Malea, who took care of most of the meals and cleaned the house. Nick had joked that she seemed to be talking herself out of a job. Ali responded by saying that she wouldn't be able to commit to spending more than twelve months with them. There was more laughter as Ali unwittingly proved their point.

Then they said that if she agreed to an extra six months they would pay her a bonus worth two terms of tuition fees. It would mean that Ali wouldn't return to her course the following academic year, but she didn't hesitate as she agreed to their terms. It was just eighteen months of her life, Ali argued.

"Is there anything more you want to know about me?" Ali asked. She thought of a recent discussion with Rosa about how everyone had three significant events that defined their character for better or worse. Rosa cited her mother's alcoholism, the way she moved school every four years because her father was in the forces, and how her younger sister had stolen her boyfriend.

"I am a good person who has done a bad thing. I once helped my sister score heroin. I don't inhale," Ali had told Rosa. These three had come to mind straight away and then just as quickly been forgotten.

"Obviously you'll have to sign a confidentiality agreement. And we would like you to agree to cancel your Facebook account. We are a family that values its privacy," said Bryony. "Is that a problem?"

"Not at all," said Ali, ignoring their invasion of her privacy.

"And if you have a boyfriend, we'd prefer you to stay with him," said Bryony.

"I don't have a boyfriend," said Ali firmly.

"Then I think that we've covered all the ground," said Bryony, efficiently organizing papers until the file that said "Nanny No. 6" was on the top of the pile. "How many families are you choosing between?"

"Sorry?" said Ali in confusion.

"How many other interviews are you doing?"

Ali was unsure what to say. She glanced from Bryony to Nick and saw that he was holding up three fingers away from his wife's field of vision.

"Er, three," said Ali.

"Your room would be on the fifth floor, across the landing from the twins and round the corner from Izzy," Bryony said. "It's got a wonderful view over the garden, and there's a small kitchenette and sitting room. The only downside is that you don't have an en suite. I hope this isn't a big problem."

"Not at all," said Ali, who didn't want to tell them she had never had her own bathroom.

"And we have a busy social life," said Bryony, looking up from her list. "So you'd sometimes need to be around in the evenings to help look after the children. We used to have a weekend nanny, but it's too disruptive, so we're looking for someone who can do everything."

"Great," said Ali.

4

. . . .
. . . .

September 2006

"Olio Chesterton," Foy Chesterton called out in a singsong voice as though he was manning a market stall. "First press. Extra-virgin. Get Malea to use it to make a *stifado*." He stood on the bottom step of the stairs that led from the raised ground floor down into the kitchen on the lower ground floor until he was certain that everyone was looking at him, and then triumphantly removed a bottle of murky liquid from a beach basket.

Improbably for London in September, Foy was wearing a pair of muddy-brown shorts, a perfectly ironed short-sleeved shirt, and deck shoes with ankle socks. His calves and thighs were tanned and hardened from two months of playing tennis every day in Corfu, his face as dark and wrinkled as one of the olives picked from his farm. When he stepped into the kitchen, Foy instinctively stooped, as tall men do, and then quickly unfurled again. The huge room didn't seem big enough to contain his energy. The twins surged forward to greet him, and clung on to his legs like limpets. He didn't flinch.

"Where's Cerberus?" he boomed. On cue, Leicester barked from the garden, furiously throwing himself against the glass door as he realized he was excluded from the festivity inside.

"Thanks, Dad," said Bryony, stepping forward to take the olive oil from his hand. "Maybe we should save it? Does olive oil have vintage years? Does it improve with age?" She quickly kissed him once on each cheek.

"Like me, do you mean?" said Foy, bending down extravagantly to pick up a twin under each arm. "You should drink a spoonful of that stuff every day so that your bones grow as strong as your grandfather's," he told them as they tried to wriggle free. Making suitable noises of disgust, Hector and Alfie buried their noses into his neck and ruffled his soft, gray hair until it stood on end.

"Do you have something for us?" they pleaded. He unceremoniously dropped them on the floor, slapped his pockets, and shrugged his shoulders.

"I forgot," he said dramatically. He noticed Izzy standing by the kitchen table and gestured for her to come forward. Like a magician, he pulled out a brightly colored sarong and matching bikini from the basket and threw it toward her in a high arc over the twins' heads. She caught it as it fluttered between her outstretched hands. The twins took advantage to make for the bag, but Foy caught them and held them aloft, laughing as their little legs hopelessly pedaled in the air.

"For my most beautiful granddaughter," he said dramatically.

"Thanks," said Izzy cautiously. Izzy glanced at the bikini long enough to see that the top and bottom consisted of little more than bits of string with four triangles attached. She stuffed the bikini inside the sarong and made a careful ball until it was small enough to hide behind the toaster. Even in the heat of the Corfu summer it had been difficult to persuade her out of jeans and long-sleeved T-shirts. When she swam in the pool she wore a conservative black swimsuit and a top. It was ludicrous to consider she would ever wear something so skimpy. She rubbed her tummy, loathing the plump childish contours, and breathed in until she could feel her ribs. Then she relaxed again and began reciting one of the mantras she had found on a pro-anorexia website: "Nothing tastes as good as thin feels."

"What else do I have in here?" asked Foy, rummaging in the bag and pulling out a chess set carved from olive wood. "Where's my cleverest grandson?" Jake lazily raised a hand from where he was sitting at the kitchen table. Foy pretended not to see him. So Jake stood up and went over to collect the chess set. Foy pulled him close and ruffled his long hair, muttering something about how he was looking forward to being taught how to play by his oldest grandson and how pleased he was that he had been tipped for Oxbridge by his school.

"Pull your trousers up, Jake," he called out as Jake slouched back toward the kitchen table. Jake made a perfunctory gesture, grabbing the belt loop at the back, but the trousers immediately slumped back down to reveal his underpants.

"Big oversight, Tita! We didn't get the twins anything," Foy called upstairs for his wife to come down. Tita slowly emerged. She came down the stairs cautiously, with a sideways step, holding firmly onto the banister because she had recently developed a fear of falling. She hadn't told anyone this, and people sometimes mistook her slow, dig-nified descent down stairs and across rooms for imperiousness.

On the floor by the bottom step, the twins feverishly searched in the bag at Foy's feet, their faces growing redder as the tears pricked. They pulled out an unread copy of *The Telegraph*, a packet of photo-graphs, and a swollen copy of a novel by John Grisham that had spent too much time getting wet beside the swimming pool. They ignored their grandmother, who was carrying an identically shaped package under each arm.

"They're wrapped up." Tita gestured to the parcels.

"Of course," said Foy. By now it was a double bluff. Tita had clearly done the shopping, and it wasn't clear whether Foy really had forgot-ten to bring them something or was pretending to have forgotten. The twins were too worked up to absorb what their grandmother was telling them and continued to skirmish in the bag like stray dogs searching for food.

Tita now stood on the same step as Foy. Beside him, she looked pale. It wasn't just her skin—she wore a wide-brimmed hat whenever she went outside in Corfu, even if it was just to count how many cars were in the Rothschilds' driveway—it was the pale linen dress that she had chosen and the pink Elizabeth Arden lipstick that always left comedy kiss marks on people's cheeks. He was so vital and present. She looked as though she should be staked to the ground to avoid floating away.

Foy took the parcels from Tita and presented them to the twins. They whooped and ripped open the plain brown packaging to reveal two ships hand-carved in wood from their grandfather's olive grove. One said "Hector" on the side. The other said "Alfie." They ran around the kitchen table, boats held aloft, shrieking wildly.

"Did you give Nick and Bryony the olive oil?" Tita asked over the din.

"I couldn't wait any longer," Foy said apologetically. "What were you doing up there?"

Tita glanced over at him disapprovingly. She pouted petulantly and put a hand on her hip. It used to be her most flirtatious look. Now she looked a little like a drag queen. Her lips pinched together tightly, creating tiny ragged islands of cracked lipstick.

"You have no self-control, Dad," Bryony quickly chipped in, then looked as though she immediately regretted saying it.

"Just as well you don't take after me, then," said Foy. It was a rebuke. Ali soon learned that Foy claimed responsibility for the positive traits in his children and grandchildren. Any bad characteristics were blamed on Tita's side of the family ("stubborn, overcautious and overbearing") or Nick's ("intolerant, anal and passive-aggressive"), even though he had met Nick's parents only once, at his daughter's wedding more than two decades earlier.

"In answer to your question, I was parking the car," Tita explained as she finally stepped into the kitchen and took a drink from the tray that Malea was holding.

"Thank you, Malea," she said, without looking down at the tiny housekeeper.

"Granny, I can't believe that you get in the car to drive four hundred meters down the road," commented Jake. "What about your carbon footprint?"

"What about yours?" countered Foy. "When I was your age I

hadn't even been to the continent. You fly abroad at least once every holiday."

"What's the continent?" asked Alfie, putting down his boat on the kitchen floor.

"It's when you pee in your pants," Izzy responded. "Like Hector."

Hector surged toward Izzy, throwing himself with all his strength at her thighs in an effort to topple her. He failed and instead battered her legs with angry fists until she pleaded for mercy.

"That's incontinent," pointed out Jake over the noise.

"That's where I'm heading," said Foy, but no one was listening. Everyone shouted at Hector to stop. Instead he continued to hurl himself at Izzy like a battering ram. Izzy was sturdy and gave no ground, which further infuriated Hector.

Ali stood back, taking stock, unsure whether to intervene. On the one hand, she was farthest away from the fracas, sitting on the edge of the sofa, beside the enormous sliding doors into the garden. On the other, Bryony had asked her to join them for lunch to keep an eye on the twins. Bryony had emphasized the need to keep them reasonably quiet at the other end of the table and the importance of making sure they didn't use their fingers to eat. She hadn't mentioned anything about mediating fights.

Nor was Ali sure what to do as Hector grabbed at Izzy's long, dark hair and Izzy responded by kicking him in the calf with a heavy-looking leather ankle boot. None of the child-care books that she found carefully piled on the desk in her bedroom at the top of Holland Park Crescent when she moved in the previous Saturday addressed the issue of children physically fighting with one another. She could vaguely remember squalling with her sister, but she couldn't recall how her parents responded. And surely if Nick and Bryony were in the room, then she shouldn't undermine their authority by getting directly involved.

"Stop that, you two," bellowed Foy, who was closest, but they took no notice of their grandfather.

Alfie headed purposefully toward Hector, carrying his brother's ship, apparently unperturbed by the noise and managing to avoid the flailing limbs. At least Ali assumed it was Alfie, because in less than a week he had already proven himself to be less volatile than Hector. Hector hurled himself at life, while Alfie was more reticent. Their temperament was their only distinguishing feature, although some days Ali suspected they pretended to be each other.

Alfie said something unintelligible to everyone but his twin brother. *"Tigil mo yan, Hector."*

Their identical blue eyes met, and Hector let Izzy's hair gently slide through his fingers. Just as suddenly as it had started, the argument fizzled out. Hector took the ship that his brother was proffering him, and they headed off to play together. Bryony shot a look at Ali.

"What did he say?" Tita asked. "Was that English?"

"Twin-speak," said Bryony dismissively. "Now, Mum, tell me what you've been up to this week."

She linked arms with her mother and led her toward the nearest sofa at the garden end of the enormous open-plan room. They were now close enough to Ali that she could hear Tita mutter something about the pace of retirement not suiting Foy. Expecting to be introduced, Ali pushed a stray strand of hair behind an ear, but neither Bryony nor her mother looked up at her.

Instead she stood alone by the sliding doors. Ali's anxiety pricked again. She wondered whether she had done something wrong. Bryony was difficult to read. She gave meticulous instructions for apparently trivial tasks and then never bothered to follow up to see whether Ali had fulfilled the brief.

At the beginning of the week, for example, she spoke to Ali for almost twenty minutes about the optimum method for testing times tables. "Forward, backward, forward, backward, random. Backward, forward, backward, forward, random," she had said in a tone as rhythmic as a metronome, "and then forward, backward, forward, random, forward, backward." She made Ali repeat a couple of times what she had said, and then explained that research showed that it was essential for children to recite things three times to ensure the memory was properly laid down in the frontal cortex.

"Surely the twins don't do times tables yet?" Ali had asked.

"If they learn some of them now, then it will be easier later," Bryony said. "It's good to be ahead of the game."

On Tuesday she had even called to check exactly how many times Ali had tested them the previous day.

"I can't remember exactly," Ali had said.

"Then you should write it down in the daybook," suggested Bryony.

The following evening Bryony had spoken to her about her worries over the secret language the twins sometimes used to communicate with each other. Apparently the boys were late talkers, and their language emerged in tandem with their first words. Bryony had asked Ali to research the subject and see if it was something common to twins and get back to her in a couple of weeks with her conclusions. She had also instructed her to analyze the words to see if she could decipher what they meant and to compile a rudimentary dictionary. Not wanting to be awkward or appear unwilling, Ali had quickly agreed.

It occurred to her that if Bryony was as worried as she professed to be, then it was surprising that she hadn't done anything before about the problem. But equally she was gratified to be entrusted with such a serious issue after just a couple of days into the new job.

So far Ali had only two words to show for her efforts. Right now, however, she was too far from them to hear what they were saying. She could see Bryony looking up from the sofa and pointing toward the twins, mouthing, "pen and paper." Using a similar gesture, Ali pointed upstairs to indicate her notebook was in the bedroom. Bryony stared at her for a little longer than was comfortable but was quickly distracted by Jake, who had begun to question his grandfather about the smoked salmon business he used to run.

"How many flights did you clock flying smoked salmon around the UK?" Jake asked Foy as they sat at the kitchen table. "You told me once that it was all flown to Poland to be packaged and then back here again to be sold. You'd need to buy a slice of the Amazon to compensate for that kind of level of carbon emissions."

"We're not talking about that," Bryony interrupted.

Earlier in the year Foy's business partner of twenty-five years had mounted a coup to get him taken off the board of the company that he had founded back in the seventies. Although it was couched in friendly terms as retirement and Foy retained an important-sounding but ineffectual title, he had effectively been bought out and left without a job. The hasty purchase of the olive grove the previous year was Bryony's idea to lift his spirits and give him a new project. Everyone was under strict instructions not to mention fish of any kind.

"That smoked salmon is paying your school fees," said Foy. "Don't knock it. Just wish I'd thought of pickling it in formaldehyde and selling it to Tate Britain."

"Actually, I'm paying the school fees," Nick interrupted loudly.

He was standing on one side of the long, thin island that dominated the other end of the kitchen, examining bottles of wine he had brought up from the cellar. He looked like a lonely plane that had fallen off the edge of a runway. It was the first time he had spoken since his father-in-law had come into the kitchen. Now it was his turn to admonish himself. What was he trying to prove?

"Hello, Nick, how's business?" Foy asked, moving swiftly toward the end of the kitchen island to shake his son-in-law's hand. For a man of sixty-eight, he moved remarkably fluidly. "Is it a bull or a bear?"

Nick laughed loudly, as though it were the first time Foy had ever posed this question. Over the years Nick had tried to explain to his father-in-law that the vagaries of the stock market didn't have any impact on the daily rhythms of his work, but Foy simply ignored him because he liked the sound of the question.

"Actually, we're still benefiting from the fall in interest rates. Means people aren't getting a good return from government bonds or savings," said Nick, putting down the bottle of wine he had been examining. "We're making a killing on these investment products called collateralized debt obligations. It's like a never-ending party."

Foy looked at him quizzically, because Nick wasn't following the established routine. Foy's question was usually the cue for Nick to ask him about his latest news.

"Sounds fascinating," said Foy, unable to disguise his lack of enthusiasm.

"It is," said Nick, deliberately misreading his father-in-law's tone. "House prices are rising, people are taking out loans to spend on cheap goods made in China. Everyone is getting rich, especially the Chinese, and they're keeping interest rates low by buying U.S. treasury bonds."

"Are you going to open that bottle of wine, or do you want me to?" asked Foy jovially, stretching toward the Girardin Puligny-Montrachet that Nick was holding. Nick possessively held on to the neck of the bottle. The bottle opener remained on the worktop.

"We're pooling debt, adding it together, and selling it on as bonds paying different interest rates depending on the risk," said Nick. "Most of it is subprime mortgage debt but it could be credit-card debt or emerging-market debt, doesn't matter, really. We sell it on to a company we've created to buy it so the risk is off our books, and then it gets sliced and diced. We get a fee on every deal, and there's revenue from repayment."

"Who buys debt from people they don't know?" asked Foy incredulously.

"People like your pension fund, for example, or your bank," said Nick. "They're looking for the best return on their investment."

"Surely you need to know who's borrowing the money in case they can't pay it back?" pointed out Foy.

"We have formulas to assess risk, and agencies like Moody's who rate the debt," Nick said, and shrugged. "It's practically infallible. Anyway, as long as people are making money, they don't ask questions. They're riskier for investors, but the returns are much higher."

Foy shook his head and picked up the bottle opener. It was clear from the way he kept turning it in his hands that he had no idea how to use it.

"The more leverage, the more potential return. That's our mantra," continued Nick. He knew from meetings with investors that there came a point in the discussion where people were unwilling to admit they didn't understand and simply capitulated to his superior knowledge of the jargon. "We're operating in the outer frontiers of finance."

"To go where no man has ever gone before," joked Jake.

"Like the olive, the stock market is both a good servant and a hard master," said Foy eventually, misquoting Lawrence Durrell.

"It is," agreed Nick.

"So you're still just selling bits of paper," said Foy.

"Yes, but the color of the ink is different," replied Nick firmly, finally releasing the bottle from his grip.

"There's got to be something wrong with a world where people aren't just spending what they earn but spending what they don't earn, too," said Foy finally.

He made no attempt to put forward his favorite argument that the growth of the financial sector in London was killing innovation in British manufacturing. It was clear to everyone in the room that Nick had just won an argument. It just wasn't obvious what it was about.

"You're being boring, Dad," Jake shouted grumpily from the middle of the room, where he was leafing through a copy of *Kerrang!* at the kitchen table, one iPod earphone in his ear, the other drifting across a plate of butter.

"What's Dad talking about?" Izzy asked her mother.

"His work," said Bryony. "Don't worry. No one understands what he does. Not even me."

"Are you going to open that bottle? Or are you waiting for us to pay further homage to the high priest of finance?" Nick picked up the bottle opener. "Nothing's obvious anymore," Foy complained, "just look at that gadget. You need to read an instruction manual to operate it."

"That was a present from my team," said Nick. "It's probably the most evolutionary bottle opener on the market. You can open two thousand bottles of wine before you even have to think about recalibrating it."

"It's like your electric salt and pepper mills," continued Foy. "I can't help thinking that the phallic nature of all these inventions is to compensate for the fact that men spend so much time in offices staring at spreadsheets on computer screens and so little time outside hunting and gathering. At least the smoked salmon industry kept me fit."

"I'm perfectly fit," said Nick. "I run four times a week. And there's not much need for hunting and gathering in the age of Internet shopping."

Foy retreated from Nick like a kicked dog and headed open-armed toward Malea, who had emerged from the storeroom in the basement beneath the kitchen. The area below the kitchen was Malea's domain. It was the beginning of the production line for the three meals she prepared each day. It was where she slept and bathed, and the front line for the laundry effort. There was a room at the back on the garden side that doubled as a playroom during the day and a place for Jake and his friends to watch TV and play snooker at night. It was also Malea's favorite location for ironing. Malea looked pleased but embarrassed as Foy picked her up and hugged her.

"Honey with walnuts," he said, pressing a couple of jars into each hand.

"Mr. Chesterton," she said in embarrassment, "you are spoiling me." Everyone giggled. Jake shifted uncomfortably in his chair because he was the one who had taught Malea to say this without telling her about the Ferrero Rocher advert. Although his worldview was limited by his parents' wealth, at seventeen he had enough insight to know that it wasn't cool to take the piss out of the person who ironed his pants.

"A taste of Greece, to entice you to visit us," Foy said.

Nick busied himself with bottles of wine, trying to hide his annoyance with his father-in-law. It wasn't for Foy to invite Malea to

Greece. She worked for him and Bryony, not Foy and Tita, and they needed her at home even when they were away. Besides, the idea that his father-in-law's indomitable Greek housekeeper would ever accept such an interloper was ridiculous.

"Stop pissing all over my territory," Ali was taken aback to hear Nick mutter under his breath. He tried to focus on the bottles of wine. Malea, who obviously wasn't privy to the fish embargo, told Foy proudly that she was cooking salmon en croute in his honor. Foy didn't flinch.

"Hope it's wild salmon. The farmed stuff is full of crap," he said virulently.

Nick looked up at him in surprise. Foy normally talked about the salmon business in terms of revolution. Of how he had introduced salmon to the masses, how he had brought democracy to the dining table by selling it in supermarkets, how he had improved the nation's health long before fish oils had become fashionable. But the Che Guevara diatribe was gone. This was a new angle.

"Those fish are no better off than battery hens," he said. "Covered in fleas, pumped with more chemicals than an East German weight-lifter. God knows what they do to a man's libido."

"Damn," said Nick suddenly. "The bloody cork has broken." He held up the bottle to the window and saw tiny pieces of cork floating on the surface.

"I thought it was an infallible bottle opener," said Foy wryly. Nick picked up the bottle of Puligny-Montrachet and started pouring it down the sink. He assumed a pose of utter nonchalance that he knew would irritate his more frugal father-in-law.

"Why don't we put it through a sieve?" suggested Foy.

"There's plenty more where that came from," said Nick, pointing at the floor beneath him, where his wine cellar was located. "We'll just have the Meursault instead. Salmon needs something a bit stronger than a Montrachet, don't you think, Foy?"

Foy wasn't listening. He had just noticed Ali standing awkwardly by the window.

"And who are you?" Foy boomed. Ali stared at him vacantly. She pointed at herself with one hand and tried to say "Me?" but no sound came out. In the week since she had moved into Holland Park Crescent, Ali was growing accustomed to the idea of being invisible. In Cromer she was always coming across people she knew, whether it was queuing in the butcher's or walking along the beach. Even in Norwich she often ran into fellow students or friends who had moved to the city in search of work.

In London, there were no familiar faces. She was neither a parent nor part of the group of Eastern European nannies who stood together, laughing and chatting in guttural strange languages in the park. It made Ali realize how much of her identity was formed from her relationship with the familiar. She regretted not taking up her father's recent offer to go out to sea with him. She hadn't been for years. She might have seen which parts of her were exposed in heavy seas when everything nonessential was stripped away, and this would surely have helped her now. Foy turned away from her.

There had been times this week when she went the entire day without speaking to anyone apart from the children and Malea, who was clearly more interested in the soaps she followed daily on the TV in the kitchen than in talking to Ali. The first two evenings she had dutifully waited downstairs at the kitchen table until eleven o'clock at night for Bryony to come home from work. She had compiled a careful list of the day's highlights, hoping for reassurance that she was doing things right. But she never appeared. On the third night, Ali gave up and took herself off to bed at ten o'clock. She walked past Izzy's door and could see her on the computer.

Above her, she could hear Jake padding about in his bedroom on the top floor, occasionally singing to a song on his iPod. She longed for company and scrolled down her contacts in the new BlackBerry that Bryony had given her. It was a spartan list. There were three numbers for Jo, but they were probably all defunct because her sister would have either lost her phone or run out of credit. And even if she managed to get hold of her, at this time of night, the chances of her being off her face were too high to risk a call. Then there were Rosa, Tom, Maia, her parents, and Will MacDonald. Impulsively, she deleted her tutor's details as surplus to requirement. Rosa, however, picked up straight away.

"Hello, stranger," Rosa said warmly, even though it was less than a week since she had organized a party to celebrate Ali's departure. Ali understood. University friendships depended on day-to-day contact, and she was already out of the loop. "How's it going?"

"Good," said Ali. "More complicated than I imagined. Difficult to form relationships with so many different people in such a short space of time, but Hector and Alfie are really sweet. And my room is enormous. You'll have to come and stay. I'm allowed girlfriends."

"Great," said Rosa. Ali could tell her attention was already wandering and knew it would be difficult to lure her away to London from the intense self-contained world on campus.

"How's your new flatmate?"

"What?"

"The girl who took my room."

"You chose well," said Rosa. "She's great." Ali heard a voice in the background.

"Who's with you?"

"Can't talk," Rosa said, and giggled.

"New love interest?" questioned Ali.

"New lust interest," confirmed Rosa. "Can I call later?"

"I have to get up at six-thirty, so maybe tomorrow," said Ali.

"Sure," said Rosa.

It was a phone call that reinforced Ali's sense of isolation. Of course Bryony communicated with her. But it was a virtual relationship conducted by BlackBerry in short, terse sentences at odd times of day. "Izzy cello?" read one. "Jake weekend plans?" read another. "Twins MMR?" Nick was out of the picture. She had seen him only once the whole week.

. . .

"And who are you?" Foy turned his attention to Ali again. "Apart from being the kind of person who requires people to ask the same question twice."

Ali found Foy's sudden attention almost more unwelcome than the previous neglect. She regretted the denim miniskirt and leggings that she was wearing and wished she had put on something more sober. She wrapped her cardigan tightly around her and pulled down the sleeves. She lacked gravitas.

"Sorry, Dad, I should have introduced you," said Bryony apologetically. Ali stuck out her hand as far as it would stretch in an effort to keep Foy at bay.

"This is Ali, our fantastic new nanny," said Bryony, an approving arm resting protectively around Ali's shoulder. "Be nice to her, because she only moved in this week."

"What happened to the other one?" asked Foy.

"She got pregnant," Tita reminded him.

"I thought that was the one before?" Foy said.

"No, she was the one who kept locking the twins in the playroom when she—" said Tita.

"We don't talk about that anymore," Bryony interrupted.

"You can't have a nanny this pretty with a teenage boy in the house," said Foy dramatically. Fortunately, Jake was sitting at the table wearing his headphones and didn't hear him.

"You can't say things like that, Dad. She's an English-language graduate from the University of East Anglia," Bryony explained, trying to divert her father. "She's helping the children with their schoolwork as well as looking after them when I'm working. Like Jane Eyre."

Ali looked embarrassed.

"What do we have for Ali?" Foy shouted over to Tita. Tita glided toward Ali and silently held out her hand for Ali to shake it. It was small and bony, and reminded Ali of the swallows that used to nest in the eaves outside her bedroom in Cromer.

"Pleased to meet you, Mrs. Chesterton," said Ali nervously.

"How about a jar of honey?" suggested Tita.

"What's a young girl like this going to do with a jar of honey?" said Foy dismissively. "Do we have an extra sarong, Tita?" Tita shook her head.

"Then we'll have to get you something when you come to Corfu," said Foy. "You'll be coming out in the summer, of course."

"I'm not sure," said Ali, again a little nervously, because it wasn't clear whether he was making a statement or asking a question, and although Bryony had mentioned family holidays in the interview, she didn't specify the destination or whether she would be invited.

"The nanny usually brings the children for a month," explained Foy, "and Bryony and Nick join us for the last couple of weeks, although Nick generally spends more time with his BlackBerry than he does with us."

His tone was jokey, but no one laughed apart from Ali, who quickly stopped. Bryony looked offended. Ali assumed it was because Foy had criticized her husband.

"You know I work pretty hard, too," said Bryony defensively.

She muttered something about going in search of Nick, who was now delaying lunch by heading back downstairs to recover another bottle of wine from his cellar. The twins were nowhere to be seen. Ali was unsure whether she should go and look for them.

"Maybe I could help with the olive harvest?" she suggested politely.

"That happens in the winter," said Foy. "It goes on for months." To Ali's relief, Foy excused himself and went back upstairs, muttering something about a weak stream and the perils of a dodgy prostate.

"The honey would be lovely." Ali turned to Tita. Tita smiled benevolently but it was her piercing green eyes, not her lipstick-smudged mouth, that captivated Ali. They were eyes that saw every-thing but revealed nothing. Even through the unforgiving glare of youth, Ali could appreciate that Tita was a woman whose life had been defined mostly by her beauty. Her hair might be gray and scooped up into an unfashionable bun at the back of her head, and the way she stood with her legs slightly too far apart may have made her look rather sturdy, but she was still a woman who commanded attention.

"Ignore him, my dear," said Tita. "He's like a child in a sweetie shop when he meets someone new, but he quickly loses interest. It's all about the first five minutes. He means no harm. Foy is a very obvious person." She sounded dismissive, but the comment was said with pride.

"With a big personality," agreed Bryony, who had come back into the room with Nick and another bottle of wine.

They could hear the Big Personality thumping back downstairs with the twins in hot pursuit.

"Look at this," he said loudly. He was holding a picture that usually hung on the wall of the upstairs bathroom, a location that was meant to lend it an air of casualness that it wouldn't have had if, for example, it had been hung in the drawing room. It was a framed photograph of Foy taken in the 1980s, outside 10 Downing Street, after a meeting of business leaders with Margaret Thatcher. Mrs. Thatcher, dressed in a blue skirt and jacket, was leaning toward Foy, ignoring the person on her left-hand side. It looked as though she was asking him an important question. He leaned toward her so that her face almost touched his neck.

The photograph had appeared in a couple of broadsheets. Foy had managed to get the original picture and had written a small caption at the bottom that read, "Let them eat fish!" He had given it to Bryony "for inspiration" after she set up her own financial public-relations company sixteen years earlier. Bryony had been touched until she realized that he had given a copy of exactly the same photograph to her sister, Hester. But by then it was too late to remove it from the bathroom wall without offending her father.

Foy held the photograph up in its frame and urged everyone to come closer. A small group gathered around the bottom step. At the front were the twins, sucking intently on sweets they had found in their grandfather's pocket. Behind them stood Bryony and Tita, standing in exactly the same pose, arms crossed and feet sticking out at right angles. Izzy hung behind with Jake, who had obligingly taken the iPod headphone out from his ear. Nick strolled over, holding another bottle of wine. Even Malea came away from the cooker to see what was going on. Only Ali hung back.

"What's wrong, Foy?" demanded Tita.

"Can't you see?" said Foy, pushing the photograph into her hands.

Everyone crowded round. Foy's face was flushed, but when they tried to reconcile its familiar features with the photograph in his hand, it became apparent that something was wrong. The face in the picture had become a smudge. It was as though Foy's face had overflowed so that his aquiline nose and jaunty chin merged into each other. The eyes, no longer blue, were in the wrong place. Foy's face was almost indistinguishable from Mrs. Thatcher's, who had undergone a similarly radical transformation. The surface had concertinaed in parts, and the corners had curled.

"It's got damp," said Bryony in wonder. "I can't believe I didn't notice before."

"Maybe there's a leaking pipe?" suggested Nick helpfully. "Or did someone leave the window open?"

"It's the only picture that's been damaged," said Foy.

"Such bad luck, Foy," said Jake, and for once he wasn't taken to task for calling his grandfather by his first name.

"Smell it," urged Foy.

Bryony leaned forward and sniffed deeply, and then immediately recoiled. She passed the photograph back to Nick, who tentatively smelled the surface and swallowed a couple of times, as though trying to prevent himself from retching.

"What does it smell of?" demanded Foy.

"Urine," said Nick in disgust.

"Someone has pissed all over me," shouted Foy. His eyes flashed accusingly around the room.

"It must have been the twins," said Tita.

"How could they reach the photograph?" Foy rounded on her.

"They could have stood on the loo seat," suggested Nick.

"It was probably part of a game," said Izzy. "They're always trying to see who can pee the farthest."

"It's just bad luck that you were used for target practice," said Bryony.

"When did they do it?" demanded Foy. "It must have been today."

Ali, who had been rooted to the same spot by the sofa, realized that all eyes were on her.

"It wasn't me," she said nervously.

"Of course we know it wasn't you," said Bryony in exasperation, "but you've been monitoring the twins all morning. When could they have done it?"

"I'm not sure," said Ali, looking over at the twins. They were whispering together in their strange language.

"Stop it," shrieked Bryony. "Speak normally. Stop all this weirdness."

"What are they saying? What are they saying?" Tita repeated, until Foy suggested it wasn't helpful to ask.

"We didn't do it," they said in unison.

"Ali, I want you to get to the bottom of this," said Bryony. It wasn't clear to Ali whether the severity of Bryony's tone was to instill fear in the twins, who were standing on either side of her, boiled sweets stuck in their cheeks, or to appease Foy, who was demanding immediate retribution.

"Yes, of course," said Ali, wondering how on earth she was going to conduct such an inquiry.

Nick's BlackBerry started to ring. He glanced down at the screen.

"Sorry, I've got to take this," he said, looking relieved to have an excuse to leave the room. "It's about the deal. The numbers are so complicated it takes the whole weekend for the computer system to crunch them." Then he left, and as far as Ali could remember, he didn't come back.

"Sum ergo edo," Foy said, and smiled, invigorated by the arrival of food, his outburst seemingly forgotten. "I think, therefore I'm hungry." Malea set down the salmon en croute on the kitchen island, and Foy leaned over to savor the smell. He gave a hyperbolic sniff and extolled the virtues of her cooking until Malea retreated in embarrassment back to the stove, where she began serving small portions of asparagus onto plates.

"All the more welcome after a month of Andromede's *spetsofai,*" he declared. "It plays havoc with my digestion. I have to sleep every afternoon."

"Needs ten more minutes, Mr. Chesterton," said Malea, lifting the salmon back into the oven. "First the asparagus."

"You do the same in England," pointed out Jake. "In fact, wherever you are, you always sleep after lunch."

Foy picked up the carving knife that Malea had placed on the worktop. He held it up so the light caught the white blade, turned it from one side to the other, and examined the handle as though he had come across an ancient artifact.

"What's this? It looks like a samurai sword," said Foy.

"It is Japanese," said Bryony. "It's meant to be one of the best knives in the world. It was a present for Nick after he closed some deal. Careful with the blade, it's ceramic."

Shepherded by Malea, Foy headed back to the table and sat at the head in the only chair with arms. Ali hovered behind him, unsure whether she was meant to join them or go upstairs so that the family could eat alone. She didn't offer to help Malea, after an attempt earlier in the week to serve pasta to the twins had been rebuffed. The message was clear: The kitchen was Malea's territory, and any attempt to help could be construed as interference. Ali counted places, trying to work out whether there was one laid for her.

"What are you doing?" asked Foy impatiently, sensing her presence. "You're making me nervous. Come and sit down."

"I'm not sure . . ." mumbled Ali.

She looked across at Bryony for direction, but she was embroiled in conversation with Tita about her younger sister's plan to reinvent herself as a life coach.

"Why would anyone pay Hester for advice?" asked Tita incredulously, pulling out a chair next to her husband. "She can't make her mind up about anything."

"Maybe it's the homeopathic approach, treating like with like," Bryony said, and laughed, sitting opposite Tita. "Anyway, it's more mainstream than crystal healing."

"I'm very relieved she's given up on that idea," said Tita. "I cannot be doing with all her New Age mumbo-jumbo. Do you know, the last time I saw her she suggested that we might all benefit from family therapy?"

"What did you say?" Bryony continued to question Tita.

"I asked her why," said Tita. "She started telling me that when you were children you drew a line on the bedroom floor to mark your own territory. Apparently you awarded yourself a much bigger space, and we allowed it to happen."

"Anything else?" asked Bryony.

"She said that I was a distant mother and Foy was an overbearing father, and that we stymied her ability to think for herself. So I asked how she could explain that you were so decisive," said Tita, obviously troubled by this turn of events.

"Well, it took her a while to decide which man she wanted to marry," Foy interrupted. "Poor Felix Naylor was still on tenterhooks even as I led Bryony down the aisle."

"Ali, please sit down," commanded Foy.

"I'm not sure whether I should be here." Ali laughed nervously, moving away from Foy, toward the middle of the table.

"That's a big existential question," said Jake, sitting down next to Tita and pouring his grandmother a glass of water.

"Is there any fizzy?" he shouted over to Malea.

Surely Jake could sense her discomfort? Ali looked at him for solidarity but found none. Jake's indifference to her stung more than Izzy's careless rudeness. His ambivalence reinforced her sense of disconnection from this new life. If you were defined by the people around you, then what did it mean if you were largely ignored? She had tried to engage with him, offered to help him with an essay on relationships between men and women in *The Handmaid's Tale*, or asked him about music that she knew he liked (The Libertines, Daft Punk, Kaiser Chiefs—Ali had cheated and looked at his iPod). But he wasn't interested.

"For God's sake, Bryony, where should the Sparrow make her nest? She's floating around the table like an escaped salmon trying to get back into its cage," Foy boomed.

Bryony pointed to the seat opposite Foy at the other end of the table and indicated that Alfie and Hector should sit on either side of her, with Izzy and Jake acting as a buffer zone between the twins and the adults.

"It's just an informal lunch," said Bryony distractedly. Ali eyed the intimidating, neat lines of cutlery, the different-size wineglasses, and the place mats, and the folded napkin atop the side plate. She sat down, feeling exposed at the end of the table. Malea put a plate of asparagus in front of her, and Ali muttered an embarrassed thank-you. She picked up a knife and fork to start eating. Hector giggled beside her.

"You don't eat asparagus with a knife and fork," said Alfie with a shy smile. "You can use your fingers."

"Thanks," said Ali, putting the butter-smeared knife back down on the table.

"Where's your dad?" Ali asked Hector.

"On the phone," said Izzy, pushing blades of asparagus lazily around her plate.

"Daddy is always on the telepono," chorused Hector and Alfie. They were eating bread rolls instead of asparagus. They took bites at exactly the same time and then swapped rolls across the table until they were finished.

"You mean the telephone," said Ali, correcting their pronunciation but not their table manners because it seemed a bit rich coming from someone who was picking up cues on which cutlery to use from a pair of five-year-olds.

"It's his job," said Izzy, as though his absence needed explaining.

Malea came round with wine, and Ali put her hand over the glass.

"Are you not a big drinker?" asked Foy, as though this made Ali suspect.

Ali jumped, and water from her glass spilled onto the table. Hector dipped his finger in the tiny pool and began drawing circles on the table.

"Not really," said Ali.

"Where are you from?" asked Foy. Ali was unsure how this connected with the first question.

"Cromer," said Ali. "It's a small town in north Norfolk." Malea cleared the plates, including Ali's. It made Ali feel even more uncomfortable, as though underlining Malea's unequal status. None of the children got up to help. They remained seated until Malea returned with plates of salmon for everyone.

"I sometimes shoot near there," said Foy.

He turned to Bryony and started asking her about her plans to come to Corfu the following summer. Ali tentatively cut a small slice of salmon and pushed it onto her fork, but it wouldn't stick, so she turned to the vegetables, which were more cooperative. She had no appetite. But then neither apparently did Tita, and Bryony's plate was piled no higher than a child's. There was debate about whether she should come for one or two weeks.

"Leave Nick behind to get on with his work," said Foy.

"It's just as hard for me to take time off," Bryony admonished him.

"Well, bring the Sparrow and then at least you'll get a proper rest," said Foy. "Have you been to Greece, Ali?"

He didn't wait for her to answer and instead began extolling the virtues of Corfu. Ali recognized Foy as someone for whom questions were really an excuse to expound his own opinions.

"We bought an old olive farm in the northeast before it became fashionable," he explained, "and I have just acquired a twenty-acre olive grove. It's a wonderful retreat for us all, and it's big enough to have several families to stay at once. Even Nick manages to come. Present at least in body, if not in mind."

This drew attention to Nick's continuing absence at the table, although Izzy and Tita had managed to slowly absorb the space where he should have been sitting.

"You'll get used to Nick's disappearing acts, Ali," Bryony said, and smiled. "He's here but he's not here. Like the invisible man."

Like me, thought Ali, the reality dawning on her that the role for which she had auditioned with the Skinners was far more complicated than she had anticipated. The Skinners needed her around but didn't really want to feel her presence. They wanted someone who could tread on the map of family life without leaving a big imprint. She would need to learn to be a chameleon.

Their detachment heightened her loneliness. Later she would realize it could also buy her freedom. But right now, Ali found herself missing her parents. She imagined Sunday lunch, albeit a couple of hours earlier, her father falling asleep because he had been out since three o'clock in the morning checking his crab pots. Her mother noisily clearing away plates as she asked Ali questions about what books she was reading for her course.

It was an idealized version of family life, because in practice all her mother would have talked about was her sister. Eighteenth-century literature couldn't compete with the drama of Jo's life, although perhaps Hogarth could have drawn inspiration from the dissolute underworld that she inhabited. For a moment, Ali even missed Jo, the old days, at least. She imagined Sunday afternoon with her friends in Norwich, the easy banter, the cheap laughs, and the comfort of knowing that she could get back to Cromer quickly if there was a problem. She wished her evening could be spent babysitting her tutor's children instead of Alfie and Hector.

She thought of the timetable of activities that hung in her room and wondered how she could monitor whether Izzy was really reading Henry James, or force the twins to sit down to do half an hour of maths with her when they got home from school, or listen to their piano practice when she couldn't read music. As for Jake, she had given up on him before she had started.

5

·······

September 2006

"Accelerator on the right. Brake in the middle. Clutch on the left,"
Ali repeated to herself like a mantra as she tentatively emerged from a
side street onto a busy main road on the first morning of the new term
for the twins. She congratulated herself for managing to drive from
Holland Park Crescent to this point entirely in second gear. Her left
calf ached from the strain of pressing on the clutch whenever she
stopped in traffic, her hands stuck to the leather steering wheel of the
BMW SUV, and there were dark shadows of sweat under her arms.
But by avoiding unnecessary gear changes she had reduced the risk of
stalling. She licked her upper lip slowly. It tasted of salt.

The radio was switched on. News about more terror alerts made
Ali feel more relaxed, as though there were worse disasters than driving through London in someone else's manual car for the first time
since she had passed her driving test two years ago. When Bryony had
casually tossed the keys across the kitchen table, asking Ali to drive
while she made calls, she had assumed it would all come back to her
naturally. Like riding a bicycle. But right now she felt as ill at ease as
an elephant on an ice rink. The car, a huge four-by-four with three
rows of seats, was a great unwieldy beast, unwilling to cooperate with
its inept mistress, and overreacting to the slightest change in pressure
from her hands and feet. Ali nervously looked at Bryony, wondering

whether she had noticed. To her relief, she was scrolling through messages on her BlackBerry.

"Ali," said Bryony without looking up, "did I mention Nick and I will be away for four nights over the last weekend in October?"

"I don't think so."

"We're going to Idaho to stay with Nick's boss on his ranch. It's an annual event. You'll know your way around by then, won't you?"

"Sure," said Ali, who wanted to appear willing but couldn't talk and drive at the same time. Then, mercifully, traffic slowed and she stopped in the road, her foot resolutely pressed on the clutch.

"I'll e-mail you the details," said Bryony. "Izzy has a party on the Saturday night, but we'll get a cab to collect her at midnight." A couple of seconds later Ali heard her brand-new BlackBerry give a satisfactory ping as the message landed in her inbox.

Bryony switched the heater on to maximum. She was always cold. Probably because she is too thin, thought Ali, recalling how every morning she was woken at six o'clock by Bryony's personal trainer ringing the doorbell. The hot air blasted in Ali's face, making her eyes feel dry and filling her nostrils with the smell of burned dust.

Bryony's phone rang. It was Nick. He wanted to talk about fine-tuning the guest list for their Christmas drinks party in light of Tony Blair's announcement that he would be standing down as prime minister in less than a year.

"Brown will get it, but Cameron will win the election," said Bryony confidently, "and we're too associated with Blair. So let's strike off Ed Balls and Yvette Cooper and invite the Camerons and the Goves instead."

The call ended as abruptly as it had begun.

Ali's back stiffened. Even without her employer sitting beside her in the front passenger seat, this maiden voyage would have presented a challenge. But Bryony's last-minute decision to show Ali the quickest route to the twins' school had amplified the pressure, especially when she suggested that Ali should drive, in case she had to take a call.

Bryony was wearing a floaty chiffon shirt that billowed gently as the heater blasted hot air through the car. The shirt was in a plum color that most people with red hair would have assiduously avoided. But somehow Bryony managed to pull it off. The early-morning sun through the windshield caught her hair and set it ablaze, turning her into something magnificent. If she were a man, people would say Bryony had a commanding presence, Ali decided.

Bryony opened an envelope, and Ali could see that she was going through photocopies of stories from today's newspapers. Every so often she would read something out loud.

"'French Connection sinks into the red' . . . Let's see what *The Times* has got to say . . . 'August terror alert cost BAA thirteen million pounds' . . . Could be worse . . . 'Scottish Power in merger talks' . . . Felix did well to get someone to spill the beans on that one . . ."

"Is this part of your job?" Ali eventually asked, as Bryony reached into her handbag to pull out a packet of seeds. She tore them open and elegantly began eating them, one by one, even though they were tiny and she could have consumed the entire packet in a single gulp. Bryony looked surprised, because although she was accustomed to being driven to work and often talked to her driver, she clearly wasn't used to someone asking her questions.

"It is," she smiled.

"What exactly is your job?" asked Ali.

"I run a financial PR agency," said Bryony, who liked the fact Ali was the only nanny they had interviewed for the job who clearly hadn't bothered to do a Google search on her family. "My clients are companies who pay me and my team to advise them on media relations. I talk to journalists on their behalf. If one of my companies is being bought by another company, or they are about to release their results, or someone is being recruited or fired, then we come up with a communications strategy to explain all this to the media."

"That sounds pretty interesting," said Ali.

"It is," said Bryony, leaning over to switch on Radio 4. "I need to listen to this. One of my clients is being interviewed."

Ali fell silent as the *Today* presenter introduced the CEO of a British company that had just bought one of its rivals, catapulting it to the top of the house-building league. It was a punchy debate that seemed to consist of John Humphrys suggesting the property market was about to lose steam and Bryony's man avoiding the question by talking about the surge in one hundred percent mortgages to enable first-time buyers to purchase the properties his company was going to build. Then it was over.

"Brilliant," said Bryony. "He managed to stick to the brief for a change. Now, tell me, what books are you reading?"

"I'm reading *Feminism in Eighteenth-Century England* by Katherine Rogers," said Ali. "It's for my coursework. I'm trying to keep up with the background reading so that I don't have so much ground to cover when I go back next year."

"What I meant was what books have you recommended the children should read?"

"Oh, sorry. I've left Jake to his own devices. Izzy is reading *To Kill a Mockingbird*, and I've introduced the twins to the joys of *Horrid Henry*."

"Can you write that in the daybook so in the future I don't need to ask?"

Bryony got out another bunch of papers from her bag. "Private and Confidential," it read on the front: "Project Odysseus." Bryony began to skim-read the document. Ali caught a glimpse of its content. A Ukrainian company wanted to buy a British counterpart. Interesting, thought Ali, who wanted to ask more questions. But Bryony's phone rang and their conversation was over.

The traffic was beginning to unravel. Ali could see the twins in the rearview mirror. They were tightly strapped in their car seats, but they each had an arm stretched toward the other so that their short, stubby fingers were entwined. When they saw her watching, they each put their index finger to their lips at exactly the same time, warning her not to say anything. Their connection was both spooky and touching. She was pretty sure that Alfie was on the left and Hector was on the right. Clutch and accelerator. Or was it accelerator and clutch? She quickly looked down at her feet for reassurance. Even if she couldn't tell the twins apart yet, she needed to be certain about the pedals of the car.

From the back of the car, Ali could hear them muttering words to each other in their strange secret language. *"Nakakatawa sya,"* one of them said seriously. The other nodded. *"Alam ko."* The words sounded ancient, like an impenetrable lost language rescued from the depths of the Amazon. Ali repeated them under her breath, and they giggled uncontrollably. They didn't seem upset about going back to school after the holidays, a relief to Ali, who was taken aback by the intensity of all their reactions.

They were due to review how to deal with what Bryony called "the language issue" at the end of the week. Ali had little concrete to report other than the fact that it seemed surprising they needed to use it when they seemed to communicate subliminally anyway. She wanted to say to Bryony that perhaps drawing attention to it might exacerbate the problem. She knew she wouldn't dare. She already understood that for Bryony, identifying problems was halfway to solving them. She lived her life by lists. How else could she be so organized?

Ali managed to persuade the car back into a more controlled rhythm as she headed down a wider street, grateful for the bus in front that meant she didn't have to pick up speed. The road ahead looked vaguely familiar. But it might have just been the generic nature of the shops. Starbucks. Habitat. Marks & Spencer. The kind of shops you found in places occupied by people in upper tax brackets. Not a Costcutter or a Sue Ryder in sight. She relaxed enough for the blood to return to her hands and began to pick up the threads of Bryony's conversation.

Ali knew from the ringtone (a song by the Black Eyed Peas downloaded by Jake) that Bryony was speaking on her private line. She also knew from the way Bryony had chewed her lower lip and stared at the screen until the chorus of "Where Is the Love?" began that she was in two minds about whether to take the call.

"Maybe it's a good idea to go organic, Dad," she heard Bryony say in an even tone. "You're always complaining that the supermarkets are squeezing your margins. Then you could sell at a higher price to more niche outlets. The other day you were complaining to Nick that the fish were full of fleas."

She was talking to Foy. Ali could hear his voice booming back down the phone. Old people always shouted into telephones, especially mobiles.

"Bloody organic," Foy shouted back at her. "It's total bunkum. We're going to the dogs in this country. Do you know, when I went to the doctor about my back last week he suggested acupuncture in my sacrum?"

"Acupuncture is very effective," Bryony interrupted him, clearly hoping to move the conversation in a different direction.

"No one's sticking a needle in my arse," said Foy, "and I'll never agree to organic salmon. God, by the time I need a hip replacement they'll be offering Dark Rescue Remedies instead of morphine."

"Bach Rescue Remedy," Bryony corrected him.

"I blame your sister," Foy continued. "All her homophobic mumbo-jumbo. Bloody yogurt knitting brigade."

"Homeopathic," Bryony corrected him. He ignored her.

"I can't think what's got into Fenton. He's spent too much time with bloody Prince Charles. I swear I saw him talking to the fish last time we were in Scotland," Foy rambled on, "asking them whether they had enough room to swim."

"How did you respond?" asked Bryony, wondering how her father's younger business partner coped with him.

"I reminded him that fish have a three-second memory," shouted Foy. "He's taking the idea to the board, you know. He's got this big idea to bring in ballan wrasse fish to eat the fish lice instead of using chemicals, because they're bad for the environment."

"That sounds like a good idea," said Bryony.

"It's a fucking awful idea. It could turn on the salmon, like the gray squirrel did with the red. It could turn out to be an invasive species like the American signal crayfish. It could . . ."

"Look, even if they decide to run with it, you'll be long gone, Dad," Bryony interrupted him. She immediately regretted her mistake. "What I mean is that it will take years before the fish can be certified as organic, and by then it will probably have gone out of fashion." But this didn't placate Foy. Ali winced on her behalf.

"They'll have to drown me in the fucking fish farm before I retire from fucking Freithshire Fisheries," said Foy. "I'm not going to leave my lifetime's work in the hands of that fucker Fenton." Bryony held the phone away from her ear until he stopped to ask if she was still there.

"*Illegitimi non carborundum,*" responded Bryony, adopting one of Foy's favorite phrases, when he finished his diatribe. There was a silence. Then Foy laughed.

"I won't let the bastards grind me down," he agreed, his mood lifting.

"Now, can you please stop swearing, because I've got the children in the back of the car and Ali sitting beside me," said Bryony, breathing a sigh of relief as she realized his spleen was finally vented. "And her first impression of you wasn't favorable."

"I see, I see," said Foy, sounding interested. "Tell me, has the Sparrow managed to get to the bottom of who defiled that image of me in your toilet? Hester is right, there's something wrong with those twins. Too much organic food, probably. Same with that bloody dog."

The bus turned off, leaving the road ahead worryingly free of traffic. She would have to go faster. Ali tentatively pressed the accelerator. The car lurched in protest. She cursed Foy for bringing up what happened at the weekend. Apart from a couple of jokes by Jake about "pissgate" on Sunday evening, the subject had slid down the agenda, to be replaced by more trivial concerns. Had Nick put Ali on their car insurance? Which of the children had been using Bryony's laptop without permission? Ali had been waiting to ask Bryony for some guidelines on the best way to extract a confession from the twins for the past three days, but she hadn't really seen her until this morning, and there had been no opportunity for small talk.

The first breakfast of the school term had been a catastrophic affair. Persuading Alfie and Hector into their uniforms proved more challenging than sliding jelly into a cashpoint machine. They insisted on getting dressed in reverse, putting socks and shoes on first and underpants and shorts last. Every pair of socks was rejected because the seams were in the wrong place and scratched their toes.

"Are you trying to wind me up?" Ali asked them.

"They're always like this," Izzy said from the other side of the table. She had painted her nails with black nail varnish. Ali pretended not to notice. Eventually Malea silently presented Ali with a couple of oversize pairs of seamless ankle socks. Her round, flat face was expressionless, but Ali thought she could detect pity in her dark eyes. Or it might have been suspicion.

Then they insisted they wanted to wear underpants with exactly the same characters from Thomas the Tank Engine. Ali went upstairs again and came down with at least a dozen pairs, which she spread over the kitchen table. She counted seventy-six stairs from the top of the house back down to the basement. On the way down she had tripped over Leicester, who liked to sleep on the bottom step of the staircase in the hallway. He had growled menacingly, and Ali had growled back at him, baring her teeth, because she had read somewhere that it was important to show dominant dogs who was boss.

"Snap," she said breathlessly, picking out a couple of pairs of pants with green trains on the front. She checked the BlackBerry Bryony had given her and calculated that she had about five minutes in hand before they were late for their first day at school.

"That is Daisy and Henry," said Alfie in disgust. "Daisy is a girl train."

"How can you tell the difference?" asked Ali, frantically searching the underpants for clues.

"She's wearing blue eye shadow," said Hector.

"You can only see that if you look really closely," said Ali, "and I'm sure no one else will notice."

"But we know," they both said simultaneously. They sounded almost apologetic.

"They're on the spectrum," Izzy chipped in, as she wolfed down two pieces of toast coated with a thick slick of chocolate spread before Bryony came down. Izzy looked up over the book she was reading at the breakfast table. *Twilight*, it said on the front. Definitely not *To Kill a Mockingbird*. Her schoolbag sat on the table beside her. It was a large pink leather bag with lots of buckles. *Chloé*, said the label on the side.

"What exactly do you mean?" asked Ali.

"Autistic children love Thomas the Tank Engine," Jake shouted from the other end of the kitchen. It was the first time he had spoken since he appeared downstairs.

"Is it an official diagnosis?" asked Ali, annoyed that Bryony had mentioned nothing to her. She carefully flattened another pair of pants with a green train on the front on the kitchen table.

"That's Edward," said Alfie and Hector in unison, sorrowfully shaking their heads as they fondly stroked the pair of pants.

"It's what our aunt says about them," explained Izzy, "when she's trying to wind up Mum. Aunt Hester always knows exactly which buttons to press. That's what Granny says."

"They're just control freaks," said Jake, pointing his phone at them. "It's in the genes. Look at Mum."

Jake stood up. He left a plate of half-eaten toast on the table and asked Malea to fetch a pair of white cricket trousers.

"Why don't you get them yourself?" Ali suggested.

"Is fine, Ali," said Malea, who was already heading downstairs to the laundry room. It was practically the longest sentence she had ever addressed to Ali. Malea knew where everything was kept. She spent her days fetching and carrying objects from one room to another, magically transforming tiny scenes of chaos into perfect order.

"I don't know where Malea keeps them." Jake shrugged.

Fully unfurled, he was several inches taller than Ali, but he had the hunched insecurity of someone who hadn't yet grown into his body. He was still sprouting. His hands were so big that the breakfast bowl he was holding looked like a small cup. He put it down on the table and sauntered toward the stairs, carefully untucking his shirt from his trousers.

"Could you ask her to bring them upstairs to the front door, Ali?" he asked. Ali stared at him, wondering if he was trying to provoke her. Then he said "Please" in a way that implied Ali was being pedantic. "I've got to find my Oyster card."

Jake got the Tube to school. It seemed an incredibly sophisticated mode of transport to Ali, who had ended up at the wrong end of the District Line with the twins the previous Friday. As he reached the bottom of the stairs, he turned around and then almost as an afterthought came back over to Hector and Alfie, and bent down until his face was at their level. He ran his fingers through his hair until it stood on end.

"On the island of Sodor, the trains are never late," he said sternly to Alfie and Hector. He picked out a couple of pairs of pants from the table and gave each one a pair. "Donald and Douglas," he said seriously to them, pointing at the trains. "They are twins, like you, and they want to go to school with you. They don't want to be late." Alfie and Hector compliantly put on the underpants, staring at Jake in wonder through their long brown eyelashes.

"What's the island of Sodor?" Ali asked.

"It's where Thomas the Tank Engine lives," chorused Hector and Alfie.

"Thanks, Jake," said Ali, but he had already left the room. Then Bryony came in, noted the time, and insisted that she accompany Ali to school in order to show her the fastest route.

. . .

Noticing the queue of traffic behind her, Ali tentatively pressed the accelerator until it could go no further. The car growled in protest as the rev counter hit five. The engine pleaded for mercy. It couldn't be so difficult to get from first to second, Ali told herself. She looked at the gear stick to get her bearings. First to second was no more than a single downward motion, a simple flick of the wrist. Surely it couldn't be so difficult to execute? Second to third was the nightmare. Up to the no-man's-land that lay in the middle and then across and up again. Fourth to fifth was unknown territory. Not something Ali had ever experienced. But first to second was surely within her grasp.

Ali thought of things she had done that required far more courage than a gear change. She had pulled the emergency cord on the Norwich-to-Cromer train when her sister, tripping on magic mushrooms, had tried to climb out of the door to get onto the roof; she had swum out of a riptide on the beach at Cley; she had slept with a married man. She had moved in with a family she didn't know, to take a job for which she was completely unqualified, in a city where she knew no one. Bryony was on the phone again. This time it was her work line that had rung.

"You're the journalist, Felix, just do your job. All I can tell you is that you're asking the wrong person the right questions." Bryony laughed. "There's going to be an announcement tomorrow, so you've got about six hours to get ahead of the crowd."

"Can't you give me a bit more than that?" Felix asked. The volume of Bryony's phone was switched so high that Ali could hear every word.

"No," said Bryony firmly. There was a long pause.

"Come out for a drink with me tonight."

Sometimes the simplest requests concealed the most complicated motives, thought Ali.

"I can't do that. I'm going to a closing dinner," Bryony said, her tone softening. "You know how busy I am. We'll invite you to dinner instead. We're always looking for stray men to make up the numbers."

The phone call finished, Bryony immediately dialed a number from her address book.

"The *Financial Times* is onto it," she said, "I know where the leak came from. It's one of the analysts at Merrill. Brian Budd is toast. We need to get on to it now, before it becomes the main angle." She put down the phone.

"Whatever happens to you in life," Bryony said, staring straight out the windshield, "make sure that you always get out your side of the story first, Ali."

Buoyed by Bryony's apparent imperviousness to her situation, Ali put out her left hand to reach for the gear stick, hoping to impose her authority. With the other hand she intensified her grip on the steering wheel. Instead of gaining stability, however, the car veered toward the middle of the road. For a moment it crossed into the opposite lane. She could see people on the sidewalk looking at her disdainfully, no doubt muttering about mothers in Chelsea tractors they couldn't control. Ali swiftly pulled her hand away from the gear stick, back toward the steering wheel, somehow switching on the windshield wipers in the process. They angrily squeaked back and forth across the dry windshield at maximum speed.

"Shit," said Ali.

"Shit," repeated the twins excitedly from the back of the car.

"Put your hand on top of mine, and when I give the command, use the clutch," Bryony said calmly.

Ali nodded compliantly, relieved that someone else was going to take control. She was too young for this job. It was all too much responsibility. She had left Hector in the bath the evening after piss-gate and had gone back in to find him sound asleep, his head almost submerged underwater. When she pulled him out of the water in panic that he had drowned, she banged his head so hard against the tap that a small trickle of blood flowed from his nose.

She knew that whatever Izzy was doing in her bedroom in the evening, it wasn't her homework, because twice this week she had rushed through logarithms and Latin verbs over breakfast. And although Bryony insisted she monitor where Jake was going and who he was with, she felt too embarrassed to ask him, even though she lay in bed worrying until she heard him come home. And she'd forgotten to feed the guinea pigs, Laurel and Hardy, for three days.

How could they expect a twenty-one-year-old to monitor a seventeen year old? Jake understood this. And he took advantage. The truth was that despite Bryony's insistence that Ali would simply be plugging the gaps that she couldn't fill, she was actually running the show. Bryony and Nick were hardly ever at home because they worked all the time. In fact, the only day she had seen Nick at home was the Sunday when Foy and Tita had come to lunch. And there was no one to share this with. When she called her friends, they had laughed.

"Take the money and run," advised Rosa. "Stay six months and then come back here for the summer term. You can share my room."

"What about your new boyfriend?"

"He doesn't really come here unless the house is empty. Too complicated."

"God, he's not one of those married guys from that website, is he?" asked Ali.

"No," Rosa said, and laughed. "I've given up on them already. Their egos are even bigger than their bank balance. In fact, there's probably a correlation between the two."

"Is the father attractive?" asked Maia, just after Ali had described Hector's near-death experience.

"Have you been clubbing?" asked Tom.

"I saw your sister in the city center," said Rosa. "She didn't know you had gone."

"Too much, too much, too much," the windshield wipers seemed to be saying as they hurtled back and forth. Bryony reached out to turn them off, leaving her right hand hovering over the gear stick.

Ali glanced at Bryony's hand to get her bearings. It was pale and infused with tiny blue veins like an underripe Stilton. She reached out for the gear stick again and felt Bryony's small bony hand atop her own. It was warmer than she'd expected. Her graceful fingers were intertwined with Ali's. Her nails were painted the same color as her shirt.

"Clutch," said Bryony, digging her nails into Ali's hand to reinforce the command. Ali pressed down hard.

"And down," said Bryony. Together they pulled down the gear stick.

"Driving is like life," Bryony said, as they successfully executed the maneuver. "It's a combination of bluff and skill. I can help you with the skill, but you need to develop the bluff. London is full of bluffers." She pointed out a mother driving past them.

"She drives with a sense of entitlement," Bryony pointed out. "You, too, can drive like that. You just need to develop the right attitude."

Ali felt a small drop of sweat trickle down the side of her face. She stuck out her tongue to catch it. But she was too late, and it dripped down onto her blue T-shirt. Another drop fell onto her T-shirt, joining the two sweaty stains together. Bryony pretended not to notice. Instead she instructed her to turn the next left and park on a single yellow line.

They all got out of the car in silence. On the sidewalk, the twins held on to Bryony. One of them, perhaps Hector, held out a hand to Ali. She took it in her own. It felt like a piece of warm fudge, soft and sticky. He looked up at Ali benevolently, knowing that the power to bestow favor was in his behest. The twins would always need each other more than they needed anyone else, Bryony had explained, in one of her chats about how to loosen the knots that bound them together.

"We'll walk the last hundred yards," Bryony said. "Then you can meet their teacher."

Bryony suggested that it might be sensible for Ali to get the Tube home, and she would take the car to work. Ali nodded gratefully, unsure what to say. She was too embarrassed to admit that she had no idea how to get back to Holland Park Crescent on the Underground.

Another mother came up to Bryony and asked questions about the school holidays. She was a large woman, the sort who wears unflattering circular skirts in loud prints and lipstick with too much pink, as if to underline her lack of vanity. Was Nick able to take time off work? Did they manage a week in Corfu? How were her parents?

"It was wonderful, Sophia," said Bryony. "We were back and forth a couple of times, but we managed two weeks there."

Sophia Wilbraham fired questions at Bryony, laughing heartily at all her responses, even though they contained only just enough information to be polite. Behind Sophia, two paces behind and two to the side, Ali noticed another woman, closer to her in age. Ali stood beside Bryony, waiting to be introduced to them all. Bryony said nothing. For a moment the four of them stood in uncomfortable silence while Sophia waited for Bryony to reciprocate.

When she didn't, Sophia proceeded to tell Bryony about their own family holiday spent in Costa Rica, where they managed to visit volcanoes, rainforests, and cloud forests, and spend a week on the Caribbean coast, all in just under two weeks. She then contrasted this with their previous holiday in Jordan, where they had trekked into the desert on camels and visited some fantastic archaeological sites.

"Less culture, but the children learned a huge amount about the environment," Sophia said. Not enough to point out the environmental cost of all their long-haul flights, thought Ali, recalling the utter boredom of her own school holidays, spent for the most part in Cromer, although there had been a couple of trips to Portugal before Jo's decline. It struck Ali that these children were already better traveled than she would ever be.

"The tour company managed to get hold of a couple of Garifuna Indians from Nicaragua so that the children could learn about indigenous culture, and they had someone to teach them Spanish for an hour each day."

The wind caught the woman's skirt so that it ballooned around her hips as though someone had inflated her. Had Jake been at the party that was raided by the police at the weekend? She smiled. There was a moment when Bryony drew a breath before replying that he had been revising for his exams on Saturday night. She glanced over at Ali, who felt another knot of anxiety in her stomach. She had no idea where Jake had been, although she knew he wasn't home until two in the morning. The woman wouldn't leave them alone. She started pressing Bryony for information about English tutors for her sixteen-year-old daughter.

"I'm looking for someone who can help unlock Thomas Hardy," she said intensely, turning her back on Ali.

"Is he stuck in your cellar?" asked one of the twins equally seriously.

"She's doing *Far from the Madding Crowd*," said the woman, smiling benignly at the twins. "But she says she can't relate to any of it. Especially all the agricultural stuff. Even though we showed her some Costa Rican peasants plowing a field with oxen. I've spoken to her teacher, and she says she just needs to read the book again." She laughed a little too heartily.

"I don't think I know anyone," said Bryony.

"Hardy's a tough nut to crack," said Ali, unable to suppress herself any longer. "And fate is a difficult concept for teenagers. I think it's better to read *Tess of the d'Urbervilles* first and then go back to *Far from the Madding Crowd*. If you get the concept of forbidden love in *Tess*, then it's easier to understand Bathsheba's dilemma."

Afterward, she tried to work out just whom she was trying to impress. Was she attempting to compensate for the muddle in the car by reminding Bryony of other reasons that she had given her the job? Was she trying to force this woman into acknowledging her existence? Or did she suddenly realize that there were other ways she could earn a living in London?

Either way, it backfired horribly. The woman asked if she was a family friend, and Ali, gratified by the attention, explained that she was working for the Skinners and that she had almost finished her undergraduate degree in English literature. The woman did a half-pirouette so that she was facing Ali, and started asking whether she would be interested in earning a bit of money doing some extra tutoring on her days off.

"Can't help," interrupted Bryony apologetically. "Ali works for us full-time, and if she has any free time she goes back to Norfolk to see her parents." It was said in a way that suggested this was an immutable routine that had evolved over years. Bryony put a protective arm around Ali's shoulders. The woman finally backed off.

"We need to establish a schedule for Martha and Izzy to practice their quartet together, don't we?" she asked. "Shall I organize it with Ali?"

"Yes, please," said Bryony.

"I'll need her details, then," said Sophia, a note of triumph in her voice, as she strode away with Ali's mobile number saved in her list of contacts.

"I knew this was going to be a problem," said Bryony so venomously that Ali was worried she would be heard. "Sophia Wilbraham won't let it go. She's like a supertanker, sweeping through the ocean, capsizing anything that gets in her way. And did you notice the way that she implied that Jake was at that party? Because I'm a working mother, she wants my children to fail."

"I'm really sorry," Ali said, unsure exactly what she was apologizing for, and taken aback by the ferocity of Bryony's reaction to the strange bell-jar woman. "I haven't really driven a car with gears since my driving test."

"I can't believe she tried to poach you so flagrantly in front of me," said Bryony more thoughtfully. "Nanny-napping on your first week of work. Extraordinary."

"What do you mean?" asked Ali in confusion.

"It's not your fault," said Bryony, as they continued down the road. "It's the risk we take employing someone like you."

"It was dangerous, and I shouldn't have done it," said Ali in confusion.

"Forget the car and move on," said Bryony almost impatiently. "We'll get you a small automatic and you can do some more lessons. Or would you prefer a G-Wiz? People your age are very environmental, aren't they? Of if you don't want to drive at all, then you can use the taxi account all the time."

"Isn't that a little premature?" stammered Ali, who hadn't yet worked out that generally Bryony posed only questions she had already answered. "I mean, I might not work out. My trial period isn't even up yet. I've only been with you for ten days."

Bryony waved away her concerns and let go of Alfie's, or perhaps it was Hector's, hand to tap a message into her BlackBerry. The private line, noted Ali.

"Jake will need a car to learn in soon," she said.

Ali felt unnerved by the generosity of Bryony's reaction. At the time she put this down to the cost entailed in buying her a car and the uncomfortable sensation that she was being bought. Then she became caught up in the idea that it didn't matter that Bryony was trying to buy her, it was the fact that she wasn't worth purchasing. Which brought into relief the idea that Bryony's judgment was somehow off-kilter. Which reminded her of the way her sister sometimes reacted to things.

It was only much later that she realized it was the inappropriateness that bothered her. She should have been the object of Bryony's wrath rather than her understanding. It was reckless of Ali to drive the car without any practice. But it was more reckless of Bryony to tolerate her behavior. Bryony's priorities were completely wrong.

"Well observed," said Rosa, during a late-night phone conversation later that day. "Professor MacDonald would be proud of your insight. He was asking how you were getting on the other day. He wanted to know whether your boss was in the mold of Mr. Rochester or Sir Pitt Crawley."

"What did you tell him?"

"I said that you'd completely forgotten about us all." Rosa giggled. "We were doing a tutorial on whether Frances Burney was Jane Austen's literary godmother."

"Of course she is," said Ali. "She mentions her in *Northanger Abbey*, and don't you remember the last line of Burney's second novel?"

"No," said Rosa.

"'The whole of this unfortunate business . . . has been the result of pride and prejudice,'" quoted Ali. "Conclusive evidence."

"This is why I miss you," Rosa said with a groan. "When are you coming to visit?"

"I'm working most weekends," said Ali.

"What about Christmas and New Year?"

"They've asked me to go skiing with them to look after the twins. If I go they'll double my salary for the week."

"God, they must be loaded."

"They are," said Ali, walking away from the chimney in case Jake was upstairs and could hear her conversation.

"At least they're not boring," said Rosa.

"The Skinners are not ordinary or average," responded Ali, "but at least I know it's them that's strange, not me." She could tell that Rosa was bored of discussing people she had never met. So instead she described how she came home from the school run to find that the pug had done a shit in her shoe.

"We're in a fight for supremacy," Ali joked.

"At least it means you're a player," said Rosa.

6

October 2006

"Are you the Skinners' new nanny?"

Ali was too taken aback to respond. She had been doing the school run with the twins for almost a month now, and this was the first time that anyone had spoken to her. Unless you included Hector and Alfie's teacher, who had taken her aside twice: once to say that the twins seemed to enjoy playing with each other more than with other children, and then again a few days later to inform Ali that they wouldn't go to the bathroom separately and were speaking a language that no one at school could identify, although the music teacher thought it might be Swahili. It wasn't. Ali had diligently gone to the bookshop at the School of Oriental and African Studies in Bloomsbury and bought a dictionary with some of the £100 spending money Bryony left out each day. But when she tried out Swahili words on them, Hector and Alfie were unmoved.

"Czy ty jesteś nianią państwa Skinner?" the woman persisted, repeating the question in Polish, as she put the brake on a heavy-looking stroller with a sleeping baby in the bottom. She was pale and small, with an asymmetrical fringe that covered one eye.

"Czy pochodzisz a Ukrainy czy ze Słowacji?"

"I'm English," said Ali emphatically, wondering if the word *nanny* didn't exist outside the English language or whether it was one of those nouns that had gone global, like *hamburger* or *pornography*. Except Ali knew it wasn't a new word. The night before her first interview she embarked on some last-minute research and discovered that "Nanny" was a nineteenth-century diminutive of Annie. An explanation as prosaic as the job she was applying for, Ali suspected.

"She's our nanny," said Alfie and Hector in unison. They had come out of school as they did almost every day, holding hands and singing "Two Little Boys," a song that they had learned in music, about a couple of friends who fight alongside each other in the American Civil War.

"Did you think I would leave you dying when there's room on my horse for two?" they sang as they marched out of the playground. At first Ali had found this touching. But as the days went by, she saw other children evil-eye them when they began. She found herself feeling protective over them as she saw how the proximity they craved alienated other children. Now lines from the song intruded on perfectly rational conversation.

"What would you like to do when you're grown up?" their grandfather had asked the other day.

"When we grow up we'll both be soldiers, and our horses will not be toys," Alfie had told Foy solemnly.

The baby in the bottom of the stroller started crying, and the woman deftly lifted him out and swung him over her shoulder. He was tiny and mewed like a hungry kitten as she soothed him with a familiar song in a foreign tongue.

Ali reflected on her interactions with the twins. She felt like a comedian trying to get a decent act together. It was mostly improvised. Hit-or-miss stuff. Mostly miss. The books on how to raise children that Bryony left in Ali's bedroom with yellow stickers marking key passages were completely unhelpful. "Silent but deadly," Izzy would say after Ali had discovered they had glued one of Bryony's favorite leather gloves onto the door of her bedroom or gone into the larder and opened every single can of Diet Coke and drank as much as they could before throwing up on the floor.

Her most successful strategy for distracting Hector and Alfie involved telling them stories in the Norfolk accent Ali had spent much of her life trying to suppress. The legend of Black Shuck and his retributions for infractions like hitting your sister or refusing to go up for a bath were far more effective than a spell on the naughty step. And they definitely had an ear for dialect.

The woman's proficiency as she quietened the baby highlighted Ali's inadequacies. When she took the twins to the park, she sat and read *Tristram Shandy*, one of her eighteenth-century literature texts, while they played, arguing to herself that if their mother couldn't be bothered to get on her hands and knees in the sandpit, then why should she? She bribed them with sugary-coated sweets that made them hyperactive and then calmed them down with all the television programs proscribed by Bryony. She had learned a lot about uppers and downers from her sister through the years.

"I'm Mira," said the woman, holding out one hand to shake Ali's hand while the other held the baby in place on her shoulder. The baby's cries became less plaintive, and it shut its eyes. Mira rhythmically jigged from side to side, the beat increasing whenever the mewing noise threatened to intensify.

"Sorry," she apologized. "I need to get him back to sleep. Just give me a few minutes."

Sophia Wilbraham had ignored Ali since the incident on the first day of term, although the impact of the perceived slight was diminished by the fact that so had everyone else. When she went to pick up the twins, Ali felt like the outsider in a Venn diagram. Everyone else was connected. The tall, shiny American mothers overlapped with their bigger-breasted, stripy-topped English counterparts and a small mutable huddle of working mothers who exchanged greetings with the antipodean nannies. The latter kept themselves apart from other foreign nannies, who herded according to nationality.

There were cheerful and noisy Filipinas who laughed more than anyone else; timid Indian women in flip-flops and saris, who never made eye contact; and then the group to which Mira belonged, who spoke whichever Eastern European language happened to be in the ascendant that day. Sometimes Ali found herself caught in the slip-stream of different conversations that wafted down the road. She closed her eyes and tried to imagine the parents at her old school in Cromer having similar exchanges.

"We're doing Cape Cod this year . . . David's trying to blag a villa in Tuscany from one of his clients . . . Bombay is too wet in sum-mer . . . There's a five-star hotel where you can stay to see the Komodo dragons . . . Forget the Portland, have the baby at Cedars-Sinai . . ."

Then yesterday: "He bit my son . . . He bit my daughter . . . He needs to be assessed by the ed psych . . . He has a new nanny . . . His parents are never around." Ali knew they were talking about Hector and must have realized she was within earshot. She felt a sting of hurt and anger on his behalf but was too unsure of herself to retaliate.

Ali was aware that Mira had carefully deposited the baby back in the stroller and was waiting for her to say something. Worried that she might appear unfriendly, she began to describe herself in greater detail, mentioning that she came from a coastal town in East Anglia and had come to London to find a job to pay off her student debts.

"It's the bit of England that looks like a head," Ali explained. "The east wind comes straight across the sea from the Urals. So do some of the birds, the starlings for sure, and sometimes we get tiny song thrushes. We've probably grown up breathing the same air. Where do you come from?"

"We were wondering if you wanted to have coffee with us," Mira said, ignoring Ali's attempt at geographical inclusion. Ali flinched. No one she had met seemed to have any interest in her life before she began working in London. Maybe that's what happened in a city of migrants. Life was lived in the present tense. She thought of the occasions that she had tried to engage Malea in conversation about the Philippines. Where exactly are you from? Do you still have family there? Will you go back one day? Malea sidestepped every question with an enigmatic laugh, as though Ali was making a joke.

Then yesterday, as Jake passed her on the top flight of stairs, he had stopped to explain how Malea had three children of her own, who lived with their grandmother in a village five hours by bus from Manila. The youngest was the same age as the twins, and she hadn't seen him for almost two years.

"That's so awful," said Ali. But Jake had already disappeared up to his room.

"I'm meant to go straight home and do half an hour of maths with each of them," Ali told Mira. "We have quite a strict timetable."

"Please, Ali, can we go to Starbucks?" pleaded Hector, pulling on her hand.

"I beg you," said Alfie melodramatically.

Ali laughed.

"We won't tell Mummy," said Hector.

Ali did a quick calculation in her head. Bryony was working late. By tomorrow, today would be a distant memory for the twins. "That would be really nice."

"We couldn't decide whether you were lonely or aloof," said Mira.

Ali was uncomfortable with the way she had been the subject of their conversation. Neither *lonely* nor *aloof* was an adjective anyone would want to attach to herself. But she did like the way Mira said "aloof," emphasizing the final consonant so that it hung in the air like smoke rings. It was obviously a word she had learned recently, because during this first encounter she used it several times. It reminded Ali of the way Hector and Alfie experimented with new words.

"Lonely," Ali said. "But not terminally." She wondered whether Mira would understand but didn't want to patronize her by searching for another word.

"Benignly lonely," said the woman with approval. "You must have a Ukrainian soul."

They headed into the busy road that Ali recognized from the first and last time she did the school run in the car.

"There are still punks, but they are paid by the council to attract

foreign tourists . . . They are very aloof . . . An almond croissant at the
Bluebird Café costs three pounds . . . Tesco Metro stays open until
almost midnight . . . The number twenty-two and number eleven are
the only buses that don't turn off into side streets . . ." said Mira,
thrilled to be in a position where she could educate an English person
about her own country.

"What's this road called?" Ali asked as they passed a tall man with
a red Mohawk and so many rings in his eyebrow it resembled a Lilliputian curtain rail.

"The King's Road," Mira said. "I can't believe you don't know it.
It's so important it has the definite article in front of it. Only the most
important roads in London have an article." She began running
though a list: the Earls Court Road, the Portobello Road, the Finch-
ley Road, the Limehouse Link . . ."

The way she spoke was odd. She enunciated each word carefully,
and her grammar was almost perfect, but it sounded so old-
fashioned.

"How long have you lived in England?" asked Ali.

"Many years," said Mira vaguely.

"Where did you learn to speak English?" Ali asked.

"I studied English literature at Kiev University years ago." Mira
shrugged.

"Literature?" asked Ali. Mira nodded.

"What books did you read?" Mira didn't reply straightaway. Instead
she stopped the stroller, fussed with the baby, and asked Hector and
Alfie whether they were enjoying school.

"*To Kill a Mockingbird, For Whom the Bell Tolls*, Shakespeare, Byron,
anything we could get our hands on," she said eventually. "It was a
long time ago."

"So how did you learn to speak with such a good accent?" Ali
persisted.

"We listened to tapes," said Mira, "and sometimes my father listened to American radio, but it was dangerous for him to do that."

"Why?" asked Ali.

"Under communism, it was prohibited," she explained.

"Were you happy when the wall came down?" Ali asked.

"New regime. Different problems," said Mira.

"Like what?" asked Ali.

"Corruption," said Mira abruptly. "We've arrived."

They went into the café, and Mira adroitly weaved the stroller between tables. There was a small group of women, whom Ali recognized from outside school. They were all sitting beside identical multistory strollers with babies tucked in the bottom and the occasional toddler sipping organic juice in the seat above.

She sat down, grateful for the company, and managed with surprising proficiency to order a skinny latte with an extra shot of coffee. Hector and Alfie sat at a table beside Ali with another boy, whom she recognized from their class.

She was intrigued to find these nannies speaking English to one another. Except because of the mispronunciation, the heavy accents, and the hesitant cadence, it sounded like a different form of English. They all mispronounced words in the same way. A rolling r that came from the front of the tongue rather than the glottis had been introduced. Maybe this is how everyone will speak in fifty years' time, thought Ali, as she sipped at her coffee. At the very least it might become a dialect or a kind of patois.

Mira introduced them to Ali. They all had exotic-sounding names: the one with the toddler was Raisa, the older woman with the perpetually worried expression was Ileana, then there was Katya. They all smiled warmly and shook her hand. Ali recognized Katya as the nanny standing beside the woman in the circular skirt at the beginning of term. Actually, Ali recalled, Katya had stood unobtrusively three paces behind Sophia Wilbraham and one pace to the side, a technique she noticed other nannies adopt when they were with their bosses. The etiquette between nanny and employer was as byzantine as the court of Louis Quinze.

Katya was tall and pale. Her hair was harshly scraped back off her face into a ponytail. She wore no makeup and a shapeless white shirt over a pair of jeans, but even despite this minimalist attire, Ali could see she was beautiful. After acknowledging Ali with a quick smile, she continued with the story she was telling.

Ali sipped her coffee, grateful for an excuse to stare at her. She was wasted spending her days looking after someone else's children, thought Ali. She should be on MTV or modeling for Stella McCartney or presenting a cookery program on Eastern European cuisine.

A small child sat on her lap, nestling into her breast. He was half asleep, his thumb was in his mouth, and he kneaded a scrap of rag with his remaining fingers. She stroked his blond curly hair, winding it round her finger into ringlets.

"Thomas's mother is away for a long weekend in New York," she explained. "I say he misses her terribly but only because his mother needs to hear that. Which I find odd because if I were his mother I would want to know that he is happy, don't you agree, Ali? Wouldn't you be happy that he is happy with me?"

Ali nodded, grateful to be included in the conversation.

"In truth, life is easier when she is away, because we get into a good routine. He goes to bed earlier because he's not waiting for her to come up at night, and Leo is kinder to him." She leaned over, patted the boy sitting next to Alfie and Hector on the head, and bestowed a small kiss on Thomas's hot-looking face. The child opened an eye and smiled up adoringly at her. "If he can't sleep, I let him come and lie on my bed, and sometimes he ends up spending the whole night there."

"Doesn't the mother mind?" Ali asked, feeling grateful the twins showed no similar urge. "I mean, the twins' mother is very particular about their routines, and I can't imagine her allowing them to do something like that."

"Sophia doesn't know, and her husband doesn't mind." Katya smiled. "But I think if you leave a child for thirteen hours a day with another woman, then you have to expect the child will become fond of her. Don't you think? We are happy together." She gave him another kiss and put a protective arm around him.

"Of course," said Ali, who didn't agree at all. The idea that she would fill any maternal void for Hector and Alfie was appalling. She didn't want the responsibility.

"What does she do all day if you're looking after Thomas and she's not working?" asked Ali.

"She goes to the gym," said Katya. They all laughed.

"Molokho, Katya, molokho bud'laska." The little boy stirred. He didn't open his eyes. Katya pulled a bottle of milk from her handbag. *"Dakoyu."*

"He speaks better Ukrainian than English," said Katya proudly.

"Why do you all speak to each other in English?" Ali asked.

"Because not all of us understand each other." Mira smiled, smoothing down her bangs so that they covered one eye. "Ukrainians in the south can understand Polish because we were invaded by Poland, and those in the north can understand Russian because they were invaded by the Russians. I speak both because I learned Russian at school when Ukraine was still Communist."

She went on to explain that although the Czechs and the Slovaks could understand each other, since partition their languages were beginning to drift apart. Both, however, could understand Polish, because they were all West Slavic languages that were written in the Latin alphabet. Macedonians and Bulgarians could understand each other, but Bulgarian was a South Slavic language that used the Cyrillic alphabet.

It would make a good topic for the linguistics component of her degree, thought Ali. Perhaps she could even write a paper in her spare time to prove to Will MacDonald that she was serious about returning to finish her course.

"But Ileana is the real problem, because she is Romanian." Mira smiled again. "She speaks four languages, but none of us understand any of them." She asked Ileana to translate an English sentence into Italian, French, Spanish, and finally Romanian to demonstrate the similarities.

"She always closes the window before dinner," Ileana said seriously, smoothing down the front of her A-line skirt.

"*Illa semper fenestram claudit antequam cenat* is Latin," she said, making Ali repeat the sentence out loud. She did the same in Italian, French, Spanish, and Portuguese, finishing up with Romanian.

"*Ea închide totdeauna fereastra înainte de a cina,*" Ileana said triumphantly. Everyone applauded, including someone at another table.

"How come you've ended up in London, Mira?" asked Ali. There was an uncomfortable silence. Ileana looked at her hands. Katya put a lid on the bottle of milk.

"Is long story, Ali," said Mira, making a rare grammatical mistake.

"So what's it like?" Katya asked suddenly, turning to Ali.

"What's what like?" replied Ali.

"What's it like working for the Skinners?"

"It's fine," said Ali, checking to see whether Alfie and Hector were listening, but they were too involved in scooping froth off the top of their babyccinos to make milk mustaches. She could see the disappointment on Katya's face.

"Early days. All a bit strange. They look after me well."

She fell silent, aware that she hadn't delivered. If they became friends she might tell them that after almost two months living with the Skinners, this was what she knew: Bryony didn't eat; Izzy ate a lot but then threw up, mostly Cumberland sausages that cost £11 a pound from the butcher in Holland Park Avenue; the twins' friends all had strange names (Star, Ocean, Canteloupe); Nick didn't need much sleep; and the under-floor heating was perpetually switched on in the kitchen, even when it got so hot that Malea had to open the sliding doors into the garden. She might have told them how music could be piped through the ten rooms on the bottom two floors from a centrally controlled panel in the kitchen and that as recently as this week she had discovered a new room in the basement: a home cinema with seats wide enough to fit two adults. Or she could have mentioned the bags of clothes that arrived from Net-a-Porter every other week.

Some of the dresses cost thousands of pounds. Ali knew because she had seen the receipts in the top drawer of the desk in Bryony's office. Many of the bags sat in Bryony's dressing room, the clothes wrapped in tissue paper, never to be used, because she didn't have time to try them on.

She thought of the £100 spending money that Bryony left on the kitchen table every morning, and the irritation on her face if Ali tried to return the change in the evening; the way the larder was stacked with food and drink from floor to ceiling, like a supermarket, because Bryony made exactly the same Internet order every week, even when the huge American fridge was already full. She recalled waking up a couple of nights earlier and hearing raised voices arguing somewhere in the house and assuming it was Nick and Bryony, only to discover the next morning that Nick was still in Asia, and she thought about the apologetic expression on Jake's face when he told her about Malea's children. Although she was sure that he lied to her more than any of the other children, Jake occasionally demonstrated random acts of kindness that made Ali feel less alone at Holland Park Crescent.

"Nick and Bryony aren't around very much. They seem to work very hard," she explained. "Nick travels a lot. I've only seen him four or five times since I started the job."

"That's good," said Katya. "It can get a bit confusing for the children if there are too many people telling them what to do."

How could it be good that the twins hardly ever spent any time with their dad? Ali wondered. She spent long hours with her father as a child. But would it have mattered if she hadn't? She wouldn't have known that if the wind was blowing off the land, then it was safe to fish. More significant, she wouldn't have known that if the wind was blowing from the northeast round to easterly, then it was best to stay on land. When it was like this her father described it as "blowing up a hooligan." She smiled at the memory. Nor would she have known that the seabed in Cromer is made of sand, chalk, and flint, and that it was this combination that made the crabs smaller and sweeter.

"Is that what you find?" asked Ali, wondering what it would be like to work for someone like Sophia Wilbraham.

"No," Katya said with a smile, "there is a very clear chain of command and room for only one person at the top. We call Sophia the dominatrix." She laughed loudly. Mira looked at Katya disapprovingly, as though Ali wasn't quite yet worthy of such confidence.

"She is someone who is not afraid of her own tongue," said Mira, muddling metaphors in a way that made Ali smile. "But she has a big heart."

"And a big arse," said Katya.

"Katya doesn't like her anymore, because she thinks Sophia wants rid of her," explained Mira.

"Sophia's husband told me that she thought I was too good-looking to live in a family home and that I cooked too many meals with him in mind," said Katya, rocking Thomas in her arms. "As though I was trying to seduce him with my *kapusniak*."

"*Kapusniak* is a Polish dish," Raisa interjected.

"Actually, it is also Ukrainian," said Mira. The conversation descended into a discussion about the origins of various Eastern European dishes.

"So what did you do?" interrupted Ali, who was intrigued by this dynamic.

"I found out her favorite dishes and started to cook them," Katya said, and shrugged.

"So will you be going to Corfu with the family like the other nannies?" asked Mira.

"Of course," said Ali, although Bryony had mentioned nothing.

Why did she lie to Mira? She decided later that it was because she didn't want to acknowledge how dislocated she still felt from Bryony. Although they spoke two or three times a day and it was rare that Bryony didn't send an e-mail every couple of hours, their relationship was functional and devoid of any context. This week Ali had received an e-mail outlining the problems of underbrushing the twins' teeth, followed a couple of days later by an e-mail warning her of the perils of overbrushing. This had rapidly been followed by a magazine article about how to encourage intellectual curiosity in small children, suggesting Ali cut out a piece from the newspaper each day to discuss with the twins in between their maths homework and piano practice.

She thought of the most recent e-mail, sent at five fifty-three a.m., when Bryony was probably warming up in the basement gym. Subject matter "Snagging," a hybrid of snogging and nagging, Ali assumed, until she read the attachment instructing her to go through every room in the house looking for problems the builders might have overlooked at the end of their recent refurbishment. Light fixtures missing from wardrobes and bathroom cupboards, unstable bathroom sinks, missing curtain hooks, loose wires, defunct lightbulbs, sloppy paintwork, grouting issues, leaking radiators. Bryony's list was exhaustive.

Then she remembered their first meeting after she had been given the job. On reflection, it was little more than an elaborate list of dos and don'ts. The dos included reading to the twins each night for at least twenty minutes, but no more than thirty, alternating between fiction and nonfiction in a ratio of roughly sixty-forty. At this point Bryony had suggested Ali might want to take notes, and had pushed a pen and notebook toward her across the dining room table.

Then there was an extensive discussion on healthy snacks and a list of forbidden foods, including most sweets. This was particularly important for Izzy, Bryony said, because she was ill disciplined and putting on weight. Ali could, however, ask Malea to make blueberry muffins using honey instead of sugar, and on Fridays everyone was allowed an organic chocolate bar (as long as it contained at least sixty percent cocoa solids). She then talked about carbohydrates in terms that reminded Ali of the war on terrorism. They hid in foods. They needed to be routed and exposed and made accountable for their actions.

"Definitely on the axis of evil," Ali had joked, but Bryony hadn't responded, because she had moved on to screen time. She accepted

Ali's assertion that it would be difficult to monitor how much time Jake and Izzy spent on their computers because they were in their bedrooms. The twins were allowed to watch no more than half an hour of television each day. Computer games were completely off-limits. At the end Bryony casually suggested that Ali might want to avoid "getting embroiled" in the nanny mafia that spent too much time gossiping in cafés.

"How long have you been with Thomas?" Ali asked Katya, in the same way she might ask a friend about a new boyfriend.

"Since he was born. Almost." Katya smiled. "They had a maternity nurse at the beginning. But they discovered that she was giving Thomas medicine to make him sleep through the night. I'd been working as their cleaning lady for six years, and so they fired the maternity nurse and I got the job."

"That's awful," said Ali. She paused for a moment. "What's a maternity nurse?"

"It's someone who gets paid to look after newborn babies," Katya explained. "Really good money, but you change jobs every three weeks. The mothers can be really neurotic, and you have to get up in the night all the time."

"Unless you drug the baby," said Ali. Everyone laughed. Hector and Alfie came over to see what was going on.

"I love it here," said Hector, leaning in toward Ali. She put out her knee and pulled him into her lap. This was the first time she could remember him spontaneously seeking her affections. She gave him a piece of half-eaten cake, and his body relaxed into her own until he was almost supine. He began humming the same song again. Ali gently wound one of his curls around her finger, and it slipped through like threads of silk.

"You need a haircut, Hector," she said, remembering Bryony's latest e-mail.

"No," responded Hector adamantly.

"If you join the army, they cut off all your hair," she teased him. He frowned as if unsure whether to believe her. Alfie came over and stood beside them. "In the army they shave it down to your scalp." She made a noise like an electric razor and pretended to cut their hair with her fingers, tickling the backs of their necks until they crumpled into a giggling heap.

"I have something for you boys for being so good," said Katya. She searched in her handbag until she had found a lollipop for each of them.

"Thank you, Katya," they trilled in unison, ripping off the wrapper. This afternoon's sugar intake represented the biggest lapse in rules since Ali had started work. On balance she would get away with it. They would probably be in bed before Bryony was home. And tomorrow night she was unlikely to ask about whether they had eaten any sweets the previous day. If they ate the lollipops now it would buy her another twenty minutes of company with Mira and her friends. She had enjoyed sitting with this group of women in the warm café, even if her contribution to the conversation was sporadic. She liked the way they gently chided and teased one another and gave one another advice about how to deal with tantrums or cook custard without burning the bottom of the saucepan. Katya was indiscreet and entertaining. Mira's employers were seeing a marriage guidance counselor. Sophia's oldest daughter was sleeping with her English tutor. Bryony had turned down an offer to appear in *Vogue* as one of Britain's top businesswomen. Mira admonished Katya without conviction.

"Don't tell Mummy," Ali told Hector and Alfie. "Otherwise we won't be able to do this again." They nodded seriously. Ali turned to Katya again.

"How did you meet Mira?" she asked.

"On the journey from Ukraine," she said.

"You must have been very young," said Ali.

"Seventeen," said Katya. "But I am an older and wiser woman now."

"Were you on the same flight?" said Ali. Katya smiled.

"We came overland, Ali," she explained, giving Mira a nervous look. "It was a long journey. There was a lot of time to get to know each other. I was in trouble. Mira helped me."

"Would you like to meet up with us at the same time next week?" Mira suddenly asked.

"I'd really like that," said Ali immediately. It would be good for Hector and Alfie, and it would be good for her. They would all be less lonely.

"And the twins can come and play with Thomas and Leo," said Katya.

"That would be great," said Ali. "They don't often get asked to go to anyone else's house."

"I'm cooking dinner for everyone this weekend," said Katya. "Would you like to come, too?"

"Nick and Bryony are going away," explained Ali. "Another time. Maybe I can cook for you."

"Can you cook?" asked Katya.

"Actually, no," Ali said with a laugh. The talk of food reminded her that the Skinners were throwing a dinner party that evening and that Bryony would be arriving home early.

"Shit," she said, looking down at her watch.

"Shit," the twins repeated, as she hurried them out of the café and searched for a cab. It would have been quicker to catch a bus home, but Bryony didn't like the twins' using public transport.

When they arrived at Holland Park Crescent, Bryony was too busy worrying about a couple of guests who had canceled at the last minute, and a wine waiter who had called in sick, to preoccupy herself with Ali's violation of the afternoon schedule. As she closed the front door behind them, Ali overheard anxious voices rippling from the drawing room.

"It leaves a big hole in the seating plan," Bryony said. "We built the party around them. I really wanted him to meet Felix so that he could assure him about Northern Rock being on target to meet analysts' forecasts so that we can avoid any nasty pieces about how the U.S. housing market could be contagious." Nick was on speakerphone. Ali heard him swear under his breath.

"Politicians are so fucking unreliable," he muttered. "Piss-poor judgment, if you ask me. We'll be around long after Blair's star has bloody well fallen. They're all a bunch of cunts."

The twins looked at Ali, wide-eyed.

"What does 'politician' mean?" asked Alfie eventually. Ali smiled with relief and whispered a brief explanation.

"He was really apologetic," said Bryony. "Something's come up. He got called back in to write a speech for tomorrow. It's probably got something to do with Blair's announcement at conference." She paused for a moment. "I was wondering whether we should invite my mother and father instead? They won't mind filling empty seats, and the wife of the private equity guy wants to buy a house in Corfu. They can talk olives together."

Nick groaned.

"Look, if I can put up with the Wilbrahams, then you can put up with Foy and Tita," Bryony deftly negotiated. Why invite people you don't like to dinner? wondered Ali, as she hung up the twins' coats in the cloakroom adjacent to the drawing room. Why go to all that trouble for people Bryony would avoid if she saw them on the other side of the street? Although, of course, to judge from the van parked outside with "Dinners of Distinction" painted on its doors, Bryony wouldn't be doing the cooking. Or the washing up. Or even pour a glass of wine. Ali picked up the internal phone and called downstairs to ask Malea if tea was on the table or whether she should bathe the twins first.

"Ali, is that you?" Bryony called from the drawing room. "Can I have a quick word? Send the twins downstairs to Malea."

Ali removed her shoes and went into the room. Bryony was sitting at the small table beside the window. A file labeled "Dinner Party

10/06/06" sat beside her. Two BlackBerrys flashed messages. A woman sat at her feet doing a pedicure, efficiently buffing nails and pushing back cuticles.

"Would you be an absolute star and step into the breach?" Bryony asked.

"I'm very flattered, but I couldn't possibly hold a conversation," said Ali. Bryony laughed so loudly that the pedicure was momentarily halted.

"I didn't mean at the dinner table," said Bryony, "although you'd do a lot better on the latest literary news than I would. I wondered if you would mind acting as wine waiter for the evening. You only need to do red." It was an order dressed up as a favor, Ali decided.

"Sure," Ali said, and smiled, relieved rather than offended by Bryony's proposal.

"I'll pay you, of course. Malea can put the twins to bed. You could probably do with a night off."

That was certainly true. Getting Hector and Alfie to bed involved more rituals than a Russian Orthodox wedding. The water in the bath had to be a certain level. She had to locate identical pajamas, then these had to be hidden from Bryony beneath dressing gowns because she didn't like them wearing the same clothes. She had to read *Did I Ever Tell You How Lucky You Are?* by Dr. Seuss three times and couldn't miss a single word, because Hector and Alfie noticed immediately. The gap between the curtains had to be exactly right, and Ali had to lie on the bed between them until they went to sleep. She had tried and failed to break this last habit, finally giving up when the twins revealed that every nanny they could remember had done this.

"What happens if your mum and dad put you to bed?" she had asked. They had looked at her blankly.

So later that night, Ali found herself standing discreetly in the corner of the dining room, holding a bottle of red wine swaddled in a stiff white napkin waiting to refill glasses.

She wore a black pencil skirt and white shirt loaned to her by Bryony. Her hair was pulled off her face. On the other side of the room

stood another wine waiter, a Latvian boy who looked far too young
to be living in London without his parents. He helpfully raised an
eyebrow at Ali whenever he noticed an empty glass. His kindness
made Ali's eyes water, but it might have been the smoke from the
scented candles.

The other waiters had just finished clearing away a starter of crab
risotto and were now serving veal paupiette with onion jus. The crab
reminded Ali of home. She wondered whether it had come from the
potting grounds fished by her father, although this year had been the
worst season he could remember. She remembered his favorite spots:
Back High Hole; Cistern Hill; Foulness shoal, for early summer, then
Brown's Ledge later in the season. He always knew the best places,
where the water had a bit of color and a lot of movement. "Crabbing's
a waste of time when the sea is sheer as piss," he used to tell her.

The female guests, apart from a woman sitting next to Nick, pleaded
anything from migraine to lactose intolerance to avoid eating a full
plate of food. So the risotto was hidden under lettuce leaves. Did
women in London ever eat? Ali wondered. At least it meant there
would be plenty of carrot and white chocolate fondant pudding left
over.

There were ten people at the large circular table, including Bryony,
Nick, Tita, Foy, and Sophia and Ned Wilbraham, a small but stocky
man with sharp features and cold eyes. If anyone recognized her, no
one gave anything away.

Then there was the man who owned a private equity company and
his wife, a superthin blond woman who could have been anything
between twenty-five and fifty-five. Downstairs, Ali heard the waiters
and waitresses place bets on whether she was the first, second, or third
Mrs. Gressingham. Ali knew from discussions over the seating plan
that the woman sitting beside Nick used to work in the City and now
advised the government on banking regulations. She had come alone.

The only guest who might genuinely qualify as a friend was Felix,
who had come straight from work to take his place between Tita and
Bryony. Ali recognized him immediately from the wedding photo in

the drawing room. He sidestepped into the room, shook hands with Nick, amid effusive apologies for his tardiness, and congratulated him on a deal that had just closed. Bryony didn't bother to stand up, so Felix hovered by her chair for a little longer than was comfortable while she gave him access to her right cheek, where he planted a slightly sloppy kiss. He reminded Ali of a faithful Labrador, grateful for the occasional patronizing pat on the head and tolerant of the odd kick in the ribs.

Ali knew from Foy that not only had Felix gone out with Bryony for more than a year at university, he had also introduced her to his old school friend, Nick Skinner, at a party after they left Oxford. Allegedly Felix had gone to this party with a ring in his pocket, intending to ask Bryony to marry him.

During one of his late-morning visits to Holland Park Crescent, Foy had given an extended version of the drama, using language so flowery that at one point Ali had to bite her lower lip to stop herself from laughing. "Felix had vituperated Nick for his *legerdemain*" was the most memorable line.

Foy described their relationship as a *"coup de foudre,"* because within a week of their first encounter, Bryony had abandoned Felix. She was bowled over by Nick's confidence, his charm, his "protean nature," and all the "accoutrements" that went with his lifestyle as a successful banker. Foy couldn't resist adding that perhaps Nick reminded Bryony of him. They were married a year later, and she was pregnant with Jake within a couple of months.

Felix went abroad for three years, working for the *Financial Times* in Washington. He came home with an American girlfriend, whom he "virtually jilted at the altar," Foy breathlessly explained. He had remained friends with Foy and Tita, and confessed to them that no one matched up to Bryony. Whether this was true or not, it had seeped into family mythology so that even Ali now viewed Felix with pity. It was an account that was convenient for both Nick and Bryony, because it diminished Felix in Nick's eyes and allowed Bryony to remain friends with him.

Ali observed him now. He was a little pasty-faced, as though he didn't see enough daylight, and his eyebrows were arched in a way that made him look permanently surprised by life. But despite his bumbling self-effacement and penchant for telling stories against himself, he quickly emerged as the most intelligent and likable person at the table. He had an endearing habit of looking at Bryony whenever he thought she wasn't watching. It was a gesture that reinforced his canine credentials.

Occasionally, he apologetically left the room to deal with a phone call. Ali heard him in the hall running through last-minute changes to a story when she went downstairs to fetch another bottle of red wine.

"The deal will definitely be announced on Monday morning," he shouted into the phone. "I've just had confirmation that the lawyers will wrap it up over the weekend so that the stock doesn't move." There was silence as someone responded. Then Felix spoke again. "It's the biggest M-and-A property deal this year. My sourcing is impeccable. In fact, I'm having dinner with them."

Foy was flanked by Bryony and Mrs. Gressingham. During the main course, he had given Mrs. Gressingham invaluable advice on buying a property in Corfu, including the name of his lawyer, the best place to buy furniture, and an insight into the rhythms of the olive harvest. He had even offered to have her to stay for a couple of days during her next trip to scout properties. By pudding, however, Ali knew that he had drunk more red wine than anyone else round the table. As the chocolate fondant was served he turned his back on Mrs. Gressingham and leaned toward Sophia Wilbraham to stare leerily down the front of her dress, muttering something through wine-stained teeth about how he was glad to see the Wilbraham cleavage had been passed down to the next generation.

"Do you like dinner parties?" he addressed Sophia's breasts.

"Of course," she answered. "I enjoy cooking." Bryony narrowed her eyes at the obvious barb.

"I think dinner parties are what couples do when they stop having sex," Foy declared loudly.

Overhearing this comment, Tita immediately turned toward Mr. Gressingham to question him about his job. What was private equity? How did they decide whether a company was worth buying or not? How long did they keep the company before it was sold? Mr. Gressingham, relieved and flattered by the diversion, gave a long-winded explanation of how he identified potential businesses and made them more profitable by borrowing more money cheaply. Tita listened carefully.

"Don't you sometimes worry that this urge to buy businesses to make them part of something bigger and make more and more profit every year just makes the people working for them feel smaller? I always think of our gardener in Corfu. He has a small family business landscaping holiday homes. He could probably make more money if he expanded, but he is perfectly happy with the status quo."

"I'm in the business of trying to make the world a richer place, not a happier place," replied Mr. Gressingham. "The way property prices are rising, we'll all need to earn a lot more money to help our children buy homes in London. You can't really live on less than two hundred fifty thousand pounds a year."

Ali heard herself gasp and saw Nick glance over at her. He gave Ali a quick, tight smile.

"I read something in *The Telegraph* today that said working women are responsible for the rise in house prices," chipped in Sophia.

"What on earth do you mean?" asked the woman from the Treasury who was sitting next to Nick. Sophia looked taken aback by her intervention, because the comment was intended to make Bryony squirm. But it was too late to backpedal.

"It said that if two parents work there is more money available to spend on housing, and that this has fueled the housing boom," she explained.

"I read that piece," said Foy excitedly. "It was the one that said that one in five women think mothers who work are bad mothers and that working mothers think stay-at-home mothers are idle. No wonder Bryony and Hester don't see eye to eye."

"The truth is that children are a twenty-year project, and so is a career, and there is an essential incompatibility for women in reconciling these two important strands of their life," said the woman from the Treasury, sounding a little as though she was delivering a speech. "And housing inflation is a problem in many countries where women aren't represented in the workplace."

"Like Iceland?" suggested Sophia.

"I'm thinking about moving my money to one of those Icelandic accounts," said Foy. "Six percent interest if you put it in Icesave."

"I wouldn't if I were you," said Nick.

"All I know is that if you love your job, then you have to keep going," said Bryony in a conciliatory tone. "I never had any desire to have a career break or set up my own business icing cupcakes."

Mrs. Gressingham remained silent during this conversation. Her face was so Botoxed that Ali couldn't read her expression.

"Did you manage to find a decent new nanny?" She leaned toward Bryony across the gap left by Felix, who had left the room again to take another call. "I remember you were looking at the end of the summer."

"Our concierge agency came up trumps," said Bryony. "She started a couple of months ago, and we all love her. She's English, fresh out of university, so she can deal with all the homework. And she's got endless patience with the twins." Ali stepped uncomfortably from one foot to the other, staring at her shoes as she felt her face turn the same color as the bottle of wine in her hand.

"Have you left her on her own with the children yet?" the blond woman asked.

"Next weekend will be the first time," said Bryony. "We're off to Idaho to stay with Dick Fuld and his wife for the weekend."

"You must be inner-circle," said Mr. Gressingham, clearly impressed by this invitation.

"That's always the big test. It all runs beautifully until we go away. The moment we step out the front door, it always falls apart," said his wife. Nick turned toward her to listen to the conversation. He was running his finger around the edge of his wineglass, making a high-pitched humming sound that signaled his boredom.

"Tell them what happened last time we went away," her husband urged, sensing his wife was already losing Nick's interest.

"We came home a day early because Dan had to get back to work, and I found the nanny in bed with the housekeeper," she said triumphantly.

"Our bed," chipped in her husband. "Not even her bed. A lesbian tryst under our own roof."

"At least they were taking exercise," joked the woman from the Treasury. "Our nanny's food bill is bigger than her salary."

"It's so difficult to find decent staff in London at the moment," said Mrs. Gressingham.

"We've been very lucky," said Bryony, sounding just a little too pleased with herself.

"It's a competitive market," said Nick. "London is a global financial center, and everyone wants to live here. And everyone wants good people to work for them."

"Have you tried any Poles? Apparently they are very good with children," said someone else.

The conversation turned back to property prices in London and the way that rich foreigners were at an unfair advantage because they didn't have to pay the same taxes as ordinary British families.

"How come?" said Mrs. Gressingham, leaning in toward Nick, so that you could see visible evidence of her daily two-hour gym schedule in the sculpted muscles of her upper arms.

"They buy houses through a holding company so they don't have to pay taxes," explained Nick.

"Anything over five million gets snapped up by Saudi princes or East European oligarchs," complained Foy. "Soon there won't be anyone English living in Kensington and Chelsea."

"Someone should start a campaign," said someone else.

"It's a bit of a minority issue," said Felix Naylor. Ali caught his eye, and he raised an eyebrow. "Wouldn't get much traction with the British public, methinks. Millionaires complaining about billionaires doesn't exactly engender much sympathy."

"Nick, tell me about these formulas the credit agencies are using to measure risk," said the woman who worked at the Treasury. She spoke in a soft drawl, with an accent that slipped from English into American, depending on the vowel. It was difficult to place her geographically. "These derivatives have got so complex that you need an economics degree and an MBA from Harvard to understand how they work."

"The Gaussian copula is used most widely," said Nick, scribbling an unintelligible formula onto a napkin "In statistics a copula is used to couple the balance of two or more variables."

"Do you foresee any problems with it?"

"I'm concerned it doesn't use historical data going back far enough to measure the risk properly. It just uses market data that's been around for less than a decade. And I worry that everyone is using the same formula. But it's helped us to speed up the issue of CDOs."

"There was a piece in *BusinessWeek* about the boom in these hybrid securities and how even though they're backed up by complicated derivatives, they're packaged like triple-A bonds so they appear as safe as houses. Sometimes I think they look like a giant Ponzi scheme."

"So what do you think Brown will do?" Nick asked.

"He'll continue with the light touch regulation," she sighed. "New Labour is in thrall to money. They're dangerously obsessed with the idea that there is a correlation between wealth and intelligence."

"Do you think he'll force banks to increase their capital reserves?"

"He's more Greenspan than Greenspan," she joked.

The geeks have inherited the earth, thought Ali. Felix rushed back into the dining room, having tended another call. He knocked Tita's arm, and a small pool of white wine tipped onto her pale silk dress.

"God, Tita, I'm so sorry," said Felix, using his shirtsleeve to absorb the wine.

"Don't worry, my dear. Now, tell me when you are going to come and visit us in Corfu."

Across the table, Ali saw Bryony shake her head at her mother. Everyone left before midnight. Not a sign of a great evening out, thought Ali, as she went into the drawing room to tell Nick and Bryony that she was going up to bed. They were sitting on the pale beige sofa. Nick had his arm around Bryony and her head rested against his shoulder, the cascade of red hair tickling his nose.

"It was a very productive evening," said Nick. Bryony wordlessly concurred. It struck Ali as a strange adjective to use. Surely a party was meant to be fun. "You're so good at this kind of stuff."

"Isn't Sophia Wilbraham ghastly?"

"Awful," agreed Nick. "But at least we don't need to invite her again for another year."

7

. . . . . .
. . . . . .

November 2006

By the time Nick and Bryony were settling in to early-evening drinks at Dick Fuld's ranch in Idaho after a strenuous day hiking up and down Bald Mountain, their daughter Izzy had drunk rather more than half a bottle of vodka and was inexpertly smoking her first joint with a boy from Jake's school at a party in Notting Hill. As her mother gratefully accepted a glass of Clos du Mesnil 1995 from a Salvadoran maid in full uniform, Izzy followed the boy into a room with a view across London and a large double bed that wouldn't be occupied that night by the owner of the house or his new girlfriend, because they were in Marrakesh for the weekend.

At more or less the same time, Ali found herself wandering into Nick and Bryony's bedroom to keep vigil for the taxi that was due to bring Izzy home from the party. It was already ten minutes late. Of course, Ali could have observed the street from the drawing room, but the same impulse that led Izzy to allow a boy she didn't know to guide her hand inside his trousers compelled Ali into the forbidden territory of the second floor of Holland Park Crescent. Like Izzy, she was marginally surprised to find she felt less like an intruder and more like an explorer mapping new territory.

Ali closed the door behind her and stood for a moment to admire the daring gold-and-black wallpaper, the crystal light fixture, and the gold mirror above the original fireplace. Bryony and Nick's bed was enormous, and the duvet as smooth as glacé icing. There was no trace of the couple that slept there. No wrinkles in the sheets. No tissues on the bedside table. No stray hairs on the pillow. She tried to imagine them in a state of abandoned entanglement and found she couldn't.

She went into the bathroom. There were matching gray towels as thick and smooth as Leicester's coat, reconditioned silver art deco bath taps shaped like fish, and a rolltop bath that matched the bed for scale. Room for three, thought Ali. The room made her think of Miami—haughty pink flamingos on a pale gray background—even though she had never been there. Not surprising, because the interior decorator was American. Ali had met her the other day. All smiles and sunny Californian bonhomie until she realized she was speaking to the nanny, not Bryony's daughter.

The bathroom cabinet exceeded expectations: Seconal, Restoril, and Ambien for insomnia (prescription in Nick's name), Vicodin and Percocet to relieve pain (also in Nick's name), and Xanax and Ativan to treat anxiety. There were also two full packets of Fluoxetine. But no Citralopram or Sertraline, which was a good sign. Bryony was on the Pill.

Ali undid the zipper of her jeans and pulled down her knickers to pee in the minimalist Philippe Starck toilet. The contrast with the overembellished sink and bath was too obvious to be accidental. It seemed to suggest a kind of shyness with bodily functions that was totally at odds with the vast floor-to-ceiling mirror that covered the wall opposite. She wondered if Nick and Bryony ever had sex in front of it. There was a hint of narcissism in their worked-out bodies, and she could imagine Nick admiring the way his buttock muscles clenched as Bryony wrapped her legs around his thighs. Ali watched her reflection and used the loo roll with particular flourish, trying not to imagine Nick and Bryony doing the same. Then she flushed the loo twice, in case they noticed that someone had used it.

Izzy was meant to be home by midnight. Ali didn't need to consult the two pages of typed instructions that she found when she went back down into the kitchen to know Izzy should have been collected in a cab at eleven-thirty. Ali stood by the kitchen island, staring at her crumpled Tube map, trying to make sense of how long it might take a taxi to drive from a party in Notting Hill to Holland Park. She now understood that the scale of the Underground system bore little relation to the actual topography of London. But when she saw the two were adjacent on the Central Line, her stomach knotted, because it certainly shouldn't take an hour.

She called Izzy and left another message, this one more frantic than the last.

"Izzy, you are now more than half an hour late, and we're all worrying about you," she said into the phone, making a swift decision to suggest that others were now involved in the drama. "Please call us as soon as you get this message."

She checked that there were no messages on the answering machine and then called the taxi company that was meant to bring Izzy home. Ali had learned from her mother that action was nearly always the best antidote to anxiety over children who had missed their curfew. Sensing he wasn't the object of her attention, Leicester came and sat on her foot. Ali tried to shake him off, but he growled so grumpily that she relented.

The woman who answered the phone told her that Izzy's friend had been dropped in Warwick Gardens at around eleven forty-five but that the journey to Holland Park Crescent had been canceled. Izzy must still be at the party, concluded Ali, because there was no way that she could walk far in the high-heeled ankle boots she had pilfered from Bryony's wardrobe.

"You were meant to drop her home," Ali rounded on the cab operator.

"We're a taxi company, not a child-minding service," said the woman. "The driver says she refused to come. Imagine the aggro if he'd forced a drunken teenage girl into the car."

"You could have let me know," said Ali truculently. "Can you please send a cab to come and collect me and take me to the same address right away?"

"Not for another hour," the woman said. "It's Saturday night."

"This is an emergency," insisted Ali.

"Then dial nine-nine-nine."

Ali turned to the last page of Bryony's instructions. There was a comprehensive list of people she might want to contact in an emergency, even though she was unsure whether Izzy's failure to come home yet constituted an emergency because she was still only three-quarters of an hour late. The ill-defined parameters of the crisis preoccupied her. Ali lurched from benign explanations—Izzy waiting for a cab that hadn't turned up, Holland Park Avenue closed because of an accident, a drunken friend who required assistance—to malevolent images inspired by incidents in the past involving her own sister. Her father finding Jo in a park being held down by a group of teenage boys (the details were never talked about), Jo found by the police in a pool of her own blood in Norwich (she was sleeping on the street and had her period), Jo taken to hospital from a party with chest pains (incompatible drug experience involving cocaine and ecstasy).

Images of Jo and Izzy became entangled in Ali's mind, and she felt a familiar pressure in her stomach, as though someone was squeezing her very tight. It was a sensation she associated with living at home. She suddenly remembered a weekend almost three years earlier, just before her A-levels, when Jo had arrived home unannounced after another long period "away" and told her parents she wanted to clean up.

By this time Ali's parents were fluent in the language of rehabilitation. Experience, however, had made them wary, and they huddled together at the table in worried silence as Jo outlined her plan. She stood in the middle of the floor, niggling a piece of loose linoleum with her toe, unable to look them in the eye. Ali had melted into the background, both repulsed and compelled by her sister's appearance: the pale doughy skin, the dead brown eyes, the scabby arms, the bony legs encased in a pair of sticky jeans. She reminded Ali of an insect. There was no attempt to hide what was going on, which meant that either she had reached rock bottom and wanted to find a way out of the nightmare she had created for herself or she no longer cared what people thought.

"What can we do to help, Jo?" her mother had asked. Her tone was guarded, as though she wanted to believe Jo might go through with her plan but didn't want to fully embrace it in case she was disappointed.

"I'll need lots of bottled water, Gatorade, Night Nurse, and peanut butter sandwiches," Jo began earnestly.

"Peanut butter?" Ali questioned, knowing that her interest signaled involvement.

"It's what they feed prisoners who are detoxing in American jails," Jo explained. "It's easy to eat, and it raises endorphin levels. And if they've got any valerian root, that would help with the anxiety. I'll need lots of clean sheets, because I'll get the sweats, and hot baths to stay warm, so can you leave the hot water on all the time please?"

The whole process would take no longer than ten days, a period that coincided almost exactly with Ali's exams.

"What about me?" Ali wanted to ask. "How am I going to revise? How am I going to get enough sleep? Who is going to make sure that I'm fine?" But she didn't, because she knew that if she had, no one would have responded. Jo hadn't done it on purpose, Ali kept telling herself. Heroin was worse than the most jealous lover: it didn't allow for anyone else in her life.

Her mother had diligently made a list. Ali was instructed to take Jo for a walk to the end of the pier and back, nothing strenuous, while her parents went shopping. It was cold and windy, and the sea was angrily foaming around the steel girders of the pier. Jo and Ali walked as far as they could. Ali could tell she was getting twitchy for her next fix.

"If I jump in over the edge, will you promise to give up drugs forever?" Ali asked her sister. Jo had nodded, and Ali had climbed onto the railing, stood there for a moment, and then jumped, fully clothed, into the sea. It was a reckless act. Her long coat weighed her down. She held her breath underwater for as long as she could. She wanted Jo to know what it was like to worry that someone might die. When she came up Jo had disappeared.

She had already gone into town and scored again. When her parents came home, Ali told them what had happened. Ali watched her mother's face and felt anger and pity for the concertina of lines across her forehead. It occurred to her as she remembered this incident that her mother was probably younger than Bryony but looked at least fifteen years older.

Ali ran her finger down the list, pressing the paper hard to stop her fingers from shaking. It stopped beside Nick and Bryony and tapped their names. There were details of where they were staying: Short Hill Ranch, Bald Mountain, Sun Valley, Idaho, read the address. Bryony had left four mobile phone numbers and a landline number of the country retreat that belonged to Nick's boss. *Where the fuck is Idaho?* thought Ali in panic, as she tried to work out what the time might be there. Were they seven hours ahead or seven hours behind GMT? She needed a map. One that stretched from Notting Hill to the Rockies. She searched for an atlas in the bookshelf, Leicester trailing behind, viewing her presence without the master and mistress of the house with snuffling disapproval.

The temptation to call Bryony and Nick, to pass on responsibility, was almost overwhelming. As Ali punched numbers into the phone she realized that this weekend was the first true test of her competence, and she didn't want to admit defeat quite so readily. Besides, there was nothing they could do. It struck Ali that a man who missed the birth of his first child because he was on a business trip might not bother to come home because his daughter was late home from a

party. And if Bryony panicked and opted to return alone, their weekend together would be ruined. They barely spent more than a couple
of consecutive nights under the same roof each week.

Not that Bryony had relished playing the role of corporate wife.
Ali recalled the scene in their bedroom on Friday morning, when she
had been called upstairs as a last resort after Malea couldn't find a pair
of walking boots that needed to be packed for the trip. Ali found
Malea silently packing suitcases, carefully wrapping dresses in tissue
paper and laying out cosmetics for Bryony's approval. She noticed that
not only was Malea well versed in the rhythms of Bryony's menstrual
cycle, she had also lined up a packet of diazepam and a half-consumed
packet of antidepressants.

"Can you believe we all have to go hiking together?" Bryony asked
Ali as she emerged from the walk-in wardrobe carrying shoeboxes.
Ali sensed no response was required. "A bloody forced march through
the Rockies with a man who calls his wife by her surname. The first
year we went a woman turned up with a fake plaster cast to avoid any
exercise and then another appeared with a real cast announcing that
she was still planning to head up the mountain. That's what I'm up
against."

Her face was flushed as she recklessly pulled out shoes and Malea
carefully placed the rejects back in boxes.

"During the day you have to wear this ridiculous walking gear,
and then the evening is like a Paris catwalk. And Fuld questions you
about your children as though he really cares, when it was his fault
that Nick wasn't there when Jake was born."

"Ridiculous," Ali agreed when Malea didn't respond, although for
someone who had never left Europe the prospect sounded enticingly
exotic.

"The wives are all suspicious of me because I have a proper job,"
Bryony continued furiously, "and on Sunday the men have to play golf
and they all wear shirts with the logo from their country clubs, apart
from Nick, who doesn't belong to a golf club and spends so much time
in bunkers that he comes home with his feet practically exfoliated.

While he's undergoing this ritual humiliation I have to trawl antiques shops. Then we all go to a restaurant and order a lunch that no one eats. God, it's all so suburban. I hate fucking smart casual."

Remembering this outburst, Ali allowed her fingers to run farther down the list. She immediately ruled out the GP, the dentist, and Leicester's vet. Sophia Wilbraham lived a couple of streets away, and her number was at the bottom of the list, but Ali knew that Bryony wouldn't want her to bear witness to a domestic crisis involving one of the children, because her version of the story would reflect badly on everyone involved: Bryony would be cast as the feckless working mother, Ali as the incompetent nanny, Izzy as the way-ward teenager deprived of parental attention at a crucial stage in her development.

Ali penciled a star beside Foy and Tita, knowing that although Foy would overreact and possibly be drunk, he would at least be available. Bryony's sister was out of the question, because Stoke Newington was so far away it didn't even seem to warrant its own Tube stop, and she had noticed the current of tension whenever Bryony spoke to Hester on the phone.

Malea's name didn't appear. She rarely left the house of her own volition except to take Leicester for a short walk to the end of Holland Park Crescent once a day. She famously once got lost going to Sains-bury's. Ali could now at least trace the route to school from the back of the cab that picked them up every morning at eight o'clock. She could negotiate her way round Holland Park. And she had discovered a cut-through to the butcher, where Bryony frequently sent her to pick up the sausages that Izzy favored during her binges.

But as far as she was aware, she had never been to Notting Hill cen-tral, although she was fairly sure that it was due north. For a moment Ali wished that her father were here. He could negotiate the North Sea in the thickest pea soup, when you couldn't see more than a cou-ple of feet in front of you. As a child she remembered making him close his eyes, spinning him round so fast that his waders creaked in protest, and then asking him to point north. He was always right.

Malea might have an appalling sense of direction, but at least she was here and could wait with Hector and Alfie while Ali drove to the party to search for Izzy. Her decision made, Ali got up so abruptly that she sent the heavy oak chair flying. Leicester growled and followed her down into the basement, where he sat proprietarily in the middle of a step so that Ali had to negotiate her way around him.

Once downstairs, she switched on all the lights and made as much noise as possible in the hope of rousing Malea. She glanced into the huge playroom, wondering if Jake might be there listening to music with friends. Although the television was switched on, nobody seemed to be watching it.

Ali hesitated in front of Malea's door, knocking into thin air a couple of times before allowing her knuckle to make contact with the wood. She reminded herself of Malea's acts of kindness: the way she would put out Hector and Alfie's clothes every night, neatly stacked in the order they preferred to get dressed; how she offered to bath the twins if Ali was busy helping the other children with their home-work; and the Cromer crab waiting on the kitchen table for her one afternoon last week.

Ali gave a couple of quiet taps with her knuckle. When Malea didn't appear, she used the flat of her hand to bang against the door. Finally Malea emerged, half asleep, wearing a dressing gown tied in a neat bow in the middle of her waist, like a present waiting to be unwrapped. Her cheeks were shiny with face cream.

"What is it, Miss Ali?" she asked sleepily.

"Just Ali, please," said Ali, as she always did when Malea addressed her. A small lamp was switched on, and Ali could see a couple of pairs of flip-flops neatly stacked in the bottom of a wardrobe containing three pairs of trousers in the same color and a few striped shirts. On the bedside table was a photograph of three small children smiling cheekily at the camera, gap-toothed and tousle-haired. The youngest still has his milk teeth, thought Ali with a pang. Beside them were a picture of the Virgin Mary and a Bible. Otherwise, the room was bare.

"Izzy hasn't come home and I'm not sure what to do," said Ali, try-ing to sound more controlled than she felt.

"Have you tried Mr. Jake?" Malea asked calmly.

"No," said Ali. "I think Jake is out." She said his name emphati-cally.

"He called me an hour ago to bring a snack to his room," said Malea, trying him on the internal phone on her bedside table. There was no reply. Malea paused. "I think he has girl with him."

"I will go upstairs and watch the twins so you don't have to worry about them," said Malea, going back into the room to fetch her shoes. "Then you can wake Mr. Jake." Ali followed her inside.

"Thank you," she said. "Has Izzy done anything like this before?"

"I not think so," said Malea, "but she always has her troubles. The other nannies found her tricky."

What other nannies? Ali wondered, suddenly curious about her predecessors. She had never asked any questions about the women who had worked here before her, an oversight that now struck her as both arrogant and ignorant. She should have asked to speak to one of them, to glean their opinion on the Skinners, before she had ac-cepted the job. Now it was too late. She was already involved. She was embedded.

She could tell whether Hector had had a bad day at school simply by observing the angle of his shoulders as he came out of the classroom. Worse, if he emerged with shoulders slumped it affected her mood; she worried about the sweet wrappings and empty packets of laxatives she found behind the radiator in Izzy's bedroom and the sticky labels with Izzy's thinspiration mantras. ("Eating is conforming." "Anorexia is a lifestyle, not a disease.") Poor Izzy. She would never be as thin as the tiny girls in skinny jeans that congregated in her bedroom on a Friday afternoon after school to experiment with makeup and one another's clothes. Ali felt another pang of worry, and checked her phone to see whether Izzy had sent her a message, but she hadn't.

"Are those your children, Malea?" she asked, pointing at the photo-graph on the bedside table.

"Yes," said Malea, who was searching in the wardrobe for shoes, her back to Ali so that her face was hidden.

"Where do they live?" asked Ali.

"They live in our village with my mother," said Malea.

"You must miss them," said Ali gently.

"Of course," said Malea, turning round to face her. "But I am giving them a better life by working here than I would if we all lived together at home. They are well fed. They are going to school. They will go to university."

"What about their father?" Ali asked.

"He was killed in a bus crash," said Malea simply.

"I'm sorry," said Ali, berating herself. Malea shrugged.

"It is the way of the world," she said quietly.

"Wouldn't you rather be poor and be with your children?" Ali found herself asking.

"I don't think you understand," said Malea. "Where I come from, people are so poor they have to choose which child to sell to help the others survive."

"I'm sorry," stammered Ali. "I shouldn't have asked."

"It's okay, Ali," said Malea, pulling on her shoes, "no one has asked the question the whole time I have lived in England. Let's go."

Ali went upstairs, two steps at a time, until she found herself outside Jake's bedroom. She knocked a couple of times, but there was no response so she listened outside the door and then gently turned the handle. It was the first time she had been in his room since she moved into the Skinners' house, even though the staircase to the converted attic began right outside her bedroom door. Jake's door opened into a cavernous space running the entire roof span. A dull light shone from a red-and-purple lava lamp. She squinted to get her bearings. On the wall was an Arsenal shirt in away colors signed by the victorious 2005 FA Cup team. There was a photo, presumably of Jake, although it was difficult to tell, skiing in a downhill slalom wearing a bib sponsored by Vodafone. On the mantelpiece above the fireplace were school photos of him playing football. He was in the first team for everything.

Ali went over to the end of his bed and stared at the tangled duvet for a moment. There were definitely two bodies beneath. He had a double bed. For someone who had slept with a boyfriend only in the back of a car or in a single bed, this proved strangely irksome to Ali, a measure of the gulf between them. Jake's attitude to his family's wealth was indifference rather than arrogance, but Ali held him more accountable because he was closest to her in age. She recalled the cricket bat Malea had found last month, already lost and replaced with a more expensive model; school ski holiday paid up unquestioningly; stolen BlackBerry substituted with the latest Nokia; latest MacBook on his desk; £50 spending money for a night out.

Ali moved toward the left side of the bed, where Jake's head was just visible. She noisily pulled out the drawer of the bedside table, hoping to wake him up without touching him. There was a familiar jumble of spare iPod headphones, a small plastic bag containing cigarette papers and tobacco, and a small packet of grass. She opened and shut the drawer a couple more times. Jake didn't stir, although the body next to him rolled closer.

Ali sat on the bed close to his head. She tentatively touched his hair, gently ruffling the fringe as she did when she woke the twins in the morning. He sighed deeply. She took the edge of the duvet and pulled it back to expose the top of his shoulder. Ali's hands were cold, and he tried to push her away as she shook the top of his arm. A naked leg emerged from beneath the duvet. His eyes remained closed.

"Jake, please, it's me," whispered Ali, prodding his shoulder again. Jake put an arm out of the bed and rested it on Ali's thigh.

"Please open your eyes," pleaded Ali.

"What do you want?" he mumbled.

"I need your help. Izzy was meant to be home over an hour ago and she's not picking up her phone."

"Relax," said Jake, patting her leg. "She'll come home when she's ready."

"She's only fourteen," pleaded Ali.

"A fourteen-year-old London girl is like a twenty-one-year-old girl from Cromer," he said. The girl beside him stirred. "Sshh, you're going to wake Lucy." He closed his eyes again.

"I don't know how to get to Notting Hill," Ali pleaded.

"What do you want me to do?" he mumbled. He tried to pull Ali onto the bed, as she pummeled his shoulder. Unsure how else to respond, Ali picked up a glass of water from the bedside table and threw it over his face.

"Are you pissed, Ali?" asked Jake, gripping the side of the front seat of the car half an hour later as they pulled up outside the house in Notting Hill where Izzy's party was being held. Apart from giving instructions on how to get to the Bassetts' house, he hadn't spoken during the journey. Occasionally he ran his fingers through his hair to see if it was still wet. "Or are you just a crap driver?"

"Crap driver," admitted Ali. To her relief there were hardly any cars in the road, which meant she didn't have to reverse into a space outside the house.

"I'm just a bit out of practice," said Ali, as they parked, although actually she had managed a couple of smooth gear changes. They got out, went to the front door and rang the bell a couple of times. No one answered. The house was ablaze with light, and they could hear the dull throb of music emanating from the basement. It's amazing that the neighbors don't complain, thought Ali, looking up and down the street.

"Everyone's in the country for the weekend," said Jake.

They peered through the letterbox, called Izzy's mobile phone, and heard it ringing from a pile of coats carelessly stacked along the hall-way. A teenage boy knelt down and started searching through pockets to locate the phone. Jake called to him through the letterbox to let them in. He half opened the door, and when he realized he recognized Jake from school, he allowed them both inside.

"Sorry, mate," he mumbled, glancing from Ali to Jake in confusion.

"Where are Mr. and Mrs. Bassett?" Ali asked the boy.

"Away." He shrugged, then headed back downstairs into the basement. Ali and Jake followed him. They walked past a huddle of girls queuing outside a bathroom on a landing halfway down the stairs. Even in the dull light, Ali could see that the pale beige carpet was covered in muddy footprints.

"Sasha, have you seen Izzy?" Jake shouted up at one of the girls.

Ali thought she recognized Sasha, although perhaps it was because she looked exactly like the girl that Jake had just brought home.

"Hi, Ali," Sasha said, standing up. Even without shoes she towered over Ali. She was wearing a pair of tiny denim shorts that accentuated her improbably long legs and a checked shirt knotted at her stomach to reveal a pierced tummy button. Her hair tumbled in blond waves around her shoulders and down her back. Her eyes were dark with kohl. Ali realized that she was simply a much older version of the Sasha who periodically appeared in the kitchen at Holland Park Crescent after school and politely asked for a snack to take upstairs to do her homework with Izzy.

"Dance, Jake?" Sasha asked, swaying her hips to the music.

"I'm looking for Izzy," Jake shouted, as Sasha stepped downstairs until she was standing beside him. She was the same height as Jake. She stretched out her arm and let it rest on Jake's shoulder.

"Most people bring a bottle of vodka to a party, but you bring your nanny," she shrieked with laughter. She leaned over to Jake and kissed him on the lips until he relented. "Enjoy," she said, rewarding his lack of resistance. "I think Izzy is upstairs."

The layout of the house was similar to that of the house on Holland Park Crescent, but it was on a smaller scale, which made it easy for Ali to get her bearings. It was funkier, too. Although the upstairs sitting room was lit by a single lamp and precariously pitched tea candles, Ali could see that the walls were painted a deep blood red and the sofas were covered in throws in exotic colors. There was a loose Oriental theme: the cupboards were painted in gold lacquer; the fireplace was guarded by a four-armed Vishnu.

Ali stood by the mantelpiece to scan the room for Izzy. In the center of the mantelpiece there was a sculpture of a man's head, the same color as the walls, and a couple of photographs, including one of Mick Jagger holding a baby, Jerry Hall draped gracefully across his shoulder. There were tiny trinkets: a pipe from India, a small clay band of animals playing musical instruments, a pencil box from Iran, and a collection of Gandhara Buddha heads. On the walls were black-and-white photographs of rock bands, including the Rolling Stones. She could see Jake approaching in the mirror above the fireplace.

"I can't see her," she said anxiously.

"Did you see the photos?" asked Jake, tapping the glass frame. "Sasha's dad works in the music industry. Her mum used to be a model."

"Gosh," said Ali, impressed. "Do you think they'll be home soon?" Jake laughed.

"They split up years ago. Her dad's new girlfriend is younger than Sasha's older sister. She's a younger model of the older model. This is his house. But he's in Marrakesh for the weekend."

"What about Sasha's mum?"

"She's at home with her boyfriend. It's not her weekend to have Sasha," Jake patiently explained.

"So Sasha is having a party without any adult supervision?" Ali asked in astonishment. "I'm not sure I approve."

"Please don't have one of your Mary-fucking-Poppins moments here," said Jake.

"What do you mean?" asked Ali.

"What I mean is that in my world life isn't supercala-fucking-fragilistic all the time," said Jake. "It's up and it's down."

Jake took Ali by the arm and led her back toward the staircase. She noticed a couple entwined on the sofa, a half-drunk bottle of wine on its side beside them, its contents seeping into the carpet. Ali couldn't help bending down to right it. Out of the corner of her eye she caught a glimpse of Sophia Wilbraham's daughter, Martha, glancing across at her, eyes glazed. Ali was taken aback to notice that one of the girl's breasts was exposed and was being inexpertly kneaded by the boy who lay on top of her. He suddenly leaned over and took the perfectly shaped nipple into his mouth and chewed it as though he was trying to nudge a stone from a cherry. Poor technique, thought Ali. Martha lazily put a finger up to her mouth, looked at Ali and whispered, "Sshh." Ali felt Jake nudge her.

"Did you see that?" asked Ali.

"She's doing a GCSE in Westminster boys." Jake laughed dismissively. "Her older sister has even slept with the tutor her mum got to help her get to grips with Thomas Hardy."

In the master bedroom on the first floor, there were so many bodies draped across the bed that it was difficult to work out how they fitted together. There was a boy in the middle, a girl lying under each arm, except one of the girls was deep in conversation with another boy draped over the legs of the first one. They were all sharing a cigarette. At the foot of the bed were another couple of bodies. One of the girls was curled up in the fetal position, sound asleep.

"She's in a K-hole," said Jake.

"What do you mean?" asked Ali.

"Vitamin K," said Jake knowingly.

"Ketamine?" confirmed Ali. "As in horse tranquilizer?" Jake nodded.

In the corner a girl was trying to play a song by the Stereophonics, but every time she pressed play someone else changed the music. For a moment Ali envied their careless intimacy. She resolved to call Rosa the following day and arrange a weekend in Norwich. At the dressing table a bare-torsoed boy was busily dividing up lines of white powder. He left a particularly large one for himself.

"Banker's bonus." He laughed, noticing Ali's expression. She said nothing.

"Line for the road?" he asked Ali.

"No. Thanks," said Jake on her behalf.

"Izzy won't be here," said Jake, hurriedly urging Ali out of the room.

"How do you know?" asked Ali.

"Don't you think if she did coke she'd be thinner?" Jake pointed out.

"I can't believe this," said Ali as she closed the door behind her.

"Don't say anything to Mum," said Jake.

"About what?" said Ali.

"About any of this," said Jake. "She'll just get worried."

"She should get worried," said Ali.

They continued upstairs to another floor. A couple of girls walked past and told them the loo was blocked because someone called Suzi had been sick. It was quieter. Ali could feel the dull throb of music through the floorboards, but it was no longer too loud to speak. As they passed the loo, she noticed a pair of legs sticking out the doorway and the putrid stink of vomit.

"Must be Suzi," said Ali, relieved to hear the girl groaning on the marble floor. "At least it's not carpet."

There were two doors before them. Ali chose the one farthest away from the landing. They found themselves in a poorly lit bedroom. Then they saw Izzy. She was kneeling on the floor beside the bed. Apple bobbing, thought Ali in confusion as Izzy's head moved rhythmically up and down in the lap of a boy sitting on the bed. His eyes were closed, but in his hand he held up a mobile phone above his head. Surely he wasn't making a phone call and having a blowjob at the same time? Could boys multitask like that? Jake was quicker off the mark.

"What the fuck are you doing?" he asked. Izzy half turned her head and smiled inanely at Ali and Jake, trying to force herself to focus. She attempted to push herself up from the floor, using the boy's knees as ballast, but she couldn't get up. Ali grabbed the phone from the boy's hand and dropped it into a half-drunk beer that sat beneath the lamp.

"Nice one," said Jake approvingly.

Izzy turned round and squinted up at them. She tried to say something, but instead of words a stream of vomit came out of her mouth. The boy stood up and backed into the corner of the room, pulling up his trousers and muttering apologies about how it was all Izzy's idea.

"She's not in any fit state to make decisions," said Ali angrily. "What should we do about the carpet?"

"They'll get industrial cleaners in before her dad comes home." Jake shrugged.

They got Izzy on her feet, and between them began the slow process of bringing her downstairs, step by step. It was like carrying a corpse. Her eyes were rolling into the back of her head, and Ali was relieved when she was sick again on the front doorstep, in part because it lessened the likelihood that she would need to be taken to hospital to have her stomach pumped but mostly because it reduced the risk of a vomiting incident inside the car.

"Poor Izzy," said Ali, stroking her hair as Izzy slumped beside her in the front of the BMW. After a couple of false starts she managed to get the car into gear.

"Poor me," said Jake from the back. "I'm meant to be revising."

"It's just one of those things," said Ali, repeating a phrase her mother used.

"You're so tolerant," said Jake.

"I'm paid to be," said Ali.

Malea was waiting by the front door. Ali and Jake paused in the hallway for a moment to catch their breath, balancing Izzy between them, an arm under each shoulder. Izzy was breathing too quickly. Her rib cage rose and fell so fast that Ali was worried she might hyperventilate. Her skin had a grayish hue. When she opened her eyes Ali could see her pupils were as big as marbles.

"We need to get her horizontal as quickly as possible to bring down her heart rate," said Ali.

Suddenly Izzy slid out of Ali and Jake's grip and lurched forward to knock the vase of flowers from the hall table. It smashed on the floor. Leicester came up from the kitchen and sat by the stairs, maintaining a grim and disapproving vigil over the proceedings.

"Shit," said Ali as they pulled her upright again.

"Don't worry. We'll frame Leicester," Jake consoled her. He kicked pieces of porcelain under the table while Malea got down on her hands and knees to retrieve handfuls of flowers. "Mum probably won't even notice. The interior decorator chose the vase."

"Do you think we could mend it?" asked Ali.

"Don't be ridiculous," said Jake.

Malea touched Izzy's face tenderly and muttered something in Filipino.

"What did you say, Malea?" panted Ali.

Malea repeated the word. It was something Ali had heard Hector and Alfie use.

"What nationality was the nanny who looked after the twins before me?" Ali asked.

"Filipina," said Jake.

"And before that?"

"Also Filipina," said Malea.

"Why are you asking about this now?" asked Jake impatiently.

Somehow between the three of them they managed to haul Izzy upstairs to her bedroom. Ali laid out towels from the bathroom on top of the duvet, and Malea went down to the basement to fetch a bucket.

"We need to get her to lie on her side," Ali instructed Jake. "Then there's less chance of her choking on her own vomit or swallowing her tongue." Ali checked her pulse.

"Are you from the Saint John Ambulance service?" Jake joked.

Ali bathed Izzy's face with a cool flannel and was heartened to see a little color return. Izzy opened her eyes for a moment, gave a small smile, and tried to say something. Her lips moved, but no words came out. Her makeup, a mess of mascara, sparkling green eye shadow, and eyeliner, had spread over her cheeks. She retched a couple of times. A thin pool of liquid, like a snail's trail, slid down the side of her cheek. Ali gently wiped her face, and Izzy fell asleep again.

Ali got up to stretch her legs. She encouraged Jake to go back up to his room, but he insisted he wanted to make sure Izzy was fine before he went back to Lucy.

"Who's Lucy?" asked Ali. "Does she qualify as revision?"

"My girlfriend." Jake smiled.

Ali drifted over to Izzy's desk and unthinkingly pressed the computer mouse to see what the time was. A picture of an emaciated girl popped up on the screen. Her cheekbones were so sunken that it looked as though someone had drawn two black lines across her face. Her hip bones and ribs jutted out through her skin. "In control," read a caption at the bottom of the photo. Ali checked the name of the website: "Ana and her friends." She looked at Izzy's history and noted that the last three sites she had visited were all pro-anorexia websites. She read the messages in the chat room and in particular one to Izzy from a girl in Manchester suggesting that she sprinkle pepper over her food and sniff cat litter to curb her appetite. It was three o'clock in the morning, and in less than four hours the twins would come and wake her up.

"Her eyes are open again," Jake called over to Ali as she switched off the computer.

"Then she's definitely conscious," said Ali.

"Do you want to share a cigarette? It's my last one. There's a little balcony where we can sit outside Izzy's window."

"I'm not sure that's appropriate," said Ali.

"It's more appropriate than anything else that's happened tonight," said Jake, opening the window. "Everyone in this house has secrets. Apart from the twins. You'll settle in quicker if you develop a few of your own."

Ali climbed out. The balcony was long and thin, designed for pots, not people. She sat down beside him and tucked her thighs to her chest, grateful for their warmth. A security guard from the private company that patrolled the street shone a flashlight up at the window, and Jake waved to reassure him. He took a couple of drags from the cigarette and then passed it to Ali. She took a deep drag and felt her shoulders finally relax.

"What a fucking evening," said Jake, taking back the cigarette from her hand. Their fingers brushed against one another. "And I've got an essay to finish tomorrow."

"You mean today." Ali pointed out the time. Jake grimaced.

"What's it about?" she asked.

"It's a comparison between *King Lear* and *A Thousand Acres* by Jane Smiley," said Jake. "Any ideas?"

This is a breakthrough, thought Ali, as he passed back the cigarette.

"Both are about patriarchal rule and the relationship between fathers and daughters," said Ali. "Larry is Lear, and Ginny is Goneril. Both fathers have so much power they're driven to insanity; both youngest daughters rebel and end up with nothing. The big difference is that Lear thinks he's a changed man, whereas Larry Cook is just the same. It's basically Lear told from a female point of view."

"Very good," Jake said. He stubbed out the cigarette in the gutter.

"Did you like the book?" asked Ali, who didn't want to let the conversation drift.

"I can relate to some of the themes," said Jake cautiously.

"Go on," said Ali.

Jake paused for a moment. "The tension between living life for yourself and fulfilling other peoples' expectations, mainly." He looked startled at this disclosure.

"I can relate to that one, too," said Ali.

There was a noise in the bedroom as Malea came in with a bucket. They climbed back in through the window. Malea gave Ali a long, impassive stare.

"You've done this before, haven't you?" asked Jake, as Ali gently opened Izzy's eyelids to check her pupils. Ali nodded but didn't allow herself to think about Jo. Instead she took the bucket from Malea.

"What do you think I should say?" Ali asked Malea.

"Say nothing," Malea said, putting a finger to her lips.

8

. . . .
. . . . . .

Ali slept fitfully. At four-thirty on Monday morning, as the first light shimmered through the gap in the curtains, she finally gave in to insomnia. A couple of months earlier she might have got up to look out of her bedroom window to admire the garden five floors below, but she was already bored with the view. The neat rows of dead alliums imprisoned in the box parterre at the center, the carefully weeded beds where nothing was left to chance, and the flawless, vivid lawn all created an image of clinical containment. Whenever she saw Leicester squat to spill the remains of his organic diet on the lawn, a shudder of pleasure crept up her spine. It was the kind of garden that made you want to sow wheat seeds that would grow tall among the grass, to read something like "Shit happens."

It was the same with her bedroom. Everything was new: the electric kettle, the wide-screen TV, and the small fridge that mysteriously replenished itself with apples and milk. Not for the first time, she felt a sense of claustrophobia. Bryony had explained that this embarrassment of new gadgetry was to give Ali privacy. But they had slowly mutated from symbols of freedom to oppression. They weren't to keep others out at awkward times of day after the twins went to bed: they were to keep her in.

Ali had brought a couple of pictures with her from her student digs to hang on the wall. One was a poster from a Francis Bacon retrospective at the Sainsbury Centre in Norwich. The other was a photograph of her with some friends from university on the beach at Cromer. Both now sat at the back of the big wardrobe that dominated one wall of her bedroom.

She was reluctant to hammer picture hooks into the new wallpaper, and it was embarrassing to put up a Francis Bacon poster in a house where an original hung over the fireplace in the drawing room. To impress Bryony with her interest in child development, Ali had put all the books that she had bought for her on a bookshelf that ran along the opposite wall just above a desk. Beside these was a single carefully chosen photo of Ali with her family, taken on the beach in Cromer.

"People don't like nannies with fucked-up families," Rosa had warned her before the interview, without mentioning Jo by name.

Jo was twelve and she was ten. They had identical haircuts, short brown bobs with long fringes, cut at the local hairdresser. Jo was pulling at Ali's hand pointing at the camera. Ali smiled as she stared at the photo from her bed. She had idolized her sister back then, and Jo had basked in the adulation. Everyone used to comment on how well they got on together. Their roles were clear: Jo was the responsible older child and Ali her adoring younger sister.

Her father had his arm around her mother, pulling her toward him. He was wearing swimming trunks, and his chest was muscular and tanned. Her mother looked glowing and carefree. The bad times were still two years away. It spoke of a happy uncomplicated childhood before the narrative of family life was hijacked.

The subject of why Jo had slipped off the edge of the family map was much debated in the ensuing crisis. There was a neighbor she hung out with when she was fourteen who smoked dope and took magic mushrooms. Since he was now a hygienist at the dentist's, while Jo was in India on another "voyage of self-discovery," he could no longer legitimately be blamed; still, Ali's mother got angry with her father for allowing him to clean his teeth once a year. A couple of dealers had moved into a house behind the train station in the early nineties, but Jo had already moved to a squat in Norwich, so the chronology didn't fit. Then there was Ali, who was much the brightest pupil the school had seen in years and would have easily made it to Cambridge, had she not messed up her A-levels. Over the years it had become clear to Ali that she was the problem. Drug addiction was a self-esteem issue, the family therapist had explained. Ali's success highlighted Jo's failings. No one said anything, but it was obvious to Ali that if she disappeared for a while then Jo might feel better about herself.

Ali's quarters were swiftly dubbed "the eyrie," even though, strictly speaking, they weren't at the top of the house but on the fifth floor overlooking the back garden, and Jake's bedroom was directly above her. Foy had come up with the description, and everyone had laughed, partly to indulge him, because everyone knew he was having trouble with his business, but mostly because it skirted the more embarrassing fact that Ali's bedroom was where the servants quarters used to be.

Knowing it would impress them, Ali had waited until Nick and Bryony were in the kitchen one morning to explain that in *Hamlet*, Rosencrantz talks about an eyrie of children, and since she was at the heart of the network of rooms used by the younger Skinner children, Foy was more accurate than he realized. Bryony had laughed with approval at the literary reference and had thrown a "Told you so" glance at Nick.

"More songbird than eagle," Ali said, as she now lay on the bed, promising herself that she would leave when she had managed to pay off her debts and saved a further £5,000 to cover the rest of her university course. If she was cautious she could be free within a year.

She wondered whether Jake was upstairs. They shared the same chimney flue, and Ali had discovered that if she sat close to the fireplace she could hear strands of conversation and music from the room above. She was going to point this out to Jake, but as the weeks slipped by and her questions about his plans or whereabouts were resolutely rebuffed, Ali decided it provided a useful means of monitoring what he was up to. The other night she could clearly smell cigarette smoke. Once he cried out in his sleep.

This morning there was silence. The only noise she could hear was a stray wisteria branch scratching against the window. She forced herself to lie in bed completely still. Outside in the garden she could hear Leicester barking. In a few minutes, Malea would appear with a small bag and scoop up his early-morning offering. Bryony was insistent it should be dealt with swiftly and efficiently because not only did it burn the grass, it offended Leicester's sensibilities. Urine was even more acidic, and a watering can with a dog-shaped mouth stood permanently by the back door to dilute his pee. What about Malea's sensibilities? Ali wondered. Clearing up crap on an empty stomach was not the best way to start a new day. But she said nothing, in case her criticism was misinterpreted as an offer to help. Leicester growled menacingly every time he saw her, and to Foy's delight she had already lost another pair of shoes to one of his dirty protests.

Nick and Bryony should have returned from Idaho late Sunday evening, and Ali was still unsure what to tell them about Izzy. She ran through the options again: full disclosure, partial disclosure, or silence, which was more complicated than it might seem because it involved both Jake's and Malea's complicity. She tried not to be influenced by Izzy. Ali had spent almost an hour with her in the afternoon. Izzy had pleaded with her not to say anything, as big, silent mascara-stained tears meandered down her cheeks.

"I promise I've never taken drugs or got so drunk before," she had said when Ali brought toast and orange juice to her room, urging her to eat.

"What about the boy?" Ali had asked, puzzled that Izzy would assume she would be more worried about the drugs and alcohol than the possibility Izzy had lost her virginity on Ali's watch. Or perhaps this was how Izzy always behaved at parties? Either way, Ali needed to know because she was pretty sure that Izzy wasn't using contraception. How easy would it be to get the morning-after pill on a Sunday afternoon in London? The Skinners didn't use the NHS, and Ali couldn't possibly call their Harley Street GP. She was somewhat reassured by the fact that they had found Izzy fully clothed, but she was assuming that she had only just gone into the bedroom. Perhaps she had already been there for hours and oral sex was dessert rather than an hors d'oeuvre?

"Did you have sex with him?"

Izzy had looked shocked.

"I'm not that kind of girl, Ali," she had said as she nibbled the edge of the piece of toast.

"Can you remember?"

"It's all a bit hazy, but I'm sure nothing like that happened."

"If we hadn't come in at that moment, you would have been the kind of girl who allowed herself to be filmed giving her boyfriend a blowjob. People might have felt sorry for you for getting into that situation, but they would have judged you all the same."

"I didn't know he was filming me. I thought he liked me. For a couple of hours I stopped feeling fat and ugly."

Izzy had put down the plate of toast, leaned toward Ali, and rested her head on her shoulder and sobbed. They were real tears, Ali had decided, not the tears of a fourteen-year-old girl trying to negotiate her silence.

"Imagine how let-down your parents would feel if they knew about this."

"But they won't know, because you won't tell them."

On the desk beside Ali sat a telephone and her BlackBerry. She would have liked to consult someone. To phone a friend. However, it had slowly dawned on her over the past couple of months that although the Skinners weren't celebrities in the conventional sense, they were newsworthy, and Rosa's discretion wasn't guaranteed. There had been a profile of Nick in the *Financial Times*; there were photos of them attending a fund-raising dinner at the Tate in the *Evening Standard* magazine; and Bryony had recently turned down another offer from a magazine to write a diary of her typical week and be photographed wearing Marc Jacobs.

Besides, it was too early for e-mails, and the phone was a red herring. Ali had discovered it was an internal phone when she tried to call her parents on the night she moved in and found herself instead talking to Jake. The architects had put in a planning application to build an elevator, but it had been turned down, so an internal phone system was installed to save people the bother of walking up and down stairs. Jake's number was 012. Ali's was 013, he had politely explained. There was a laminated list stuck in the top drawer of the bedside table.

Impulsively, Ali decided to go downstairs. It was only five in the morning, but she could sit in the drawing room and run through her reasons for not telling Nick and Bryony anything of what had happened. She pulled on a short cardigan on top of her T-shirt and pajama bottoms and carefully opened the bedroom door. As Ali made her way past Bryony and Nick's bedroom the staircase made uncomfortable groans, as though it wanted to expose the impostor treading its boards. She continued down into the hallway, shivering as her feet touched the York stone floor.

The drawing room door was open. The set of curtains at the far end was drawn, leaving one end of the room veiled in shadow while the other half was bathed in early-morning light. Ali surveyed the scene slowly, scrunching up her toes in the thick carpet as she used to do in the sand on the beach in Cromer.

She remembered the snagging list Bryony had sent her and checked the grand piano. Bryony was correct: there was nothing beneath its legs to protect the carpet from its weight, there was no bulb in the

light fixture above the Francis Bacon, and the decorators had forgotten to paint the skirting board on the right side of the room. She
marveled at Bryony's capacity to retain so much information.

Ali walked toward the marble mantelpiece that dominated the
drawing room. It was heavy with invitations. An art opening at Blain
Southern, weddings, fiftieth-birthday parties, a school reunion for
Bryony at Wycombe Abbey. She picked up one—an invitation to
drinks at the Treasury in honor of Warren Buffett—and traced her
finger over the gold-embossed lettering, closing her eyes as though
reading Braille.

"What are you doing in here?" a voice asked. Ali jumped and
turned to find Nick sitting on a sofa at the other end of the room. It
was too dark to see his face, but his tone betrayed his impatience.

"Sorry, I didn't know you were back," said Ali, knocking the invitation on to the carpet. She bent down to pick it up, self-consciously
putting a hand across her chest, suddenly aware that she was wearing
nothing beneath her T-shirt. "I mean, I thought you might be back,
but I didn't think you would get up so early."

And now he was here, sitting in semidarkness with one portable
computer open on his lap and another beside him on the sofa. All
around his feet lay piles of paper and magazines. *The Journal of Fixed
Income. Journal of Corporate Finance. Risk. Euromoney. Fortune.* He leaned
down and started stacking them in a single precarious pile.

"I'm doing a list for the builders of things they need to put right,"
explained Ali. "Bryony asked me."

"At five o'clock in the morning?" he questioned, but his tone had
softened.

"I couldn't sleep," Ali apologized as she stepped away from the fireplace and toward him.

This was the first time she had seen him in more than ten days.
Now that she was closer, Ali could see he was wearing a crumpled
white shirt with the sleeves carelessly rolled up. The top buttons were
undone. His jeans were creased. Ali couldn't help noticing that his belt

was too loose and his zipper half undone. He put down the computer. Even though the screen was facing the back of the sofa away from her, she could see from the dim purple glow that it was still switched on. She also recognized from the Arsenal sticker on the lid that it was Jake's computer. There was a shared moment of embarrassed silence.

"I was going to try and sleep for a couple of hours before I go to work, but it proved elusive," Nick said smoothly as he snapped the lid of the computer shut. "I'm leaving for the States again in a couple of days."

"Where are you going?" asked Ali politely, trying to avoid staring at the computer.

"To Boca, for an off-site," said Nick.

"Boca?"

"Boca Raton in Florida. Brainstorming session with the boys from my team. And the girls. We do it a couple of times a year to try and come up with ever more ingenious ideas to make money as people copy our previous ingenious ideas and render them inert."

"Oh," said Ali, surprised by his unusual verbosity on the subject. "It must be great traveling so much."

"After a while every hotel room looks the same and the piped music has the same bland quality wherever you are. It's the downside of globalization."

There was an uncomfortable silence.

"What's keeping you awake?" Nick asked. Ali was relieved when he switched on a small radio that sat on a table beside him.

"And now the shipping forecast, issued by the Met Office on behalf of the Maritime and Coastguard Agency, at 0520 GMT, Monday, the twenty-seventh of November . . ."

"Your radio has seen better days," said Ali stiffly, noticing the bent aerial and scratched face. She picked it up.

"It's the one I had at university. It's survived several of Bryony's purges." He smiled.

"Humber, Thames, southeast four or five increasing six or seven veering south four or five later. Occasional rain, with fog patches becoming moderate." The voice on the radio filled the silence, its familiarity giving Ali more confidence.

"No gales," she said. "They always do them first."

"Do they?"

"Anything over gale force eight." She nodded seriously. "Then it's the general synopsis, then the forecast for each area."

"I don't understand what any of it means."

"Once you understand the formula, it's easy," said Ali. "He's telling us that the wind is coming from the southeast, at Beaufort Force four or five, and that over today it will increase to Force six or seven but not for the next twelve hours. Veering means it's changing in a clockwise direction to the south, and moderate is the visibility. If visibility is less than a thousand meters then it's poor."

"I'm impressed," said Nick.

"My dad taught me," said Ali, presuming that Nick had read the file on her family and knew that her father was a fisherman. "Humber and Thames are the areas where he fishes off the east coast."

"As in Humber Light Vessel Automatic?"

"That's just the coastal weather station in that area."

"I've always rather liked the sound of North Utsire and South Utsire," said Nick, warming to the theme. "They sound so ancient and exotic. One day I'd like to visit."

"It's Norse. They were named after an island off the Norwegian coast called Utsire. They used to be part of Viking, actually. It's another shipping area. The names are very atmospheric."

"Darkness outside. Inside, the radio's prayer—" Nick began.

"Rockall. Malin. Dogger. Finisterre," Ali responded.

"Carol Ann Duffy," they both said simultaneously. There was a brief moment of connection. Then Ali looked down at her feet and it snapped.

"I never have time to read anymore," Nick said. "I can't remember the last novel I finished, and I haven't been to the cinema for about two years. I lead a life largely devoid of culture."

It didn't sound as though he felt regret, so Ali was unsure what to say, other than perhaps he should pick up a book instead of downloading porn or whatever he was doing on his son's computer. Nick slumped back into the sofa and closed his eyes for a moment, rubbing his hand over the stubble on his chin.

"So how has your first month here been?"

"It's my third," Ali pointed out, even though she knew that he was hoping for a bland one-word answer.

"How has your third month been?" he asked lazily.

"Better than my first and second."

"And how did you cope without us?"

"Everything was fine."

"Children?"

"Good."

"What did Izzy get in her maths review?"

"Eighty-nine."

"Class average?"

"Ninety. That's an improvement."

"But still not good enough."

"The twins have gone up a level in reading, and Jake got an A on his English essay."

"Did he go out?"

"Only at the weekend."

"Foy?"

"Fine."

"Watch him after a glass of wine, he can get a little leery."

Ali looked down at her feet in embarrassment.

"Did he mention the photo again?"

"A couple of times. Your mother-in-law is trying to get hold of a duplicate. He's stopped bringing sweets to the twins until they confess. But they're sticking to their line."

"What do they say?" There was another long silence.

"They say it was you."

Nick opened one eye.

"They say that you went into the toilet as they came out."

"And who do you believe?"

"I re-created the incident. The picture was too high for them to reach."

"And what were your conclusions?"

"That Hector and Alfie are right." Nick leaned back into the sofa and started laughing.

"A regular little spy in our midst." He laughed even harder. "Did you tell anyone else?"

"No."

"Are you going to?"

"No."

"Good girl."

The shipping forecast finished.

"What else have you discovered?" Nick teased.

"The language the twins speak is Filipino," said Ali. "I cross-referenced the list of words with Malea."

"Really?"

"I found out that Malea's friend looked after the twins until I got here, then Malea helped out," said Ali. "That's almost the entire period that Hector and Alfie were learning to speak."

"Didn't you know any of that?"

Ali shook her head.

"Bryony should have told you." He shrugged.

"She's always very busy—there isn't much time to chat," said Ali, surprised to find herself defending Bryony. "But I feel bad I took the job from Malea."

"If it wasn't you it would have been someone else," Nick said, his impatience tempered by Ali's loyalty to his wife. "Malea was a good stopgap, but she would have never worked out as their nanny. She's too indulgent. You can see they need more structure. Especially Hector. Don't worry about it."

"Did she used to sleep in my room?" Ali asked.

"She was always in the basement, but the twins used to go down every night and sleep in her bed. Since you arrived they haven't. It's a result."

"I feel bad about it," Ali said. "I think maybe they filled the space in Malea's life that her own children should have filled."

"You think too much. You know, guilt is one of the most useless emotions known to man. It wastes a lot of energy. If you feel really bad then give up the job, but it won't achieve anything because some-one else will replace you and you won't have saved enough money to go back to university. Would it have been better to get rid of Malea so that you would never have known? She earns the same amount of money doing what she's doing. It's actually a better situation for her, because she can go back to the Philippines every couple of years for six weeks to see her family."

"There are more important things in life than money," said Ali primly.

"Not in the world Malea inhabits," he said smiling, "nor the world I live in."

"What exactly is it that you do?" Ali asked. She was uncomfortable with the enforced intimacy of their situation. Yet she didn't want the conversation to end. The weeks of loneliness had heightened her need for meaningful exchange with other people.

"Are you really interested?" he asked. "It's the kind of job that no one really understands. It's a mystery, even to some of the people that I work with."

"I am." She nodded vigorously.

"Why don't you sit down?" he said, moving both computers onto the floor so that there was space beside him on the sofa. She remem-bered Rosa's warning about predatory fathers and glanced nervously from Nick to the sofa a couple of times. His face was pale, as though he had spent too much time indoors. His eyes were bloodshot and puffy. Her own face, open and youthful, hid nothing of her feelings.

"Whatever you think I am, I am not."

"What do you think I think you are?" Ali would have liked to ask. Instead she looked down at her feet.

"Now, do you want me to explain what I do?" Nick asked with faux impatience. "It's a great cure for insomnia."

He leaned back into the sofa, seemingly unaware his zipper was half undone, and a pile of papers on the arm fluttered to the floor. "Strictly Private and Confidential," it read in big black letters at the top of the page that landed on Ali's bare foot. She bent down to pick it up, her T-shirt billowing. He swiftly averted his eyes. "Project Odysseus." The same document Bryony was reading in the car a couple of months earlier. How amazing that they are both so involved in each other's professional life, thought Ali, as she handed back the paper and sat down beside him, taking care to make sure no part of her body touched his. But close enough that she could see the grime collected on his collar.

"I'm in charge of fixed income for a bank. An American bank. It's not the kind of bank where you or I would have an account or go and withdraw money," he started. "It's a bit like running a shop. You work out what your customer wants, get stock in, and sell it at a profit as fast as possible. I'm in charge of two areas: principle finance, where we lend directly for projects, like building Wembley Stadium, for example, and securitization, the racier part, where we repackage investment contracts called derivatives."

"So far so good," said Ali.

"Do you want me to go on? It's not something that you can explain in a sentence."

Ali nodded. If she was being paid from the money he earned, then she should at least understand where her salary was coming from. Besides, she had never seen him so animated.

"The derivatives desks makes more money for the bank than any other," he said. He waited for Ali to react.

"Millions?" she complied.

"Billions." He smiled.

"The trades involve bits of paper, not goods. Sometimes people use them as a way of controlling risk. For example, if your father thought the price of crab was high and that next year it might drop, then he could buy an option for an agreed sum to sell the crabs at the current price in twelve months' time. That way he would know how much money he stands to make and ensure he has a market for his product."

"Surely the person selling the crab option at the lower price would lose money?" Ali pointed out.

"Good question. But what if there is an oil spill and there is a shortage of crabs, then your father loses out on the chance to make more money and the person who bet against him Hoovers up the difference?"

"So it's like gambling," said Ali.

"But more scientific and creative, because whenever someone comes up with a clever plan to make money, the next person copies him, and profits fall. So you have to constantly innovate."

"It's not really like inventing penicillin, though, is it?" Ali asked nervously. Nick smiled benignly.

"No, but I guess we're giving loans that allow millions of poor people in the U.S. and the UK to buy their own homes," he said, repeating a line he frequently used during meetings at the Bank of England. "We repackage debt from these mortgage companies and bundle it into bonds called collateralized debt obligations—CDOs—and sell those on to investors, like an IOU. The investors earn interest, and they get their money back at the end. The more bonds we sell, the more money we make and the more mortgage companies have to allow other poor people to buy their own home."

"But how does anyone make money?" Ali asked.

"The CDOs are divided into different tranches. Some are higher risk than others. The higher the risk, the greater the return," said Nick. "Subprime loans have higher interest rates, so people who invest in them take more risk but earn more money. And every time we sell a bond, we get a fee."

"How can the people who don't have enough money for a deposit on their house afford to pay a mortgage?" Ali asked. "Who picks up the bill if they can't pay?"

"The housing market is booming," said Nick, as though he was addressing an audience. "Every week house prices go up, so they can take out equity to pay the interest. There are mathematical formulas to work out the risk, and we take out insurance so that if something goes wrong we get paid. It's beautiful maths."

"So can I get paid in CDOs?"

Nick chortled loudly, and Ali felt gratified. They heard a noise in the hall. Nick stopped laughing, and they simultaneously turned toward the drawing room door. It slowly pushed open, the bottom of the door scraping against the deep carpet. Jake emerged. He was wearing his favorite pair of black jeans and a grubby white T-shirt with the White Stripes on the front.

For a moment he stood before them, arms curled above his head, eyes closed. He lifted his chin in the air and stretched, the corners of his plump mouth pulled down so that his lips parted. He smiled. All this with his iPod turned up so loud that Ali could recognize "Seven Nation Army" playing. He had obviously just come in.

On the sofa Nick looked down at his trousers, aware for the first time that his zipper was half undone and this might not look good. He pulled at it, but his hands were clumsy and it was stubborn. He tugged again, but the zipper wouldn't budge. He gave Ali a panicked look. She instinctively moved farther away from him. But it was too late. Jake sensed the movement at the other end of the room. He opened his eyes, and his gaze fell on the two people sitting on the sofa. His eyes darted back from Nick to Ali. He took in the flimsy T-shirt and his father's dishevelment and drew all the wrong conclusions.

That night, for the first time in weeks, Ali called her parents. She was relieved that her father picked up the phone, because he was less recriminatory than her mother about the increasingly long silences between them. He certainly wouldn't be measuring them. Nor was he threatened by Ali's urge to separate herself from her family, perhaps because it was a similar impulse that compelled him out to sea every day.

Ali would have liked to discuss what had happened with Nick. Should she preempt Jake by mentioning something to Bryony first? Get her side of the story out before anyone else? Or perhaps she would end up looking defensive? Should she try to reason with Jake?

Instead she remained silent and listened to her father talk about what he had been doing that day. His steady tone soothed Ali. He'd gone out to the deeper waters by the shipping lanes and landed his best haul of the week. The mechanical shanks meant it was easy to pull in the pots without any help.

Ali lay on the bed and closed her eyes as she listened to him describe how a live bottlenose whale had washed up on the beach that morning. A group of locals had spent the day trying to keep it alive by throwing buckets of water on its flesh and using brooms to try to sweep it back toward the sea. The tide came in, and the whale finally found itself in water that was deep enough to swim. They persuaded it away from shore. Less than an hour later it came back and grounded itself on the beach again. It reminded her of the stories he had told her as a child.

"Why?" asked Ali. "Do you think it wanted to die? Why didn't it choose life?" He could hear the note of anxiety in her voice but didn't question it.

"It was probably confused. Animals are bent on survival, not self-destruction," her father pointed out. "Only human beings have the self-awareness to kill themselves."

"If I was there I might have been able to save it," said Ali.

"Perhaps it didn't want to be saved," said her father. "Some people don't. Jo will do what she does whether you are here or not."

There was a muffled exchange, and then Ali's mother came on the

line. They spoke at cross-purposes, her mother struggling not to mention Jo, and Ali struggling not to mention Jake.

"How's it all going?" her mother asked.

"Generally fine," said Ali. "It's a bit complicated sometimes—"

"But nothing you can't handle," her mother interrupted.

9

∷ ∷ ∷ ∷ ∷ ∷ ∷
∷ ∷ ∷ ∷ ∷ ∷ ∷

December 2006

The morning before the Skinners' much-anticipated annual Christmas drinks party, Bryony revealed to Ali "in total confidence" that the surprise entertainment that evening would be provided by Elton John. A member of his entourage would be coming at eleven o'clock that morning to run through last-minute details, and Bryony would be grateful if Ali was on hand to deal with any final tweaks, because the party planner might arrive at the same time.

"Elton likes a glass of still water, no ice, no lemon, on top of the piano. Lots of flowers in the room," said Bryony, glancing down at her notes, "and if it's warm he needs somewhere to put his jacket. He'll sing for about half an hour and then mingle with guests for twenty minutes. We're trying to create an air of intimacy and informality, so he won't be using a microphone. We're not sure whether David will be coming. It's always everything at the last minute with them."

All this was said in a relaxed tone, as if to underline Bryony's familiarity with the habits of Elton John and his husband, David Furnish, and her nonchalance at having such illustrious visitors to their party.

Nick and Bryony hosted dinners roughly every two weeks, but this was the first time any of their guests held interest for Ali, although sometimes their names sounded familiar. This time, she was so astonished that she dropped Alfie's bowl of Cheerios onto the oak floor, where it shattered into tiny pieces. Sensing an opportunity, Leicester tripped across the room and began scoffing cereal and licking up pools of milk.

"God, how amazing," gushed Ali.

"No one knew until today, apart from Nick, otherwise we'd have photographers turning up," Bryony explained.

For once she said nothing about the importance of Leicester sticking to his fully organic diet, and instead of the tongue twirl in her cheek that usually indicated disapproval, Ali saw that Bryony was gratified by her response. Her guests' reactions would be more sophisticated. Some would feel awe, others jealousy—Bryony didn't much mind which—but none could feign indifference. The presence of Elton John at your party was an almost unsurpassable public-relations coup, even if he was being paid to perform.

"Don't worry about the bowl, Malea will clear it up," said Bryony.

Three months earlier, shortly before Ali began working at Holland Park Crescent, Bryony had first mentioned that a party was held every year on the first Saturday in December. She had said that she would be grateful if Ali could save the date in her diary to help look after the children that evening. They would include not just the twins, Izzy, and Jake, but also her sister's two children, Maud and Ella. She would be "generously compensated."

Ali had nodded as Bryony outlined the details. There would be food and drink for one hundred fifty people, some music in the middle, and a decorative theme that reflected all these elements. Ali recalled the neurosis of her own mother before Christmas dinner in Norfolk when there were only fifteen guests. Although, of course, her mother's mood was always infected by uncertainty about whether Jo would make an appearance. But at least she could synchronize a meal, thought Ali. Mira and Katya complained that their employers were lazy about cooking for their children. Bryony, however, was in a different league. It wasn't that she didn't cook. She couldn't cook. On the single day a month that Malea took off, both lunch and dinner were eaten at restaurants, and if Nick was there he cooked breakfast. Even with Malea's help, how could Bryony possibly do food for more than a hundred people? How could she organize such an event?

"Will you make everything in advance and freeze it?" Ali had asked tentatively. Bryony had burst out laughing as she explained to Ali that a party planner would organize everything from invitations to food and entertainment for the evening.

"Can you imagine the chaos if I was doing it?" she asked. "One of the most important lessons I learned early on in my career is the art of delegation, Ali. My biggest chore will be deciding what to wear and who not to invite."

Bryony wore her lack of domestic skills as a badge of feminist honor, although it struck Ali as somewhat hypocritical that her solution was to pay an impoverished student and a Filipina to fill the vacuum. She frequently complained about 1950s values creeping back into contemporary parenting culture. Her nickname for Sophia Wilbraham was Cupcake, a reference not simply to Sophia's penchant for fresh baking but also her large girth, and her fondness for pleated skirts that resembled bun casings and neatly ironed white shirts the color and texture of white icing. "What's Cupcake up to this week, Ali?" Bryony would nonchalantly ask as they reviewed the daybook on a Sunday evening, looking at the agenda for the following week.

And courtesy of Katya, Ali would generally be able to satisfy her curiosity with a few choice tales from the Wilbraham household. (Katya had been made to remove all the name tapes that she had carefully ironed on to four sets of children's uniforms and replace them with sew-on tapes; Martha had been caught with a boy in her bedroom; Ned had got drunk and called Sophia's mother a bitch in front of the two oldest children.) As she told these stories, Ali wondered why, if Bryony loathed Sophia so much, was she so interested in what went on under her roof?

Which was why, when Bryony suggested Ali sit down at the table with her to familiarize herself with the order of events for the evening, she was taken aback to see Sophia Wilbraham and her husband on the list of confirmed guests that the party planner gave her.

"Any last-minute no-shows?" Bryony asked the woman running the event.

"Four," said Fi Seldon-Kent, director of Elite Entertainment, as she cast a glance down at her list. "David and Samantha Cameron have sent their apologies. And the Campbells are stuck in Saint Barts," said Fi, referring to her notes. "A problem with flights."

"I can't believe they fly on commercial airlines," said Bryony incredulously.

Fi shook her head as though she couldn't believe it, either. She was probably in her early thirties, Ali decided. She was one of those shiny, polished public-school types who seemed to begin all her sentences with the phrase "Would you mind awfully" and typed everything in italics. She was kind to Ali, in the sense that she at least acknowledged her presence.

Ali glanced up and down the guest list. Combes, Crichton–Millers, Cullens, Lord and Lady Rogers, Lady Townshend, Peter Mandelson, Robert Peston, Marjorie Scardino, Caspar Simpson, Skeets, Southerns, and Strachans. Some people had their job titles listed against their name, so Ali could see that the editor of the *Financial Times* and several journalists from *The Economist* would be coming, as well as the chief executives of a couple of High Street banks. Bryony's closest friend, Holly Long, was coming without her husband. The list ran to three pages. Apart from Elton John, the only names Ali recognized were those that belonged to Bryony's family: Foy and Tita Chesterton; Bryony's sister, Hester Chesterton, and her husband, Richard (Rick) Yates, and their two children, Maud and Ella Chesterton-Yates, an amalgamation of their surnames that always generated arch comments from the rest of the family. She also recognized Bryony's "old friend" Felix Naylor. She searched for Nick's parents, knowing she wouldn't find them. The children said they had never met their paternal grandparents because they were dead.

"Ali is looking after the children. The younger ones are allowed to stay up until about nine-thirty, then she'll take them to bed," Bryony explained.

"Just before Elton starts his set," Fi confirmed, looking at her timetable.

"Exactly," said Bryony briskly, overlooking the disappointment on Ali's face as she realized that she would probably be reading Dr. Seuss as Elton John belted out "Don't Go Breaking My Heart" in the drawing room. Bryony told Ali that the children could come into the drawing room and dining room to mingle with guests for no more than an hour. She had bought a strappy dress with sequins for Izzy, and she would be grateful if Ali could make sure that she wore it rather than one of her "grungy" outfits, and stay with the twins at all times. Hector and Alfie should wear identical blue corduroy trousers with white shirts and sleeveless cashmere pullovers.

"Well, that is great," said Fi Seldon-Kent enthusiastically as she picked tiny balls of fluff from the wrist of her cashmere sweater. Fi believed fervently in the art of positive affirmation, and Bryony relaxed in the warm glow of approval.

They turned to the question of flowers. The tone of the party was "lazy decadence," Fi explained, "Chateau Marmont meets Marrakesh," which meant naturalistic flower schemes everywhere, apart from the room where Elton John was due to sing. The railings leading up to the house were already a riot of purple hydrangea, chocolate cosmos, and silver foliage. In a couple of hours, the florists would have finished replicating this scheme up and down the banisters, spraying the flowers with water every couple of hours until the party started at six-thirty, to avoid any danger of wilt. Bryony joked that she might require similar treatment, and everyone laughed a little too loudly.

Cocktails would be served to guests as they arrived, Fi continued, reminding them about the specially created Winter Solstice cocktail

containing Polstar cucumber vodka and champagne with a hint of
elderflower in the background. Dom Pérignon would be served all
evening, as well as a selection of red and white wine chosen by Nick.
A ticketed cloakroom would be run by a team of girls who would
collect coats in the hallway and take them upstairs to Bryony's office.

Fi handed out a canapé menu to everyone round the table. It was
written in the same eighteenth-century typeface as the invitation, Ali
noted. Edwardian Serif. Uptight with a hint of decadence.

VEGETARIAN

Creamed Stilton served on a Rosemary Scone

Creamy Wild Mushrooms on Brioche Toast

FISH

Potted Brown Shrimps with Crème Fraîche on Sultana Bread

**Smoked Haddock & Chive Fishcakes
with Lemon Crème Fraîche**

MEAT

Thai Beef Rice Paper Roll with a Soy & Honey Dip

Parsnip Falafel with Baba Ghanoush & Smoked Chicken

SWEET

Apple & Cinnamon Turnovers

Spiced White Chocolate & Candied Fruit Biscuit

Fi confirmed that six parking spaces had been reserved outside the
house: two for Elton John, one for a former Northern Ireland minister who still had a security detail, and another for the director of the
Tate, where Nick was a major donor. The Darkes next door had

kindly offered to give up two residents' spaces "for unforeseen emergencies."

One had already presented itself, because the chief executive of Nick's investment bank, Dick Fuld, had suddenly announced late last night that he would be flying over from New York in one of the company's private jets with his wife, Kathy, just for the party. On one level this represented a social coup, because Dick's presence was a barometer of Nick's current status at the bank. Ali had overheard Nick telling Bryony that it was the first time he had bothered to turn up to a party for any of his European employees, a reflection perhaps of the fact that Nick's department had earned more than any other for the bank that year.

It would give Nick a chance to say thank you in person for the £8 million bonus awarded to him earlier in the week (£6 million in share options, £2 million in cash). On the other hand, it would require a whole barrage of additional planning to draw up a list of people to whom Dick should, and, even more important, shouldn't, be introduced (the latter included all journalists; Foy; Bryony's sister, Hester; and a couple of eager beavers from the London office who wouldn't know how to handle themselves in the face of such power).

Foy had requested the other emergency space, but Bryony had managed to persuade him and Tita to either walk the four hundred meters from their house or get a local taxi company to drop them. "Couldn't Mr. Artouche oblige?" Foy had whined. He had always coveted the Armenian driver that drove his son-in-law to work every morning.

"He's busy," Bryony had said firmly.

Bryony had suggested Ali wear something that would distinguish her from both the guests and the waitresses, to avoid creating confusion. Bryony was good at dressing up orders as advice, thought Ali, as she reviewed the contents of her wardrobe an hour before the party was due to start. It had seemed a simple enough request at the time.

She had one dress, but it was too short and flimsy for such a formal party. There were jeans, T-shirts, leggings, and a denim skirt. So wearing the skirt and leggings, she decided to head down into Izzy's room to see if she had anything that she could lend her, even if it was only a top that she could wear with her jeans. She knocked on the door a couple of times, and when no one answered she turned the handle to go in.

She found Izzy lying facedown on the bed, wearing a T-shirt and a pair of Jake's pajama bottoms. She made no noise, but Ali could tell from the way her shoulders were shaking that she was crying.

"What's wrong, Izzy?" Ali asked, going over to her bed to put a hand on her shoulder.

"I can't find anything right to wear," said Izzy, her voice muffled by the duvet. She was marooned in a sea of clothes strewn from the bed onto the floor and back to the huge built-in wardrobe across the side of the room.

"Neither can I," said Ali, patting Izzy's shoulder.

"That's because you don't have any clothes," said Izzy, "not because none of them suit you. You look good in anything." Still lying on the bed, she turned her head to face Ali. "Why can't I be thin like Mum?" Her pale cheeks were red and blotchy, and her eyes were swollen from crying so much.

It was not a question that Ali wanted to address, although the answer was simple: Apart from her dark hair, Izzy was built like Nick's side of the family. There was a single photo of his parents on a chest of drawers in Nick and Bryony's bedroom. They stood in a line, legs slightly apart, squat and stout and sure of the ground beneath their feet.

"It's what's inside that counts," said Ali.

"That's not true, Ali," said Izzy. She sat up on the bed. "Look at the people here tonight and tell me tomorrow whether you still believe it's what's inside that counts. In Mum's day you could get away with being either beautiful or clever. Now you have to be both, and I'm neither."

"Everyone loves you the way you are," said Ali. But what she really meant was that people loved Izzy the way they thought she was. Bryony and Nick described her as the fulcrum between Jake's moody cynicism and the twins' excess of temperament. Her friends found her sweet-natured and easygoing. Malea said she was the most softhearted member of the family. Did they not sense her fragility, or did they not want to see it? Ali wondered.

"If Mum loved me the way I am, then she wouldn't go on about what I eat all the time," said Izzy, "and she wouldn't need someone like you to help me with my schoolwork. She'd just let me be me."

"She just wants the best for you," said Ali, searching for a pot of moisturizer on Izzy's dressing table that would simultaneously remove the small rivers of mascara flowing down Izzy's cheeks and soothe her skin. It was Crème de la Mer. For a moment Ali hesitated as she shook a gloopy lump onto cotton wool and handed it to Izzy. Over the previous four months she had developed some immunity to the scale of the Skinners' wealth, but somehow this £50 teaspoonful of face cream shocked her more than the man who came once a month to check whether any lights needed new bulbs, or the gardener who threw away annuals from pots in the back garden after they finished flowering like a man discarding his middle-aged wife for a younger model.

"Actually, it's got nothing to do with me, it's all about her," said Izzy quietly. She looked at Ali from behind the sticky mask of face cream. "Have I returned to my former state of mediocrity?"

"You're not mediocre, Izzy," said Ali. "You're a talented musician. You're brilliant at sport. You got an A for your last English essay."

"None of it comes naturally. I have to work hard at everything I do. And everyone gets A's at my school. Getting A's is what's expected. You're practically prevented from doing a GCSE in a subject where you might not get an A."

"And you're really good at lacrosse," said Ali, reminding Izzy that she was part of the team that played in the final of the UK schools' championships as she watched Izzy trace lines through the cream on her face.

"Did you know Mum got a scholarship to Wycombe Abbey and a first at Oxford, and that she was the woman everyone wanted to marry?" said Izzy. "It's such a burden being her daughter."

"You don't have to plow the same furrow," Ali said.

"There are girls at my school who do internships in the holidays with Marc Jacobs. Three others are already signed up with the Royal Ballet. One has started a year-nine magazine with an interview with Cherie Blair on the cover of the first issue. Another is signed to Select Models. I'm just a humble little Christmas tree in a wood full of oaks. That's why you are here. You are part of the great master plan to secure ten top-grade GCSEs for Isabella Skinner and work experience doing something glamorous in the media. Anything else would be catastrophic. I once heard Mum telling Dad that I would need to get a decent job because I wasn't cut out to be a City wife."

"Well, it would be a shame to work so hard and then be condemned to a life shopping at Selfridges and acting as a tutor to your children," said Ali, trying to lighten the mood.

"Especially if I end up being a size sixteen," said Izzy. "In Mum's book, that's worse than being dumb."

"All parents worry about their children," said Ali, thinking about her own mother and the way her face had become frozen in a permanent mask of anxiety over the past ten years.

"She only worries about the things that reflect badly on her," said Izzy resolutely.

"You'll find your own way, Izzy," Ali reassured her. "You'll find something you love doing, and then life will fall into place."

"Is that what you really believe, Ali?" asked Izzy. "Because if it was, then you wouldn't be working here."

"I like working here," insisted Ali, surprised to find this was true.

"Why?" asked Izzy.

"I feel free," said Ali, "I feel unconstrained. I know that I could leave whenever I want, but I love living in London, I really like living with your family, and I know you won't believe it, but it's great looking after Hector and Alfie. I find them interesting and unpredictable.

And it's just a phase. Like being a teenager. This isn't the rest of my life, and it isn't the rest of yours." Izzy's eyes brightened for a moment. Something had resonated. "I'm trying to find my center of gravity. So must you."

But sometimes you need to get away from your family to do that, Ali thought to herself. Her phone rang. It was Bryony.

"Can you come down right away, Ali?" she said brusquely. "There's been a disaster. I need you."

"I'd better go, Izzy," she said apologetically.

"Don't worry, Ali, I'll put on the dreadful dress that Mum bought me. I won't let you down. Even though I'll look like a sausage decorated with sequins." Izzy smiled. It was a sad smile of resignation rather than rekindled joy. "Then tomorrow the diet begins."

Ali went downstairs to find the ground-floor rooms transformed. The grand piano, tuned earlier in the day, had been moved into the dining room in a cloud of disapproval from Tita, who said that Steinways were "uniquely sensitive" to subtle changes in room temperature, movement, and humidity. The enormous round dining table had disappeared, and half a dozen smaller tables covered in white linen tablecloths and flower arrangements that matched the color scheme in the hall filled half the room. Each table was surrounded by half a dozen gilt-colored chairs with pale linen seats.

Ali glanced round the room, then headed toward the drawing room. She could hear raised voices, male and female, all speaking at once. The sofas and armchairs had been reconfigured to maximize the space in the center of the room, giving two intimate seating areas at either end. Bryony was standing by the fireplace, shouting at Hector and Alfie, who were huddled on either side of their grandfather on the nearest sofa.

"I can't believe they chose this moment to do something so monumentally stupid," yelled Bryony. "Have they got any idea how stressful it is organizing a party like this?"

"It shows quite sophisticated comic timing," said Foy unhelpfully.

"Calm down, Bryony," barked Nick, noticing Ali's presence in the room. "He can wear a hat, for God's sake."

"A hat at a bloody drinks party? He'll look ridiculous," said Bryony. "People already think they're weird without them doing this kind of thing. Sophia Wilbraham is going to have a field day."

"Who cares what that gossipy barrel of a woman thinks about anything," said Nick. "I don't know why you even bother to invite her."

"To remind her that whatever she does, I do it better," retorted Bryony. "And because you like her husband."

"He's useful to know," said Nick.

Ali stared at Hector. His luscious curls had disappeared, apart from one sole survivor curled just above his right ear. His hair was so short that in parts Ali could see his scalp. On the right side of his head were a series of tiny cuts from a razor blade. His face was completely brown.

"Why have you done this?" shrieked Bryony, moving toward him.

"It's because we want to be soldiers," said Alfie, shrinking back into the sofa. "Ali told us that soldiers always have shaved heads. I cut Hector's hair, and now he must cut mine, otherwise we won't look the same and we can't be in the army together."

"You are not cutting your hair, Alfie," Bryony said firmly. He started crying and punching one of the sofa cushions.

"What have you put on your face?" asked Ali.

"Camouflage," said Hector.

"What did you use?" she persisted.

"Shoe polish," they both shouted out at exactly the same time, stoking Bryony's fury. "It's behind the curtain."

Ali went over to the window and found two tins of open shoe polish, one black and the other dark brown. The curtains were covered in a series of perfectly shaped shoe-polish handprints. She resolved to tell Bryony about this part of the disaster later.

"Why did you tell him that soldiers have shaved heads?" Bryony asked Ali.

"Because they do," said Ali, trying to bind apology and reason into her response. "It was a passing comment. I didn't suggest they should actually cut their own hair."

"You can't blame Ali," said Nick. "Think of all the things they did when we had the other nannies."

"Ya ha mimusch," Alfie shouted. Hector repeated the phrase until everyone was staring at them.

"What are they saying, Ali?" asked Bryony.

"I don't recognize those words," said Ali.

"Why weren't you watching them?" Bryony turned on Ali again.

"I was helping Izzy choose what to wear," said Ali.

"She knows what she has to wear," said Bryony impatiently.

"She was upset about something, I was trying to help her," said Ali.

Bryony sat down on the sofa, suddenly deflated. "I'm really sorry, Ali, I know that you can't be with them all the time. Can you just take them away and deal with them?"

"Shall I cut Alfie's hair a little, just to calm them down?" suggested Ali, as the twins walked over to her and each took a hand.

"Yes," said Bryony, wondering how she could be so easily defeated by a pair of five-year-olds.

"What would we do without her?" asked Nick as Ali left the room. "She's brilliant with them. Far better than the rest."

"You're very lucky," agreed Foy. "Imagine if you had to look after them on your own. Like Hester."

Twenty minutes later Hector and Alfie sat on either side of Foy on the closest sofa, avidly listening to a story he had told them many times before about how he escaped through enemy lines after being shot down by Germans during World War II. Like most of Foy's stories, the content was entirely fictional. He was far too young to have fought in the war, and he had never been a spy, but the twins were enraptured.

Ali had done her best with the kitchen scissors, and although Hector looked dreadful she had managed to placate Alfie without cutting his hair quite as short. They had both refused to wear hats, and Bryony had acquiesced.

"I think Dick should sit there," Nick said, pointing to the sofa at the end of the room. "Then I can control who he meets more easily. People can informally congregate here for an audience. Tell Ali to keep the twins well away from him. He doesn't do mess."

"Good idea," said Bryony, looking over at Ali to make sure she had heard. Ali nodded.

"Will you keep an eye on his wife, Bryony?" he asked. "For God's sake, don't let Hester near her."

"Maybe I should get Felix to charm her?" suggested Bryony.

"Maybe you should get Felix to mark Hester," retorted Nick. "He's about the only person who can rein her in. By the way, I've just been sent an e-mail saying that we've been voted *Risk* magazine's structured finance bank of the year for 2006."

"Darling, that is great news," said Bryony, quickly kissing him on the lips. Nick leaned toward her, but she pulled away as the doorbell rang.

"Whoever that is, tell them to piss off, because they're early," said Nick.

"It's Hester and Rick," Bryony said, and sighed. "Why are they always the first to arrive and the last to go?"

"Nunc est bibendum!" declared Foy. "Shall we open some champagne to get us all in the mood before Mr. and Mrs. John arrive?"

"Everyone calls them Elton and David, Daddy," insisted Bryony.

"I'm not addressing a couple of poofs that I've never met by their first names," said Foy. "I will be introducing myself to Mr. and Mrs. John as Mr. Chesterton."

"Your homophobia betrays your age," said Hester coolly, "and they might not find an audience with you such an interesting prospect.

Anyway, once they've fulfilled their side of the contract, I don't imagine they'll stick around for small talk. Especially not of the smoked-salmon variety."

Ali stared at Hester in fascination. She was wearing a mid-length shift dress and leather boots, as if deliberately underplaying the glamorous dress code. As far as she could tell, Hester wore no makeup, but she had inherited the quiet beauty of her mother, so that even the unflattering hemline just below the knee somehow looked elegant.

"I was just joking, Hester," said Foy, standing in the path of a waiter who had just appeared with a tray of champagne. "Mr. John might be interested to meet another self-made man."

"Remember to pace yourself, Foy," warned Tita, who had just appeared in the drawing room, wearing a cream diaphanous dress and a diamond necklace that Ali had never seen before. She seemed to glow in the soft light. Her hair was scraped off her face and twisted into an elegant bun at the back of her head, accentuating her cheekbones.

"Rick, Hester," she said, the palms of her hands suspended in the air as though blessing her son-in-law and daughter. "So lovely to see you." She waited for them to come over to her.

"You look beautiful, darling," she said to Hester. "But perhaps the boots are a little clunky."

She would never learn, thought Ali. Hester wore the boots precisely because it would provoke this reaction. Everything Hester did was still in opposition to her parents, most significantly her choice of husband. Rick stood beside Hester, clearly there under duress. His jacket was too big, his trousers were too short, and he wasn't wearing a tie. From the neck down he reminded Ali of a bouncer you might find outside a nightclub in Norwich. From the neck up he looked like an irascible romantic poet with his tangled hair, brown eyes, and round glasses.

"Have you broken up for the holidays yet?" Tita asked as she kissed Rick on both cheeks, her lips barely touching his skin. Ali thought she saw Tita's nose crinkle as she glanced down at the chest hair peeking out of the top of his shirt, but it might have been Rick's aftershave that offended her olfactory sensibilities.

"I've got a couple of weeks off," said Rick, "but now that I'm deputy head I have to go in for planning meetings."

"How marvelous," said Tita, who always adopted a melodramatic tone when talking about Rick's job teaching in the state sector, as though he were fighting in Afghanistan. "Do they pay you more for doing extra days?"

"Unfortunately not," said Rick, rocking backward and forward on his shoes until Tita looked almost seasick.

"At least he still gets to spend a lot of time with me and the children," said Hester, linking arms with Rick. "He's always around for them."

"Wonderful," said Tita cautiously, as though she suspected this might be a barb aimed at her. According to Bryony, Hester had never fully forgiven Tita for forgetting to pick them up at the end of her first term at boarding school because she was grouse-shooting in Scotland.

"So what are you doing in the holidays?" Tita asked.

"We'll probably dig up the allotment," said Hester zealously, "we're almost completely self-sufficient in vegetables. Doing our bit to reduce the carbon footprint."

Bryony rolled her eyes. Ali knew all about the fault lines in Bryony's relationship with her sister from a discussion she had overheard between Nick and Bryony in the kitchen earlier in the week. The general facts were these: Hester had always found life more complicated; Bryony was hard pushed to identify any period of equilibrium between them; and having children had turned the cracks into permanent fissures. Nick had been satisfied with this analysis, but Bryony had wanted a more exhaustive examination.

So Ali knew that from the outset Bryony had been an easy baby, while Hester was colicky and tricky. Hester had apparently never settled at the tiny nursery set up by one of Tita's friends in Chelsea, while Bryony had cried when it came to going home. In the sink-or-swim environment of a girls' boarding school, Bryony hadn't simply managed to navigate an adequate survival strategy. She found long-lasting friends, like Holly Long; she had captained the regional lacrosse squad; and her trajectory to Oxford was effortless, apart from a glitch in her final year when her first boyfriend, Felix Naylor, appeared on the scene.

Hester, by contrast, who followed Bryony to Wycombe Abbey two years later, had never enjoyed school, and after a year and much discussion was removed mid-term and sent to a girls' day school in London. An incident that Foy had never forgiven because it had ruined the salmon fishing season on the beat he had bought on the Tay in the mid-1970s because it meant Tita had to be at home to look after Hester. Although it did allow his "close friendship" with Eleanor Peterson to flourish unencumbered by his wife's presence.

By their late twenties this state of imbalance had become ingrained. Hester floundered from one job to another. She dated men whose only common theme was the fact that they were as different as possible from her father. Bryony left Oxford, went to work at a financial PR agency that a friend had set up, and within four years owned half the shares in the company. Then, just before her twenty-ninth birthday, Hester met Rick. She fell pregnant with Maud almost immediately. And she took to parenting with all the zeal of a mother who wanted to redress the inadequacies of her own childhood. She decided not to go back to work. Never to employ a nanny. She read books about attachment theory, became a militant breast-feeder, experimented with co-sleeping and home schooling, and refused to immunize her children.

"Of course, we don't have any staff to pick up the slack in the holidays," said Hester.

At the mention of staff, Foy asked Hester whether she had met Bryony and Nick's new nanny. Using his index finger, he beckoned for Ali to come over.

"This is the wonderful Ali Sparrow," he said so loudly that Ali blushed with embarrassment. "She's an expert in twin control and eighteenth-century English literature. We all adore and worship her. Why haven't you got a drink, Ali?"

"I don't drink when I'm on duty," Ali said, shaking hands with Hester and Rick. The twins snuggled into her side.

"Hello, Aunt Hester," they said.

"God, what on earth have you done to your hair?" Hester asked Hector and Alfie, bending down to examine Hector's scalp more closely.

"Is it so obvious that it's a self-inflicted haircut?" said Bryony, trying to tread lightly over the issue. "Ali has done a splendid job on damage limitation." She smiled at Ali apologetically.

"Did it happen while you were at work?" Hester questioned Bryony.

"Actually, it happened while I was at home," said Bryony. "It's got nothing to do with the fact that I work."

"I was simply asking when they did it," protested Hester. "Although, of course, it could be interpreted as a kind of protest, a cry for attention. It must be difficult being the youngest members of a family when both parents work such long hours. And a new nanny."

"They wanted to look like soldiers," Ali explained in an even tone. "So Alfie tried to shave Hector's head. It's because of a song they learned at school."

Alfie and Hector began singing "Two Little Boys," and Foy immediately joined in.

"I have a record of this song," said Foy excitedly, "from when I was a child. Would you like to have it, boys?"

The twins jumped up and down in excitement.

"I don't think they should be learning songs that glamorize war," said Hester.

"I think if it was a number-one hit for Rolf Harris in the seventies, then we can assume that its underlying message is pretty benign," said

Nick, who seemed adept at avoiding the undercurrent between Hester and Bryony, no doubt worrying he might get pulled under.

"My only problem with it is the homosexual undertone," said Foy.

"Don't be ridiculous, Dad," said Bryony and Hester together.

Rick turned to Ali and began bombarding her with questions that no one else had asked for months. "Where are you from? When are you going to finish your degree? Are you studying Sterne? Have you made friends in London? What do you parents think of your job?"

"I've met a really nice group of nannies from Eastern Europe," she told him. "Sometimes we have dinner at each others' houses. They don't go out much, because they're trying to save as much money as possible. But it's really interesting meeting people from different countries."

"Are they all legal?" Rick asked.

"I'm not sure," said Ali, who had recently learned that Mira and Katya both came illegally to England from Ukraine. "I don't really like to question them too closely about how they got here."

"Polish is the second most widely spoken language in the school where I teach," said Rick.

"The Poles are good workers," said Foy, whose innate Conservatism didn't stretch to immigrants, because for the past twenty-five years Freithshire Fisheries had expanded on the back of the labor of its migrant workers.

Ali noticed Jake come into the room. He was dressed in the same suit and tie that he wore for school every day. Ali smiled at him, but he quickly looked away. Nick headed toward him holding a glass of champagne.

"There are some people I want you to meet tonight," he told Jake, putting an arm around his shoulder. "They might be able to give you work experience. You could end up with a great set of contacts."

"Dad, I've told you I don't want to work in a bank," said Jake. "You have to accept I'm not motivated by the same instincts as you. And although I know this is a fabulous networking opportunity dressed up as a family party, I'd rather let everything happen organically."

"That's not how the world works, Jake," said Nick.

The doorbell rang again.

"That will be Elton and David's people," said Bryony to everyone. "Take your positions, everyone."

A current of excitement charged round the room.

10

∷ ∷ ∷ ∷ ∷ ∷

Parties were like relationships, and this one was in its honeymoon period. Everywhere people were laughing and talking, feigning nonchalance when they recognized a well-known face. Elton John was working the room. Bryony had introduced him to a government minister who was lobbying for HIV medicines to be made cheaper in Africa. They were talking animatedly. Bryony was anxious about his vocal cords. How much should a singer talk before he gave a concert? she worried. Would they reimburse her if he strained his voice? Or would they sue her for damages?

"Relax, Bryony," said a woman Ali had never seen before. "It's all going to be fine." They stood together in the center of the room, and Bryony apologized for canceling lunch earlier in the week.

"I had lunch with my husband instead," the woman said. "It was the first time I'd seen him for almost a week. He's been in the States on a yoga course."

"How is everything, Holly?" Bryony asked, glancing around to check that there was no one cast adrift. Nick was spending too much time with Dick Fuld. She should go and rescue him, but then she might get entangled with his wife.

"I think we're making progress," said Holly. "We're trying to go out together once a week and just enjoy ourselves. We're not allowed to talk about anything that has come up in the counseling sessions."

"Like what?" asked Bryony.

"Mainly about our mother–child relationship," Holly said. "I have to stop trying to organize him, and he has to stop assuming I will do everything. I'm meant to make myself more vulnerable, and he's meant to try and become more assertive. But we have to do it uncritically."

"Sounds complicated," said Bryony.

"Basically we have to reach a point where we agree on more issues than we disagree—then we'll have reestablished equilibrium. But as long as he doesn't find another job, it's going to be difficult. That's why I'm keeping Mira. I don't want him to feel like a househusband, and she's so good at keeping everything organized."

"And the new job? Caught any white-collar criminals?" Bryony asked. "I've always wondered how the Financial Services Authority works."

"It's great. I love it."

"Well, I'd better not be seen consorting with the enemy for too long," joked Bryony.

"Boom times encourage the risk takers." Holly laughed.

"Anything interesting?" asked Bryony.

"Nothing I can talk about. But I should warn Nick that there is serious discussion in some circles about banks' balance sheets. They're all overleveraged. How's your new nanny working out?"

"Ali's brilliant," said Bryony. "I live in terror that she'll leave."

Waiters and waitresses brought in tray after tray of drinks and canapés on cool slate platters. Ali mingled, threading her way through the room, holding on to Hector and Alfie on either side of her. Occasionally, an adult bent down to speak to one or the other of them or pat them on the head, as you might a friendly Labrador. They answered questions politely. If they began to speak whole sentences in unison, Ali tried to distract them. She knew that Bryony didn't like people to notice this particular quirk.

She passed Sophia and Ned Wilbraham. How did they fit together? wondered Ali.

"Impressive guest list," he said from behind a glass of champagne.

"She's showing off," Sophia retorted. Then she noticed Ali.

"Have you settled in?" she asked. Ali smiled and mumbled something about how she felt like part of the furniture.

"Well, if you get fed up, then let me know," Sophia said, beaming. "I'm at home a lot more, so you wouldn't have so much responsibility for small children and you could get some useful teaching experience with my eldest. She's very gifted."

"Thanks," said Ali, unsure what else to say. She pulled the twins away, and they circled Foy, who was holding court.

"When Mrs. Thatcher came to power you couldn't take more than five hundred pounds out of the country at a time," he said. "Now you can move millions at the flick of a switch." He clicked his fingers like castanets. Tita was standing close to him.

"I can't understand why basic things like cooking and gardening and sewing have suddenly become so fashionable when we did these things completely unthinkingly," she was telling Eleanor Peterson.

"Tita, we paid other people to do them," said Eleanor.

Ali caught the threads of other conversations, but the twins acted as an invisible cloak so she didn't have to face the embarrassment of being mistaken for another guest or, even worse, a member of the Skinner family. They headed for a quiet corner of the room, where Nick was now huddled in conversation with Ned Wilbraham, who worked as a broker at a rival investment bank. She made the twins sit down to sip fizzy lemonade from zany spiral plastic straws. Nick turned his back on them.

"There was a piece in *Barron's* saying that the average price of new homes in the U.S. has fallen three percent in eight months. What does that tell you?" asked Nick. It sounded like an argument, but Ali had overheard enough of Nick's conference calls to know that the under-current of aggression and hostility was born of an inalienable sense of his own rightness rather than any call to arms.

"That the housing boom is either coming to an end or going through a temporary glitch," said Ned. "If it's the end of the world, Nick, you only get to bet on it once, you don't want to get short too soon."

Ned stood with his legs a little too far apart, cowboy style, as though using his muscular frame to compensate for Nick's superior height. He was a pale man, with deep-set eyes and a haircut almost as short as the twins'. Not conventionally good-looking, thought Ali. A man who would burn in the sun and freeze in the cold.

"You need to know where the emergency exit is before the fire starts," said Nick. "I went to a conference on credit markets a couple of months ago. There were about fifty guys in the room. I calculated their income last year was more than two hundred fifty million pounds." He paused to sip his Winter Solstice cocktail. "It suddenly occurred to me that there was no connection between their intellect and their unbelievable accumulation of wealth. What if they're not right? What if they're wrong?"

"The mathematical modeling shows the risk is negligible," said Ned. "The Gaussian copula is a beautiful thing."

"I think the models are underestimating the risk of credit prod-ucts," said Nick. "They're measuring correlation, not risk. And every ratings agency is using the same models."

"The risk is spread so widely that even if some of those loans default, and I agree some of them are chicken shit dressed up as chicken salad, then the others won't," Ned said.

"What happens if there are unmanageable and undetectable amounts of risk spread through the entire financial system?" said Nick. "It's just a hypothesis."

"Look, if Alan Greenspan believes we're in the new paradigm, then we are. We're living the dream. Just enjoy it."

"Look back," said Nick, "the tulip bubble, the dot-com bubble.

Historically every credit boom is followed by a credit bust. I look out there and I see overextended consumers, negative savings rates, and a profligate government. Repossessions are up, prices are down, defaults are climbing. Why should this be so different? How can ever-increasing debt be sustainable?"

"Christ, you're beginning to sound like fucking Hayek." Ned laughed. "If Fuld knows you're thinking like this you'll be kicked out on your arse."

"I'm having a crisis of faith," Nick said, smiling. "I no longer believe the markets are self-correcting."

"Well, keep it to yourself, because while everyone is making money no one wants to listen to bad news," said Ned. "If the seller doesn't believe in his product, then the buyer is going to sense his indifference. Just park the doubt and pick up the fee. You can't be fucking agnostic in this business. You have to keep dancing until the music stops. Shall we get back to the party? We shouldn't be seen together."

"Why not?" Ali wanted to ask, as she bent over to wipe lemonade from the twins' hands. Was it because of the hostility between Bryony and Sophia? Or more likely the fact they worked for rival banks?

"We want to go and talk to the man who looks like a Vulcan," said Hector, pulling at Ali's arm. Ali glanced over at the direction in which they were pointing and saw that they meant Nick's boss, Dick Fuld.

They pulled past Bryony and Felix.

"I've had wind of a deal," Felix whispered to Bryony. "You should see if you can get on the pitch list. You don't have any retail clients, do you?"

"Why are you so good to me?" Ali heard Bryony ask him. Felix stared at his scruffy leather shoes, and by the time he responded to her question, Ali and the twins were too far away to hear his answer.

"Daddy says his boss's nickname is the Gorilla," said Alfie, "but I definitely think he should be called Mr. Spock."

Alfie shook off her hand and, because he was smaller and more adept at running between the legs of party guests, Ali soon lost sight of him. Hector pulled her along, and she trusted his instincts, but even before she reached the sofa where Dick Fuld was sitting talking to Nick, she knew that this was where Alfie was heading.

"I want to talk about your forward pathway," she heard Dick Fuld tell Nick. "If you can beat Goldman and make fifty percent of next year's profit on new products, then you'll be one of the people in line to head up Europe." Dick Fuld was lying against the back of the sofa, legs splayed, hands behind his head; the pose of a man who was used to bestowing power.

"Thanks, Dick. We're already contributing fifty percent of Lehman's revenues in Europe through CDOs," she heard Nick say. "And we're in the middle of putting together the biggest CDO deal in the history of the bank, so we should be back up at the top of the league table next year."

"Good job, Nick." Dick Fuld nodded. "Go make the world a richer place."

Ali could hear his wife talking to Julian Peterson about various pieces of art that they had bought.

"I'm on the board of the Museum of Modern Art," she drawled comfortably, "so I've been in a privileged position when it comes to buying art because I know what's coming on to the market early enough to be a player. That's how I secured the Gorky, but I also love de Kooning and Barnett Newman."

"Would you let us interview you for an arts program we're making for the BBC?" Julian asked her.

"We don't want that kind of publicity," said Kathy Fuld politely.

Ali hovered close to the sofa, using Alfie as bait, hoping to divert Hector from his target when he emerged from the sea of people. But before Hector appeared she saw Hester coming into range.

"Nick," Hester said sweetly, "I've always wanted to meet your boss."

"Dick," said Nick slowly, the muscles in his cheek twitching, "this is Bryony's sister, Hester."

"Pleased to meet you," said Dick Fuld, standing up to his full height to shake hands with Hester. Ali could see him looking her up and down, absorbing the hokey dress and wondering where on earth they were going to find any common ground. He didn't need to worry because, like her sister, Hester was an opinionated and confident product of her class and education and had no qualms about engaging him.

"I wanted to ask you, Mr. Fuld, how people like you and Nick can justify earning such extortionate sums of money for what you do when my husband works long hours in a state school for a fraction of the salary?" said Hester in a way that sounded as though she had been rehearsing this moment for a while. "Don't you think it's unethical? Surely people's significance should be measured by what they contribute, not what they earn?" For a moment, Dick Fuld looked truly alarmed. This was, after all, a man who had his own private lift in the Lehman office in New York, so he could avoid speaking to colleagues. Then he leaned toward Hester.

"London is the financial capital of the world, and we're all sucking from the breast of the same whore," he snarled. "I bet you and your husband own your own house, and that you've taken out equity on its ever-increasing value over the past ten years to pay for holidays abroad and such like. We're all benefiting from this financial stability. And if you don't like it, go and live in Cuba."

"I'm sorry, Dick," muttered Nick. Hester opened her mouth to respond, but she was interrupted by Hector, who crawled through her legs and stood in front of her, looking up at Dick Fuld.

"Are you a Vulcan?" Hector asked. "Can you cry?"

To Nick's relief, Dick Fuld took Hector onto his lap and began telling him just what it was like living on the Red Planet.

"Did you bring your gorilla with you?" Alfie asked.

"It got left behind in the Twin Towers," said Dick Fuld, rubbing the top of Hector's head as though shining a cricket ball. "That's some haircut you've had, little boy."

"It's because I'm joining the army," said Hector, as Alfie came and joined him.

"Time for bed," said Ali.

"I was kicked out of the Air Force," Dick told Hector. "For insubordination. So I'd listen to your commanding officer if I was you." They meekly took Ali's hands.

"You lifesaver," whispered Nick. "Now, where's that fucking suicide bomber of a sister-in-law so I can give her a piece of my mind?"

The following evening Ali stood in the hallway of Holland Park Crescent and inspected herself one last time in the lavish eighteenth-century gilt mirror that dominated the entrance to the house. According to Izzy, it had once hung in the drawing room in Regent Street, where Samuel Johnson had compiled his dictionary. Ali wanted this to be true, so she never confirmed its origin with Bryony, preferring instead to imagine Johnson at his desk, checking himself in the same mirror, as he tried to find the best definition of a word like *discombobulate*.

Apart from a huge flower arrangement on the table, there was no trace of last night's party. No stray glasses, no stains on the floor, no half-drunk bottles or crisps trodden into the carpet on the stairs. It gave the whole event a dreamlike quality. Over breakfast the following morning Nick had leaned over to Bryony and kissed her on the lips to thank her for organizing "a wonderful event." Foreheads touching, hands entwined, they both agreed that it had been a triumph and that despite Hester's intervention, Dick and Kathy Fuld had stayed much later than anticipated. Nick's breath probably didn't even smell of the night before, thought Ali, who had been gripped by this rare display of intimacy.

Perhaps this was why Bryony always had a photographer on hand. The normal mess of family life disappeared so quickly that they needed constant visual reminders of what they had actually done together. The shelves in the den were stacked with up-to-date photo albums in chronological order. The kitchen walls had a montage of carefully chosen pictures of the family at play.

The staircase was filled with tasteful black-and-white portraits of the children at various stages of their life. There was one of Hector and Alfie as toddlers, sitting on the branch of one of the beech trees at the end of the garden; there was Jake surfing, and Izzy riding a horse. The pictures had a deliberately casual feel, as though the photographer had caught them off guard, but Ali already knew this was an illusion: there was nothing spontaneous about the life of the Skinner children. Their schedules were as tightly controlled as the flight plan at Heathrow Airport.

On the landing outside Nick and Bryony's bedroom there was a huge picture of them taken at a party. They were dancing together, Nick pressed against Bryony's back, the sun on their face, so they stood out among the crowd of people as though they were blessed. Nothing can go wrong for these people, thought Ali, whenever she walked past it. All this visual suggestion had the effect of making people think they weren't having quite such a good time as the Skinners, which made Ali wish she hadn't agreed to go out with Katya and Mira.

"When a man is tired of London, he is tired of life," Ali said, quoting Johnson to give her courage on her first night out alone in the city. One eye on the mirror, she settled on the jauntiest angle for her woolly hat, checked her eye makeup for any smudging, and rummaged in her bag to make sure that she had her map of London, wallet, cigarettes, the piece of paper with the security code for the front gate, and keys. Then she left the house unchallenged. It seemed incredible that no one had asked where she was going or who she was meeting.

The twins were asleep upstairs. Izzy was having dinner with her parents in the kitchen, a painful process that consisted of Bryony trying to avoid eating while monitoring every mouthful that Izzy consumed. Jake was going out with Lucy. He hadn't told her, but standing by the fireplace in her bedroom, Ali heard him agreeing to meet her in a bar in Kensington High Street.

Desmond Darke was standing on the sidewalk as Ali shut the gate behind her. He emitted a reluctant grunt of recognition. She hurried down the street, aware that Katya and Mira would be waiting for her, rehearsing what she would tell them about the party. If people didn't share any past, it left only the present to rake over. Ali enjoyed living life in the moment, but their collective lack of history added a certain edge, as though the narrative of life had to be written even faster.

Ali was meeting them in a pub in the Portobello Road. She walked down Holland Park Avenue, past Jeroboams, past the butcher's, past the estate agent's, and turned the first left after Daunt Books. Two significant thoughts suddenly occurred to her: For the first time she had got her bearings without having to consult her map, and the pub was very close to the house where she and Jake had rescued Izzy from the party.

She walked faster, London speed, hoping that Bryony had worn in the ankle boots that Ali had found outside her bedroom this morning with a note saying they were too big for Izzy and too bohemian for her.

The pub was a cozy hum of Sunday-night drinkers. It was Victorian, with a series of wood-paneled rooms constructed around a long thin bar. Ali traipsed through a couple before coming across Mira and Katya sitting at a table at the far end. The Romanian nanny that she had first met in Starbucks was also there. They were all drinking Guinness, and Ali ordered the same, even though she had never really enjoyed its bitter taste. They got up and hugged her. Ali sat down beside Katya, feeling vaguely self-conscious that she was the only obvious native English speaker. Ileana was talking about a Romanian film that had won a best first film award at the Cannes Film Festival.

"It's called *A Fost Sau n-a Fost?* in Romanian," she explained. "In English I can't remember. Maybe *East of Bucharest* or something like that."

"What's it about?" asked Mira.

"It's about a man who claims he was part of the revolution in Romania but actually was drunk most of the time while other people were overthrowing Ceauşescu. It questions the nature of historical memory. It's very, very funny. We all wanted to be heroes, but most of us weren't."

"What was it like back then?" Ali asked. "I was only four years old in 1989."

"Put it this way, Ali: I thank my lucky stars every time I take the Pill." Ileana laughed. "My mother had ten children. No one was allowed to use birth control. Until she was forty, my poor mother was constantly pregnant."

"What happened then?" asked Ali.

"After forty, as long as you had at least four children, you were allowed to have an abortion," Ileana explained.

"Do you know what Thomas said to me today?" Katya asked. Mira looked at her watch.

"Eleven minutes forty-six seconds." She laughed as she turned to Ali. "I time Katya to see how long it takes before she mentions Thomas. This is a record, actually."

"He told me that he only wants to eat food that I cook," said Katya triumphantly.

"That's a big compliment," said Ali.

"It is because Sophia is such a terrible, terrible cook." Katya laughed. "Her meals look like her. They are legendary." She said the last word carefully, as though she had learned it only recently. "The other day I cooked the food for her dinner party. She always makes me promise not to tell anyone, but then she had an argument with Martha because she came home late."

"Where was she?" asked Ali.

"Some party near here," said Katya vaguely. "So Martha took revenge by telling everyone that I had done it all. She pointed out that the person with the purple hands and fingernails had obviously made the beetroot soup. Sophia tried to laugh it off. After everyone left she had a big, big tantrum." Katya stretched out her arms to demonstrate its breadth. "She told me that now everyone knew, I would have to leave and that I had betrayed her trust."

"What happened next?" asked Ali.

"Her husband, Ned, tried to reason with her. He told her that it wasn't my fault and that if anyone was to blame, it was Martha for revealing the truth or Sophia for creating a dinner built around a lie. So Sophia threw the remains of the beetroot soup at him, and he called her a fucking cunt."

"God, how awful," gasped Ali, trying to imagine a similar scene in the Skinner household. To judge from Mira's and Ileana's muted response to this drama, it was not an uncommon occurrence.

"So what did you do?" asked Ali.

"I cleared up the broken dish," Katya said with a shrug. "She's looking for an excuse to get rid of me."

"Well, you just have to make sure that you don't give her one," Mira warned.

"Her husband sounds kind," said Ali.

"He is very nice." Katya nodded so vigorously that the head of the Guinness slopped over the edge of the glass. "But he is very chicken-pecked."

"Hen-pecked," Ali corrected her, giggling.

"One day he will rise up against her," said Katya.

The conversation turned to food. There was a shop in South London where you could buy *horilka z pertsem*, announced Katya. "In Old Kent Road."

"In *the* Old Kent Road," said Mira. "It is one of those streets that takes the article."

Mira countered with another shop in West London where you could buy authentic *pampushki*.

"You can make that yourself," said Katya. "Yeast, sugar, egg, garlic sauce. Thomas loves *pampushki*."

"What do you eat in Romania?" Ali asked Ileana.

"Our food has the same influences as the rest of Romanian culture," said Ileana. "From the Turks we have meatballs, from the Greeks *musaca*, from the Bulgarians vegetable dishes like *ghiveci*, vegetable stew and *zacuscă*, chopped peppers and eggplant, *snitel* from the Austrians." As she spoke Ileana closed her eyes.

"Are you remembering meals from your childhood?" Ali asked cautiously. Ileana's eyes flashed open.

"God, no! There were food shortages all the time. That is why we talk about food so much now."

They all laughed again.

"Do you know why I will always love England?" asked Mira. She didn't wait for Ali to answer. "Because I learned English from listening to the BBC World Service, and speaking English has saved my life." She leaned back in her chair for dramatic effect.

Katya teased her for going native.

"She even eats Marmite," she said.

"If I didn't speak English I wouldn't have made it here," continued Mira, ignoring Katya.

"Mira is a political refugee," said Katya. "She can get very serious about things." Ali saw Katya give Mira's calf a gentle kick under the table.

"What did you do before you came here?" Ali asked Mira.

"I was a bank manager," said Mira. "When I got to London I worked nights cleaning offices in the City. Then I became a cleaner. Then the family I worked for hired me to help with their children."

Ali stared at her.

"You are wondering how someone who had a good job ended up degrading herself by cleaning other people's toilets?" asked Mira. "It's simple. I could only keep doing my job in Kiev if I was corrupt. After the wall came down there were a lot of problems with corruption. Businesspeople made a lot of bad money through selling natural resources. They wanted me to siphon it off to American bank accounts with a cut for myself. I refused. They came after me, and I had to leave the country."

"Let's not talk about the past," urged Katya, fidgeting in the hard-backed wooden seat. "It's too gloomy."

PART
TWO

11

. . . .
. . . .

August 2007

"The house is on the right side of the island but the wrong side of the road." Nick smiled, turning round to face Ali in the middle row of the Land Rover. "I'm afraid you have to deal with the worst excesses of Greek drivers before you manage to get to the beach."

Since the driver sitting beside Nick in the front not only was Greek but also spoke reasonable English and the precipitous route down to the village of Agios Stefanos from the main road was almost deserted, Ali was unsure how to respond. She didn't want to contradict Nick but it felt wrong to cast aspersions on a house she had never visited, especially one that occupied such a disproportionate place in family mythology. The comment reflected his mood, more mercurial and impatient of late, and Ali was relieved when Bryony intervened.

"It's hardly a busy road, and the view over the bay more than compensates, doesn't it, Nick?" said Bryony. She leaned across to give Ali a reassuring pat on her arm but missed because the driver was negotiating another hairpin bend. "It's fabulous."

"Fabulous," agreed Nick.

"Fabulous," trilled the twins from the row of seats in the back.

"I've seen the pictures," said Ali politely. "It looks like paradise." Actually, she had seen just one and that had only recently replaced the picture Nick had defaced in the downstairs bathroom a year before. It was in soft focus and steeped in muted yellow, but Ali could just about make out an old farmhouse in the background. To tell from Tita's caftan and Foy's flared trousers, the photo dated from the 1970s.

"The house is constructed around an old olive press," explained Bryony. "The main building dates from the seventeenth century. Foy built another wing about twenty years ago and then another, and now, of course, there's the olive farm."

"A work in progress," said Ali, using one of Foy's favorite phrases. Nick and Bryony laughed, as she knew they would at this blend of affectionate familiarity and confidence.

Ali's currency in the household had never been higher. At Christmas she had accompanied the Skinners on a family ski trip. She had picked up the twins from their lessons with a private instructor just before lunch and looked after them for the rest of the day so that Nick and Bryony could make the most of their holiday. She had won plaudits for ensuring that the music practice regime seamlessly continued. And she had finally dared to tell Bryony that the language the twins spoke was Filipino, without insinuating that it was because they had spent so much time with Filipina nannies when they were little. It was one of the few times she saw Bryony look embarrassed.

In the Easter holidays, when Izzy's obsession with losing weight had become more than a passing fad, Ali decided to tell Bryony about her visiting websites that promoted anorexia. Bryony had seemed more concerned about the amount of time Izzy spent on these sites when she should have been doing homework rather than their content, but was nevertheless very grateful to Ali for alerting her to the problem in the months leading up to Izzy's end-of-year exams. She agreed that Izzy should see an eating-disorders counselor that Ali had researched. When Izzy came top in English, Ali was given credit for all the hard work she had put in, helping with homework.

At the beginning of the summer holidays Ali had organized a party for the twins' sixth birthday, themed around SpongeBob SquarePants. A replica of SpongeBob's pineapple home and the Krusty Krab restaurant had been set up in the garden. Inside the restaurant a man dressed up as SpongeBob served hot dogs disguised as Krabby Patty burgers. His sidekick, a Latvian woman, dressed up as Squidward, organized games themed on the sea, and painted portraits of the children. Everyone agreed it had been an even bigger success than the Clifford party the previous year, when the old nanny had merely commissioned bone-shaped cupcakes. At Christmas, Ali had been declared "responsible" and "reliable." By the summer she had become "indispensable" and "essential," and had even heard Bryony describe her as "the bedrock of the family."

Jake was the only thorn in her side. Their communication remained a muddle of misread signals, mangled questions, and confused responses. All seen through the prism of false assumptions drawn from that encounter in the drawing room, when Jake had wrongly concluded he was witnessing an uncomfortable piece of postcoital choreography. Ali had tried to talk to him about it after New Year's, but had been so violently rebuffed that she swiftly retreated back into uneasy silence.

Holland Park Crescent now felt more like home than anyplace else. There were pictures that the twins had painted with Ali hanging in frames on the walls of the playroom in the basement. A couple of photos of Ali with Hector and Alfie had made their way into the montage of family pictures hanging on the kitchen wall. The weekly supermarket order had been updated to include some of Ali's favorite foods. Most significant, at the beginning of the summer, someone had stopped to ask Ali the way to Earls Court from Bayswater Road, and she found she could describe the best route without referring to her *A–Z*.

Ali smiled as she weighed up all this. They were passing through a small hamlet. The sun beat on the white walls of old houses so that they seemed to glow. Ali picked out the tall, stabbing shape of a cypress tree silhouetted against the blue sky. Every element of the landscape was perfectly outlined against the vivid blue canvas. The cypress seemed always to grow alone, unlike the friendly clusters of olives, whose branches stretched sociably toward one another. But there were compensations for being on your own, thought Ali. There was no one else to block out your sunlight.

"Alfie and Hector will probably want to spend all their time in the pool, anyway," said Bryony. "Then you can concentrate on your suntan without worrying about the Greek drivers."

She smiled across at Ali. Bryony had a clever way of couching work as pleasure, making Ali feel as though she was the object of her munificence rather than her bidding. She wasn't wearing makeup, and her cheeks revealed previously unnoticed constellations of freckles. She had gathered her hair into an unruly ponytail, from which rebellious strands of red curls escaped. Without lipstick her lips were too pale, but she looked younger than ever.

"How's their swimming?" Bryony asked.

"They're very buoyant," said Ali. Once a week she took Hector and Alfie for private lessons at a center where instructors taught children to feel an innate connection with the water before learning any strokes, a technique that Ali felt had more to do with avarice than science because it was taking them so long to learn. "Their floating technique is amazing. Almost balletic. Everyone comments on it." She didn't mention the fact that it was the way their swimming was completely synchronized that caught people's attention. Over the past year she had grown to understand that Bryony favored a sanitized version of her children's daily life.

"Can we go in the pool as soon as we get there, Ali?" pleaded Hector.

"Ali needs time to settle in," said Bryony firmly, tending to a message on her BlackBerry. "Traveling is always so exhausting. I'll take days to recover."

Except that the journey couldn't have been less stressful. Nick's driver, Mr. Artouche, had delivered them to a hangar beside Heathrow airport, where a small private plane, a six-seater Hawker, was waiting for them. A NetJet pilot had shaken hands with each of them, raising a laugh from the twins by shaking Leicester's paw up and down. Their luggage was transferred from the back of the car to the back of the plane, and within ten minutes they were in the air. There were no queues to try the patience of parents and children, they were liberated from the stench of a hundred pairs of shoes being removed as people were slowly herded through security checks, and no squabbling over window seats because there was one for everyone.

The tensest moment was trying to persuade Leicester into his dog harness for takeoff. Nick and Bryony had sat in a couple of seats at the back of the beige cocoon with its leather upholstery and suede walls while Ali had sat opposite them and the twins, with Leicester beside her, howling during takeoff. Lunch, including Leicester's scrambled eggs, was served in bamboo containers with wooden cutlery, a recent trend to underline the company's ecological credentials, the air hostess had explained with no trace of irony.

The funny thing about Bryony was that she could cope with life's tsunamis but she couldn't deal with the tiniest unpredictable swell. When Ali had driven the brand-new G-Wiz into the side of a stationary bus, Bryony had barely flinched, calling the garage, making tea, and sorting out the insurance within minutes of being told. Professionally she was utterly unflappable. But if she discovered that Jake had trodden mud onto the drawing room carpet or Izzy had lost another coat, everyone ran for cover.

When Sophia Wilbraham revealed that she knew the twins spoke their own language, Bryony had mounted an inquisition to uncover the source of this information, Ali as chief suspect coming under greatest scrutiny. It turned out it was the twins who had taught Leo a few words. Ali tried to persuade Bryony that this could be the loose thread that could lead to the gradual unpicking of Hector and Alfie's relationship, but Bryony couldn't see it. In the end she was appeased only when Ali told her another nanny had reported fetching her charge from a party and finding Sophia Wilbraham's daughter semi-naked on a sofa with a boy clamped to her left breast. For a moment Bryony's face was in perfect repose.

Bryony had worked throughout the journey, reading through a thick envelope of press cuttings about a retail client that had announced it was moving into High Street banking. Shares in the company had gone up by four percent when the deal was announced at eight o'clock that morning.

Ali knew this because Bryony had spent most of the car journey to Heathrow talking to the chief executive of the company on her mobile phone. Now, buoyed with the positive press coverage, she was intent on relaxing, challenging Nick to a game of tennis that night and promising to take the twins to dinner at their favorite restaurant.

Ali stared at the sea out of the Land Rover's window, pressing her nose against the glass. She wanted to wind it down to feel the heat of the sun on her face, but Hector had just been told off for doing the same thing. In the distance she could see the rocky coast of Albania sketched in the haze. It was the ribbon of brilliant turquoise that stretched between the two coastlines, however, that captured her attention. She had never seen the Mediterranean before. She removed her sunglasses and gasped.

It was so still that it looked almost fake, like the motionless faces of the American mothers at the school gates. The North Sea was like an unreliable friend with its constantly changing currents and moods. The Mediterranean was friendly and benign. No hidden depths, thought Ali, relaxing under its warm caress.

"Someone described it as a 'conspiracy of light, air, blue sea, and cypresses,'" said Nick. "And I can't do better than that."

"I think it was Lawrence Durrell," said Bryony.

"It's such an astonishing color," said Ali.

"There's no phosphate in the Mediterranean, which means there's no phytoplankton to cloud the water," said Nick, glancing at Ali in the mirror above the sun visor. "That's why it's so vivid. You should try and go out in a glass-bottom boat. There are all sorts of fish: wrasse, sea bream, cardinal fish."

Ali saw Bryony catch his eye. "Ali is here to work," the look said. Ali didn't mind.

Nick had little idea of the complicated labyrinth of arrangements between her and Bryony that allowed him to go out to work each day unfettered by domestic demands. Corfu was a break from the routine in London, but it wasn't a holiday. Ali certainly didn't feel exploited. Even less since a salary increase after a new plot by Sophia Wilbraham to entice her away from the Skinners had been uncovered in the New Year.

"I'll go out with Alfie and Hector," she promised Nick.

Bryony turned to Ali and began outlining logistical arrangements for the following three weeks. Breakfast and dinner were always eaten at home. Lunch was flexible. It was up to Ali what she wanted to do with the twins. She could walk to a taverna on the beach or have lunch at home as long as she let Andromede the cook know before ten o'clock in the morning. There was a motorboat moored in the harbor that they could use during the day but not at night, because it was the favored mode of transport to reach early-evening drinks parties.

Bryony explained that Ali should eat with Hector and Alfie in the evening. Izzy and Jake would have dinner later with the rest of the family. Izzy would be arriving with Hester, Rick, and their children because she had been staying with them in North London. Her sister's family would be in Corfu until the end of the month. Bryony called up dates on her BlackBerry to double-check details, but her memory was flawless.

"How can Hester take so much time off?" Nick interrupted. One of the few traits he shared with his father-in-law was a barely disguised intolerance of anyone deemed to be lazy. Nick believed that if you weren't at work, then you should at least be playing competitive sport or doing something self-improving. Until recently, Hester had done neither.

"She's a life coach," said Bryony.

"Life doesn't stop in the summer," said Nick.

"Maybe people feel better about themselves in the heat," said Bryony. "In the summer it's enough to exist. You don't need plans. Please don't ask Hester. It will cause an argument."

Nick began a familiar diatribe about how it was possible that someone as inconsistent as Hester could tell other people how to run their lives.

"She's so contrary. Whatever she's doing is marvelous and whatever anyone else does is wrong. Remember when she found out your father had invested in your business? She went ballistic for a couple of months about children who sponge off their parents, then when he offered to give her a hundred grand to buy their house in Stoke Newington it was absolutely fine to take the money. And God, didn't she give you a hard time about being a working mother until she decided to reinvent herself as a bloody soothsayer."

"You're talking about my sister," said Bryony without conviction. It was unclear to Ali whether she agreed with Nick or was trying to avoid further argument.

"Be careful that Hester doesn't exploit you," said Bryony, turning to Ali. "I'll lay the ground rules, but she'll probably try and redefine them." Ali nodded, unsure what to say.

Nick chipped in. "Hester likes to go off on her high horse about people who take their nannies on holiday and then offloads her children all the time. She seems to develop a headache at exactly the same time every day."

It was widely acknowledged among members of the family that Hester was "difficult" and Rick was known as "the drudge." At first Ali thought this meant he was boring, but over the past twelve months she had realized that a drudge was someone who simply espoused ideals that didn't fit with the rest of the family. Although Rick was defined by what he didn't believe in (private schools, four-by-fours, having dogs in London, skiing, designer clothes, cleaners, Tesco, and salmon farms) rather than what he believed in.

"Why did she marry him?" Bryony had once asked Nick.

"To take revenge on your family," Nick had joked.

Bryony continued with arrangements. Jake had already arrived with his girlfriend, Lucy. She paused for a moment, as if considering how this newcomer might fit into the family map. Lucy's status was undergoing some kind of transition since Jake's request to bring her on holiday.

"What's she like?" Nick asked Ali. "You've seen more of her than we have."

"Who?"

"What is Jake's girlfriend like?" repeated Nick.

A year ago Ali's description of Lucy might have included an account of her blue eyes, waist-length blond hair, and impeccable manners, and she might have hinted at the slightly strange flirtatious manner she adopted with Foy. She now understood that a brief précis of her social background was the required response.

"She seems very nice," said Ali. "Her father is a doctor, I think he might be a neurologist, and her mother has an interior design company."

If Nick was in a better mood she might have added that Lucy was the sort of girl who saw university primarily as a hunting ground to find a rich husband and that it might be sensible to warn Jake of her intentions.

"She's the perfect starter girlfriend," said Bryony approvingly, "although I could do without the public displays of affection. I hope they've managed to restrain themselves in front of Mum and Dad."

"Can Thomas and Leo come and stay with us in Corfu one day?" asked Alfie.

"Only if they come with their nanny, not their parents," Bryony joked. "You know their nanny quite well, don't you, Ali?"

"Yes," said Ali cautiously, knowing that as much as Bryony enjoyed hearing gossip about other families, she didn't like to be reminded how this information was obtained. She searched for a suitably neutral comment.

"Katya has been very helpful," she said.

"She's been with Sophia for years," said Bryony, as if Ali might not know this already.

"She's gorgeous-looking," Nick chipped in. "I'm not sure Foy's heart would hold up with her lounging around the pool in a bikini."

"She is very beautiful," agreed Bryony.

"When God created woman, he had Katya in mind," said Nick.

"Hmmm," said Bryony vaguely.

"She's also a great cook," Nick added.

"How do you know all this?" asked Bryony.

"Ned told me," said Nick.

"When do you see him?" Bryony asked.

"I bump into him sometimes. In the street," said Nick.

"She's very good with the children, isn't she?" asked Bryony, turning to Ali.

"Yes," said Ali, although she loves Thomas more than Leo, she thought to herself.

"Who is Thomas's real mummy, Sophia or Katya?" asked Hector thoughtfully.

"Sophia," said Bryony and Ali simultaneously.

"Why?" said Alfie.

"Because she is the person who grew him in her tummy," explained Bryony carefully. "She is the person who loves and cherishes him most and makes sure that he has enough clothes and eats well."

"Katya feeds Thomas and gets him dressed and takes him to school," said Alfie. "And when Sophia's not there he sleeps in her bed."

"And she gives him milk," said Hector.

"Yes, but Sophia buys the food," said Bryony impatiently.

"Katya does the milk," argued Hector, as though milk was the sacrament through which motherhood was channeled.

"Sophia is the mummy," said Bryony firmly. She circled her tongue around her cheek a couple of times, a gesture Ali had come to recognize as a sign that Bryony was either nervous or losing patience.

"Ali," said Hector, "which animal do you think has the worst life?"

"An animal that is used to having freedom and then loses it," Ali suggested.

"Like a young student who comes to London to work as a nanny to a demanding professional family with four children," joked Nick.

"I was thinking more of a lion that is captured to live with a circus, perhaps," said Ali cheerfully. Actually, she felt freer living with the Skinners than she had ever done before, mostly because she no longer had to answer to the demands of her own parents whenever there was an emergency with her sister.

"A Greek cat," proffered Nick.

"A South Korean dog," suggested Bryony.

"You're all wrong," said Alfie triumphantly.

"A tapeworm," the twins said simultaneously, "because it lives in your poo and can only escape through your bottom." They giggled wildly.

"I don't think a tapeworm qualifies as an animal, does it, Ali?" said Nick.

"It's an arthropod, which means it has its skeleton on the outside," Ali explained to the twins. "But it's still part of the animal kingdom."

"If I had a tapeworm, could I keep it as a pet?" asked Hector.

The Land Rover slowly meandered around another corner. This one was so sharp that the driver was forced to make a three-point turn. Leicester woke up and jumped on Bryony's lap, took one look out of the window and turned round to Bryony as if to ask what she was doing bringing him here. He started to shake.

"Can you turn down the air-conditioning for Leicester?" Bryony asked. "I think he's cold."

Ali put her hand out to stroke him, but he emitted a low throaty growl of grumpy disapproval.

"God, couldn't we have sent him to the Philippines with Malea?" asked Nick.

"Too humid," said Bryony, as if it had been a possibility. "So how is your week looking?"

She put away her BlackBerry and tickled Leicester behind his ears. This was the signal for Ali to slip into the background. The first six months she had fluffed these cues, but now her entrances and exits were as well stage-managed as those of a spear carrier who has done a couple of seasons with the Royal Shakespeare Company. She used to feel put down when Nick and Bryony started talking as though she wasn't there. Now she saw it as a sign of confidence: their trust in her discretion.

"Not good," said Nick, craning his neck to turn to face Bryony in the seat directly behind him, "although some of my colleagues might be pleased to see the back of me."

"Why?" she asked.

"They think I'm losing my nerve," said Nick with a smile that quickly faded. "Where I see impending meltdown, they see opportunity."

"People don't want to listen to bad news, they just want to keep going with what they know," Bryony reassured him. "It's human nature."

"Every five years something bad happens," said Nick. "I reminded them that I was around for the Japanese property bubble, the collapse of the peso, the devaluation of the ruble, the dot-com bubble. Do you know what one of the traders said?"

Bryony shook her head. "Tell me," she said.

"He said I was so old I could probably remember the Dutch tulip crisis," said Nick. "That was in the seventeenth century."

"That's quite funny," said Bryony.

"He was implying that I've lost it," said Nick. "I'm telling them to slow down the CDO machine or at least insure against losses on every deal, and they want to crank it up. Fucking lunatics. Goldman sold all their mortgage positions at the end of last year and are betting on a crash. Hedge funds are shorting investment banks that are overexposed. They're betting their share price will go down."

"You said Lehman's second-quarter profits were up twenty-seven percent," Bryony countered.

"It was all M-and-A," said Nick. "Fixed income was down fourteen percent."

"Hank Paulson said yesterday that volatile markets are a fact of life and the credit crunch will work its way through the system," said Bryony. "If the U.S. Treasury secretary is saying that, surely it's going to be fine. Then you'll be the clever guys who called it right. Maybe the market has overreacted?"

"Look at the facts, Bryony," said Nick. "Accredited Home Lenders is going bust. New Century has filed for bankruptcy. Bear Stearns has bailed out two of its hedge funds. Moody's and S-and-P are cutting credit ratings on bonds backed by subprime mortgages. The only surprise is they didn't do it earlier, because the U.S. housing market is in the middle of the fastest default rate in history. If the price of bonds and loans is dropping you have to ask if there's a change in the weather, right?"

"But not right now," said Bryony, gently stroking on his cheek. "As long as everyone holds their nerve it will be fine. M-and-A was losing steam, and now there's a couple of deals coming my way."

"I'm so lucky to be married to a woman who understands what I do," mused Nick, turning toward Ali as if suddenly aware of her presence. "No one else does." His right cheek was red from the heat of Bryony's hand.

Ali was transfixed by this exchange. She rarely saw Bryony and Nick together. They were hardly ever at home at the same time, and when they were, they were either going out or having people over for dinner. Sometimes she wondered whether their relationship existed only in front of an audience.

In the time she had lived at Holland Park Crescent, she had rarely seen them sit down to eat alone together in the evening, although she sometimes came across Bryony eating with Jake and Izzy, especially since the worries about Izzy losing weight. True to her word, after the Christmas party Izzy had taken up dieting with the same zeal that she had once invested in binging, cutting out food groups until all that remained were steamed vegetables.

Ali's own parents by contrast rarely socialized, and ate together at six o'clock every evening. What did they talk about? Ali tried to remember. Lots of discussion about diminishing crab stocks. The fishermen blamed overfishing, the experts blamed global warming, "because then no one needs to do anything about it," her father would say bitterly. Whether it was a good thing the crab season had extended until December. They talked about money a lot. Sometimes her parents talked about Jo. A friend of her father's had seen her in Norwich. She had called to say that she would visit and then never turned up. She was thinking about moving abroad for a while.

"The break will give you new perspective. You'll come up with something. You always do. That's why those headhunters are always knocking at your door. Nick Skinner is never far from the next big thing," said Bryony.

"Maybe I should get out now?" said Nick in a jokey tone, but in a way that suggested this wasn't the first time he had mooted such an idea.

"You're too young to keep bees," said Bryony abruptly. "Why don't you take a look at these?" She pulled out estate agent's details for a couple of houses in Oxfordshire, the county where Foy had grown up. "I love this one. Thornberry House. It needs a lot of work, but it's got forty acres and a swimming pool. It will be a great place for you to relax at weekends."

"Looks great," said Nick, barely glancing at the enormous Jacobean house.

"You know, I really think Sophia should think about getting another nanny," said Bryony. "It complicates family relationships if they stay more than four years."

"Forget the country, I really think we should consider getting our own place out here," said Nick, as the vehicle turned into the long driveway up toward the Villa Ichthys. "I'm not sure I can face a week with Foy at the Villa Fish."

"One more good year and we'll be able to do both," said Bryony, ignoring the way he facetiously translated the name of her father's house into English.

. . .

"Welcome to the Château Chesterton," said Foy exuberantly, as he urged them inside the house through an imposing eighteenth-century doorway that was the entrance to the original olive press. He closed the old oak door behind him, abruptly cutting off the shrill love songs of the male cicadas.

Tita stood in the hallway, pale and statuesque, one hand resting on a simple round wooden table. She put out her cheek to be kissed and allowed first Nick then Bryony to pay homage to its powdery surface. She didn't bend down for the twins and instead let them kiss her hand, which they did with flourish, taken by the novelty of it all. She was wearing a pair of simple white trousers and a silk Liberty-print caftan that Bryony had given her for Christmas.

"Hello, Daddy," said Bryony, hugging Foy. He was baked as hard and brown as the earth in the flower beds that flanked the road to the house.

"You look like a lizard," cried Hector, rushing toward him.

"And you look like a stick insect, and lizards love eating stick insects," said Foy, nuzzling Hector's neck.

"You, on the other hand, look gorgeous," he said, stepping back to admire his eldest daughter. Her phone rang. "Switch off that wretched thing. You're on holiday."

"I'm at the tail end of a huge deal," said Bryony, glancing down at the number. "It's only Felix. I can call him back." Ali waited expectantly for Foy to question Bryony about the deal, to ask the name of her client, to discuss which newspaper had devoted the most coverage. "It's the biggest takeover this year," Bryony said hopefully. Foy didn't take the bait.

"All well in the big smoke?" Foy turned to Nick. "Still shuffling all those bits of paper?"

Nick winced.

"What will you have to show for it all at the end?"

"I certainly won't be able to claim that I introduced smoked salmon to the masses," said Nick benevolently. "But I have in my own small way enabled millions of people to own their own homes."

"Mrs. Thatcher was doing that a quarter of a century ago," Foy said.

"Well, we all owe her a big debt of gratitude," said Nick.

Bryony shot him a grateful look. When he was on his own territory Foy could be insufferable.

"I thought we would have a simple dinner tonight and save ourselves for tomorrow's celebrations, when Hester and Rick are here," said Tita, looking straight ahead at the door, even though it was now closed. She said Rick's name as though she was spitting out an orange pip. "You don't mind, do you . . . ?" Her voice drifted away.

"Sounds perfect." Nick smiled agreeably.

Bryony's attention swiftly moved to Jake, who drifted into the hallway wearing a pair of baggy swimming shorts with an improbably bright sea anemone print. His arm was around Lucy. They were sharing a towel across their shoulders. Bryony hugged him.

"You look like a piece of mahogany," she teased him, patting his solid, polished torso. She then kissed Lucy once on each cheek. Lucy and Jake held hands throughout.

"They're actually glued together," joked Foy. "We haven't yet seen either of them without the other. They leave their billet together in the morning and retire there together at night." Everyone laughed. Lucy had tied a sarong around her hips, and everyone was doing their best to look away from her white bikini top.

"Shall we go back in the pool, Lucy?" Jake suggested.

"I was hoping you might show Ali around," suggested Bryony. Jake winced.

"Hector and Alfie would probably find it less of a chore," he said.

"We want to go in the pool," they protested.

"If you point me in the right direction, I'm sure I'll find my bearings," said Ali awkwardly. To her surprise, Tita offered to give her a tour.

. . .

"I'm a member of the Mediterranean Garden Society," said Tita, as she led Ali into the garden. "I've tried to stick to as many indigenous plants as possible. My only weakness is for Chinese jasmine. Its smell is enchanting." She pointed to the front of the house, where the jasmine ran unfettered up the entire right side, infusing the area around the front door with its heady, sweet mustiness. Tita closed her eyes and breathed in deeply through her nostrils. It was a curiously unself-conscious gesture from a woman whose personality was defined by what she held back. Out of politeness, Ali did the same, keeping one eye open to make sure that Tita wasn't waiting for her.

Ali understood at once that although Foy might talk more about the Villa Ichthys than anyone else, its soul belonged to Tita. It surprised her, because Tita mentioned Corfu less than even Nick. Perhaps her silence was a way of keeping the relationship secret. The best love affairs were clandestine, thought Ali wistfully.

Tita referred to the plants like old friends, "the oleanders, my dear myrtle, sweet arbutus, stoic salvia," occasionally reaching out to touch a leaf or a flower. Otherwise, she didn't say very much, a trait that Ali appreciated because it allowed her to form her own relationship with the landscape.

"Jasmine is used in ayurvedic medicine to calm the nerves and heal anxiety," said Tita, "so if Hector and Alfie are playing up and you need to unwind, then come here to relax. I've planted it around the terrace beside the pool, too, but there are always so many people . . . Go to the bench at the front of the house. No one ever thinks to sit there."

Her sentence drifted into the air, and Ali was once again unsure whether she had finished. She opened her mouth to say something, but then Tita started up again. "You wouldn't guess to look at it, but jasmine is related to olive. They're all from the Oleaceae family. Like forsythia, privet, and lilac."

"I'd never seen an olive tree before today," said Ali.

"Well, you'll see more than your share here," said Tita. "Some of the trees have been here since the twelfth century. When Corfu was occupied by the Phoenicians, they paid people for every olive they planted. The Corfiotes could even pay taxes in olive oil."

Tita stopped for a moment to describe the layout of the garden. Ali would have felt guilty for removing her from the relative cool of the house into the midday heat, but she quickly realized that the tour was for Tita's diversion, not her own. Tita continued. There was an orange grove at the bottom of the house, away from the pool. They were picked daily and squeezed to make juice. To the left of the house was a large courtyard covered in vines, where most meals were eaten. There was a more formal terrace at the front and a parterre with a mirror sculpture by Barbara Hepworth at the center.

"She came to stay after it was installed," said Tita. "Just before she died."

"I've seen this before," said Ali.

She realized that during a visit with the twins to Foy and Tita's house she had spent some time staring at a large landscaping plan framed on the wall. It was drawn in black ink, with small symbols to indicate different shrubs and plants.

"You notice everything, don't you," said Tita. Statement not question, decided Ali quickly. "I planned it all myself, and then Christos the gardener followed my instructions. We had to ship in fourteen thousand cubic feet of soil from another part of the island to encourage the roots to grow. Plants need to feel sure of the soil beneath them to flourish. Like humans, really."

"It's beautiful," said Ali, suddenly feeling thirsty.

"Do you feel sure of the ground beneath your feet?" Tita asked. "I used to think I did, and now I'm not so sure. Maybe it's because every day another part of me is slowly disintegrating." She laughed.

"A garden is a good legacy," said Ali, pleased to find the right words for once.

"It's taken years," said Tita, staring over Ali's head to the sea beyond.

"Before Foy retired I used to spend quite a lot of time out here on my own."

"It must be nice for you to spend more time here together, then," said Ali, knowing even as she said it that it wasn't true.

"As you can imagine, Foy isn't good at pottering," said Tita, with a vague smile. "You know a bit about gardens, don't you?"

Ali couldn't remember Tita ever asking her any questions about herself, and felt shy about responding. "I've seen you deadheading the roses in London."

"My mother gardens," mumbled Ali. "It's difficult by the sea. The salt and sand take their toll." Tita ignored her response.

"*Lavandula pinnata*, looks lovely but smells of nothing," Tita said, thoughtfully addressing another plant. "A plant of no substance. A bit like Lucy."

They walked silently down a winding path flanked by olive trees at the back and lines of santolina at the front. Every step took them closer to the sea. At the bottom of the path the landscape opened out to a swimming pool that overlooked the ocean.

It was enormous and pleasingly unsymmetrical. At one end, built into one of the original terraces, were a couple of artificial waterfalls. The pool was painted cobalt blue to match the Ionian Sea. There was a covered pavilion with a large marble table at its center, where people could have lunch.

"It's a saltwater pool," said Tita. "The waterfalls block out the sound of the traffic on the road below. It can get quite busy in the summer."

"Nick mentioned the cars," said Ali.

"And probably nothing else," murmured Tita. "He resists the lure of Corfu. It's probably Foy's fault. Most things are."

"What's that?" asked Ali, pointing to a small building to the right of the pool, built in the same style as the main house.

"The changing rooms," said Tita, waving her hand dismissively. "I never go in there."

Tita sat down at the table. She put the palms of her hands on the flat marble surface. Her hands were large, totally unlike Bryony's. They were starting to twist with early arthritis, and their gnarly appearance reminded Ali of the corkscrew hazel that her mother had in the garden at home. Tita stared silently out to sea. She explained that Ali's bedroom was in the annex built on the side of the building that housed the original olive press. On the third floor, opposite the twins. Her voice had shrunk to a whisper.

"Go back to the house now," she instructed.

"Can I get you a drink of water?" Ali asked.

"I'm happy here," said Tita, smiling at her. Her face was lit by the late-afternoon sun creeping across the sky, and for a moment Ali wondered whether she might simply float, Chagall-like, into space.

Ali heard voices from the olive-tree path and decided to return to the house on the route Tita had pointed out through the orange grove. The front door was still open, and the hallway blissfully cool with its stone tiles. On the left was a small cloakroom with bundles of hats, tennis rackets, and walking sticks hanging on old oak pegs. Ali went in and washed her face with water, drinking thirstily from the tap.

She went past a sitting room and saw Nick on the phone through the half-open door. It was an old-fashioned phone with wires, which meant he couldn't pace up and down the room as he did normally. So he sat on a white sofa, crossing and uncrossing his legs. He was delivering instructions to someone.

"We need to get this on by Tuesday," he repeated a couple of times down the line. "Tuesday, not Thursday, otherwise we'll be too late. Have you got that, Ned?"

They must be working together on a deal, thought Ali, as Nick gently pushed the door shut with the tip of his foot.

12

Ali sat on the terrace, eating breakfast with Hector and Alfie. They had insisted she should join them at the far end of the huge marble table at the center of the open-air pavilion, even though no places were laid there and all the food was set out in a picturesque arc of baskets and ceramic bowls at the opposite end.

It was a quirk that would irritate Bryony if she appeared, because she would see it as part of Hector and Alfie's desire to be separate from everyone else. The fact that Ali not only was invited to join them but had been asked to position herself between them would also be viewed with suspicion, as though she condoned their eccentric behavior. But Bryony never seemed to emerge before eleven and it was too hot to argue, so they sat in a neat row, contentedly glued to one another's thighs with a viscous mix of sweat and suntan cream.

They faced the door that led back into the house from the terrace as though willfully ignoring the more obvious and spectacular view out to sea. Hector and Alfie each picked out a croissant and a *pain au chocolat* from the basket carried from the other end of the table by the elderly Greek housekeeper. They took a bite out of one, then the other, their movements as rhythmic as a metronome. Ali ruffled their hair and put an arm around each of them, and they snuggled into her ribs.

"What shall we do today?" she asked.

"Palanguyan," said Hector immediately.

"Yes," agreed Alfie, *"palanguyan."*

"Pool it is, then," confirmed Ali, who had compiled a list of more than a hundred words and phrases for the educational psychologist, who had seen them the month before. They reached for their glasses of orange juice. Ali tried to break the pattern by holding down Alfie's arm as Hector struggled to stretch his small fingers around the glass. But Alfie, generally the more malleable of the two, roughly shook her off and muttered something incomprehensible to his brother.

"Please try and do things at different times," pleaded Ali.

"Why?" said Alfie.

"Because it upsets Mummy," said Ali, choosing her words carefully. "She's worried that as you get older if you keep doing everything at the same time then you'll be different from other people."

"We are different from other people," protested Hector.

"We are genetic clones," agreed Alfie, repeating a phrase he had heard the educational psychologist use.

"She wants you to learn to do things on your own because one day you'll each meet a girl and fall in love and you'll have to learn to live apart," explained Ali.

"We'll fall in love with the same girl," insisted Alfie.

"And live in the same house," added Hector.

"Maybe we'll marry you," said Hector.

"Then you won't ever leave us," said Alfie, leaning back into his seat as though he had resolved some great conundrum.

"I'm not going anywhere for a while," Ali reassured them, "and the more you do things apart from each other, the longer I'll be able to stay."

Ali had recently sent a carefully worded e-mail to her tutor, asking to defer her place at university for another year. She had pleaded continuing insolvency and the chance to earn enough money to graduate without any debt. Will MacDonald had immediately sent back an e-mail agreeing to her request. It seemed a simple negotiation. But the truth was as gnarly and twisted as the raspberry plants that Tita was growing below the terrace.

Katya, clearly suspicious, had questioned Ali closely when she brought Thomas and Leo to play with the twins. They had sat in the playroom and talked while the children watched television. Ali explained to Katya that she wanted to stay with the Skinners because life with them was more entertaining than life without them. She was too attached to Hector and Alfie to leave suddenly. Bryony needed her. And she didn't want to become embroiled in her sister's problems again.

She told Katya how she had overheard Bryony on the phone telling someone that she couldn't run her life without Ali. Katya pointed out that the Skinners had managed their affairs perfectly well before Ali's arrival and would probably do so after her departure.

Ali dismissed Katya's comment as jealousy. Perhaps she even wanted Ali's job. The widely held view among the nanny community was that Ali had landed the plum but lacked the credentials to endorse her as its rightful owner. Then Katya had hugged her and said that she was delighted Ali was staying but wanted to make sure she was doing it for the right reasons.

"You mustn't live your life through another family," Katya warned her.

"You do," Ali retorted.

"That's because I have no choice," said Katya.

"Well, this is my choice," said Ali.

Ali would have liked to tell Katya the truth, but she worried it might have weakened her resolve. Besides, she was pretty sure that Katya had secrets of her own and would forgive the deceit. So she mentioned nothing of the lust-fueled, hurried entanglements in pitch darkness in the back of Will MacDonald's Volvo station wagon after babysitting his children. She had never told anyone about their relationship, not even Rosa, not because she feared their disapproval but because she wasn't convinced by it. It reinforced Ali's sense of being an observer to life rather than someone in charge of her own destiny.

Ali considered the outbreak of the relationship. One minute she was in the passenger seat of her tutor's car discussing whether *Tristram Shandy* was the first postmodern novel, the next he pulled over on the side of the road, confessed that he had never got beyond volume three, and kissed her chastely on the lips. No warning. No preamble. Until that moment she had never even fantasized about Will MacDonald. I am a homunculus, Ali remembered thinking, as she kissed him back, eyes open. There followed a more disorderly kiss that lasted so long that the next day the muscles in Ali's cheeks ached.

Nor did she mention the way he carefully put the children's car seats in the trunk to make room in the back, or how he used baby wipes to clean the sperm from her thigh and his stomach. She didn't mention how she believed in Will's desire for her but couldn't quite believe in her desire for him, which meant she often felt curiously detached from the sexual act. As though she was both performer and critic. Nor did she describe how the initial thrill of illicit attraction had curdled into a sour mixture of passion and guilt, until all that remained was the guilt.

He had tried to convince her to stay. His relationship with his wife was as cold as permafrost. They hadn't been happy for years; they no longer had sex; she didn't understand him. It all sounded so passive, thought Ali, who imagined marital disharmony as a dramatic plate-throwing affair. The day after he said he might leave his wife for her, Ali had cut out the advert in *The Spectator*. Perhaps she wasn't so dissimilar to her sister: they both ran for the hills in a crisis.

"Did you know we are made from the same egg, Ali?" asked Alfie self-importantly.

"And it's impossible to separate yolks," said Hector.

"One day you will have to go your own way," said Ali firmly.

"One day," conceded Alfie.

"But not today," said Hector adamantly.

Ali looked down and saw that both of them were gripping her arms. Then she leaned over to kiss each of them, but it was no more than an excuse to sniff the small craters in their napes. Why had no one ever mentioned how small children smelled so beautifully sweet? It was the scent of innocence, before the false trail of hormones was laid.

She stroked their hair gently at the line where their necks became visible, aware that she was now synchronizing her movements to mimic theirs. She remembered how at the end of term the teacher had taken Ali aside to tell her about another incident on the playground. Hector had been bitten on the arm. Her relief that Hector was the victim rather than the perpetrator was immediately tempered by the teacher's description of how Alfie unexpectedly started crying and rubbing his arm, even though he was inside reading to a classroom assistant. Ali couldn't bring herself to tell Bryony that the teacher thought they could feel each other's pain. It could undermine the reprieve she had won, allowing them to be in the same class the following year.

Bryony couldn't see the magic in their relationship. She found their closeness spooky and blamed herself for compounding it by going out to work. As far as Ali was concerned, it was the purest form of love that she had ever seen. There was mutual support, understanding, empathy, generosity of spirit. They shared everything, they hardly ever argued, and they were always there for each other.

"If you hurt him, you hurt me," Alfie told the boy on the playground who specialized in winding up Hector.

Once Ali had shared a similar relationship with her sister. Now it was difficult to believe that Jo used to be the filter for all Ali's uncertainties. Why did her mother view the sea as a rival to their father's affections? Why did Jo fancy only other girls' boyfriends? Why didn't she think the air in Cromer smelled better than anywhere else she had ever been? But then came the drugs, the psychosis, and the uneasy march toward recovery and the disappointment of relapse, where the person she knew turned into someone else and their relationship became a lopsided affair in which one of them cared too much and the other not at all. She was determined that the bond between Hector and Alfie should not be prematurely severed.

Ali breathed in deeply. The heady, sweet-smelling jasmine growing up the columns of the open-air pavilion and the strong odor of fish from the rice dish Andromede had just brought out on a tray made her feel nauseated.

"What is this?" she asked, stirring the yellow rice mixture to unearth hard-boiled egg, mushrooms, smoked haddock, and a strong smell of curry.

"It's kedgeree," said a voice emerging from the terrace below. Nick appeared, wearing a pair of soggy swimming trunks, a copy of *The Economist* tucked under one arm. When he saw Ali, he wound a towel around his waist and sucked in his stomach. Hector and Alfie ran across to throw themselves at him.

"Why are you all cramped so closely together around this huge table?" Nick asked, as Hector and Alfie clung monkeylike to each leg. His tone was bemused rather than belligerent. He put down the magazine on the table beside the rest of his holiday reading. It was an eclectic mix, giving away nothing about the personality of the reader: *The Assault on Reason* by Al Gore, *The Girl with the Dragon Tattoo* by Stieg Larsson, and *The Black Swan* by Nassim Nicholas Taleb. No doubt he would plow through them in the same methodical way he swam fifty lengths up and down the pool each day.

Searching for a talking point, Ali looked at the cover of *The Economist*. It depicted a businessman constrained in a tight corset. "A good time for a squeeze," it read. Ali understood that it related in some way to Nick's conversation in the car.

"Will you come swimming with us, Daddy?" the twins pleaded, pulling at the towel.

"I've got to get on with some work this morning," Nick said, bending down on one knee until he was at their height. "Maybe later."

It wouldn't happen, thought Ali. Bryony and Nick always seemed to have reasons not to spend time with their children.

"But I will have breakfast with you now," he added.

He sat down and began spooning the kedgeree onto his plate. The twins started playing a rhyming game.

"A tiger from Niger."

"A squid from Madrid."

"A bongo from Congo."

"An impala from Kampala."

"A loon from Cameroon," suggested Nick. They looked at him in astonishment.

"How do you know how to play, Daddy?" they asked.

There was a bell on the table, which he rang, and Andromede appeared. He politely requested fresh coffee and orange juice. She gave him a long, silent stare and went back into the kitchen.

"Isn't she terrifying?" said Nick. "She is Foy's eyes and ears."

"Does Andromede speak English?" Ali asked.

"Not a word," said Nick, "but she understands everything." He put a spoonful of kedgeree onto Ali's plate. Ali was grateful for the gesture, even though she didn't want any. He held the serving spoon awkwardly in his fist, and she could see the skin around his nail was shredded until it was raw. When he saw her looking he hid his thumb inside his fingers.

"Is this a Greek dish?" Ali asked.

"Couldn't be more English, really," said Nick. "It dates from the Raj. Fits with Foy's postcolonial pretensions. They always ate fish for breakfast in India, because it would have gone off by the evening. It's one of the Corfu rituals."

He laughed and Ali smiled, uncertain whether it was permissible to laugh with him. His attempts at intimacy always seemed to be at someone else's expense and had the unfortunate habit of reinforcing their distance.

"I was thinking maybe you could go out together with Jake and Lucy one evening?" Nick proposed. "There are a couple of bars in the village. All very low-key. You might want to escape from the fray. It's difficult to be alone here, and it can get a little intense when the whole family is together."

"I think I might cramp their style," said Ali politely.

"Isn't it a burden, always being so sensible when you're only twenty-two?" Nick suddenly asked. "You hardly ever take a weekend off, and when you do, you never seem to go out."

"I don't mind staying at home. I've got quite used to it, really," said Ali, getting up from the table and urging the twins toward the pool.

They followed the path that Tita had shown Ali the previous day. Hector and Alfie arrived at the pool before her, and she found them staring open-mouthed at Lucy, who was lying on her stomach on a comfortable-looking sunbed while Jake coated her in suntan oil. She was wearing the same white bikini bottoms from yesterday but no top. Jake was in a different pair of shapeless trunks in similarly loud colors. They billowed around his thighs in the faint breeze that blew from the sea.

Jake sat upright, assiduously rubbing Lucy's back. He started at the top, spending equal amounts of time on each shoulder blade before squeezing a trickle of coconut suntan oil down the back of her spine to the spot where flesh met bikini bottoms. His finger traced a line back toward her neck through the trickle of suntan oil, and she stretched appreciatively, like a cat in the sun.

Ali coughed and the twins shouted, but Jake and Lucy couldn't hear them over the sound of the waterfalls. After a while the babbling started to grate on your nerves. Corfu was surprisingly noisy. Last night the cicadas chattered nonstop, occasionally outdone by screaming owls that pierced the stifling hot night air. Could you turn the waterfalls off? Ali wondered. The idea made her want to giggle. But it also made her nostalgic, because the reason she found it so intrusive was that these weren't the sounds that she associated with the sea. She missed the greedy, reckless emotion of the North Sea and its loud, noisy seduction technique. She loved its uncompromising quality.

Then, in the middle of the night, the sound of Lucy and Jake having sex in the room above had woken her. At first she had tried to ignore them, but when Lucy's cries got louder she got up to search through the bookshelf, hoping to find something to distract her. She quickly realized she was in a room intended for children. It was all *Alice's Adventures in Wonderland*, Dr. Seuss, and Enid Blyton. So instead she went out onto the balcony that led from her room.

On the balcony outside his bedroom in the main part of the house, Ali had noticed Nick sitting on a chair with his laptop on his knees. Once or twice he glanced over to Jake and Lucy's room. She could see in the hazy light of the computer screen that he was chewing his upper lip. He stretched his arms, and Ali was surprised to see his hands were trembling.

When she was sure he couldn't see her, she stood for a moment with her eyes closed, listening to the voice of the Mediterranean. Its whispered promises and dull lapping couldn't compete with Lucy's high-pitched animal cries, and in the end Ali resorted to a pair of earplugs that she found in the bathroom alongside small bottles of shampoo and body wash. They muffled the noise, but she could still feel the vibrations of the headboard beating against the wall. At least Jake knew how to give a girl a good time, thought Ali, although Lucy was undoubtedly the kind of girl who was polite enough to fake it.

Remembering this, she now waved at Jake, hoping to catch his attention, but he was focused on Lucy's long brown legs. He began rubbing oil into her feet, paying equal attention to each toe. Ali watched with the twins in fascinated silence as his hand began a slow-motion drift to the edge of Lucy's bikini bottoms. His hand lingered between her legs, and she turned onto her back to face him. The twins drew closer.

"Bosoms," they shouted in unison. Lucy sat up in shock and reached for her bikini top from a small mosaic table. Jake stood up in front of her to provide a screen and walked toward them.

"You should have said you were here," he reproached Ali, as Hector and Alfie jumped into the pool. "It's not fair on Lucy. She needs her privacy."

Ali glanced over at Lucy, who looked gratified by Jake's response.

"We tried," said Ali, demonstrating to Jake how she waved at him and how the twins jumped up and down shouting.

"Is this revenge for me sneaking up on you and Dad?" asked Jake, with a half-smile.

"What do you mean?" asked Ali.

"You know what I'm talking about," said Jake.

"You've got it all wrong," said Ali.

"I know what I saw." Jake shrugged.

"Ali, would you be an absolute star and fetch a couple of Diet Cokes from the house?" shouted Lucy. "Andromede failed to stock up the fridge in the pool house last night. I'll have a swim with the twins while you're gone. And if you could bring my book I'd be so fantastically grateful."

"Sure," said Ali, going into the pool house to check whether Lucy was correct or just wanted to assert her authority. She was relieved to escape. Tita hadn't shown her the inside of the building yesterday, and it gave her an excuse to stand still for a moment and get her bearings. Her breath was uneven. She was shaken by Jake's outburst. It wasn't the substance that bothered her. She could see how he had come to the wrong conclusions. It was the way his emotions were so close to the surface, threatening to spill over at any moment. Perhaps he would tell his mother what he had seen. And then Ali would lose her job and return to Cromer in disgrace, punished for the wrong affair.

"Why now?" she wanted to ask him. "Just when I'm almost perfectly happy."

Ali looked round the pool house. It was so much more than a changing room. From Tita's remark, she had imagined something like the garden shed where her father kept his fishing tackle and an old transistor radio that ran on batteries. Instead it was a perfectly formed Lilliputian house complete with a kitchen, bar, and sofas.

The fridge door was neatly packed with rows of beer, cans of Sprite, and orange juice. There was a large plate of watermelon on one of the shelves and half a dozen oranges on another. But there was no Diet Coke. She glanced out the window toward Lucy. Lucy caught her eye and shrugged apologetically without making any attempt to get up. She was playing Uno on the sunbed with Hector and Alfie, Jake straddled behind her with his head leaning on her shoulder. Ali slammed the fridge door in anger at Lucy's demands. A couple of mobile phones tumbled into the sink. They must belong to Nick, thought Ali. She would take them back to the house immediately. It would take the sting out of Lucy's request.

Ali set off back up the hill to the house, her breath quickening as the path got steeper. She enjoyed the sensation of the sun burning deep inside her lungs. When she was halfway up she stopped for a moment and sat down to look at the view across the bay. In the distance a huge passenger ship slowly crossed her line of vision. She squinted to try to make out its flag. In her hand one of the Black-Berrys vibrated. Ali looked down at the screen and pressed the e-mail icon to check whether she was delivering the phone to the right person. She was gratified to see a raft of messages relating to Nick's deal.

"Congratulations," read one. "Only you could make junk look so beautiful."

There was a request from the World Economic Forum asking Nick to discuss credit markets at their next meeting in Davos. "I'm not worried about flat yield curves . . ." began another. Maybe he wouldn't need to fly home after all, thought Ali, turning her attentions to the second BlackBerry. It would be great for the twins to spend some time with their father. They spent too much time with women.

Glancing through the e-mail messages, Ali quickly realized that the second BlackBerry belonged to Bryony. The top three messages were unread. "*FT* daily brief," "4am cut," "Lex." The fourth one was marked confidential and had been opened. "Project Beethoven," it said. "Russian energy bid—private and confidential."

"Your phone," said Ali, finding Nick still sitting at the breakfast table.

"Thanks so much." He smiled, pushing his sunglasses onto the top of his head so that she could see his eyes. "It's a good sign that I forgot to bring it up with me. Means I'm not resisting the holiday. Did you bring the other one, too?"

"Do you mean Bryony's?"

"I'm tending her phone so that she can have a lie-in." He smiled through recently rewhitened teeth. Nick was sitting in his swimming trunks, and Ali couldn't help comparing his upper body with Jake's. The frame was identical, but the contours were softer. Like raw meat wrapped in cellophane. When he was home, Nick went running almost every day and came home to complete a grueling circuit of stomach crunches and weights in the basement gym.

"There's something I wanted to mention to you," Ali said impulsively.

"Go right ahead," said Nick, looking amused. He closed *The Economist* and put it neatly on the table beside him. "I'm all yours. For the next five minutes, at least. Then I need to make some calls."

He glanced down through the new messages on his BlackBerry. "Bear Stearns triggers Dow crash," read the headline of a Reuters story. He opened it and swore under his breath.

"Has something happened?" Ali asked.

"One of the ratings agencies has downgraded Bear Stearns's debt to negative from stable," he said vaguely, as though unaware he was talking to Ali. "It was heavily invested in subprime."

"Is this a bad moment?" Ali asked.

"A bad moment for the world economy, but actually it strengthens my argument," said Nick, looking up from his BlackBerry. "What did you want to say?"

"Do you remember when Jake came into the drawing room in London last autumn and found me sitting on the sofa with you at five-thirty in the morning?" she said, deciding that precision was the only weapon with which to fight the embarrassment of what she was about to say.

"Vaguely," said Nick.

"Well, he seems to have drawn the wrong conclusions," said Ali, adopting a forthright tone that seemed appropriate in the circumstances.

"What exactly do you mean?" asked Nick, leaning forward to squint at Ali with his piercing blue eyes.

"He thought that something had happened between us," said Ali, staring at Nick without blinking.

"Why on earth would he think that?" asked Nick in astonishment.

"Your zip was half undone, and I suppose I was only wearing a T-shirt and cardigan, and maybe we looked as though we had been . . . as though we might have been . . . intimate," she continued, immediately berating her absurdly Victorian choice of adjective.

"I see," said Nick in a neutral tone. "Is this what Jake has indicated to you?"

"He has always been cool toward me, but today he specifically insinuated that this is what he believed," said Ali, sounding calmer than she felt.

"And what do you want me to do about it?" asked Nick.

"I don't know," said Ali, looking down at her feet. "Maybe tell him the truth?"

"What did you see when you came into the drawing room?" asked Nick. Ali was surprised by the question.

"I saw you sitting on the sofa with your zip halfway down, looking at something on Jake's computer," she said.

"And what did you assume?" he asked.

"I'm not sure," Ali lied.

"I think that you thought I was looking at porn," said Nick, "and that I was using Jake's computer so it wouldn't come up on my history." There was a long silence.

"I never imagined having this conversation with my children's nanny," said Nick, shaking his head. The sunglasses slid onto the table, but he didn't attempt to pick them up.

"I don't judge you for looking at porn," said Ali quickly, "but you need to tell Jake that's what you were doing, because frankly it's the lesser evil."

"How about I had just come home from the mother of all trips and I was assuming that no one would come into the room, so I'd undone my trousers and let it all hang out and was using two computers because I wanted to look at yield curves on one screen and write a document on the other?" said Nick.

"Then I would say that I made the wrong assumptions, too," said Ali. Nick gave a hollow laugh.

"I'll have a word with Jake," he said, tapping the table with his fingers. "You know there is a historical precedent for this."

"What do you mean?" asked Ali. Nick took a deep breath.

"When Jake was little, about ten years old, he caught Foy having sex with Julian Peterson's wife, Eleanor, when they were on holiday here together." Nick sighed. "It was before they had bought their own house. Jake went down to the pool house one night to fetch a jar of grasshoppers that he had collected. The door was open, he went inside, and he saw Foy screwing Eleanor Peterson. They didn't see him. Can you imagine what a sight that was? Foy's trousers halfway down his arse and Eleanor's skirt up around her waist. Granted, Eleanor is a good-looking woman who has grown old more gracefully than many, but she was almost sixty at the time. Between them, there was more than a hundred years of flesh lying on the table."

"The table?" repeated Ali.

"She was lying on the table, like a buffet," said Nick distractedly. "Jake came and found me and told me what was going on. We never said anything to anyone else. Tita must have known. Bryony and Hester have no idea."

They heard the sound of voices approaching.

"Can I have Bryony's phone, please?" said Nick, holding out his hand. He took the phone and for a brief moment their fingers clumsily touched. Ali blushed with embarrassment. Foy appeared from the front of the house wearing a pair of sandy-colored shorts that did up above his belly button, emphasizing his girth.

"*Les invités sont arrivés!*" Foy announced triumphantly. He came outside with Hester's daughters under one arm and Izzy under the other, commenting on how tiny Izzy felt in his embrace. But it was a ruse to underplay the more conspicuous changes to Izzy's appearance: she had dyed her hair crow-black and cut a ragged fringe high on her forehead; her nails were painted with black nail varnish, and she was wearing purple lipstick; her eyebrows were dyed black. She was wearing a shirt with the sleeves cut off, a short miniskirt, and big black boots.

"God, Izzy, what have you done to yourself?" said Nick. "Bryony! Bryony! Come out here."

Bryony emerged from the house with Tita and Hester. Hester had obviously added to the drama of the occasion by mentioning nothing to her sister or mother.

"She's become a post-punk," said Hester in the face of Bryony's awed silence.

"Why have you made yourself so deliberately ugly?" asked Bryony. She looked as though she was about to cry. She turned to Hester.

"How could you let her do this?" she asked.

"It had nothing to do with me," Hester protested. "She went to Camden Market looking perfectly normal and came back looking like this."

"It's all about self-expression," said Izzy. "Hester had nothing to do with it."

"If you try and tell me that this has happened because I work full-time, I will probably resort to physical violence," Bryony shouted at Hester.

"I think you can safely assume that Izzy doesn't want to model herself on you," said Hester, stung by Bryony's criticism.

"Are they old enough to celebrate with a small glass of champagne?" Foy asked. He urged Andromede to search immediately for a bottle to celebrate with.

"I guess so." Nick smiled as Izzy came over and sat on the edge of his knee.

"Will you at least get rid of those great clunking boots, otherwise you'll get trench foot in this heat?" Izzy shook them off her feet to reveal a small tattoo of a yin-yang symbol on her left ankle.

"What is that?" Nick asked.

"It represents peace and harmony," said Izzy.

"Well, we certainly could use that," said Nick.

"It's so long since I've seen you, Daddy," she said, clearly enjoying all the attention. "Where have you been?"

"Working hard to earn enough money to keep you afloat," said Nick. He stared at Izzy sitting on the end of his knee as though she was a strange mythical creature come to torment him.

"I can't believe you've done this, Izzy," shouted Bryony. "Why do you want to punish me?"

"Calm down, Bryony," urged Foy.

Ali retreated into the jasmine to observe the elaborate ritual of greetings, aware that her presence would make things more awkward. People were never sure whether to ignore or acknowledge her. Silence was preferable to the misfired kisses and clumsy hugs that people sometimes undertook. Their intentions were well meaning, but it highlighted her confused status. She was relieved that Izzy's metamorphosis had occurred away from her.

She watched as Nick gripped Rick's hand and put the other hand on his shoulder in a manner that could have been interpreted as patronizing, except that Rick retaliated with a bear hug that definitely left Nick on the back foot. The twins and Lucy and Jake appeared, and Rick gave an ebullient round of high-fives. Hector took one look at Izzy and burst into tears. Lucy gave a disapproving glance up and down her body. Jake chewed his lower lip and stared at Ali.

"I want Izzy back," Hector cried. Izzy went over and knelt down to reassure him that she was the same person.

"It's a disguise, Hector," she explained.

Foy demanded that everyone admire the pair of handmade slippers that Tita had bought for his birthday. There was an olive tree embroidered in the velvet over the left toe and a salmon on the other. Tita walked slowly toward Hester, arms outstretched, and embraced her daughter.

"So lovely to have you all here together," Tita said, her eyes filling with tears.

"It's wonderful to be here, Mum," said Hester, embracing her mother.

Foy vigorously shook Rick's hand.

"Happy birthday, Foy," he said, carefully placing a present on the marble table.

Foy stared at it for a moment, until he was sure that everyone was watching. Then he carefully peeled back layers of paper and Bubble Wrap until he reached an oil painting of the Villa Ichthys that Hester had commissioned from an English artist resident on Corfu.

"It's marvelous, Hester," said Foy, although the lines were perhaps a little too abstract for his taste and the blocks of color too muted for such an obvious man. "How clever you are."

"It was Rick's idea," said Hester, looking at him sharply, as though searching for any signs of insincerity.

"We must put it up at once in the drawing room so that Julian and Eleanor can admire it when they come over," he said.

"If Foy is in the mood for presents, then maybe we should hand over ours," suggested Nick.

"Although I have no idea what he's got for you, Daddy," said Bryony. "It's been his big secret."

"We need to go down to the beach," said Nick.

"Can't you just give it to him here?" asked Bryony, nervously eye-ing Hester.

"Indulge me," said Nick, putting his arm around Bryony.

"On the Koloura or the Kassiopi side?" asked Tita.

"The Koloura side, in case we make the Rothschilds jealous," joked Nick.

"Come with us, Ali," said Bryony, noticing she was hiding under-neath the jasmine. "You'll love this beach."

Ali could hear Nick and Bryony's argument, even though their room was on a different floor in the main part of the house, where the olive press used to be kept, and their shutters were closed. The old stone walls couldn't keep secrets. In summer nothing moved, the air stood still, and noise floated in mysterious patterns from one end of the estate to the other. She knew without listening that the argument was about the boat that Nick had bought Foy for his birthday.

She remembered Nick standing beside Foy on the beach, one hand covering his father-in-law's eyes. Nick had dramatically removed his hands to reveal the twenty-three-foot speedboat. Foy had waded into the water and immediately got into the driving seat, laughing at the way Nick had called the boat *The Menace*.

"What a beast," Foy kept saying, unable to suppress his joy. Alfie and Hector had climbed in the back, demanding to be given the first ride around the bay. Izzy had scrambled onto the prow with her cousins, Maud and Ella. Jake had even managed to disentangle him-self from Lucy to climb on board. Foy had asked Tita if she wanted to join him, but Tita knew the motion would make her dizzier than usual. Hester and Rick had stood on the beach, unsmiling.

"How much did it cost?" Bryony kept asking.

"Does it matter?" responded Nick. To judge from the lazy tone of his voice, he was lying on the bed, sipping beer.

"You're the one saying that we shouldn't buy this house in Oxford-shire," said Bryony.

"I paid for the boat a year ago," said Nick. "Things were different then."

"How much did it cost?" she insisted. "I can look it up on the Internet, so you might as well tell me."

"Three hundred thousand pounds," said Nick, as though this information would miraculously cauterize the argument. "It's a Silvestris."

"Why did you get it?" asked Bryony.

"I wanted to buy your father something that he will really love," said Nick.

"I don't believe you."

"Why do you think I bought it?"

"Because you want to show my father that you can afford to buy him a present that he couldn't afford to buy for himself. It's part of this ridiculous one-upmanship that you have with him, this need to prove yourself against him. There's more to life than money, Nick."

"You don't believe that or you'd let me give up my job," Nick shouted back.

"It wouldn't work," said Bryony.

"What wouldn't work?" said Nick.

"We wouldn't work if you didn't work," she said.

13

Foy stood up in *The Menace*, one hand on the steering wheel, the other saluting Julian Peterson, as he navigated his way rather too fast toward the small jetty at the foot of the Petersons' house on the edge of the bay at Agios Stefanos. The nose of the boat bumped the newly built wooden gangway, wrong-footing Julian, who for a moment looked perilously close to toppling into the water beside them. He stepped back to regain equilibrium, and Ali could see that his beige shorts and blue short-sleeved shirt were spattered with sea-water.

"Let the party begin," Foy shouted triumphantly as he finished his salute by doffing his panama hat toward Julian. Bryony put an arm on his shoulder to restrain him because he was rocking the boat, but Foy resisted. His sudden enthusiasm at the prospect of drinks at the Petersons' was all the more astonishing, given the way he had spent most of the ten-minute journey complaining that they should bring their own food and wine because Julian was so stingy.

"What's all this?" Julian asked as he leaned forward to read the boat's name and get a better view of the hand-stitched-leather interior.

"Birthday present from my son-in-law," Foy said, struggling to feign nonchalance.

"God, it's a Silvestris, isn't it? You lucky bastard," said Julian, react-
ing in exactly the way Foy hoped he would. "Nick must be doing
well. Either that or he's trying to kill you."

"Requires a clear head and a steady hand, and fortunately I still
have both," said Foy, unable to contain his excitement. "Isn't it a
beast? Glides through the water like a torpedo. I'll take you and Eleanor for a spin later."

"Grandpa needs a parrot for his shoulder," shouted Hector
excitedly.

"Please get a parrot," pleaded Alfie, "please get a parrot." If someone could get a boat that cost more than a house for his birthday, then
a parrot didn't seem so outlandish, thought Ali, as she helped the
twins onto the jetty. Bryony, Tita, Maud, and Ella followed close
behind.

Ali stood awkwardly as everyone kissed Julian hello. She knew the
routine by now. Two kisses, one on each cheek. Would Julian remember her? If not, would Bryony remind him? In the event, both forgot.
Foy, who was generally better than everyone else at including Ali in
a round of greetings, was too wrapped up talking about the engine of
his boat to notice her unease. For a moment she considered introducing herself, even though she had met Julian several times before. It
was a less embarrassing prospect than coming across him later and
having to explain that she was neither a friend of Jake's nor one of
Hester's daughters, and was, in fact, the nanny.

Foy strode up the steep pathway toward the Petersons' new house,
leaving Julian breathlessly trailing behind him. Now it was Foy's turn
to muster enthusiasm appropriate to the purchase of an eight-bedroom
villa overlooking the Ionian Sea.

"Stunning location . . . beautiful garden . . . fantastic house . . ." he
said effusively, sounding like an estate agent. "It will be so lovely having you and Eleanor close to us in the twilight of our life."

"Have you decided to retire here?" questioned Julian. "What about
your business?"

"Can't retire yet," said Foy gruffly. "Fenton's not ready to take responsibility. Too much of a loose cannon. Requires a steady hand on the tiller to negotiate with these bloody supermarkets. They're squeezing our margins so tight that you can barely fit a piece of paper between profit and loss anymore." It was all bluster. Even Ali knew Foy's opinion no longer held any sway with Freithshire Fisheries.

Ali hung back with the children, behind Bryony and Tita, who were discussing Izzy. This was the first time that Tita had joined the family on an outing since they had arrived. Generally she was invisible. In the mornings, when Ali was down by the pool with the twins, Tita visited famous Corfiote gardens in search of new ideas. Occasionally she went to see a friend or accompanied one of the guests to a local market. In the afternoons Ali usually took the twins down to the beach, and when they came home Tita was shut away in the drawing room, sticking photos in albums or reading. Always biographies. Never fiction. Sometimes they happened upon her in the pool in the late afternoon. She wore a swimming hat with purple and orange plastic flowers and swam the slowest breaststroke Ali had ever seen, her head held erect above the water.

Tita had reluctantly decided to go in the boat at the last minute, after a great deal of persuasion from Bryony and Foy, who both insisted she should be present during *The Menace*'s first proper maiden voyage. How everyone would travel to the Petersons' had been the catalyst for a long argument that spluttered on from breakfast through to lunch. Far longer than it took to get there, Ali now realized.

Hester and Rick had announced they would walk, even though it was so hot that Leicester's paw had blistered on the terrace. It was a point of environmental principle, Rick had sanctimoniously explained. Izzy had refused to go in the boat because it would interfere with her makeup. Nick had really wanted to travel in *The Menace* but had caved in to pressure from Bryony to take Jake, Lucy, and Izzy in the Land Rover. Bryony had insisted he needed to spend more time with his troubled teenage daughter. As she had waited outside the house for the boating party, Ali heard Nick impatiently revving the Land Rover in the driveway and pressing the horn nonstop for almost a minute until Jake and Lucy finally emerged. Then, just as they were all in place, his phone had rung.

"Sorry, Izzy, I'm dealing with a bit of a crisis. I'll make it up to you."

"Every day is a crisis in your world, Dad."

"You're not far from the truth at the moment," Nick had muttered as he worried about the e-mail he had just received, subject: "something spooking markets, source unknown." He flicked up and down his messages. "I'm going to have to go back to London for a couple of days."

"Izzy is becoming difficult to manage," said Bryony as they headed up the hill. "And she was always so easy."

"It's a difficult age," said Tita.

"I wasn't like that, was I?"

"I don't think so," said Tita vaguely.

"I can't understand why Izzy has such low self-esteem. We've given her the best of everything. We got her into a great school. Against the odds, frankly. She's a talented musician. If she doesn't blow it, she's on track to get a couple of fistfuls of A's in her GCSEs. Honestly, we couldn't do any more for her than we've done, and then she turns up like this. I can't help thinking if she hadn't gone to stay with Hester then this wouldn't have happened."

Bryony stopped for a moment to allow Tita to draw level with her. Tita walked straight-backed, as though she had spent the best part of her adolescence in posture classes with a copy of Mrs. Beeton on her head.

"Do you think it's because I work?"

"Darling, you and Hester were practically reared by nannies and it never did you any harm."

Ali would have liked to add that the work thing was a red herring and that some people were born with a propensity for self-destruction. Her mother stayed at home until she and her sister were teenagers, and Jo had still ended up with a drug problem.

"That's not what Hester would say."

"Hester always has to blame someone else for her own problems. She's like her father that way. Doesn't want to take responsibility for her actions. I think it's fabulous that you love your job. It means you always have your freedom. If I had been born in a different era I might have done something like you."

"Do you regret being so reliant on Dad?" Bryony asked suddenly. It was a question that Bryony had spent a lifetime wanting to ask, but now that the opportunity had arisen she was afraid of the answer. Tita stopped for a moment and stared up at Foy, who had reached the top of the steep track and was holding Eleanor in an extravagant embrace on the edge of the terrace that ran along the front of the house.

"I love your father very much. But greater independence might have provided solace in difficult periods," she said with an economy of language that made Ali wince at the turbulence it concealed. In modern parenting manuals Tita might have been classified as a distant parent, but she understood enough about human emotion to know that her daughter didn't really want full disclosure.

They could see Izzy waving at them from the terrace. The Land Rover crew had beaten them. The intense heat wasn't conducive to the kind of outfit appropriate to a teenager who wanted to show off her neo-Goth credentials. Ali was relieved to see that Izzy had abandoned her black leather boots in favor of flip-flops. She was wearing a very short denim skirt, a ripped T-shirt, and the same purple lipstick that gave her face a cartoonish look. Her proximity to Foy made her arms and legs look even spindlier.

"Look how thin she is," said Bryony. "I thought it was good that she lost a bit of puppy fat, but of course Izzy has to take it that one step further. Do you think she's properly anorexic? We've taken the computer out of her room so she can't go on those wretched websites. She's even seeing an eating-disorders counselor. We've gone with her a couple of times for a family session."

"She has an unhealthy attitude toward food," agreed Tita, who was rarely seen eating. Bryony continued to meander around the subject of Izzy as they finally reached the terrace at the top of the slope. Her solutions were all so extreme that it was difficult for Tita to find any middle ground worth debating.

"Should we push her harder or not push her at all? Should we let her eat what she likes or take her to an eating-disorders clinic? What about boarding school or home schooling?" Tita stopped and turned round to face the sea. She put out a hand to steady herself on a flimsy oleander, and for a moment Ali thought she might fall. Perhaps the conversation was making her dizzy.

"Is that you, Ali?" she asked, narrowing her eyes against the sun. "Would you mind taking my arm?"

Julian and Eleanor Peterson hadn't mentioned any other guests when they invited the party staying at the Villa Ichthys for early-evening drinks at the end of the first week of the holiday. So it was doubly enervating for Bryony to find Sophia and Ned Wilbraham sipping champagne cocktails together with Rick and Hester.

Nick was standing in a huddle with Ned. Their heads were bent so close to each other their foreheads were almost touching. They stared at their feet, and Ali wondered if they noticed they were wearing identical brown deck shoes and beige chinos, the uniform of the banker at leisure. Nick glanced at the group emerging from the path onto the terrace but didn't react.

"I've just had an e-mail from a colleague in London saying there's something strange going on with the markets. The price of U.S. gilts and gold is up, and investors are dumping anything with default risk. But no one knows why."

"There's definitely a perception that there's a liquidity problem, but I'm sure it's a case of short-term jitters," agreed Ned. "It's because BNP Paribas stopped investors' withdrawing money from those three funds."

"I think it's more serious than that. Either trust has gone or people are running out of cash," Nick argued.

"I saw the ECB has announced it will provide as much funding as banks need to keep up with demand for capital. That should reassure people," said Ned.

"Defaults on subprime mortgages are the highest they've been since 2002," said Nick. "If the money isn't coming in to pay the bond holders, then who's left holding the baby?"

"Surely the risk is dispersed through credit derivatives and CDOs so that any shocks can be absorbed?" questioned Ned.

"It depends on your view on fat tails," Nick responded.

"You've lost me now," said Ned. "I'm not a Harvard MBA, remember. I'm just a humble M-and-A type."

"It's when the medium-term stability of the system is built on a painful readjustment at the end. Those credit derivatives might make the system look more stable, but in fact there could be a big fat whale-sized tail waiting to sweep us all overboard when the boom slows down," Nick explained.

"But according to Greenspan we're all enjoying the great moderation," said Ned. "It's always a question of perception in these markets. And the models can't all be wrong."

"Maths tools are a compass. They're not infallible, and it worries me that everyone is using the same models. What happens if the basic premise is wrong and extreme negative events occur more often than the formulas are telling us?" asked Nick.

"Then we're all fucked," said Ned. "Don't let what happened to those Bear Stearns funds make you feel gloomy. They were overleveraged. There was a maturity mismatch. They'd got too many long-term mortgage-linked assets that you can't shift in a hurry, funded by short-term debt that dissolved overnight."

"Look at those boats out there," Nick insisted. They both turned toward the sea, where an array of cruise ships, sailing boats, and ferries were purposefully striking their way up and down the channel. "The statistical likelihood of them all capsizing at once is tiny, but it's not impossible. And it is possible that the system could de-leverage all at the same time."

"So what would you advise?"

"I'd get rid of all the liability on our books today. I'd dump all of the mezzanine debt and most of the super-senior tranches, or at least try and get some insurance."

"What about your lords and masters? Have you convinced them of your strategy?"

"No." Nick gave a hollow laugh.

Ali turned her attention to the other end of the terrace, where Sophia was questioning Rick about education. Was it really easier to get children from state schools into Oxbridge? Should she consider sending Martha to a sixth-form college for the last two years of her education, to secure a place? Did he really think an intelligent child would do equally well in any school? Did he know a good English tutor, because her eldest daughter's last tutor had recently resigned, citing irreconcilable differences over Thomas Hardy. Sophia sprang up from her seat as she saw Bryony.

"What a fantastic coincidence," she trilled.

"Yes, lovely to see you, too," said Bryony, trying to muster enthusiasm.

Sophia was wearing an expensive-looking floaty silk top over a pair of white trousers, and when she stood up she reminded Ali of a sailing boat turning toward the wind.

"I bumped into Sophia in the supermarket. We know her parents. So do Foy and Tita." Eleanor beamed at Bryony. "Such a small world."

"I didn't realize you were planning to come to Corfu," said Bryony, in a tone that suggested had she known she might have reconsidered her holiday plans.

"I booked it ages ago, then completely forgot to mention it to you. I'm here for the whole month, but of course I don't have to rush back to work. Martha would love to see Izzy. Did she bring her cello? They could practice their quartet together."

Izzy made throat-slitting gestures behind Sophia, in full view of Eleanor Peterson, who nervously suggested she might like to go and swim in the pool with the other children. "Sophia's nanny is down there, looking after the little ones."

"Do you fancy a swim, Martha?" Izzy asked, peeling off her T-shirt to reveal a black bikini top and a rib cage like a rack of lamb. It was for Martha's benefit. Ali knew she was the one who had instigated the snide comments about Izzy's weight the previous year. Martha remained sullenly in a chair beside her mother. There was nothing in her demeanor to suggest she relished the prospect of spending time with Izzy.

"Would you like a towel, Izzy?" Eleanor inquired.

"I'm fine. Thanks."

"How about you, Jake? Would you and Lucy like to swim?"

"The cold water would do you good," said Foy.

"I'm fine, thanks, Eleanor," said Jake, his voice muffled because Lucy was draped over his knee, obscuring his mouth. He was unerringly polite to Eleanor, but he couldn't look her in the eye. Lucy shifted in his lap. They settled still and sticky on each other. At one point Ali caught Jake lazily licking Lucy's shoulder blade.

Sexual attraction is exhausting, thought Ali. Like eczema. The more you scratch, the worse the itch. A memory of her at university, sitting in a lecture on Daniel Defoe, suddenly came to mind. Will MacDonald had been speaking about Defoe's representation of women. His mouth had opened and shut, but she could hear nothing of what he said, and the sheet of paper on which she was meant to take notes was blank. Yet she could recall the exact sensation of his finger trailing up the inside of her thigh the previous evening as he drove her home from babysitting.

Immediately after the class she went up to his office in the English faculty. She couldn't speak as he opened the door and then locked it behind him. "Ali," he whispered throatily as he pressed himself against her. Ali remembered feeling sick with longing. Entwined, they headed in ungraceful side steps toward a coffee-stained sofa beneath the window, pulling at each other's clothes. He was wearing a belt, and it seemed to take ages for them to get it undone. He pushed a couple of books on the floor, and she lay down on a small pile of unmarked essays. Then he was on top of her, and they kissed so eagerly that their teeth clashed. His hand quickly found its way inside her bra.

An image of Jake as a child stumbling upon Eleanor and his grandfather in the pool house came to Ali.

"Would you like a drink?" Eleanor asked her.

"No, thanks," said Ali, holding on tightly to the twins' hands, more for her own comfort than theirs.

"How about you, Foy?" Eleanor asked. "Shall I get your usual?"

Eleanor's face was a mass of contradictions that reflected the conundrums life had unexpectedly thrown her way since her husband's best friend first put a hand on her knee beneath the dinner table in Holland Park Crescent all those years ago. She had been one of the first women in the country to have a face-lift in the 1970s, Foy had told them over a recent Sunday lunch. If you looked closely, you could see the scars from the staples behind her ears. It was one of those dangerous facts that enthralled the twins. She had become a kind of Frankenstein figure to them.

Of course, Foy's attention had been flattering, but even Eleanor must have realized that it had less to do with her and more to do with the fact that she was married to Julian. Foy and Julian might have been childhood friends, yet his instincts were purely competitive. But Ali knew that if you have sex with someone a couple of times, it can easily develop into a habit, and she imagined that neither Eleanor nor Foy were prone to analysis.

So once the relationship had started it probably seemed easier just to keep going. Perhaps it was pleasurable. Foy was undoubtedly a more generous lover than he might otherwise have been, because he knew Eleanor would be drawing comparisons. According to Katya, who had described all this in great detail but refused to reveal her source, Foy took unbelievable risks—in a bubble lift that got stuck while they were skiing in Val d'Isère, knowing Julian and Tita were waiting in the restaurant beneath them; in the bathroom at Nick and Bryony's house, with Mrs. Thatcher watching them from that photograph; in the pool house in Corfu. Apparently this was the last time.

Which was why, when Foy had finally ended it, it must have been all the more devastating. Although she knew that she was never the only one, the relationship had nourished her for the best part of thirty years, and when it was over Eleanor must have felt as though she was finally enshrouded in the invisible cloak of old age. Undoubtedly the one person in whom she would have liked to confide was married to the man who had caused her so much pain.

"You've brought out the wrong olives," said Julian. Eleanor flushed.

"These are delicious," said Foy, cramming two or three into his mouth at once. "Much better than mine." He bent down to give one to Leicester, who spat it out in disgust. Another couple arrived as they were leaving the terrace. He looked vaguely familiar. Julian introduced him to everyone as though he had just produced a rabbit from a hat.

"Chatham House rules, please," said Julian pompously as he did a round of introductions, which included all the adults present. The new arrival was a friend of their eldest son's. They had been at Oxford together. He was staying with friends in the village.

Ali didn't catch his name, but she could tell from the way Foy headed toward him that it was someone who merited attention. They began talking about the yacht anchored on the other side of the bay opposite the Rothschild residence. It belonged to a Russian oligarch, Foy explained.

"It's one of the biggest yachts in the world. There's a helicopter pad on the roof and a swimming pool on the prow. Makes my Silvestris look like a rowing boat."

"I've been on it," said the new guest, knowing everyone would find this tantalizing.

"How was the décor?" Eleanor asked.

"All gold taps and leather," Ali heard the guest say as she headed off down the path toward the pool with Leicester and the twins.

It wasn't until the journey home that Ali realized it was the shadow chancellor and his wife.

"Do you think they're still in love?" Katya asked Ali as they sat companionably at the edge of the enormous new pool, their feet dangling in the water, watching the children swim. It was the sort of question that Katya liked to slip into conversation, and one of the reasons that made her both exhilarating and exhausting company. She stumbled from distance to intimacy like a child fiddling with a camera lens.

Ali was still struggling to adjust to Katya's surprise appearance at the Petersons' party. It said a lot for her friend's adaptability that she didn't seemed remotely phased.

"I think they're too young to know. When you're eighteen, love and lust mean pretty much the same thing."

"I didn't mean Jake and Lucy." Katya laughed as they both stared at them. "I meant the golden couple, Nick and Bryony."

Ali did a quick head count in the pool because Katya had eyes only for Thomas, even though he was wearing armbands. "One, two, three, four, five, six, seven," Ali murmured under her breath as she accounted for all the children in her charge.

Hector and Alfie were with Thomas in the shallow end, playing a game that involved rescuing insects from the pool with a fishing net and nursing them back to health in a makeshift Lego hospital they had built under the long, thin shade of a cypress tree. Leo was at the other end receiving a diving lesson from Hester's oldest daughter, Maud.

Izzy and her younger cousin, Ella, were working out a synchronized swimming routine. Izzy's black bikini showed off her newly pierced tummy button to best effect. All that remained of her post-punk credentials were the jet-black hair and black nail varnish, the pale foundation and dark lipstick that she had put on for breakfast washed away by the water, but the dyed eyebrows survived.

"Although Jake is definitely feet."

"You mean fit," Ali corrected her. Katya's English was impeccable, apart from when she attempted colloquialisms. Then it collapsed in a mishmash of mispronunciation and malapropism.

"I guess I don't look at him that way."

"Don't be so coy," Katya teased, using one of her favorite new words. "When you see him rubbing Lucy with suntan cream, don't you ever wish it was you?"

"Absolutely not," said Ali. "Jake and I have never really seen eye to eye." She was about to add that she didn't really know him, but it sounded absurd, as though she was deliberately obfuscating. She considered the facts: he slept with his light on, he didn't use a pillow, he once waxed his monobrow, he told his sister men didn't fancy thin women, he used Lynx deodorant, he said "tits," not "breasts." Intimate stuff, endearing even, but it was knowledge filched rather than tendered.

"Attraction is like temporary blindness: you don't need to see to feel," said Katya.

"I just don't think of him in that way," said Ali impatiently.

She turned around to check that no one was within earshot. Izzy, in particular, had an uncanny sixth sense for conversations you didn't want her to hear, although she professed to be completely bored by the overdiscussed subject of Lucy and Jake. Until the news of another mismanaged outbreak of foot-and-mouth disease in England, it had threatened to become the main theme of the holiday.

Lucy and Jake had disappeared again. Nick had teased Jake about being carsick when they arrived at the Petersons' house. To judge from the ill-concealed bulge in his swimming trunks, it was a euphemism for lovesick. She just hoped they had found somewhere discreet, because apart from insect hospital, the younger children's other main pastime was spying on them and writing up reports of what they had observed. Yesterday she had heard them all talking about sex.

"What's oral sex?" Alfie had asked his twelve-year-old cousin, Ella.

"It's when you have sex with someone and talk a lot afterward," replied Ella.

It was after nine o'clock. The sun was low in the sky but engaged in a last-minute burst of energy before it dropped below the horizon.

"And he is so clever," continued Katya. Ali looked at her blankly and realized that she was still talking about Jake. "Bryony and Nick wanted him to read economics at Oxford, but he insisted he wanted to stick with English. They even tried to persuade him to take a year off so he could think about it for longer, but he refused. I like a man who knows his mind."

"How do you know all this?" asked Ali.

"You know what it's like. Nannies hear everything." Katya shrugged. "So do you think Nick and Bryony are in love?"

"I guess so," replied Ali vaguely, admiring Leo's persistence as he got out of the pool after yet another painful belly flop.

"Three out of ten," trilled Maud. She was a hard taskmaster, like her mother, thought Ali.

"How can you tell?" asked Katya. "They don't see much of each other."

"That's circumstance, not choice," said Ali, "and when they're together they seem to get along fine. They hardly ever argue."

"That might mean there is no connection between them," pointed out Katya.

Ali would have liked to tell Katya that she wasn't sure that she had ever been in love and therefore felt unqualified to comment on anyone else's relationship. But if she shared a confidence, it might provoke Katya to reciprocate with one of her own, and Ali wasn't sure that she wanted to be the keeper of Katya's secrets.

She considered her situation. During their yearlong affair, she had shown all the symptoms: she had listened to music that reminded her of Will MacDonald; she had read books that he recommended; she had found ways of turning every conversation back to him; and when she lay in bed with her hand in between her legs she imagined it was his fingers instead of her own. But was this love? Because when she had finally left for London, within weeks all this had faded until she found she could recall only individual features of his face, the whole having been forgotten, and even these had faded with time.

"When I see Bryony and Nick together, I think they have a marriage of convenience," Katya continued. "It's all too quiet."

"Why is it convenient?" asked Ali, her curiosity outweighing her natural reticence about discussing her employers' relationship. If Mira had been with them, she would have questioned their loyalty.

"Simple: he gives her wealth, she gives him status," said Katya. "He comes from a really humble background."

"If he earns so much money, then why does Bryony need to work?" said Ali. It was a question that she had wanted to ask since she moved in with the Skinners.

"Also simple," said Katya. "With a father like Foy as your main role model, you would never consider men reliable, and she wants to impress him."

"I don't know about the machinations of their relationship," said Ali, annoyed she hadn't drawn these same conclusions, "but they are good to me, and that's all I really need to focus on."

"Does Nick ever flirt with you?"

Ali thought for a moment. She had never really understood flirting. "I don't think so."

"What are your parents like?" Katya asked a few minutes later.

An image of her mother and father companionably sharing toast and jam at six o'clock each evening, just before the shipping forecast, came to Ali's mind. The simplicity of her parents' relationship now seemed marvelous. She had never noticed it before she moved in with the Skinners. Even the way her mother was jealous of her father's relationship with the sea now seemed magical.

"Normal," said Ali resolutely. "Where are your parents?"

"I was brought up by my mother," said Katya. It was the first time since Ali had met Katya that she had referred to her life in Ukraine. "My father disappeared. One day he was there, and then, poof, the next he was gone."

"Where did he go?"

"My mother thinks he had another wife and family in southern Ukraine," said Katya, rippling the surface of the swimming pool with her toes. "But we don't know."

"How awful," said Ali.

"Is good life lesson," said Katya. Ali noticed the momentary lapse of grammar. "It teaches you that anything you have been given can be taken away from you. You learn to take the moment when you can." She raised her arm and grabbed a fistful of thin air to demonstrate. Ali followed her gaze to the swimming pool, where she was watching Thomas haul himself out of the shallow end. He ran toward Katya, and she shouted a few words in Ukrainian, and he slowed down. She pulled her long legs out of the pool and sat cross-legged so that Thomas could sit in the small warm space in the middle.

"Is that why you came to England?" Ali asked. Katya nodded gravely.

"I send almost everything I earn back to my mother for my brothers and sisters. It is my responsibility."

"How do you know Mira?" asked Ali.

"We made the journey together. She helped me. She saved me from some very, very bad people. But it's all over now." Ali sensed Katya had said enough. She rocked backward and forward on her haunches, singing a Ukrainian lullaby to Thomas.

"Where are the rest of the children?" asked Katya. Ali looked toward the pool and realized that they had all disappeared. The insect hospital was intact, but the patients were busily escaping back into the wild. Some were wandering back into the very swimming pool from which they had been rescued. What did that tell you? wondered Ali.

That some insects were more intelligent than others? That fate was random? Or that bad luck followed some insects around?

"I'll go and look for them," Ali volunteered.

"Will you take Thomas so I can swim?" Katya asked. She pushed him off her knees and stood up to stretch her long legs. There were tiny specks of dust and gravel stuck to her buttocks and thighs. She didn't bother to wipe them off. She was wearing a bright red bikini. She reminded Ali of an exotic fruit about to burst from its skin. Katya lifted Thomas onto Ali's hip, and he contentedly played with her hair as they headed into the olive grove at the bottom of the garden, calling for Hector and Alfie.

When she got back to the terrace, Ali found the children eating kebabs and pieces of barbecued chicken at the table. Bryony was busily piling up dirty plates and filling glasses with water. She shot Ali a disapproving look for not being there to look after the twins, even though the Petersons' Greek housekeeper was on hand to help. Hector and Alfie were sharing a seat and eating from the same plate, a double infraction in Bryony's book, although everyone else commented on how sweet it was that they were so close.

"Sorry, they all disappeared at once," Ali told Bryony. She sat Thomas down next to Hector and gave him a chicken leg coated in honey to chew on.

"This heat is so exhausting," said Sophia, fanning herself with a napkin. "I feel almost sedated."

"That's what happened in *The Tempest*," said Ali, anxious to win back Bryony's approval.

Sophia looked interested, and Ali explained that the shipwrecked souls who find themselves washed up in *The Tempest* are overcome by the dreamy quality of the island and break free of the restraints of their narrow Milanese life to become somnambulists and dreamers.

"Some people think Shakespeare set the play on Corfu," she

explained. "Caliban's mother is called Sycorax, and that is almost an anagram of Corcyra, the ancient name of Corfu."

She turned to Bryony, who gave her a broad smile.

"Do you know where Leicester is?" Bryony asked.

"We left him down by the pool," Ali explained. "We cooled him down with a bucket of water and let him go to sleep underneath a sun lounger."

"Would you mind going to get him, please?" Bryony asked. "He doesn't know his way round here."

Once again, Ali set off for the pool. Leicester was no longer beneath the sun lounger, although there was a small, dusty bowl shape where he had been lying. She searched for footprints but found only bits of Lego and a couple of dead grasshoppers. Ali inwardly cursed the dog. He was punishing her for neglecting him. Then she heard a crash in the Petersons' pool house and noticed the door was ajar.

There was a noise that sounded like a fridge door opening and shutting. Surely Leicester couldn't open it alone? She tiptoed along the stone path that led to the pool house, regretting that she had left her shoes up on the terrace because it was so hot underfoot.

These people had so many fridges, thought Ali. There were at least five in Holland Park Crescent, and more at the house in Greece. And the Petersons were no different. She remembered her parents replacing the fridge they had owned for almost a quarter of a century a couple of years ago. It had taken almost six months of poring over catalogs, agonizing over different models, comparing prices, energy costs, size, and design, before they could reach a decision. Fridges don't grow on trees, her father had joked when he saw the bored expression on Ali's face after yet another discussion. "They do for some," she could now tell him.

She went into the pool house quietly so she could catch Leicester at the crime scene. Instead she saw Ned, trousers and underpants pulled down beneath his improbably white buttocks, on top of Katya, who was naked apart from her bikini top, which was pulled up over her chest and so flimsy it barely qualified as an item of clothing. He was stroking her breasts as though they were sacred objects. They were shiny with sweat. Ned's head was turned to the side so that Ali could see his mouth was open at a funny angle as though he might have been saying a word with long vowels like *greengage*. His face was tomato red. She almost giggled out loud at the absurdity of her discovery. She was reasonably confident that Katya didn't see her, and she stepped back into the daylight.

"Can you believe the shadow chancellor was there?" said Foy on the journey home. He had persuaded Tita to accompany him in the boat again. She refused to sit down, even though she was covered in spray, preferring to hold on to the windshield with one hand and Foy's shoulder with the other. "I liked the cut of his jib. He asked me to make a donation."

"Julian has a sixth sense for the way the political wind is blowing," said Tita. "He told me that he thinks Blair might make him a peer before he leaves office."

"It's not Julian. It's Eleanor," said Foy, unable to disguise the admiration in his voice. "She's wonderfully adept at making people feel as though she is their best friend."

"What did you think of the house?" asked Tita.

"Not enough light sockets," said Foy dismissively.

"It's a shame Nick has got to go back to London," said Tita.

"It's the same every year," Foy said with a grunt.

14

September 2007

The day after Nick's bank announced better-than-expected third-quarter results, Izzy meandered downstairs wearing a slouchy mohair sweater (purple bra visible beneath), short tartan skirt, tights with carefully fashioned holes, and black leather jacket, ready for a late-evening rehearsal with her string quartet at Sophia Wilbraham's house.

They were entering a school music competition, and Sophia had asked Ali to make sure Izzy was at their house by eight o'clock at the latest, so they could run through Beethoven's String Quartet No. 14 in C-sharp minor for the last time. Ali could hear the discontent and resentment in the clump, clump of Izzy's Dr. Martens boots as she slouched into the kitchen. The cello was about to take a pounding.

It was a bad plan. Izzy was tired after school. She was bored of the cello. And she was fed up with her life being organized by other people. But Bryony had only just arrived back from Kiev and was therefore powerless to derail the plan at this late stage. And out of pity (always a questionable motive), because Sophia's husband was having an affair, Ali had allowed herself to be steamrolled into submission. She had also agreed to collect Izzy at nine-thirty because Sophia didn't want to take responsibility for her walking home alone, "given all her troubles." As Izzy explained fairly articulately to Ali earlier in the day, none of this fitted with her new philosophy of taking responsibility for her destiny.

Unusually, Nick and Bryony were sitting at the kitchen table, having an early-evening drink together. They had just closed on the house in Oxfordshire, and Bryony wanted to discuss the renovation project because she was due to fly to Moscow the following day. Since his premature departure from Corfu, Nick had hardly been at home. Ali sometimes overheard scraps of conversation when he came back at night, but she didn't ask any questions. "We've got a two-billion-dollar CDO that we can't move at par . . . We're selling it at a one-hundred-million-dollar loss . . . A quarter of Countrywide's subprime loans are delinquent . . . We're in a negative feedback loop."

From Ali's perspective the magnitude of the losses always seemed eye-watering, and somehow they impacted on Nick's self-discipline because he abandoned his late-night exercise routine in the basement gym in favor of a bottle of wine in the drawing room.

Bryony had a deal afoot. Ali had glanced at the top page of "Project Beethoven" (private and confidential, for limited distribution) in the recycling bin and understood from skim-reading the first page that one of Bryony's Russian energy companies wanted to bid for a British distributor. She also knew from Bryony's fraught phone conversations that the British government wasn't very happy about its gas supply being controlled by Russia and that most newspaper stories reflected this view. The results of the Ukrainian elections a couple of weeks earlier didn't bode well. The pipeline that supplied Europe went through Ukraine, and the Russians were already making threatening noises because they didn't trust the doll-like new prime minister, Yulia Tymoshenko.

"They already supply most of our gas, so what does it matter if they distribute it, too?" Bryony briefed journalists from the kitchen in the evening. One of her other deals was "going hostile," which made Ali think of cowboy films. Bryony's mood wasn't good enough for Ali to ask her exactly what this meant. To judge from her stress levels, it definitely wasn't positive.

The architect's plans were unfolded on the table, and Bryony was efficiently running through what she termed the "headline alterations." They ignored Ali, who was discreetly searching through the bookshelf for Izzy's sheet music, lost days ago. When Bryony was away the music practice regime dissolved.

"How much?" Nick asked.

"He's thinking seven figures."

"What?" Ali's back was turned to him, but she didn't need to see Nick's expression to catch the exasperation in his tone.

"I'm a frugal person, Nick. It's difficult to see how we could do it any cheaper." Bryony's tone was soft, almost regretful. It was as though she was playing Monopoly and apologizing for building four hotels on Park Place. Ali was grateful they couldn't see her face as she aimlessly shuffled through the same pile of papers over and over again. Not since they had appeared in *The Sunday Times* rich list in April had Ali been so conscious of the Skinners' enormous wealth.

"It includes everything," said Bryony.

"Well, that's good to know," said Nick, his voice syrupy with sarcasm.

How could anyone spend so much money doing up a house? Ali wondered. It wasn't really a moral question, although it should be. Rather, it was logistical. She now understood that a set of curtains for an early Victorian drawing room with two sash windows could cost almost £10,000, because she had seen the bill from the interior decorator to replace the set ruined at the party. Eight sets could buy you a house in Cromer, she had calculated. The new curtains were so thick that Hector couldn't hold the edge in one hand. There was lining, interlining, weights, blackout fabric, passementerie trimming, walling. When she heard the interior decorator speak to Bryony, Ali had felt like an anthropologist who had stumbled across a secret language spoken by only a very small British tribe.

"Define 'everything,'" Nick demanded.

"Building the kitchen extension, reroofing, insulation, resurfacing the tennis court, installing a security system, swimming pool, home cinema, games room, the orangery . . . It's all here." She tapped the plans impatiently, indicating that he should look at the spec. He picked up the eight-page document and started reading.

"You've agreed to spend eight grand on a reconditioned burnished-copper bateau bathtub? I'm not fucking Henry the Eighth, you know, or have you already included a velvet loo seat?"

"Copper is a great electrical and thermal conductor," said Bryony calmly. "It's the best material for a bath. Retains the heat really well, so actually you save money on hot water."

"Bryony, you cannot seriously talk about saving money on heating bills when you're washing your bits in a bath that costs more than a new G-Wiz."

"I'll pay for the bath," Bryony said with a shrug.

"Replastering, thirty thousand pounds?" continued Nick. "You're spending too much time with Russian oligarchs."

"The Jacobean ceiling moldings need to be completely reconditioned," Bryony explained. "We need to sample the original mortar to try and come up with something that matches the original plaster. The architect says it will probably be a combination of one part calcium carbonate to twenty-five parts lime. There are only about two people in Britain who can actually do it. It's a listed house. We need to be faithful to the original spirit of the building."

"I just don't get why we need to do all this. The people we're buying from have been living quite happily there for almost half a century."

"It's what we agreed. You were at the meeting. And their taste is diabolical. I can't live with all that chintz."

"We can't afford it." Now it was Bryony's turn to look incredulous. She paused for a moment, then leaned toward him on her elbows, fingers firmly entwined until her wedding ring was hidden, and smiled.

"Don't be ridiculous, Nick," she said calmly.

"Why can't we do half now and the rest later?"

"That will end up costing even more, and it will be even longer before it's all finished. I don't see what you're so worried about."

Bryony picked up the newspaper and flicked through to the business pages until she found today's story about Lehman's results.

"It says here that things are better than expected and that your bosses think the worst of the contraction is over." She ran her finger over the headline until the tip blackened. "'Lehman Net Falls Less Than Expected.' You're being too much of a bear."

"Fuld is deluded. They're on a spending spree when everyone else is tightening their belts. They're buying hedge funds at the top of the market, buying back stock to impress investors, investing in real estate when they should be selling it. We have loans on our books worth thirty-four times the value of the bank. I honestly think they've gone mad. And I'm not alone."

"Have you spoken to anyone senior?" Bryony asked in a tone that suggested she hoped that he hadn't.

"In a conference call today, I tried to point out that in June, Merrill had nineteen CDOs that couldn't be moved at the right price. They told me I was being overcautious and uncreative," Nick said. "We're at the top of the market. I can smell it. And Fuld still wants more risk."

"Lehman's shares have gone up today again, and you're sitting on a pile of stock, so please can we just give the green light to the architect, and then I can put this to one side and focus on work again?" Bryony paused for a moment. "I can always put some of my money into it and ask Dad to chip in with the rest."

"You are not to do that, Bryony," Nick said, his hand curling into a fist.

"I want to have Dad's seventieth-birthday party at the new house next June. Time isn't on our side, Nick."

So when Izzy slouched across to the table, carrying a bowl of muesli and yogurt, the early-evening snack recommended by the eating-disorders counselor, instead of praising her for eating sensibly, Bryony and Nick flew at her over her choice of outfit.

"You cannot go to the Wilbrahams' house looking like that! What will she think?" spluttered Bryony. "You look like a punk."

"I am a punk," retorted Izzy, through thick layers of purple lipstick that reminded Ali of the raspberry jelly the twins had eaten for tea.

"Punk died in the 1980s," said Bryony.

"Jacobean houses died in the sixteenth century," said Izzy. "Anyway, I'm a post-punk."

"Seventeenth, actually," Bryony corrected her.

"I don't care if you're a prehistoric punk, you look a mess," said Nick, shaking his head at Bryony as though this was all her fault. "I can't believe your school tolerates you dressing like this."

"All my school cares about is how I perform in my exams," Izzy retorted. "Anyway, I might look like a mess on the outside, but I'm less of a mess on the inside. You're always saying in front of the counselor that you love me for what I am, not how I look, so you should try and see beyond the shell to what lies beneath."

"You're being completely unreasonable, Izzy," said Bryony. Her tone softened. "Why don't we go to Selfridges this weekend? I'll call my personal shopper and book an appointment. You can buy what you like. God, I can even see the Oxfam label hanging off that leather jacket."

"Has your BlackBerry buzzed to remind you to spend quality time with your daughter?" said Izzy. She was holding a small mirror and applying kohl around her eyes. When she had finished she snapped the mirror shut and stared at Bryony.

"If I spent my days shopping and baking cakes or sat with you while you did your homework, wouldn't you question the purpose of your education?" Bryony asked. "I'm not going to apologize for having a job. And one day you'll thank me for it."

Jake came into the kitchen and announced he was going out with friends. He was meant to be working in the weeks before he started at Oxford in the first week of October, but despite endless discussion of work-experience possibilities—a week with Julian Peters at the BBC, a couple of days of filing for his godmother at the Financial Services Authority, and a stint at an advertising agency belonging to another friend of his parents'—nothing had materialized, because Jake couldn't be bothered to make the calls. Ali half wondered if she could volunteer to go instead of him.

"What makes life worth living isn't the pursuit of happiness but the happiness of pursuit. I'm trying to move away philosophically from the concept that money buys you happiness, because I don't see much evidence to endorse that particular belief system around here," Izzy continued. "And I can't do this Saturday because I'm spending the day at Aunt Hester's. Rick is giving me his old electric guitar. I'm done with the cello. The Beethoven quartet is possibly my swan song."

Ali winced. Izzy really knew how to deliver the knockout blows.

"I can't deal with this, I need to get to work," Nick suddenly announced.

"Dad, it's eight o'clock at night," said Izzy.

"Come on, Nick," said Bryony, her tone softening. She leaned over the kitchen table and rested her hand on top of his. Nick's fingers tensed beneath. "Lehman's has just written down seven hundred million dollars from their balance sheet to cover subprime losses, surely you've covered your back?"

"By my calculations we have about twenty-two billion dollars illiquid and impossible-to-price level-three mortgage assets on our books," said Nick, his nails scratching the table backward and forward beneath Bryony's hand. "No one wants to touch CDOs, Bryony." He leaned over the table toward her. "When this ship sinks, it will make Enron look like a storm in a teacup, and if you go on like this it'll take us down with it. The entire New Labour project is nothing more than temporary prosperity built on illusion. This has all the classic signs of a bubble bursting."

"So what shall I tell the architect, Nostradamus?"

"I don't care." Then he got up from the table, straightened the architect's plans, lined up pens and pencils, and left the room.

"I'm not getting changed," Izzy reiterated, as Nick went upstairs.

"Are you trying to make yourself as unattractive as possible?" Jake asked his sister as he came downstairs and headed straight to the toaster with a couple of slices of white bread. Malea rushed forward to take them from his hand and put them in.

"I want to write my own script, not follow someone else's," Izzy said. "It's a noble aspiration."

"Which self-help book are you channeling today?" Jake responded.

"At least I'm exploring my own individuality instead of subsuming my ego in a middle-aged relationship. It's pathetic the way you and Lucy are joined at the hip."

This was a new theme in Jake's post-Corfu relationship with Lucy. It had been noted by Foy in front of the rest of the family and within earshot of Ali on the last day of the holiday that Lucy referred to herself only in the first person plural. ("When we are back in London . . . When we invite friends round for dinner . . . When we go to Scotland with my parents.")

"Jake should be playing the field," Foy had drunkenly complained to Julian Peterson over a whiskey on the terrace one evening. "She's the kind of girl who'll only give a man a blowjob if she thinks there's a wedding ring involved."

"Not like my wife, then," Julian had said. Foy had looked almost hurt by the comment and muttered something about Eleanor being the type of woman that any hot-blooded man would want to "decant" from her dress, as though Julian should have taken his wife's infidelity as a compliment to his taste rather than an insult to his masculinity.

Then, back in London, Lucy had compounded the situation for Jake by buying him a pair of expensive sheepskin slippers for his nineteenth birthday and insisting that he open the present in front of the rest of his family. As if on cue, Lucy now came downstairs to let Jake know that they were expected for an early-evening drink at her parents' house.

"Don't eat white bread, Jakey," she said, removing the plate of toast from Jake's hand. "I bought you that really nice three-seed loaf." For a moment they both held the plate. Ali and Izzy watched the standoff in fascinated silence.

"Can't we just go straight-out?" asked Jake, finally allowing Lucy to take it.

"We agreed to show them the photos of Corfu," Lucy said. Ali turned round and caught his eye. He looked at his feet in embarrassment. He wasn't even a deer caught in the headlights, thought Ali, searching for the right metaphor. A deer could run away. He was more like Laurel and Hardy stuck in the cage in the twins' bedroom, eyes pleading for the purpose of their life to be revealed.

She knew from the sounds conducted by the chimney flue in her bedroom that sex between Jake and Lucy had become somewhat perfunctory. She felt mildly ashamed of herself for listening, but the dynamic of their relationship in retreat was too interesting. So she knew that Jake wanted a long, drawn-out performance. He wanted to keep the light on and observe the subtle changes in the muscles around Lucy's mouth as his hand slowly mapped previously unexplored territory. He wanted to make her come with his mouth. He wanted depth and disinhibition, while she was content to swim in the shallows, to do nothing more than keep her side of the bargain. So, while it wasn't unpleasant, and Lucy always seemed willing, there was a sense that the quicker it was all over, the better.

Ali heard Jake tell his friends that he had read enough of his sister's magazines and seen enough porn to know there was a world of pleasure that he was being denied and Lucy was denying herself. So when one of his friends started telling him how hot he thought Lucy was, Jake did nothing to discourage him.

"Shall we leave the delightful Mr. and Mrs. Skinner to their domestic idyll and head down the road?" Izzy proposed.

Lucy bristled, but her natural self-restraint meant that her fury went into angrily buttering Jake's toast. Jake simmered beside her. When Ali said good-bye, he ignored her.

Sophia Wilbraham answered the door almost as soon as Izzy rang the bell. Ali stood beside Izzy, holding the cello in front of her body, pleased to have ballast between herself and Sophia, even though she knew she looked like a bag handler.

Sophia eyed Izzy over her half-moon reading glasses. Ali noted the self-satisfaction seeping into her face as she absorbed the holes in Izzy's tights, the purple lipstick smeared on her front tooth, and the chipped black nail varnish. Not competition for Martha, Ali could see her think.

This reminded Ali of being with her mother in Cromer when she was a teenager and her sister's decline had become the talk of the town. Ali recognized the expression on Sophia's face: the self-congratulatory smile, the disapproval, and a sense of relief that her own children weren't on such an obvious trajectory to imminent self-destruction. Ali hadn't learned about schadenfreude until she joined Will MacDonald's tutor group. There was a lot of it around in the eighteenth century—Henry Mackenzie's *The Man of Feeling*, for example—and Holland Park was steeped in it.

"Such an eye-catching outfit," Sophia said as she urged them inside, out of the cold. "You put things together so . . . decoratively."

"Thanks," said Izzy, who was sufficiently aware to know Sophia's comment was dishonest even though she didn't understand her motivations.

"Sorry we're a bit late," said Ali, even though they weren't. "Bryony just got back from Russia, and she wanted to see Izzy."

She immediately regretted saying this because she knew Sophia collected information about other people and used it as a currency to be banked and traded at a later date. Even the most innocuous facts—Foy's birthday, the subject of Izzy's latest English essay (a party in which a girl accidentally falls out of a window), or the name of Jake's girlfriend—were collated and filed.

"How long has she been away?"

"Weeks," Izzy said with a sigh.

"It must be exhausting for her," Sophia said, "and for you, Ali." She gave one of her most ingratiating smiles, waiting for Ali to respond. "Such a big responsibility when I imagine Nick works long hours, too. And the twins are at such a difficult age."

"She's only away for a couple of days at a time. At most."

Sophia gave her a suspicious look, as though trying to gauge whether Ali had been instructed to withhold detail. She lacked the psychological skills to intuit that Izzy might have her own reasons for casting her mother in the worst light possible. Instead she clung on to her easy-bake stereotype of Bryony as a typical working mother paying the price for her selfish ways with a wayward daughter and freaky twins. She preferred not to dwell on Jake, who had learned he had three A's in his A-levels when they were in Corfu.

"Bryony should have come and had a drink with us," Sophia said

"She's too busy discussing the new house with Daddy," Izzy countered. Ali poked Izzy with the tail spike of the cello. Izzy ignored her and took a side step. "It needs a lot of work."

"What house?" asked Sophia.

"You know how Mum always has to have a project," continued Izzy. Sophia nodded so vigorously that her glasses nudged to the end of her nose and her double chins gently undulated. She stared at Izzy, intently awaiting further information.

"Well, they've bought a house in the country," Izzy explained, "an old Jacobean pile in Oxfordshire. I haven't actually seen it yet. But we're all going there this weekend, when Mum gets back from Russia."

"She's going away again?" questioned Sophia.

"Just for a couple of days," Ali interrupted.

"Well, at least I'm on hand to fill in the musical gaps," Sophia said.

"Thank goodness," said Izzy. Sophia gave a harrumph of satisfaction that made the button on the side of her skirt pop open.

"How much revision have you been doing for your mocks, Izzy?" Sophia asked as they trailed after her into the house.

"Four hours every night," Izzy said politely. Sophia looked at her in confusion, torn between worry over the revelation because Martha's schedule was definitely lighter and uncertainty whether Izzy was telling the truth.

"Beethoven calls," she said finally, urging Izzy into the sitting room. "We're going to focus on the third movement."

Ali went in behind Izzy to hand over the cello. Martha was tuning her violin at the piano. She gave an embarrassed half-wave to Ali, caught her eye for a moment, and then quickly looked away. Ali thought back to the party in Notting Hill. She considered the gulf between Sophia Wilbraham's perception of Martha and the reality of her life. It was the same with Bryony and Izzy. It could be argued that Bryony was even less insightful because she had worried less about Izzy when she was on track to develop a full-fledged eating disorder than she did now that she was slowly recovering.

Then Ali thought of her mother and Jo. Even when it was obvious to Ali, at age fourteen, that the way her sister came home in the early hours of the morning and then slept until four o'clock in the afternoon had more to do with drug time-tabling than the adolescent body clock, her mother still wanted to believe that Jo was simply going through a phase common to most teenagers in Cromer. Her father had been more realistic. He noticed the acne, the way Jo stopped wearing short-sleeved tops, the sunken eyes, and pleaded with his wife and daughter to get some outside help. Perhaps this blind spot was something common to all mothers. Maybe they didn't want to see, or they thought the antidote to their children's problems was simply to love them more.

She noticed Martha was wearing a shirt with the buttons conservatively fastened almost to the top. She couldn't get rid of the image of her breast in the boy's mouth. Ali felt a stab of compassion. She knew from Izzy that the boy hadn't spoken to her since and had complained on his Facebook page that she had hairy nipples. Martha had subsequently gone to a beautician and not only had all these hairs removed but had a Brazilian, too.

"Don't you think women should sign a nonproliferation of depilation treaty, Ali?" Izzy had said after she told her this story. "Or the boy who wrote it should be given a Brazilian?"

"The latter sounds more practical," Ali had said, and laughed.

Ali smiled as she recalled this conversation. Now that Izzy was eating more, she was less moody. Although she had confessed to Ali that she still kept a diary in which she recorded everything that she consumed, including the number of times she brushed her teeth each day, because toothpaste contained calories, she said she hadn't deviated from the target weight set by the counselor. Most important, she had stopped visiting the awful pro-ana websites.

Ali was reassured by her openness because she had read enough on the Internet to know that secrecy was one of the main components of anorexia. And although Bryony didn't see it this way, Izzy's imperfect appearance was a good measure of the distance she had put between herself and her eating disorder. It was Bryony who told Ali that anorexia and perfectionism went hand in hand, but she didn't seem to be able to apply the reverse logic to her own daughter.

"She's put on weight," said Sophia, as she led Ali back into the hall and suggested that she go downstairs into the kitchen to find Katya. Ali was about to explain that it was a terrible idea to say something like that within earshot of a girl climbing out of the abyss of an eating disorder. But she stopped herself because she realized Sophia was fishing for information to confirm the diagnosis.

"I'll just say a quick hello," said Ali, who had avoided being alone with Katya since the summer.

Katya was in the basement kitchen, cooking. She was cutting beetroot and cabbage on a chopping board, her precision seemingly uncompromised by the speed of the knife. Her hands were blood red with juice. On the cooker two large, spicy-smelling sausages were slow-frying in a pan.

"Hello, stranger," she said, coming over to hug Ali. "I'm making borscht. It's Thomas's favorite. He must be the only three-year-old in London who chooses beetroot soup over fish fingers. I swear his soul is Ukrainian."

Ali listened halfheartedly. When it came to Thomas, Katya was worse than the most indulgent mother or obsessed lover.

"Maybe Sophia ate lots of beetroot when she was breast-feeding," Ali suggested.

"She didn't breast-feed," said Katya a little too quickly. "I fed Thomas bottled milk."

"I just came down to say hello," said Ali, pointing at the staircase. "I'm going to come back to collect Izzy later. Bryony's just arrived home."

"You don't need to explain," Katya said in her curious clipped accent. She continued chopping, the knife now gliding expertly backward and forward across an onion. There were no tears. Her hair was tied back off her face, and she was wearing a simple vest top and black miniskirt. The ingredients and saucepans were lined up in orderly fashion beside the cooker as though trying to impress her with their cooperation.

There was no recipe book. Unlike Malea, who had taken to Delia Smith's *How to Cook* as if it were a sacred text, and then refused to deviate, Katya cooked from memory and instinct. She tore up parsley, sprinkled it into the stock, leaning over to sniff the aroma, then chopped up a clove of garlic and did the same thing again.

She had a smooth way of moving that reminded Ali of treacle sliding off a spoon.

Ali couldn't stop watching her. She wondered whether Katya was conscious of the attention she attracted. And even though she meant to leave straightaway, Ali found herself perching on a stool beside the kitchen island, observing her as she cooked and talked about Thomas.

Even when she dropped a small spice jar on the floor and bent down to pick it up, it seemed part of a single fluid movement. She was liquid. No wonder Sophia Wilbraham's husband wanted to slide into her at any opportunity.

Ali had never got beyond the front door of the Wilbrahams' house before, and she was taken aback to find that the kitchen was almost an exact replica of the one she had just left behind a couple of streets away. The stove was a different color. The worktop was a slightly darker shade of granite. But the layout was so familiar that when she opened the cupboard to the side of the staircase, she knew she would find plates on the bottom shelf and soup bowls on the top.

"She used the same architect and interior decorator," said Katya, noticing Ali's expression. "If I had so much money I would try and be more original, but Sophia has big crush on Bryony." She shrugged.

"I thought they loathed each other," said Ali.

"Love and hate often sleep in the same bed, don't you think?" Katya said.

Which bed do you sleep in? Ali wondered. Then she reproached herself. She wanted limited engagement. Low-intensity conversation. A frugality of detail that was totally at odds with Katya's personality. She knew Bryony would be at home, waiting to discuss the daybook. Ali had written a week's worth of notes the previous evening. She had used a different-colored pen for each day, and had recklessly embellished incidents involving the twins and details about Izzy's progress at school, as much for her own entertainment as to assuage Bryony's curiosity about the life her children led when apart from her. But Katya always posed more questions than she answered, and Ali always found it difficult to resist.

"Isn't she always being rude about Bryony?" Ali asked.

"Absolutely," said Katya. "She criticizes Bryony for neglecting her children in favor of her career, for wanting publicity, for the vanity of having a personal trainer, the amount of money she spends on clothes, the twins' behavior . . . everything. But really she wants to *be* her. It's because she is uncertain about the decisions she has made about her own life."

It was an unusually charitable analysis of her employer. Perhaps Katya felt more sympathy for Sophia now that she was having an affair with her husband. Ali thought back to Will MacDonald and remembered how at the peak of their relationship, when lack of detection made them ever more bold (she had started regularly visiting him at his office, they had sex in the bed he shared with his wife, and they went to the cinema a couple of times), she was ever more friendly to his wife. At one point she even imagined his wife knew about their relationship and condoned it because it made him happier and therefore easier to live with.

"I know that you saw us," Katya said suddenly, as she poured the rest of the ingredients into the stock and turned round to face Ali. Ali nodded, acknowledging the truth of her statement but unsure how exactly to respond. So she did what her father did when he found himself in a tight corner, and said nothing because people couldn't tolerate silence.

"He's in love with me," Katya explained. She said it neutrally, so that it was impossible to gauge her feelings about the situation. There was no evidence of joy or unhappiness. Was Katya in love with him? Or was she merely tolerating his love for her? Did she think she might be fired if she turned him down? Ali was still running through these scenarios in her head when Katya came over and sat down on a stool beside her and put her hand on her forearm.

Ali looked nervously toward the staircase, worried that Sophia might be coming downstairs, but she could hear her barking orders at the quartet through the ceiling. *"Andante, andante, andante,"* she bellowed.

"Ned is going to leave her," Katya said, her finger pointing up to the sitting room above, "and we are going to move in together."

"You can't do that," said Ali firmly.

"It is what Ned wants." Katya shrugged. She closed her eyes and nodded sagely, as though she had spoken some inviolable truth.

"Is it what you want?"

"She is looking for a new nanny, Ali. She wants me out of here."

"But that isn't something binary, Katya."

"What do you mean?"

"I mean that just because Sophia wants to replace you, it doesn't mean that you should move in with her husband. It's what we call fucked-up logic."

"He is in love with me," Katya repeated.

"Are you in love with him?"

"Yes," said Katya unconvincingly. Ali tried a new tack.

"What about Thomas? It will make him so unhappy if his parents get divorced."

"Ned and I will get married. I will become Thomas's stepmother. I will always be part of his life." It sounded as though she was in a language class, practicing her use of the future tense.

"He might eventually resent you for breaking up the marriage between his father and mother. Have you thought about that?"

"Thomas and I have a special bond. He loves me."

"And what about Sophia?"

"She will find someone else. Ned will give her money. He is a very rich man," she said in a matter-of-fact tone. "Ali, be happy. This is a very good option for me."

"Are you doing this because you are worried that if you lose your job then you won't see Thomas anymore?" Ali asked.

"Of course," said Katya.

"But that isn't a good reason," Ali persisted. "Have you told Mira?"

"Of course."

"What did she say?"

"She understands my struggle because it is also her struggle," Katya said enigmatically. "You are very nice person, Ali, but you can't put yourself in my boots."

"Shoes," Ali corrected her. "I can't put myself in your shoes."

"Do you know the story of how we came here?" Katya asked. She went to the fridge, took out a bottle of wine, and poured Ali a glass.

Ali looked down at her watch and saw that it was almost a quarter to nine. She might as well wait for Izzy to finish and then go home.

"I've always felt that you and Mira didn't really want to talk about it," Ali said. "But I'd love to hear it."

Katya stared straight ahead at a point located in the middle of the fridge. Ali assumed she was trying to collect her thoughts, struggling to remember an event that took place years earlier. But as Katya began to tell her story, Ali realized that it was as though she was describing something taking place before her right now. It was so vivid that she slipped into the present tense.

"I come from a village in northern Ukraine, southeast of Odessa. My family is very poor. My father leaves us, so I go to Kiev to find a job working in a bar. But I earn less than two hundred dollars a month. One day a man comes to the bar and says he is looking for girls to go and work in Europe as nannies. The man owns a travel agency in the center of Kiev. He tells me that he can get me a fake Czech passport and that I can get a student visa and work for a family in Western Europe because I speak English. He shows me pictures of different families and children, and e-mails they sent with details of the job."

The soup on the cooker had started to boil. Bubbles of purple liquid erupted on the surface, sending small jets onto the stove that Katya didn't seem to notice.

"I was seventeen. I was studying English in university during the day and working all night. I was so tired that I couldn't sleep, my vision was blurred, and I was losing weight. This man wanted to help me. Wouldn't you have done the same?"

"Yes," said Ali, who made a point of agreeing with Katya whenever possible. "So is that how you met Mira?"

"I didn't know Mira then." Katya paused for a moment and released Ali's arm. Ali looked down and saw red marks where Katya's fingers had pressed into her flesh.

"In September 1998, I meet this man at his office. There are six other girls. One of them I know from university. He points at posters of the Acropolis, Big Ben, and Florence on the wall and tells us that

within a week we will be in Europe. We set off together in the middle
of the night, heading for Poland. There are two Czech drivers. They
teach us how to say our name in Czech and how to say hello so that
we don't have problems crossing into Poland. We drive through the
night. I worry about the passport they have given me because the ink
is smudged.

"We eat some of the food we have brought with us, and we hide
any money we have in our shoes because they say it will be taken from
us at the border. I have one hundred dollars. When we get to the border they give us our Czech passports and we cross to the other side,
and then they take them away from us again."

Katya stopped and picked up her handbag from the floor. She drew
out a small leather purse and pulled out two fifty-dollar bills from
the side.

"This is the money. I keep it to remind me where I come from and
what I had to do to get to where I am." Then she took the bills, ironed
them flat with her hand before carefully folding them into four and
putting them back inside the wallet again. This had obviously been
repeated so many times that Ulysses Grant's features were completely
impressionistic.

"Once we cross the border we go in a different vehicle with different drivers. Two more girls join us. There are other men with us. I
don't talk to anyone. Not even the girl from university. We are so
afraid people might hear us. We travel at night. Sometimes we stop in
a wood to sleep. When we reach the Czech border we are divided into
small groups so we don't draw attention to ourselves. I am lucky
because the passport they have given me has two German stamps in it.
One of the girls is refused entry, and they just leave her. I wish it is me,
because I don't trust the people we are with."

"So where were you now?" Ali asked, wishing she had paid more
notice to the geography of central Europe when she was at school.

"Czech Republic," said Katya patiently. "More cars pick us up. I
am back with the original group of girls. This time the drivers speak
Russian. We leave the border, and we drive for maybe two days. My

food has run out. We stop once at a garage and I manage to fill my water bottle. Then that afternoon the car turns off the road and we go down a track through a forest."

Ali noticed that Katya's hands had begun to shake. Upstairs she could hear raised voices. Someone shouted. Footsteps stamped across the floor. A door slammed. Then there was silence. She should go up, but nothing seemed more important than listening to Katya, who was oblivious to the commotion above.

"I think they are going to kill us. One of the girls starts crying. The men just laugh and offer us vodka, but all of us refuse. I have paid one thousand dollars for the passport in Kiev, and they start saying that I owe them more money for organizing the journey. They tell me that I will have to work for them until I have paid them back. I tell them I have a job as a nanny in England, and they laugh in my face."

"Why didn't you tell me any of this before?" Ali asked.

"Because I look forward, not backward," said Katya, "and sometimes if I talk about it I have nightmares."

"Would you rather stop now, then?" Ali asked. Katya shook her head, closed her eyes, and began talking again.

"We reach a river. It is so wide you can't see the other side, and we wait there until it is dark. They get drunk and forget to take back the passports. Then they put the car on a raft and we get inside and the raft sets off across the water. It is so bumpy that some of us are sick. I put my passport in a plastic bag and hide it down my trousers. We have almost reached the other side when the raft hits something in the water and turns over. Two of the girls drown. They can't swim, and it is so cold. They scream for me to help them, but there is nothing I can do. I see them go underwater, and then they are quiet. I hear people calling us, and I try to swim toward their voices. The current is strong, but I manage to get to the riverbank. When I get out I find another group of Ukrainians. One of them is Mira.

"The man from the car comes over and says that I belong to him and they should hand me over. Mira argues with him in Russian. In the end she gives him two hundred dollars to let me go with her group. The other two girls stay with him. Mira's guide tells me the man I escaped from was working for a group of Ukrainians who traffic women to work in the sex industry. There were no jobs as nannies. It is all lies. My friend from university was never seen again. Her parents have never heard from her. They think she was maybe taken to Athens and forced to work as a prostitute. Or maybe Israel. Or England."

"That is so awful, Katya," Ali said.

"It is the way of the world. Since the fall of communism women have just become another commodity. Like oil and gas."

"Does Ned know all this?"

"Ned wants a woman who will look after him and make him feel good about himself. Anyway, my experience is worse than some but better than most. I am free."

"What happened to the man who trafficked you?" Ali asked. "Was he caught?"

"The man who owned the travel agency?" Katya asked. Ali nodded. "He is now one of the richest men in Ukraine. He's one of Bryony's clients, actually."

"How do you know that?" Ali asked.

"Ned told me."

"How does he know about Bryony's clients?"

"From Nick."

"But they hardly ever see each other."

"They talk on the phone," said Katya. She paused for emphasis. "A lot, a lot."

15

∷∷∷∷∷

On her way back to number ninety-seven, Ali's phone rang. Izzy was in the middle of a tirade about Sophia Wilbraham, which Ali was diplomatically ignoring, although she sympathized completely with its sentiment. She could easily have derailed the diatribe with a couple of questions, but she was too intrigued to hear about what had occurred upstairs. Besides, it provided a useful counterpoint to distract her from what Katya had just told her. Ali looked down at the screen, saw it was her mother, and decided to let it go on to voice mail, where it joined the other drifts of messages her parents had left over the past couple of months.

"There's no such thing as a short conversation with my mother," Ali joked, investing the relationship with a lightheartedness that didn't really exist.

"Tell me about it," sympathized Izzy, before returning to the subject of Sophia.

"She told me I hadn't practiced enough and said that if I devoted as much energy to my music as I did to chasing boys then the third movement wouldn't be such a mess."

Ali smiled because Izzy was doing a very good impersonation of the sanctimonious tone adopted by Sophia when she passed judgment on other people's shortcomings. "At which point Martha went as red as that soup Katya makes, so I knew she was the source. Then Sophia said it was a shame that instead of my mother being around to instill discipline, I was abandoned in the third movement of my childhood to the whims of an unknown and inexperienced twenty-something nanny from the sticks."

Ali bristled. The curious thing about Sophia Wilbraham was that it took only the tiniest exposure for any positive feelings you might have about her to curdle. So any residual pity for her husband's betrayal immediately evaporated.

"How did you respond?"

"I told her that most of my energy was devoted to sustaining my borderline eating disorder, and if Martha was anything to go by, then sexual abstinence was no prerequisite for musical flair, as demonstrated by the huge love bite she was trying to cover up on her neck."

"Brilliant."

"I'm always much more articulate when I'm angry. I think listening to Joy Division helps me to mine it more efficiently. It's all to do with externalizing feelings rather than being passive. Loathing rather than self-loathing."

Jake was right. Izzy was beginning to sound a little like a self-help book.

"Then she made Martha undo her shirt and saw the love bite. She started shouting at her, and Martha threw her violin on the floor, stomped out of the room, went upstairs, and Sophia declared the practice session over."

"Did she say anything else?"

"She said we needed to speed up the adagio. The other girl said the teacher had told us to slow it down, and she said he was completely wrong and that she'd heard way more live performances than he'd eaten hot dinners. She literally barked at us."

Ali's phone rang a second time.

"Bad use of 'literally,'" said Ali, glancing down at the screen to see that it was her mother again. "If you say that, it means she actually did bark."

"Don't be pedantic. Anyway, Sophia makes Leicester look submissive, and her voice sounds way more animal than human."

"Good use of 'pedantic,' though."

Again Ali ignored the phone in her bag and instead pulled out a packet of cigarettes.

"I won't say anything," Izzy promised.

"Thanks," said Ali, as she took a deep drag and considered how to handle her parents.

She had resolved to get in touch with them when she got back from Corfu at the end of August. But she'd held back because she still hadn't established when she could have time off. Bryony was working almost every weekend for the next month. This Sunday she was meant to fly to the United Arab Emirates. The following weekend she would be visiting an aluminum smelter in Kazakhstan. The Saturday after that she had another meeting with the builders and the architect in Oxfordshire. It seemed incredible how she could crisscross the globe while Ali found it difficult to leave Holland Park.

She was less certain of Nick's movements, but even if he were around he wouldn't want Ali to leave him alone with the children. Izzy had once let slip that he'd never looked after them alone for more than a couple of hours at a time.

So Ali wanted to avoid her mother until she could appease her by confirming a date. She also wanted to avoid any conversation that ended with her defending the Skinners from accusations that they were taking advantage of her good nature. It had become a bit of a theme of late, as it dawned on her parents that she wasn't going back to university this year. Just before the summer, Ali had finally told them that she was considering staying for another year, and revealed exactly how much money she was earning. Her mother had fallen silent at the other end of the phone.

"I think actually she is a man . . . her hands are enormous, like great hams . . . She clicked her fingers at Katya . . . She said Alfie and Hector made Romulus and Remus look positively domesticated," Izzy continued.

"Disturbing," said Ali, but really she was thinking about her parents.

"Is this what happens to women if they give up work once they've had children?" asked Izzy. "I thought Mum was pretty controlling, but at least she has to let go when she goes to work."

"Maybe Mrs. Wilbraham has invested her chance at happiness in just one thing. It's a high-risk gamble: it could reap huge benefits, but it also increases her exposure if things don't work out. She's over-leveraged."

"You sound like Dad talking about his bloody job." Izzy laughed. "What I don't understand is why Martha's dad married her. He's so relaxed about everything. She should have been shelf-bound, don't you think?" She was using Foy's favorite phrase to describe an unattractive woman who, in his view, didn't merit a husband.

"She probably wasn't like that when he married her. It's difficult to keep perspective when you have children. They swallow you up until they're ready to spit you out, and then you're left wondering what remains of you."

"Is that what happened to your mother?"

"My older sister, Jo, swallowed us all up."

"What do you mean? In a predatory way? Like a shark?"

"She wasn't intent on destruction, but she somehow managed to chew up everything around her. Jo had lots of problems, and that didn't leave much room for the rest of us. Mum, Dad, and I were all focused on her."

"What kind of problems?" Izzy asked. Ali hesitated for a moment, weighing up whether to tell the truth.

"Drugs," she said finally. "But don't say anything."

"Weed?"

"Everything. She wasn't picky."

"So did you come here to escape all that?" Izzy asked.

"In part," said Ali vaguely.

"Is that why you were so worried about me at that party?"

"Among other things," said Ali. "I was worried about you because you're my responsibility and if that boy had put that clip on YouTube, then it would have happened on my watch. And even if we'd managed to get it taken down, that's what everyone would remember about you."

"You really care about us, don't you, Ali? You don't just think we're spoiled and worthless?" Izzy asked nervously.

"Of course not," said Ali cautiously. "Your life is just very different from mine."

"In what way?"

"You don't have to worry about money in the same way. You have unimaginable opportunity. You take things for granted. But I don't think this necessarily buys you freedom. It just buys you choices and a bigger burden of expectation."

They had reached the steps outside the Skinners' house. For a moment, Ali stopped and stared. By night the house looked even more imposing. Two spotlights attached to the railings reflected back onto the façade, picking out the bay windows of the drawing room on one side and a huge camellia growing in a pot on the other. Ali coolly observed the blue plaque on the side of the house, the icy surface of the chrome number on the front door, and the high-gloss black railings. It was still difficult to believe that she really lived here, cheek by jowl with this family, that she was on first-name terms with the next-door neighbors, that the car sitting outside on the off-street parking had been bought for her, that she had helped the twins plant in the wildflower window boxes sitting on the window ledges on either side of the front door. What did it say about someone if she could adapt so seamlessly to the rhythms of another family's life and so quickly forget her own?

There was a light on in every room on the first three floors. In the drawing room she could see Bryony examining invitations on the mantelpiece. In the adjacent window she thought she glimpsed Foy's hair poking above an armchair. Downstairs in the kitchen Malea was scrubbing saucepans. Little vignettes of contented domesticity that reminded Ali of an Advent calendar. She smiled at Izzy as she got out her keys and expertly turned the lock. The Skinners were insulated from the outside world, and she was happy to take her place in their cocoon.

"By the way, did you know Martha thinks her dad is in love with their nanny?" Izzy said as they went into the hallway. "That's why she always whistles the theme tune to *The Sound of Music* when Katya comes in the room."

"Martha has a very fertile imagination," said Ali a little too quickly.

Down in the kitchen, Ali paused for a moment to listen to her phone messages as Izzy said good night to her mother and grandfather. There were four. The first one was from Bryony, wondering when she would be home to discuss the daybook. The rest, disappointingly, were all from her mother. Rosa had stopped phoning, no doubt fed up with the way it took so long for Ali to return her calls. She hadn't heard from Will MacDonald in more than six months.

"Jo's home," the messages from Ali's mother said. Or, more accurately, "Jo's hum."

The sound of her mother's slow, undulating accent with its elongated vowels and lilt at the end of the sentence made Ali smile. The English language was born in East Anglia, her mother had told her when she first noticed Ali's efforts to erase her Norfolk accent. She should feel proud of it. It was a piece of advice Ali remembered, because her mother's interventions in her life were so rare. She closed her eyes and for a moment allowed herself to be enshrouded in its familiarity.

Any fleeting pleasure, however, was swiftly supplanted by irritation at the deadpan tone of the rest of the message. It was impossible to tell whether her mother was elated or discomfited by Jo's return. There was no note of either triumphalism or exhaustion. Ali knew it was a ploy to force her to call back to see what was going on so that she would be drawn into another drama involving her sister. She felt guilty for feeling irritated, and further irritated that she should feel guilty. It was an old loop: Ali's desire to be free from the shackles of family expectation, followed by the claustrophobic sense of responsibility. Something the Skinner children could also identify with. She dutifully dialed her mother's number.

"Hi, Mum, it's Ali," she said as her mother picked up the phone after just one ring.

"Alison, is that you?" her mother responded.

"I said it was me," said Ali, trying to suppress her impatience. "I just picked up your message."

"I left more than one."

Outside, she could hear Leicester barking plaintively. She went to the window and saw that the sliding doors were covered in muddy paw prints. Where was Malea?

"I can't hear you, you're cracking up."

"Breaking up." Ali smiled. She opened the sliding doors just enough to allow Leicester in. He looked affronted, and Ali apologized, informing him she wasn't to blame.

"Who are you talking to?" her mother asked suspiciously.

"The dog."

"Are you listening to me?" her mother asked. "You don't call us for months, and then you give the dog more attention than me."

"How's Jo?"

"She'd love to see you."

"Why hasn't she called me, then?"

"Don't be difficult, Ali."

"Can I speak to her now?"

"She's gone out."

"How does she seem?"

"The same," said her mother carefully.

"The same good or the same bad?" Ali asked, knowing that she would never get a straightforward answer because her mother was permanently pitched between the desire to believe that Jo was all right and the dread that perhaps she was lurching into a new crisis.

"Your dad tried to get her to go out on the boat with him, but she wanted to stay in bed." This was bad news. Ali slumped down on the sofa, and Leicester jumped up to sit beside her. She was used to these vague answers, and over the years had come to appreciate that perhaps they contained a more essential truth than a simple black-and-white response. Her father believed, as did Ali, that the sea had a curative effect on the soul. Ali loved watching the lights of Cromer fade and the soft pink tones of dawn emerge on the horizon, as they headed away from shore to check the crab pots. When Jo was well, she agreed with them. When things were bad she saw the sea as her tormentor, which it could be after five hours in a boat when it was blowing up rough.

"She's thinking about another clinic. It's expensive. We're not sure whether it's the right place, Ali. We can take out more money against the mortgage, but it's a stretch."

"Do you want me to come home?"

"Yes," said her mother emphatically.

Ali took a deep breath and gently pushed open the drawing room door. Foy peered around the top of his seat by the fireplace and squinted at her.

"It's the Sparrow," he boomed. "What news do you bring from the kingdom of birds? What's your tweet of the day?"

"Hello, Mr. Chesterton," said Ali, coming into the room.

"Call me Foy, for God's sake, otherwise you make me feel old," he shouted through stained teeth. Ali noticed an almost empty bottle of red wine on the table beside him.

"One thing about sparrows that you should know, Ali. They mate for life. Although the odd single sparrow has been known to try and steal someone else's mate."

"I didn't know that," said Ali.

"Would you like a glass of wine?" Bryony asked, nodding vigorously at Ali to indicate she should say yes. Bryony filled the glass until the bottle was empty.

"I was wondering if I could have a quick word with you, Bryony," said Ali.

"It's time we went home," said Tita, whom Ali had just noticed standing by the window, staring out into the street. She turned her head slowly and smiled enigmatically.

"Where have you come from?" Foy asked. Ali explained about the music practice at Sophia Wilbraham's house, going into more detail than necessary about the technical challenges of the third movement without revealing any hint of the drama that had just taken place, in the hope of boring him into silence.

"How that woman ended up marrying Ned Wilbraham I cannot understand," said Foy, shaking his head. "I've never met a more shelf-bound female. Of course, she thoroughly disapproves of me. I think I once made a pass at her mother when I was drunk. She was all right. Less agricultural."

"Dad," Bryony reprimanded him.

"I'm saying nothing your mother doesn't know already," Foy said petulantly. "Am I, Tita?" Tita didn't respond.

"It's all in the arse with Sophia, isn't it? I saw her on the beach in Corfu. She practically blocked out the sun with her backside. It's like a planet that the rest of her body orbits around. It's funny how women get like that while old men struggle to hold a pencil between their buttocks. Not Tita, of course." He glanced over at his wife, hoping his approval met with her approval.

"You can't talk about Sophia like that. You'll end up saying some-thing in front of Izzy," Bryony chastised him.

"How can you compare Izzy to that woman?" Foy exploded.

"I'm not," explained Bryony. "I'm just trying to tell you that we don't talk about weight issues in this house. It's one of the things the anorexia counselor has recommended. We talk about healthy eating."

"God, you're all in thrall to bloody self-help gurus," Foy said. "If Winston Churchill was alive now, they'd have sent him to Alcoholics

Anonymous and got someone else to run the war. Then we'd be having this conversation in German."

"It might have made life easier for his wife, though," murmured Tita. She turned to Bryony. "He'll fall asleep in a minute. It's always the storm then the calm with Foy."

"But then he'll end up spending the night here," said Bryony. "Nick's tolerance levels are not very high at the moment. He's under a lot of stress at work."

"Stress," said Foy, repeating the word in disbelief at least a couple of times. "He doesn't know the meaning of the word. When I set up Freithshire Fisheries, I woke up every night for five years worrying about how I was going to pay back my bank loan. That's creative. He's just investing other people's money. Mine, probably."

"That's why it's called investment banking," said Bryony tartly. "He's very worried about the Lehman's board steering the bank in the wrong direction." She was trying to impress her father by underlining Nick's seniority in the bank and his courage in swimming against the tide of opinion. Ali was struck that everything Bryony had just said ran counter to what she had told Nick earlier in the evening. "He's trying to get them to write down more debt. You saw what happened with Northern Rock. There's a problem with liquidity at the moment. Markets are jittery. People want credit and they can't get it. The cost of borrowing is rising."

"He'll find a way of making money out of everyone else's misery," said Foy. "That's his specialty. Ali, have I ever told you how I set up my smoked-salmon business? Now, that's an interesting tale. It's a love story and a thriller packed into one."

"This isn't the moment," pleaded Bryony.

"You know, I think they're trying to force me out completely," Foy announced suddenly. He slumped back into the chair, his energy sapped, like Hector after a tantrum. "After everything I've done to build up the company."

"What do you mean?" asked Tita.

"The board gave me a vote of no confidence because I refused to endorse the move toward organic. They want me to resign. What's the point of farming half as many fish for twice the cost? It doesn't make financial sense."

"Dad, you knew this might happen," said Bryony. "They've been talking about it for ages."

"They're fiddling around cultivating native sea urchins to feed on the beds below, and seaweeds to take out the nitrates and phosphates the salmon put in. And they're introducing a fallowing system every other year. They're not going to use antibiotics anymore, and they've got the endorsement of Freedom Food. I'm surprised they haven't recruited a fucking acupuncturist to keep the fish relaxed."

"It's a sound plan," said Bryony. "Why can't you just agree with them? All businesses need to evolve. We're about to set up a public-affairs unit to lobby government on behalf of different clients. And sustainable development is the theme du jour for investors."

"I'm too old for change." Foy sighed, closing his eyes. Within minutes he had fallen into a deep sleep.

"Leave him, Mum," said Bryony gently. "I'll get Malea to make up a bed for him and send him home in the morning."

Bryony and Tita talked briefly about Foy's seventieth-birthday party. Should Nick make a speech? Would the renovations be finished by June next year? Should they get Fi Seldon-Kent to organize the event? Should the grandchildren play music or do a sketch? It wasn't the moment to ask Bryony whether she could go home for a couple of days over the weekend, but tomorrow would be too late. Ali walked toward Bryony and Tita and coughed lightly.

"Yes?" said Bryony impatiently.

Ali presented her dilemma in the most impressionistic terms ("Something has come up . . . an unforeseen event . . . My mother has summoned me home"). When she saw Bryony's tongue twisting in her cheek, she regretted the tactic and wished she had just come out with the truth, because then she might have shown more compassion.

"It's really inconvenient." Bryony hadn't raised her voice, but it took on that taut, brittle quality that Ali recognized as the prelude to an outburst. Struggling to keep an even tone and scratching at a small groove in the table that Hector had carved out, Bryony carefully explained that it would make life very difficult if Ali was to do this.

"When you accepted this job you promised that you would always put the needs of our family first. I know you haven't had much time off, but you can take ten days at Christmas."

"I need to help my parents with something."

"Is there a problem with money? Because if there is, then perhaps we can help you out."

"That's a very kind offer," said Ali, taken aback by the lack of imagination in Bryony's one-dimensional response to her situation. "Thank you. But it's not a question of money."

"Treat it as a bonus for your first year's work," insisted Bryony.

"I can't do that," said Ali, who thought it sounded more like a bribe than a bonus.

"Could Katya cover for you?" suggested Bryony. Ali thought for a moment. She remembered the way Katya had eyes only for Thomas in the pool in Corfu.

"I think it's a big responsibility," said Ali. There was a long silence.

"How would you feel about the twins going with you?" asked Bryony finally. "It would be lovely for them to meet your parents and have a weekend away from London."

Ali considered Bryony's suggestion. Her parents wouldn't mind. If Bryony had any inkling about her sister, she betrayed nothing.

"Is there enough room?" Bryony asked.

"It's a great idea," said Ali. "My parents love small children." Bryony beamed with satisfaction that a mutually beneficial compromise had been found so quickly.

"This is what I love about you," she said, "your ability to be flexible and think on your feet. Remind me to give you a set of Jo Malone candles for your mother and sister. What's their favorite aroma? Lime, basil, and mandarin?" She picked up her BlackBerry and punched in a reminder. Ali was relieved that she had looked away.

She was gripped by an absurd image of Jo using the scented candle to cook up heroin in a teaspoon and had to stifle the urge to giggle by pinching her hand.

16

So Ali ended up spending her first weekend at home in more than a year with Alfie and Hector in tow. And, at the last minute, Izzy, who announced that she didn't want to stay in London playing gooseberry to Jake and Lucy.

"What about me?" Jake had asked as they left the house for the train station on Saturday morning. Ali laughed until she realized he was only half joking.

"We're going for lunch with my sister and brother-in-law," Lucy reminded him, linking her arm with his. "We're going to see their new baby."

"You could spend the morning in Hatton Garden," Izzy called back to Jake as they left the house.

"What happens there?" Ali asked, as they climbed into a taxi to take them to the station.

"It's where people go to buy wedding rings." Izzy giggled. "She's got him by the *cojones*."

When they arrived in Cromer in the early afternoon, Ali's father was waiting for them at the train station. Jim Sparrow was hunched over against the wind and wearing a pair of trousers belonging to an old suit that Ali hadn't seen for years and a jacket with leather patches at the elbows. The latter she suspected had been hastily purchased from the rails of one of the secondhand shops on the High Street after her late-night phone call to warn her parents that she wouldn't be alone.

Ali felt a pang in her stomach for the effort he was making, particularly given the fact that Izzy was in one of her more outlandish ensembles, involving a pair of heavy platform lace-up boots, fishnet tights, and a very short miniskirt with suspenders. Not that her father would react. This was a man, after all, who had once gone to the squat in Norwich, where his oldest daughter was living; found Jo semiconscious, lying in a pool of her own vomit; and carried her in his arms back to his car like a small child. He had walked past the group of spotty, sunken-eyed junkies who watched him without saying a word.

Moreover, Jim Sparrow was a nonjudgmental man. "Never assume anything about anyone until you know what's going on beneath the surface" was one of the few pieces of advice he handed down to his daughters. He used the example of the sea. Just offshore of the Devil's Mouth was a chalk ridge that stretched for miles along the coast with a network of sea life that supported a whole ecosystem of marine creatures, some of which had never been identified. He had seen it with his own eyes. On a still October morning the sea might appear leaden and dull, but beneath the surface was a hidden world waiting to be explored. Human beings were no different.

It was an attitude that had helped Ali to blend in with the Skinners. She neither passed judgment on their life nor was impressed by it. Their wealth, their complicated relationships, their topsy-turvy morality all washed over her like the sea over that chalk ridge. It was this quality that came to define her life with the Skinners during this middle period, because if she hadn't been so open perhaps they would have been less inclined to drop their guard with her.

Jim gave Ali a quick hug. He smelled of cheap aftershave, mothballs, and crab. She clung on to him even after he let go.

"I've missed you, Daddy," she said.

"It's good to have you home, girl," he said gruffly.

"She's coming back with us," said Hector, holding on tightly to Ali's hand. Jim smiled at his vehemence.

"What's your name, boy?" He bent down to Hector's height.

"What's that on your face?" Hector asked suspiciously. Jim gave his daughter a quizzical look.

"It's a beard," explained Ali.

"There's a bit missing," said Hector.

"It's called a chinstrap beard," said Jim.

"*Balbas,*" said Alfie and Hector at the same time.

"What are they saying?" Jim asked Ali as he stood up.

"They sometimes have their own words for things," she explained.

She introduced Izzy, who was trying hopelessly to stop her hair from blowing about in the wind. "Thanks so, so much for having me to stay. I've always wanted to come to Cromer." The enthusiasm was an affectation. It was the same tone Tita adopted if Ali made her a cup of tea or read Foy stories from *The Telegraph* when he dropped in for coffee, the politeness reinforcing the inequality of their relationship. As usual, Izzy's purple lipstick had smudged, so she looked even more like a child experimenting with an adult world. Ali gestured for her to wipe her lower lip. Izzy got the cue but ended up spreading it across her chin.

"Now Izzy's got a chinstrap beard," said Hector.

"I'm really looking forward to going out in your boat," said Izzy.

"So you'll be up at three o'clock this morning, ready to go and check the crab pots, will you?" Jim asked. "I can see you've brought the right gear."

"Where's the car?" Ali asked, as they walked through the empty parking lot onto the main road.

"It's in the garage," he said. "Jo had an accident. She reversed into the neighbor's van last week. I can't get it mended yet."

"How is everything?" There was a long pause.

"She says she wants to have another go in a clinic. But if she goes on the NHS she has to wait six months. It will kill your mother if she moves back in with us until then."

"How about going private?"

"We can't take out any more money against the value of the house. I know it's a big thing to ask, but we were wondering whether you could help, Ali?"

He was shouting over the noise of the wind and water as they turned the corner onto the street that led to the promenade. The question was carried away out to sea. Instinctively, everyone bowed their heads and huddled closer together. Of course this was why they had enticed her home, thought Ali. She was always an adjunct to Jo's needs.

"We're going to be blown away," yelled Alfie, gripping Ali's hand.

"Like Dorothy in *The Wizard of Oz*," agreed Hector.

At the end of the road they stood for a moment and narrowed their eyes to stare at the sea. Sea and horizon blended together in smudged gray tones. The waves broke restlessly as though unable to agree on a rhythm. Some were faster moving and swallowed smaller, less decisive breakers as they came into shore before angrily spewing their double load on the beach. In the summer they sometimes broke between the sea defenses in a single continuous line. Today they were messy and confused. The wind must be coming from the northwest.

"Every wave is unique," she shouted. "Each one has its own shape, its own speed and height."

"So there aren't any twins?" shouted Alfie. Everyone laughed.

"Shall we count the waves?" asked Hector.

"Let's do it from inside the house," Ali suggested, pointing to a row of red-brick fishermen's cottages at the end of the seafront.

"Can you really see the sea from your house?" asked Izzy.

"You can watch it from your bedroom if you like," said Ali's father. "Ali's window looks onto the beach. You're all sleeping there together."

"That is completely brilliant," said Hector.

. . .

Ali tried to see her home through the twins' eyes. It was obviously much smaller. In fact, she was pretty sure that the basement kitchen at Holland Park Crescent took up more floor space than the fisherman's cottage where she had grown up. There was a single room on the ground floor: a kitchen at the back that looked onto the street and a sitting room with a view out to sea. The black-and-white linoleum floor was worn through in parts, especially by the kitchen sink and the cooker. This was the area where her mother walked backward and forward like a polar bear in its cage, waiting for Jo on the nights she failed to come home. Ali bent down and touched the holes, and for the first time, instead of feeling anger she felt something more like pity.

"What are you doing?" her mother asked.

"It must have been so hard for you," Ali murmured.

"And for you," her mother said, quickly turning away from her to open the fridge door, even though the milk was already sitting in a jug on the table.

Ali's mother had disguised the worst of the damage with a rug that wrinkled and slipped every time someone trod on it. The Formica worktop was peeling, and her father's attempt to stick it back down along the seams had failed. Everything needed exfoliating, thought Ali as she stood up again. It was a drab space.

The twins focused only on the floor, which delighted them because it resembled the outsize chess game in Holland Park. But Ali could see Izzy eyeing the double-glazed windows, the net curtains, and the place mats and knitted doilies, and measuring the distance between Ali's life and her own.

"I can give you the money to pay for rehab," said Ali, doing a quick calculation in her head to work out how much longer she would need to work for the Skinners to clear her debts and subsidize the clinic. "But I'm not going to get involved."

Ali's mother held her in a silent embrace and returned to the business of preparing lunch. She had added an extra leaf to the dining room table and put on a white embroidered tablecloth. There were china cups and saucers from a cabinet in the sitting room and a small plate of sandwiches with the crusts cut off. Ali hugged her back and thought she felt smaller and more fragile beneath one of the thick jerseys that she wore in rotation throughout the winter months.

"Thanks for coming, Ali." Her mother smiled. "We've missed you." Another stab of guilt.

"I'm going to show them where they're sleeping," Ali told her mother, urging the three children to follow her upstairs. The door of Jo's room was shut, but if she were at home Ali would have known from the tension in her parents' faces. She walked past it, wondering if the walls were still painted black and whether Jo still hid her drug paraphernalia under the mattress.

Ali's bedroom was just as she had left it. The twins fell upon her collection of Sylvanian Families. The Underwood Badger family and the Vandyke Otters were missing, presumably pilfered by Jo and sold on eBay. They turned to the objects that Ali had collected on the beach over the years. Her mother had put them in orderly rows on the windowsill.

"Tell me what they all are," Hector pleaded. There was the skull of an oystercatcher, murky green sea glass, driftwood, shells, stones with exotic red veins. They represented the flotsam and jetsam of her teen-age years, thought Ali. Izzy read a poem framed on the wall. Algernon Swinburne's "By the North Sea."

"A land that is lonelier than ruin, a sea that is stranger than death . . ." Ali could remember only the first verse. It was a birthday gift from Will MacDonald. She couldn't hang it in her room in Norwich, because everyone knew it was his favorite poem. She removed it from the wall and put it facedown on her desk.

They headed back downstairs for lunch. Izzy immediately sat at the head of the table. Ali's father raised a bemused eyebrow but said nothing. Izzy scrutinized the sandwiches with suspicion because of her uneasy relationship with carbohydrates. Compared with the biscuits neatly circling a china plate with a willow-leaf pattern, they were the lesser evil, so she took a couple and politely nibbled around the edges. The twins filled their plates high and ate biscuits before sandwiches. They were enthralled by the view from the window.

"Can we have some more, please?" asked Hector with his most beguiling smile.

"Of course," said Ali's mother, piling more biscuits onto his plate. She ruffled his hair with her other hand. His thick curls had grown even more luscious since the incident the day of the Christmas party almost a year earlier.

"Did you have a good journey?" asked Ali's mother as she filled glasses with orange juice.

"Great," said Ali, looking around the room to see if anything had changed and feeling relieved when she found nothing had. There had been a period a couple of years earlier when Jo was at rock bottom (again), when objects beloved of her parents had disappeared from walls and mantelpieces overnight. The carriage clock that lost five minutes every day, the two porcelain dogs that guarded the only shelf of books in the house, even a collection of Agatha Christie novels that Ali had amassed over the years.

Ali handed over the Jo Malone candles. Her mother put them in a drawer without opening the box. She questioned Ali about life in London, and Ali was grateful for Izzy's presence because it meant she could answer in generalities. Yes, everyone was "very kind"; it was true there were lots of women from Eastern Europe working as nannies; no, she didn't have to do any cleaning because there was a housekeeper; yes, she could find her way around on the Underground.

"Have you spoken to your tutor about taking out another year?" her mother asked after a lull in conversation. "Have you been in touch with him?"

"By e-mail," said Ali.

"He called me," her mother said. Ali looked up to see whether there was any recrimination in her mother's eyes, but could find none.

"He wanted to know whether you would be available to do any babysitting over the Christmas holidays."

A familiar sense of oppression began to settle over Ali. The tick of the new clock seemed to get louder. She remembered sitting by the old one, counting her life slipping away in the endless beat of another Sunday afternoon with nothing to do apart from listen to her parents worry about Jo, or making homework that she could have finished in an hour take the entire afternoon until the sky began to darken at three-thirty. She looked out the window and wondered whether the sea would treat her kindly if she went for a swim. Sometimes, if you broke through the capricious breakers that slammed close to the shore, you could find a different mood, especially if the swell came from the sea rather than the wind.

"I was wondering if you could look after the children so that I can go into Norwich and see my friends tonight," said Ali impulsively. "I want to see if I can photocopy a couple of reading lists and maybe borrow some books so that at least I can keep up with some of the work."

Her mother looked pleased, and Ali felt guilty.

"Of course," she said. "Maybe they'll be able to talk you round."

"I'll have to stay for at least another year," said Ali firmly.

"She will." The twins nodded.

Outside, a flock of seagulls was squabbling over a bag of chips that a child had dropped on the promenade. The twins observed in fascinated silence. Izzy watched, no doubt wondering how seagulls could get away with eating so much carbohydrate.

As she sat on the train from Cromer to Norwich that same evening, Ali recklessly sent a text message to her old tutor asking if he wanted to meet up for a drink. She wrote the message quickly, before she had a chance to analyze her motives, and immediately deleted it so that five minutes later she wondered whether she had sent it at all.

She hoped Will would sense the ambivalence implicit in such a last-minute arrangement. If she had really wanted to see him, she would have got in touch days ago. Or perhaps, it occurred to her, he might interpret it as an act of desperation. It might look as though she had struggled to resist his lure and then her resolve had disappeared as her train pulled in to a city filled with memories of him. And what if his wife picked up the phone and saw the message? Its informality, its brevity, its implied intimacy would give her away immediately.

His wife was always so nice to her when she babysat for them. Sometimes Ali fantasized that she appreciated Ali's sleeping with her husband because it was one thing that could be struck off the roster of domestic duties. Other times, Ali felt annoyed with her for not realizing what was going on. How could she be so dim-witted about her husband's motives for driving their babysitter home once a week? For her to uncover the affair now would be disastrous.

She needn't have worried. Will was well practiced in the dark arts of double-crossing his wife and wrote back within a couple of minutes, suggesting that he pick her up from the station, thus circumventing the pub and returning to their original modus operandi.

"Why did I do that?" she wondered, as the train drew in to the station. It was a fitting epitaph to her relationship with Will. Whenever she was with him, it seemed a perfectly plausible coupling, but as soon as they were apart she couldn't quite believe how she had managed to weave such a complicated web of deceit for herself. She had gone through the motions of love without really feeling it. Then it occurred to her that Will MacDonald was simply a bridge from one part of her life to another.

"You've got a new car," Ali said as she climbed into the front of the Saab station wagon just outside Norwich station. He kissed her chastely on each cheek, one eye on the other people pouring into the parking lot. He smelled faintly familiar, but it wasn't until afterward that Ali realized it was toad in the hole. She guessed he had had tea with his wife and children, perhaps helped with bathtime and then made an excuse about returning to his office to collect essays he had forgotten to mark. The persona of absentminded intellectual provided

good cover. Infidelity was easy once you had learned the basic prin-
ciples. Fidelity was the challenge. It was a lesson she was glad she had
learned earlier in life than most.

"We've had another baby," he said, pointing at a baby seat in the
middle row. "It's got a great boot. Two adults can stretch out across it
diagonally. She's six months now."

There was so much wrong with these four sentences in terms of
syntax and content that for a moment Ali was tempted to erase them
with some aggressive verbal red pen. You said you never had sex with
your wife? Was this new baby conceived while our old affair was
going on? How do you know the trunk is big enough for two adults
to lie across it? And who were you with when you made this discovery? But close questioning might make her appear jealous, and Ali
realized that she didn't care enough to make a scene.

She glanced across at him as he headed out of the city on the Yarmouth Road. He looked just the same. White T-shirt. Black jeans.
Old green jacket. Three days of stubble. Very rock-and-roll for someone who spent his life trapped in the straitjacket of eighteenth-century
literature. His hair was a little longer and a little thinner.

"How's London?" he asked. He switched on the CD player, and it
started to play "Twinkle, Twinkle, Little Star."

"Shit," he said, pushing buttons until Leonard Cohen came on.

"It's great," said Ali. He put a hand on her thigh as Suzanne went
down to her place near the river. Ali was mildly surprised to feel a
familiar throb between her thighs. It was a year since she had last had
sex, and she was relieved to discover that the chemistry of desire hadn't
been neutralized by the asceticism of her existence in London. She
wasn't sure that she wanted to pick up where she left off with Will, but
the sensation wasn't unpleasant, so she allowed his hand to linger and
leaned over toward him so that her head rested on his shoulder. She
half thought about unbuttoning his zipper and sucking his cock. They
had done this before when he was driving. It had felt pleasurably reckless, and she was worried that if he spoke anymore he might kill her
desire.

She rested her hand on his groin and started to pull down his zipper. He was already hard. His breathing became throatier, competing with Leonard Cohen. He made a noise that reminded Ali of the twins' guinea pigs. It seemed to come out of both his nose and mouth at the same time. Ali stifled a giggle. Will's foot accidentally pressed down on the accelerator as he spread his legs to give her more room, but Ali was already worrying about what would happen to the twins if he crashed the car and they woke up in unfamiliar surroundings without her to reassure them. So she sat up and adjusted her seat belt. The cord was broken. Desire was like religion, thought Ali. If you stopped believing, the other person's certainty seemed faintly ridiculous.

"I've had some problems with my neck," she mumbled by way of an excuse. She exaggeratedly rolled her head in different directions. Then she picked up his hand from between her legs and held it. It was large and heavy, and she couldn't find a comfortable way for their fingers to fit together. She was used to the sticky warmth of the twins' hands, so tiny that she could hide them within her own. "Carrying children."

"Tell me about it," he said, glancing over at her to see whether everything was still fine, because he understood better than most the ephemeral nature of lust.

"I read something about the woman you work for in the paper last week," he said. "She sounded quite impressive."

"She is," said Ali, "although, of course, close up to any family you realize there are going to be flaws. It's only from the outside that other people's lives look perfect." He took his hand away to push down the turn signal and headed along a country road that Ali didn't recognize. They didn't touch again for the next half-mile, until he turned into a lane beside a church and stopped the car.

"It said she was the daughter of a multimillionaire. That must have given her a head start."

"Perhaps."

"How are the kids? Spoiled, I imagine," he said as he got out of the driver's seat and headed toward the trunk. He climbed inside and carefully spread out a couple of tartan rugs whose last outing was probably on a family picnic. "And emotionally deprived in that way that upper-class English families specialize in."

Ali tried not to show her irritation.

"The twins are odd because they are twins, but they are really sweet," she called to him from the front. "They share this strange language and keep insisting I should learn it. They've sort of allowed me into their world because I accept it rather than trying to force them out of it. They don't have many friends, because most children are put off by their impenetrability. They have lots of stuff and they're always going on exotic holidays, but really all they care about is being together."

"You sound like their analyst," he said, urging her to join him in the trunk.

"I've probably picked it up from their educational psychologist," Ali said, resting her bare feet on the dashboard.

"Izzy is more troubled. I'd love to take her out of London and send her up here for a while so that she can forget about impressing other people and find out what impresses her. She compares herself unfavorably with her mother all the time, and because Bryony is extraordinary, she's a difficult act to follow."

"Are you going to join me, Ali?" Will asked. He held up a lit joint as bait.

Ali got out of the car and slammed the door. She turned her head skyward. It was a clear night, and she knew without looking that she would find a quarter-moon, because it had been a neap tide that morning. For a moment she stood, head craned toward the sky, momentarily overlooking the fact that she was meant to have a cricked neck.

She had forgotten how many stars there were on a clear night in Norfolk. It was as though the universe was filled with a million eyes watching over her. She remembered as a teenager going out into the garden and asking the stars to take care of her sister when she hadn't come home. Sometimes her father would join her and she would embarrassedly explain what she was doing and he would tell her that he sometimes did the same thing.

She thought of the map of the stars on the door of her old bedroom in Cromer. Her father had taught her about different constellations almost at the same time as she learned to read. So she knew that this time of year Ursa Major would be firmly in the ascendant and Ursa Minor would be nestling beneath.

"You're such an old hippie, Ali," said Will from the back of the car as she joined the dots in the sky with her finger, muttering different names under her breath. Ali didn't hear him. A familiar euphoria filled her. She felt diminished by the landscape but connected to something bigger than herself. It was a still night, and she could smell the sweet scent of marijuana emanating from the back of the car.

"If I smoke it all, you'll have to drive home," he said, remembering her hopelessness behind the wheel.

"Actually, I can get round central London now. The Skinners bought me a G-Wiz."

She clambered into the trunk. He was right. They could almost lie down.

Will had made a makeshift pillow from a couple of coats. He leaned forward to pull the door shut, and Ali asked him to keep it open. She took a deep drag of his joint.

"I want to feel the air on my face," she said.

"You didn't mention the oldest child," Will suddenly said. "I remember when I wrote your reference they mentioned a teenage boy."

"Jake's nineteen, he has a life of his own," said Ali, handing back the joint because she didn't want to be sleepy when she met up with her friends. "He's just started at Oxford. Reading English lit. Not what his parents wanted, but he was adamant."

"You must have a lot in common."

"You and I love books but we don't have a lot in common, do we?" Ali said, unthinkingly. For a moment, Will MacDonald, M.A., Ph.D., looked wounded. Ali quickly backtracked, because he was prone to overanalysis. "What I mean is that we don't really know each other well enough to know where the common ground lies." She was careful to use the present tense. "We meet each other. We talk about whether Moll Flanders was the first feminist literary heroine. We both like chocolate bourbons. We don't like Tony Blair."

"We have sexual compatibility," said Will, turning toward her with a glint of intent in his pale blue eyes.

"What does that mean?"

"It means that we can communicate without talking."

"That's something ephemeral. It's not enduring."

"But it should be exploited where it exists," Will persisted, lying on his side and putting his arm across to touch her breast. "So what's he like?"

"I'm not sure," said Ali, as various images of Jake collided in her mind. Jake coming into the drawing room and finding her with Nick three months after she started working for the Skinners. Jake carrying Izzy down to the car after the party in Notting Hill. Jake confronting her in Corfu. There was nothing easy about their relationship. In fact, their interaction was so minimal that she didn't even know if it qualified as a relationship.

"We didn't get off to a very good start, and we've never made much headway," Ali said dismissively.

"So what happened? All those boys sleep with their nannies, don't they? Did he make a pass at you and you turned him down?"

Ali smiled at his archaic use of language but decided not to pick him up on it because he was the kind of middle-aged man who liked to share a joint with his students and download music by The Libertines to establish his youthful credentials.

"Just after I started the job, he found me sitting beside his dad on the sofa in their drawing room at five o'clock in the morning, and he jumped to all the wrong conclusions."

"What do you mean?"

"I was wearing a T-shirt and Nick had been wanking and was in a state of dishevelment. Jake thought that we'd been fucking."

"Your employer wanked in front of you?" said Will.

"Don't be ridiculous. He was in that state when I came into the room. He was looking at a computer screen."

"So is this man pursuing you?" Will sounded outraged at the prospect. He must be jealous, Ali decided. He couldn't possibly be expressing any moral opprobrium, given the wild fluctuations of his own behavior.

"Is who pursuing me?" Ali tried not to sound exasperated.

"The father, of course," said Will. "It's a classic plotline, the young servant girl finding herself the object of her master's desire."

"You're too immersed in awful Richardson," said Ali, feeling a sudden urge to get away from him.

"Remember, Pamela ends up marrying the man she works for," said Will.

"This is the twenty-first century, Will," said Ali.

"So how are you going to tear yourself away from these people?"

"I'm not thinking about leaving, if that's what you mean."

"It's crazy to stay there much longer. Even if you don't want to come back here, you should finish your degree somewhere else. I'll help. You've got choices. Good choices. And I'll feel guilty if you don't."

"I like living with them. It's entertaining, and in a funny way, I feel free."

"That's what kidnap victims say. Be careful you don't develop Stockholm syndrome. Someone told me a story about a nanny who stayed with their family even after the children went to university because she couldn't bear to leave them."

The penny dropped immediately.

"You're sleeping with Rosa, aren't you?"

He looked away guiltily. They had an uncomfortable conversation about whether *The Lives of Others* was the best film ever made, then got into the car and drove back to Norwich station in silence. Ali got the first train back to Cromer.

. . .

The next morning Ali went down to the beach to swim alone. The sea always had a purging effect on her soul. She could forget herself in its embrace, especially on a morning like this, when the tide was high and the waves were big enough for some of the local kids to surf. She got in the water as she always did, running at it fast, not giving herself time to think about the numbing cold as she thrashed through the early waves. These were all bluster, like angry show-offs, wanting to impress people with their personality, and then falling into a foamy soup of anger at their inability to sustain any momentum.

Close to the shore they broke strong and hard, and Ali knew that she would find peace only if she managed to reach the zone where the pier ended at the lifeboat station. She kept well away from the structure itself, wary of the children holding crab lines over the edge and the rip tides around the girders.

She could hear herself breathing, shocked throaty breaths. She pushed forward through the waves, walking and swimming until she could no longer stand. The water got colder, and she flipped onto her back and pounded farther in, doing the backstroke until she had reached her destination. Then she treaded water for a moment and stared back toward the beach. Sometimes, at this point, she would wait there, wondering how long it would take before she would be too cold and tired to get back in. It was a comforting thought knowing that if life didn't work out for her, she could just end it all this way, and no one would ever know if she had drowned by accident or design.

On the beach, she could see the twins and Izzy standing there with her mother. They were waving at her. She lifted a hand in the air and waved back. Hector and Alfie jumped up and down. Her mother put a restraining hand on Alfie's shoulder. Ali ducked underwater and opened her eyes. She could see nothing but the murky green of the sea beneath. She held her breath for as long as she could, and then burst to the surface feeling like one of the seals that swam up and down this route every day. Her eyes were watery with salt.

Beneath the surface, where her legs flailed, she could feel the strange pull of contradictory currents that indicated to her that the tide was now on the turn. She had no idea how long she had been in. She headed back to the beach doing the crawl to find Hector and Alfie sobbing with her mother and Izzy.

"They thought you had drowned," her mother explained.

"We tried to tell you," said Izzy, who looked even more shocked than Ali's mother by the twins' reaction. They clung on to Ali's goose-pimpled legs, begging her never to go in again. She suggested that they put on their swimming trunks and come in for a quick dip with her.

"No, no, no," they chorused.

On the way back home Ali's mother told her that it wasn't healthy for children to be so attached to someone who was being paid to look after them.

"It's going to make it very difficult for you to leave them," she warned, over Hector's and Alfie's sobs.

Ali's sister appeared for the first and only time just as they were all about to leave. Ali was relieved that Jo had disappeared for the night, because she looked awful. Even Izzy, a fervent admirer of grunge, who spent hours engineering perfect holes in her tights and trying to tease her hair into dreadlocks, was taken aback by her appearance. Jo's skin was sallow, even beneath the suntan, and especially when set against the gaudy primary colors of her ankle-length skirt and tie-dye top. Instead of looking interesting and romantic, she was dirty and scabby. The woven wristbands were faded, and the clunky bracelets drew attention to her skinny arms. Her clothes smelled of stale patchouli oil. She smiled at Izzy and the twins. Her teeth were gray. One was missing. She was painfully thin, thinner even than Izzy at her thinnest. She embraced Ali.

"I'm going to do it this time, Ali," she whispered. "I won't let you down."

"I've heard it all before," Ali wanted to say.

"Maybe I should give it a go at home again? Would you help me?" Jo asked. The twins clung onto Ali's hands, as if sensing a rival to her affections. Ali put an arm around each of them. The choices with Jo were always stark: life and death, love and hate, sickness and health. How could she compare her needs to her sister's? She would do anything to help her.

"She's helping by paying for you to have another go at rehab," she heard her mother abruptly intervene. "She can't just walk away from her job. Ali has her own life to lead."

So there was an unexpected bonus to her altruism: it bought Ali unintended freedom. When she got back to London, Ali wasn't sure whether something had broken or something had been mended, but she suddenly had more clarity about what she didn't want than she could remember in years.

17

· · · · · · ·
· · · · · · ·

November 2007

A couple of weeks after the trip to Norfolk, Ali was surprised to see
that Nick had sent her an e-mail. He usually did not communicate
directly with her, preferring to use Bryony as a conduit for any special
requests (dry cleaning suits, renewing car registration, booking flights,
buying underpants). Ali immediately opened up the message. It was
written formally, like a letter, with proper paragraphs, correct punctuation, and every word written in full. He wanted Ali to bring Hector and Alfie to his office in Canary Wharf the week before Christmas
so that he could take them to the annual Lehman's Christmas party
for children.

Nick informed Ali that wives generally didn't attend these events,
to give husbands the opportunity to spend "quality time" with their
children. He then invited Ali to accompany him in case he had to take
any phone calls. He explained nothing more about the party other
than confirming the date and time in another brief e-mail a couple of
days later in which he warned Ali that people took the dress code seriously, but failed to tell her what it was.

Ali took heart from this reassuringly normal request and enthusiastically agreed to come with the twins. Over the past couple of months
Nick and Bryony seemed to be working all the time. Weekdays and
weekends blended into one another. The bimonthly dinner parties

had stopped, Sunday lunch with Foy and Tita was suspended, and the annual drinks party was canceled. Most evenings Ali ate dinner alone with the children.

The trip to Norfolk seemed to have shifted the parameters of Ali's remit so that responsibility for the weekend now fell on her shoulders rather than Bryony's. Ali knew from her phone conversations that Bryony was struggling with the same Russian energy deal, trying but failing to generate positive stories in the British press. Her client was rude and demanding, relentlessly threatening to fire her from the account. After a great deal of persuasion, Felix Naylor wrote a piece for the *Financial Times*, arguing that you couldn't be in favor of globalization without accepting that key British industries might end up being owned and run abroad. He also came round late one evening to warn Bryony that a journalist on his newspaper was digging around her Ukrainian client.

"His background is dubious," Felix had told Bryony over a bottle of wine late one night.

"It's the same with all those oligarchs," said Bryony dismissively. "If no one else is worried about their dirty money, then why should I be? They get more invitations to Ten Downing Street than I do. They've practically hijacked the entire Icelandic financial system."

"This government is totally undiscriminating about the company it keeps and utterly in thrall to anyone who waves a fistful of money in their face," agreed Felix, "but you should cover your back with this guy."

"What are they saying about him?" Bryony pressed him for details.

"Let's say that after the wall came down he was heavily involved in nontraditional exports," said Felix.

"Can't you give me a bit more than that?"

"Only if you tell me whether Northern Rock shareholders are going to be compensated."

"I'll tell you what I know."

"They say that he was the mastermind behind an international sex-trafficking ring that ran from Ukraine. But you didn't hear that from me."

"Fuck," said Bryony.

"Fuck, indeed," said Felix.

Bryony at least worked from home in the evenings. Nick rarely seemed to be at Holland Park Crescent during daylight hours. When he did appear before the twins' bedtime, he came down into the kitchen without addressing a word to anyone. Malea always brought him dinner, which he accepted wordlessly and then left half eaten. If Hector or Alfie broke through his reverie, he always responded with relevant questions that suggested he wasn't completely out of touch. When he caught Izzy smoking in the garden, he simply reminded her to pick up the cigarette butts in case Leicester tried to eat them. He stopped asking questions about schoolwork. Or music practice. Or whether Foy had been at the house. Once he asked where Jake was, and Ali gently reminded him that he was away at university.

He seemed more anxious about Bryony. Their nonchalance about each other's whereabouts had been one of the defining characteristics of their relationship. They had traveled without coordinating diaries, often relying on Ali to know which country or even which hemisphere the other was in. Now, when Bryony was away, Nick wanted to know exactly where she was staying. He made Ali forward e-mails with addresses and phone numbers in case of emergencies. He pressed her for details about whether she was traveling alone or with colleagues. He was interested in Bryony's schedule for the following week. He wanted to know when she would be home again. He made unusual requests: the recycling box should be kept in the kitchen rather than outside the back door; mobile phone bills should be filed in his office; Bryony's handbag must be left in their bedroom.

Ali found his neediness rather touching until she began to hear raised voices coming from their bedroom at odd hours on the rare nights that both of them were in London at the same time. The previous evening, curiosity overwhelming common sense, she had stood outside to hear what they were arguing about. She felt oddly self-righteous about her intrusion, arguing that she needed to know for the twins' sake. She imagined possible scenarios: Nick had lost his job; the house in Oxfordshire was coming in over budget; Nick didn't want Foy to have his seventieth birthday there; Bryony was having an affair; Nick was having an affair. What else did married couples argue about?

"Lack of libido is a sign of depression," she'd heard Bryony shout.

"Or a sign that I don't find you attractive anymore," Nick had retorted. Something fell on the floor. A book, perhaps. Or the bedside clock. Ali guiltily stepped farther into the shadows when she knew she should have walked away.

"Then why don't you go and find someone else to have sex with?" asked Bryony.

"Because I don't want to turn into your father."

"What do you mean?"

"You know exactly what I'm taking about."

"He might have had the odd fumble over the past fifty years, but at least they've managed to stay married."

"I'm not sure that's how Eleanor Peterson would see it. Or Julian, for that matter."

"He hasn't had a relationship with Eleanor. She's my godmother. And my mother's best friend." Bryony sounded exasperated.

"Foy likes to keep it close."

"Dad has not had sex with Eleanor." Then, against the odds, she had laughed. It was a tired noise. More snort than guffaw.

"Why do all our rows end up being about my father?"

There was a long silence, during which Ali considered Bryony's comment and concluded that perhaps it wasn't strange at all, because her parents argued almost exclusively about Jo; Ned and Sophia Wilbraham always bickered about Katya's relationship with Thomas; and Will MacDonald always rowed with his wife about the mess the children made in the car, which seemed particularly hypocritical, given his behavior inside it. Then Nick spoke.

"Because he's the serpent twisted around our marriage." Ali gasped and put her fist in her mouth to prevent any further impromptu outbursts.

"Don't be so melodramatic," said Bryony angrily.

"He's the problem."

"You can't blame him for what's going on at your bank. I know he's got a lot of faults, but he can hardly be held responsible for the subprime mortgage crisis."

"I can," said Nick testily, "because if he wasn't around, then I might have done something different with my life years ago and then I wouldn't be up to my neck in shit now."

"Like what?" Bryony challenged him.

"Been a playwright or an academic."

"Or an astronaut?" suggested Bryony acidly. "Well, why didn't you do any of these things? I earn enough money to support you. You could have done anything you liked."

"No, I couldn't," Nick countered petulantly.

"Why?"

"Because otherwise I'd have ended up like Rick, with my balls cut off. I'd have to put up with the snide comments and the constant barbs without responding in any meaningful way because I can't bite the hand that feeds me. And just like Hester, you wouldn't have been able to resist accepting money from him."

"I could have learned to live more frugally," protested Bryony.

"When I was trying to persuade you not to spend a million pounds doing up a Jacobean manor house that I didn't even want to buy, your first reaction was to ask for money from him."

"Are you saying that you work in an investment bank to impress my father?"

"I do it in part to maintain our independence from him. I couldn't tolerate being financially dependent on him."

"But I'm financially independent. We don't need his money."

"That would make it even worse," said Nick.

"I don't understand."

"Because it would look as though I couldn't afford to keep you."

"Are you saying that you couldn't earn less money than me because it would be emasculating?" Bryony questioned him.

"It would be easier for you to give up work than me."

"You want me to leave my job?"

"No," Nick said with a sigh. "I love the fact that you work. I'm just trying to say that it's another thing your father uses against me."

"One of the reasons I work is because of him." Bryony's voice was so loud now that Ali allowed herself to breathe properly again. "I never want to depend on a man like my mother depends on him. She would have left him years ago if she had any other options."

"So you agree that he's had an affair with Eleanor."

"I know he's probably had affairs. Just not with Eleanor. Does it really matter exactly who he's slept with? He's my dad. I can't just walk away from him the way you walked away from your parents."

The door of the bedroom opened suddenly and Nick came out, slamming it behind him.

"What are you doing here?" he asked angrily.

"You woke me up. I heard the noise. I wanted to check that everything was all right," stammered Ali.

"Well, everything is just tickety-fucking-boo," shouted Nick, storming downstairs.

The following afternoon, as instructed, Ali waited for Nick with Hector and Alfie in the lobby of Lehman's at exactly two o'clock. Knowing Nick was an aggressive timekeeper, she had arrived at Canary Wharf almost an hour early and wandered around with the twins. There was a huge Christmas tree in the main square, festooned with lights and baubles, but it was utterly diminished by the long winter shadow of surrounding skyscrapers.

Everything was gray. The water in the canal. The sky. The buildings. The only bit of color was the red blaze of ticker tape that ran around the building opposite Nick's office with up-to-the-minute news of shares listed on the London Stock Exchange. Hector and

Alfie stared at it in fascinated silence, trying to work out how long it took for the same share to appear again.

"What does it all mean, Ali?" they asked, as though posing a great philosophical question. "Why do some go up and others go down? Why does it change all the time?"

"I'm not sure," said Ali.

They walked around, heads craned toward the sky, overwhelmed by the scale of the buildings. Ali had never been to New York, but she imagined this was what it might be like. People, mostly men, rushed past them with a sense of purpose Ali hadn't observed anywhere else in London. Some smiled at Hector and Alfie, reminded no doubt of their own families. Others looked mildly shocked, because this definitely wasn't a place for children.

"It's like the bit in *Chitty Chitty Bang Bang* where the streets are empty of children because the parents have hidden them from the child catcher," whispered Alfie, searching for Ali's hand with his own. He began whistling the tune to "Two Little Boys."

"Spooky," agreed Hector, using their favorite new word.

Just before two o'clock they stood outside the Lehman's building and counted exactly how many floors there were from top to bottom.

"Thirty-three," shouted Hector triumphantly.

"Where does your dad work?" Ali asked.

"Don't know." Hector shrugged. "Never been here before."

As they worried how Father Christmas would land his sleigh on the roof of such a tall building, a receptionist called up to Nick's office and explained that Mr. Skinner was coming to the end of a call and would be down as soon as possible. Ali tried to persuade the twins to read a sign commemorating the opening of the building by Gordon Brown three years earlier, but they were more interested in sliding up and down the marble floor or playing catch around the huge brown pillars. At one point they started singing at the tops of their voices. The high-ceilinged atrium acted like an echo chamber. The receptionists smiled indulgently.

Nick eventually emerged from the elevator. He didn't apologize for being late, because he had no idea how difficult it was to entertain two six-year-olds inside such a building for more than twenty minutes. Ali searched for traces of last night's dispute in his face. The lines around his eyes were etched a little deeper, his blue eyes were cloudy, and he smiled a little too readily, as though conscious that he should make a good fist of looking happy. Otherwise, he looked reassuringly the same.

"Daddy," yelped the twins as they saw him.

Nick appeared gratified by their reaction. He proudly introduced Hector and Alfie to the receptionist, and she remarked on how they were as handsome as their father. She looked from one face to the other as everyone did the first time they met them, disconcerted by the way one was a mirror image of the other. Hector's left eyelid was slightly bigger than a half-moon, Ali could have told her. And Alfie had a birthmark shaped like an almond on his right shoulder blade. Nick smiled at the compliment, giving it enough attention to make her feel comfortable that she hadn't overstepped any boundaries but not so much that he revealed any vanity.

"Thanks for bringing them, Ali," he said as they headed toward the elevator. They passed a couple of enormous pictures. Everything in the building was oversize, thought Ali. It was a monument to the male ego. Tall ceilings, cream marble floors, black marble walls, huge pillars, and leather sofas so deep the twins' legs couldn't hang over the edge. It was all sharp edges and cool, hard surfaces.

"What exactly goes on here?" she found herself asking Nick.

"It's a place where we turn money into more money." He smiled.

Ali felt as though she were shrinking while Nick seemed to grow in stature as he led them through the security barrier deeper into the building. She was relieved to see how he dominated this environment. He was more relaxed here than he was at home, greeting everyone by name and proudly telling people that he was taking his children to visit Father Christmas on the thirty-first floor. "Where you normally weave your magic," said one of the few women Nick had greeted.

The way he occupied the space around him reminded her of Will MacDonald when he was in his faculty building: neither belonged to his environment; rather, their environment belonged to them. As they waited for the elevator to arrive, Nick took them over to see a large black-and-white photograph of soccer players with a montage of green and white circular shapes in the middle.

"What team?" asked Hector.

"No idea," said Nick. "No one has ever asked that question. But probably Mexican, because it's a piece by a famous Mexican artist called Gabriel Orozco."

"I like it," said Alfie. "Can we buy it for our bedroom?"

Nick laughed.

"We have a great collection of artwork here," he said, more for Ali's benefit than the twins'.

"Antony Gormley, Lucian Freud, Robert Rauschenberg, Gerhard Richter. But you'd probably find the antique book collection more interesting. There's an entire collection of Samuel Johnson. That's your period isn't it?"

"Actually, he only wrote one novel," said Ali, "but he was a brilliant critic."

He was trying to make her feel comfortable, but Ali wished he would just ignore her and focus on Hector and Alfie.

"We've got first editions of Byron and Shakespeare, too."

The elevator arrived. The twins jumped in and then jumped out again, worried the doors might close before Ali and Nick had gotten inside. Nick suggested they might like to see his office, because it had a really good chair they could spin around on.

"Brilliant," said Alfie and Hector simultaneously. They each took one of Nick's hands, leaving Ali standing alone in the corner. Nick kept talking as the elevator went up to the thirty-first floor.

"There's a restaurant with a chef on the top floor. We entertain clients there. On the seventh floor there are lots of restaurants. Benugo, Mongolian grill, stir-fry. And there's a gym, a medical center, and a dentist."

"Like a small town," said Ali.

Hector and Alfie weren't listening. They were too busy playing a game in which one of them closed their eyes while the other tried to guess what floor the elevator had reached. When finally it stopped, they stepped into yet another large atrium. The twins careered up the corridor like bouncy balls.

"There's the Antony Gormley," Nick said, stopping in front of a lithograph. "*Cloud Man*. I asked them to hang it here because I like its mystery. The idea that man's identity isn't fixed. Appeals to me."

"You should read John Locke, then," said Ali. "That was his theory."

Nick turned right and headed toward his office. There was a metal sign that read "Nick Skinner" on the door. His secretary came in and made a fuss of the twins, twisting their curly hair between her fingers and asking Ali the kind of questions you would normally ask a parent: did they like football, did they prefer Star Wars Lego or lorries and trains, did they go to sleep at exactly the same time? Who walked first?

Ali inspected his office. There was a leather sofa, and a large L-shaped walnut desk with three Bloomberg screens on one side and a photograph of Nick shaking hands with Gordon Brown at the Mansion House dinner in June, just a week before Brown had become prime minister. Ali remembered how Nick had come home glowing after this event. He was full of praise for Brown's "brilliant" speech and recited whole sentences by rote to Bryony and Ali when he found them in the kitchen going through the daybook. He described how Brown had congratulated bankers for inventing "the most modern instruments of finance" and how their achievements meant the country would live in "an era that history will record as the beginning of a new Golden Age." The gold had tarnished pretty quickly, thought Ali.

She went to look at a photograph on the wall taken by Sebastião Salgado. It showed thousands of miners scratching through soil at the bottom of a pit, filling sacks, and then carrying their burden up huge ladders to the top of the Serra Pelada mine in Brazil to sift for gold. It was a vision of hell. Did he not see the incongruity of this picture hanging in this place? It didn't surprise her, really. She had met enough wealthy people since she had moved into Holland Park Crescent to know that social conscience didn't really extend beyond occasional attendance at charity events.

"It's a different kind of gold rush from the one in the City over the past decade. They earn about twenty cents a day," said Nick, observing her interest in the photograph. "People do desperate things to help their family. I know I would."

Much later, after Nick's disappearance, Ali thought about this comment. It was easy to recast so much of what Nick said during this period in the light of what subsequently transpired. Everything seemed nuanced. Even something banal like his decision to take up smoking could be misinterpreted. Did he go out into the garden at night to have a cigarette? Or was he doing something else? Did he really want to go through the recycling to remove documents for shredding because he was worried about identity theft? Could there be another reason?

At the time, however, there was no reason to assume Nick was referring to himself. His phone rang soon after, and he went into his secretary's office to deal with yet another call. The twins sat behind his desk and took turns to spin each other on his chair. Ali sat down at a coffee table on the other side of the room and picked up a copy of the *Financial Times* from his open briefcase. She skim-read a piece written by Felix Naylor about the perils inherent in banks, analysts, and ratings agencies all using the same mathematical formula to measure the risk of collateralized debt obligations. Beneath the newspaper was a little diary that Ali hadn't seen before. She flicked through the past couple of months and was taken aback to see that Nick had an appointment with a therapist at the same time every Friday evening.

She quickly hid it underneath the newspaper and unearthed a small haul of cheap-looking mobile phones, a couple of SIM cards, and a piece of paper with a phone number written in pencil.

"What are you doing?" asked Nick sharply. Ali hadn't noticed him come back in the room.

"Reading Felix's piece," said Ali, nervously picking up the *Financial Times*.

"And what do you think he's trying to say?"

"I don't really know," Ali said with hesitation.

"What's the formula called?" Nick asked.

"She's not at school," Hector rounded on him.

"Gaussian copula?" Ali suddenly remembered.

"Well done." Nick gave a quick smile. "He's pointing out that the Gaussian copula doesn't use historical data to measure the likelihood of defaults, it only uses data from credit default swaps over the past decade. He's been listening to what I've been saying."

Nick spun Hector and Alfie in circles on his big black leather chair. When they were sick with dizziness they crab-walked to a walnut sideboard and picked up a photograph. It must have been taken shortly after they were born. They were in Tita and Foy's drawing room, and Bryony held a baby under each arm like a couple of rugby balls. Her hair was wild, and her mouth slightly open. She looked glorious and defiant. But who was she defying? Ali wondered.

One of the twins was leaning toward her breast, eyes shut, mouth open, as though rooting for milk through her silk shirt. It was unclear to Hector and Alfie exactly who was the greedy one. How would it feel not to be able to recognize yourself in photos? thought Ali. How could you feel unique, when every day you were confronted with an exact copy of yourself? And yet, when she had gone back to Norwich at the weekend, wasn't that almost how she felt? She couldn't recognize the person she was when she lived there. She couldn't believe that she had spent most of her waking hours thinking about Will Mac-Donald. He was so mediocre.

"Did you enjoy Norfolk?" Nick asked.

"We had a great time, thank you," Ali said. "We went to the beach, visited the lifeboat museum, and ate fish and chips on the pier. Hector and Alfie went out with my dad in his boat. Even Izzy came, although she refused to compromise with footwear and ended up going to sea in those enormous platform boots."

"It was very kind of you to take them," Nick responded.

"My parents enjoyed having them," said Ali. "They're a lot of fun." She immediately regretted saying this because it might have sounded recriminatory, as though she thought he should spend more time with them.

"Did you manage to catch up with any old friends?" Nick asked. She glanced at him. He hadn't asked her so many questions since her first interview.

"I went to Norwich on Saturday evening and the others stayed at home." She kept the answer deliberately opaque.

"Shall we go and see if Father Christmas has arrived?" Nick asked. They used the fire escape to go up to the top floor, so that the twins and Ali could admire the view over the edge of the building. They could see as far as the Millennium Dome, the other side of the river.

"Totally against all the rules." Nick laughed a little too wildly. She was unnerved by his lack of caution. When they opened the door at the top of the stairs, Ali realized they had arrived in the middle of Santa's grotto. There were excited girls and boys queuing to see him, and benevolent fathers holding the hands of children who were clearly not used to this level of paternal involvement in their daily affairs. Everyone looked faintly bemused at their unorthodox entrance, including Father Christmas, who pointed out that one of them had knocked over an elf as they pushed open the door.

An annoyed-looking middle-aged elf in an unflattering ruched skirt came over and suggested that they go out the front entrance and queue for presents like everyone else. The implication being that she obviously thought Nick felt entitled to break the rules because of his position in the company.

"Why are there donkeys, Daddy?" asked Alfie.

"So the children can have rides," Nick said, and shrugged.

"How do you think they got them up here?" Ali asked in disbelief.

"In the elevator," said Nick. "This party is all about the art of the possible."

They went farther into the heart of the room. There was a carousel with small children enjoying limitless rides. In the corner were a couple of clowns doing magic tricks. Ali counted at least three fire-eaters. There was a photo booth where children and parents (mostly fathers) could have their pictures taken together, and a three-tier chocolate machine billowing melted milk chocolate for children to dip in sticks holding marshmallows. The small child who had been sitting on Father Christmas's knee opened a present and inside found a DS that must have cost almost a hundred pounds. Ali thought it was a cross between *Charlie and the Chocolate Factory* and *The Wizard of Oz*. The noise was deafening. A singer, rumored to be Pixie Lott, was due to come and entertain everyone in a couple of hours. Ali was perplexed. This didn't look like a bank in crisis.

She put her nose in the air as she might on the beach in Norfolk, trying to get a good sniff of the salty headwind. It smelled of photocopier and air-conditioning. She felt a sense of unease that crept from the center of her body until it had reached the end of each limb. She shook out her hands and legs, trying to shrug it off. She thought of Holland Park Crescent, with its basement gym and wine cellar. She considered the basement cinema with leather chairs bigger than seats in first-class flights. The larder filled with food that more often went rotten rather than being eaten. The paintings. The antiques. The parties where famous rock stars pimped themselves for thousands of pounds. There was something wrong with a world where she couldn't go back to university because she was funding her sister to go into a drug clinic. Although, unlike Nick's CDOs, Ali's investment in Jo was already paying dividends. According to her parents, who had visited Jo on the weekend, she had gone through withdrawal and was working intensively with a therapist to unravel the pattern of her addiction.

The rich are always listened to more than the poor, thought Ali, remembering something Felix Naylor had said to Bryony during an argument about how City values had come to dominate British life over the past fifteen years.

"The trouble with people who make money is that their ego is a reflection of their bank balance," he had said. "The more money they make, the higher their opinion of themselves. They have no self-doubt, and people who don't question themselves are dangerous."

It was, as Foy might say, *le loi de l'emmerdement maximum*. Sod's law. She remembered a conversation she had overheard about subprime mortgages in which Nick was extolling the virtues of lending to families of low income because they had to pay more to borrow, which meant their debt generated more revenue. She had wanted to point out that he was talking about people like her parents but didn't dare.

"It's quite something, isn't it?" he said to Ali. "The events team organizes it."

"It's really over the top," agreed Ali. "I mean, there doesn't seem to be a liquidity problem here."

"What do you know about liquidity problems?" He laughed.

"I hear you talking," said Ali, feeling embarrassed.

"You really have three-hundred-sixty-degree vision around our family, don't you?" Nick said. "I'll have to remember to be more cautious in the future, otherwise I might be accused of revealing privileged information."

PART
THREE

18

·······
· · · · · ·

·

June 2008

It was, everyone agreed, very bad luck that Foy's seventieth-birthday
party came at the end of a week that saw Lehman's announce such
huge losses that the bank made headline news around the globe.
Doubly misfortunate, because just days before the party Nick's boss in
London called to warn he would be resigning before the week was
out and hoped they would understand if he and his wife couldn't
make it. Even Izzy felt compelled to commiserate with her father
when he returned home from his latest trip to New York, having
survived the latest cull.

"A billion is a lot, isn't it, Dad?" Izzy inquired over their first dinner together in weeks.

"It was two-point-eight billion dollars, actually," said Nick, nervously drumming the table with his fingertips. "In just three months.
Quite a feat, really, given it was the first time we've ever recorded a
loss."

"At least you've still got a job," said Bryony.

"Sometimes I really wish I hadn't," said Nick.

He closed his eyes and rotated his head in slow circles to loosen up
his neck muscles. Then he gave Bryony a smile so forced and fleeting
that its attempt to reassure was instantly undermined.

She eyed him sharply. The antidepressants should have started neutralizing the anxiety by now. In April, after some persuasion, Bryony had finally managed to get him to take her Fluoxetine, arguing that no one could trace the prescription back to him. Still, Nick was struggling to eat, cutting tiny morsels of beef and hiding them beneath upturned Yorkshire puddings that resembled small bunkers. A pile of newspapers was strewn across the table beside him. "Lehman Slumps to First Loss as Credit Crunch Takes Toll." "Wall Street's Leading Woman Pays Price for Lehman's Losses." "Lehman Chief Accepts Blame for $2.8 Billion Loss."

"This is just the tip of the iceberg," he said, and sighed.

"You're beginning to sound like Chicken Licken," said Bryony.

"Well, the sky is falling," retorted Nick.

"What do you mean?"

"The losses should have been even bigger."

"How can you hide losses?"

"Enron-style creative accounting. There's a repo fund where we temporarily sell our best assets just before results are announced, to boost our balance sheet. Then we buy them back a week later."

"Surely that's illegal?" Bryony asked.

"It's legally doable but morally reprehensible, which is why no one talks about it. I don't think any other banks are doing it, at least not to the same extent. It's a drug peculiar to us. I've been railing against it since last year."

"Why don't you just cut your losses and sell off the sticky assets?"

"Because it's too late," said Nick. The drumming fingers had stopped, and he was now running them through his hair over and over again. It was a new habit. He'd stopped getting haircuts, Ali suddenly realized. It seemed significant, but she wasn't sure why.

"All the real estate and mortgage assets are virtually illiquid. We can't sell them without taking a huge hit, and most of them are impossible to sell. The short-sellers have got their sights trained on us. David Einhorn is gunning for us."

"Who's he?" asked Bryony.

"Big-cheese hedge-fund guy. He's the one who pointed out that we've got twenty percent of cash tied up in the debt on the Archstone-Smith property deal, and he's said publicly that we're hiding losses."

"Maybe he's just looking for his big short to come good."

"He's right, Bryony. That's what he is," said Nick.

"The U.S. government isn't going to let a bank as big as Lehman's go to the wall," said Bryony, trying to reassure him.

"The Fed has no appetite for bailouts."

"Bear Stearns was different," said Bryony. She paused for a moment. "Perhaps you should resign, too?"

"Perhaps I should," said Nick enigmatically. "But then how would we pay the mortgage on our Regency villa and our Jacobean folly? The banking sector isn't exactly awash with jobs at the moment."

"Just one more year," said Bryony, leaning over to steady his restless hand with her own. "Then you can leave it all behind."

"That's what you say every year," said Nick.

"There is no education like misfortune," pronounced Izzy. "And before you say anything, it's not from a self-help book. It was Ali." Izzy was in an exuberant mood. She had just finished outlining her summer holiday plans with her parents: a week surfing in Cornwall, three weeks in Corfu with friends, a party in Norfolk (with a Latin American theme), and a party in Scotland (with a Moroccan theme).

She sat at the table, enveloped in a cloud of perfume, a sure sign that she had been smoking. Relieved that last summer's neo-punk look had been diluted in favor of a more feminine vibe, Bryony and Nick had decided to overlook the cigarettes.

"Actually, it was Disraeli," Ali called out from the table by the bookshelf at the other end of the room.

"Are you developing an eating disorder, Dad?" Izzy asked Nick. "Because I can recommend some more subtle ways of avoiding food."

Nick managed to muster a smile.

"I don't want to offend Malea," he whispered.

"Give it to Leicester," suggested Izzy, patting him on the arm. "That's what I used to do."

"Anyway, these changes at the top might be good for you," said Bryony. "Haven't they promoted people who share your view?"

"They've got rid of a couple of the lunatics who've been running the asylum, but it's too little too late," said Nick, as he carefully filled another bunker with beef. "It's like the bit on the *Titanic* where you can see the iceberg but it's too late to brake."

They began halfheartedly to debate whether to cancel Foy's party, dispassionately batting opinions backward and forward across the table as if playing a lazy game of tennis that no one really wanted to win. It was too hot for dissent, thought Ali. The temperature had crept up to almost twenty-eight degrees earlier in the week, and the under-floor heating still came on in the evenings so that Leicester wouldn't get cold at night.

Bryony held the invitation in her hand and occasionally used it to fan her face. The party planner had cleverly suggested a hologram. When she tilted it forward Ali could see a photo of Foy and Tita on their wedding day, and when she moved it backward it revealed a close-up of the photo of them dressed up as Greek peasants.

Since Nick had resisted the whole idea of throwing a party for Foy, Ali was bemused that he didn't take advantage of this latest catastrophe and at least argue in favor of postponement. Bryony reminded Nick that there had been four hundred guests at the wedding of a Lehman's colleague in New York a couple of weeks earlier and no mention in gossip columns the following day.

"They kept it deliberately low-key," said Nick.

"She didn't even wear a full-length dress," agreed Bryony. "Just knee-length Missoni."

"And they canceled Neil Diamond and got a tribute band instead," said Nick.

"Maybe we should ditch the fire-eaters, the belly dancers, and the stilt walkers, and just stick with the jazz band?" Bryony suggested. She paused for a moment. "What about the camels?"

"I hope you're taking the piss," said Nick.

"It's part of the Eastern Promise theme," said Bryony nervously.

"If I see a camel I'll shoot it," said Nick venomously.

"I promised my friends there would be camel rides," Izzy protested.

"Izzy, you sound like the spoiled daughter of a rich investment banker," said Nick. He turned to Bryony. "Why do you have to be so bloody excessive?"

"It was the party planner's idea," said Bryony defensively. "To create authenticity."

"You didn't have to say yes. If she had proposed bringing over a bunch of Tuareg nomads from the Sahara, would you have agreed? In case you haven't noticed, I am almost exactly half as wealthy as I was this time last year, because my shares in the bank have lost so much value." Nick's anxiety was so close to the surface that Ali thought it might bubble through his pores.

"I'll cancel the camels," said Bryony, in the even tone she had adopted with Nick of late, "even though they're already in the field outside the house."

"Just leave them there, then."

"I'll look after them," offered Izzy agreeably. "They'll eat anything. They're a cheap date."

"It doesn't look good to party while Rome burns," said Nick. "It's the sort of thing the tabloids could exploit . . . There's a never-ending appetite for stories about City extravagance at the moment."

"Still, we'd draw more attention by canceling . . ." said Bryony.

"And I suppose it's such a remote location it's unlikely they'd bother to send anyone . . ." mused Nick. "Everyone knows it's Foy's party, not ours . . ."

"Although they know you're paying for it . . ."

"Also, your father would never agree to abort at this late stage. He's been preparing his speech for months . . . You need to make sure that Felix is on message," said Nick finally. "I'll hold him directly responsible for any diary pieces."

They fell silent for a moment, as if surprised that they had found so much common ground.

"This probably isn't the moment to ask, but could you give me some money to go out tonight?" Izzy interrupted. "I'm going to see *Sex and the City* with a friend." Ali waited for them to ask her about the identity of the friend, but they failed to pick up the hint.

"Haven't you got exams?" Nick asked as he pulled out his wallet and peeled out £50 for his daughter.

"Only French oral left," said Izzy. "Ali's arranged for someone to spend all morning speaking French with me on Monday. She's getting together all the questions I might be asked right now."

Nick looked over to the table, where Ali was diligently typing questions in French onto Izzy's laptop and then drawing up model answers.

"Anyway, I don't know why you're so worried about gossip when all everyone will be talking about is Sophia Wilbraham," said Izzy, who had been biding her time, waiting for the perfect moment to drop her bombshell.

"What do you mean?" asked Bryony.

"She won't be coming now, will she?" Izzy asked. "Not after what has happened. Nor will Ned."

Ali stopped typing but didn't turn round.

"What's happened?" asked Bryony, narrowing her eyes, trying to gauge whether it was good or bad news, and how it could possibly impact on tomorrow evening. Izzy paused for dramatic effect and leaned conspiratorially toward her parents.

"Sophia was meant to go and visit her mother in Edinburgh yesterday morning. She took Thomas and Leo to school and then went to Euston station," Izzy began. "Just as she was about to get on the train, she realized that Katya had bought her the wrong ticket. It was for the same time the previous day." The last sentence was said portentously, as though everyone should immediately absorb its significance. Only Ali understood: Katya wanted Sophia to miss the train so that she would unexpectedly come home.

"Can you get to the point, please, Izzy?" Bryony asked. She had opened up her party file on the page marked "Seating Plan." Now that Nick's boss and his wife had backed out, she needed to find two other people who would complement the other guests at the head table. This was one job she couldn't delegate.

"She tried to change the ticket, but they insisted she had to buy a new one, so she decided to cancel the journey until the following day. When she got home she heard noises coming from the top floor. Apparently it sounded like builders."

"Please, Izzy," pleaded Bryony, sketching a couple of revised seating plans on a piece of paper.

"She went up to their bedroom on the top floor and found Ned and Katya in bed together."

"In bed together?" Nick echoed.

"Actually, on the bed rather than in bed," Izzy corrected herself.

"What were they doing?" Bryony asked in astonishment.

"That is an intriguing question, Mum," said Izzy, who had taken to emphasizing adjectives whenever she spoke so that sometimes she sounded like an advert. "Because Ned tried to convince Sophia that they were rolling around to try and get rid of air bubbles in the water-bed. Apparently, if you leave the valve open, put down a towel, and gently roll across the mattress you can release even the most stubborn air pockets."

"Air pockets?" repeated Nick.

"Sophia and Ned have a waterbed that they brought back with them from New York," explained Izzy. "Apparently they're very good for bad backs. There's even a TV that springs up from the base."

"I can't believe they've got a waterbed," said Nick.

"And what did Sophia say?" asked Bryony. Malea came to the table. Nick wordlessly pushed his half-eaten plate of food toward her.

"She asked them why they needed to take off all their clothes to do this," said Izzy breathlessly.

"They were naked?" Bryony asked disbelievingly.

"Katya was wearing a skirt but nothing else," said Izzy. "Ned was wearing a pair of socks. He said they had taken their clothes off because the heat made the bubbles burst faster."

"Sounds a convincing defense," said Nick.

"He had a huge erection, Dad," said Izzy.

"Isabella!" said Bryony firmly. "You can't speak like that in front of your parents."

"I'm not the one in the dock here," said Izzy.

For a moment Nick and Bryony stared at her in silence, clearly torn between the urge to question her further and the feeling it was somehow inappropriate.

"And what did Sophia say?" asked Bryony, unable to resist.

"She said that once they had finished popping air bubbles, she would be very grateful if Katya would go to her room, pack her bags, and leave immediately. She told her not to bother asking for a reference for the seven years she had worked for them as a nanny and said that if she ever came to the house again she would call the police. She told Ned that he should put on his clothes and go downstairs to the sitting room, where he should start researching marriage guidance counselors or divorce lawyers, depending on which route he wanted to take." All this was said in her uncannily accurate rendition of Sophia's voice.

"Poor bastard," said Nick, shaking his head.

"I don't know why you feel sorry for him," said Izzy, outraged. "He deserves to have his bollocks cut off."

"Izzy!" said Bryony.

"It's a bad situation for everyone," said Nick, trying to backtrack. "Not something you want a lot of people to know about. And everyone obviously does. How did they find out all the gory details?"

"Martha hasn't set the personal setting on her Facebook page," Izzy explained.

"Then what happened?" asked Bryony. They both turned toward their daughter, totally focused on what she might say next.

"Katya told Sophia that Ned wanted to leave her and they were planning to move in together. She said they were in love and they'd been having an affair for more than a year. Ned denied all of this, apart from the length of time they'd been seeing each other, and said straightaway that he had no intention of separating from Sophia."

"I can't believe any man would seriously contemplate divorcing his wife to marry the nanny," said Bryony.

"Easier than introducing a stranger into the family," observed Nick. "The children love her, and Ned says she's a great cook."

"When did he tell you that?" Bryony asked.

"We're getting off message," said Izzy, using one of her mother's favorite phrases.

"Poor Katya," muttered Ali unthinkingly. She checked her phone to see if there were any messages from her. Bryony and Nick turned round. They had evidently forgotten that Ali was in the room with them.

"Did you know anything about this, Ali?" Bryony asked in an interested rather than accusatory tone.

Ali stared at the computer screen for a moment, collecting her thoughts. "She's had a difficult life," she stammered, and her face reddened.

"It's no excuse," said Bryony, clearly uninterested in Katya's background. "I'll give Sophia a call right away and see if there's anything we can do to help. And I don't want Katya in this house again. Please, Ali."

"In case she's contagious?" interrupted Izzy. "Why are you all blaming her?"

"I can't believe it," said Nick, shaking his head.

"Which bit?" asked Bryony.

"I can't believe she'd sleep with an ugly bastard like him," he said, and laughed.

Bryony glanced down at the guest list for Foy's party and struck off the Wilbrahams with a flourish of black pen.

"Makes rejigging the seating plan easier, anyway," observed Nick.

"Have you got something to wear for tomorrow night, Ali?" Bryony asked. She didn't wait for an answer. "Because there's a dress that doesn't fit me that I think will really suit you. It's Marc Jacobs."

"Thanks, Bryony," said Ali, who had the distinct feeling that she was being bought off but was unsure of the exact nature of the deal. Was Bryony trying to reassure her, to underline that she didn't think Ali would do anything like that with her husband? Or was it an attempt to buy her loyalty because she thought she might?

"I'm not for sale," Ali wanted to tell her.

Thornberry Manor did not improve on acquaintance, but Ali suspected it was the style of architecture rather than the atmosphere inside the Jacobean house. The paneling and mullioned windows made the interior gloomy, and the endless carvings and cornicing made Ali feel queasy, as though she had eaten too much Christmas cake.

It was, however, a great venue for a party. It stood on a hill in twenty acres of gardens and woodlands. From the first floor there were wide views across the undulating Cotswold countryside. There were several rooms big enough to hold hundreds of guests, and even though the building work wasn't yet completed, it was far from the disaster anticipated by Bryony four weeks earlier.

A series of painted murals of sibyls and prophets in the great chamber on the first floor hadn't yet been restored, but a clever interior decorator had covered the peeling paintwork with a couple of Barcheston tapestries decorated with flowers and mythological motifs. The library was completely untouched but wouldn't be needed. And work had only just begun on the ribbons-and-roses plaster in the Long Room, where later there would be a disco with a DJ chosen by Jake. As Bryony explained, during a tour of the house for her family and Ali, these were minor details, because most of the party would take place in the tent erected on the front lawn.

The house reminded Ali of Foy. The outside was a strange combination of bluster and conservative restraint. It was built in a rigid,

symmetrical E shape. But the five tall gables and eleven heavily orna-
mented bay windows across the front immediately contradicted this
rigor. Inside were ornately carved wall panels. Then, suddenly, there
were touches of wild excess: pendants that dripped from ceilings like
icing, bacchanalian friezes painted on the walls, and fireplaces carved
with swords and shields. The roof was a garbled complex of shaped
gables and domes that could be reached from the long hall that stretched
across the whole of the third floor. The house demanded attention.

"She's got a very big house, a very big house in the country," Izzy
sang to the tune of a Blur song as she tried to keep up with her mother,
who was leading them through the arched doorway at the front of the
house and into the garden.

"I can't see," said Alfie, blinking away tears from his eyes as he
walked from the dark oak-paneled hall into the glare of the June
sunshine.

"I don't like it here," declared Hector. "I want to go home."

"You've done a wonderful job, darling," said Tita. "I can't imagine
where you find the time."

"Everyone needs an Ali." Bryony smiled warmly as she explained
that Ali had worked almost every weekend for the past couple of
months to allow her to visit the house to monitor progress. Ali would
have described it differently. It was Bryony's sheer force of will that
had driven the project. The architect was terrified of the way her
cajoling, friendly tone could so quickly turn threatening. He had once
confided in Ali that he felt as though he was involved in an abusive
relationship.

Bryony continued the tour. She explained that the Sundial Garden
adjacent to the lawn where the tent was pitched had box-edged beds
filled with the heady scent of Hidcote lavender, roses, clematis, and
salvias, planted by the previous owners of the house. And since it
looked as though the weather was going to hold, not many of the elderly guests would even need to go into the house, except to use the
bathrooms on the ground floor, where their attention would be taken

up by the restless trails of vines and flowers, ribs and pendants on the ceiling of the main entrance hall, and a montage of photos of Tita and Foy taken over the years.

"The able-bodied should go up to the long gallery on the first floor and take a look at the view across the Cotswolds before it gets dark," suggested Bryony.

"Great excuse to escape from a drudge," Foy boomed. "Don't want to get cornered by Eleanor Peterson."

"You're meant to be sitting next to her at dinner," Bryony warned him.

"Can't I have a young filly instead?" whined Foy. "How am I meant to make a speech about seventy being the new fifty when I'm sitting next to someone who makes me feel as though I'm the old eighty?"

"Like who?" asked Bryony, aware she needed to both humor her father and keep him in line. Not for the first time, she wondered how her mother had managed to walk this tightrope for the past fifty years.

"How about Sonia Gonzalez?" suggested Tita. "She's a psychologist. Very interesting—"

"I don't want interesting, I want entertaining," interrupted Foy.

"Sarah Kempe?" said Bryony.

"Too home counties and she falls asleep when she's drunk."

"Caroline Peploe?"

"Doesn't let me get a word in edgeways."

"Who do you propose, then?" said Bryony.

"Ali?" said Foy hopefully.

Everyone turned to stare at Ali, who felt herself blushing as pink as the roses in the flower bed behind her. She stared fixedly at the sundial, wondering whether the arrows were set correctly, or if the builders had inadvertently turned them the wrong way. If they asked her to sit next to Foy she would have to invent an illness or throw herself out of a window on the first floor, like the lady of the house in the sixteenth century who discovered her husband had fathered a child with a chambermaid. Foy was impossible when he was drunk.

"Ali needs to look after the twins, unless you want them on the table, too?" said Bryony, calling his bluff.

"Lucky escape," Jake muttered from the back of the group. He had just arrived from the train station, a fact that prompted a round of comments about his newfound evangelism for public transport. He explained that he'd be driving back to Oxford with friends the following day. He looked tanned and relaxed, comfortable in his skin, thought Ali. His hair was so long and curly that it reached his improbably long eyelashes. He stood slightly apart from the rest of the family, joking with Ali about the potential pitfalls of being seated next to his grandfather.

"Lucy, then," Foy proposed.

"Fine by me." Jake shrugged.

"Won't she be upset if she's not sitting next to you?" Tita questioned Jake.

"She'll take it as a compliment," he reassured her.

"She'll interpret it as a sign that she has been taken even deeper into the bosom of the Skinner family," Izzy teased him.

"What should we do with Eleanor, then?" asked Bryony, as though trying to decide how to dispose of an unwanted Christmas present.

"Stick her next to Sophia Wilbraham's father," said Foy. "Or Sophia's boring husband."

"He's not boring, Grandpa," said Izzy. "In fact, he's very unboring."

"More significantly, he's not coming," interjected Bryony. "So we don't need to talk about him at all."

As she went into the tent, Bryony fielded calls on her BlackBerry: No, it wasn't possible for the chief executive of the Ukrainian energy company to speak directly to the editor of the *Financial Times* about negative coverage; in fact, given his past, he should keep his profile as low as possible. Yes, she could pull the press release about the French supermarket chain that was going to put in a bid for its English counterpart next week, because the deal had been delayed.

In between calls she issued short, clear responses to last-minute

questions posed by Fi Seldon-Kent, who had been charged with organizing the party. Yes, Foy would need a microphone to make his
speech. No, presents shouldn't be brought into the tent. Yes, champagne should be available all evening. No, there weren't any restric-
tions on where guests could mingle. This was welcome news to Jake
and Izzy, who had each been allowed to invite twenty friends and
were now regretting the responsibility that rested on their shoulders
to make sure they had a good time.

"I can't believe this is our house," said Jake, who had seen it only
once before.

"Most of it isn't," Nick observed wryly.

"What do you mean?" asked Jake.

"The bank owns most of it," said Nick.

The only person who sounded as though she belonged to the house
was Bryony. She had already absorbed its history as if it were her own.
She explained to Foy that it had been constructed in 1624 by a merchant, during the consumer boom fueled by the price of wool. Foy
said that was more romantic than the house being bought by a banker
who had made a fortune on a credit boom fueled largely by selling
dodgy mortgages.

"He couldn't have bought it without me, Dad." Bryony bristled.
She went on with her story. The same family had stayed here for
almost three centuries. The crests depicting rams' heads and sparrow
hawks in the hall belong to them.

Their tenure ended when the then lady of the manor fell in love
with a local squire and poisoned her husband with laudanum. The
house was sold to a Victorian art dealer who then bought most of the
oak and walnut furniture that still remained. In the early twentieth
century it had been used as a billet by the army and then been abandoned until its last makeover in the 1950s.

"I see they think Lehman's is going to be the next domino to fall,
Nick?" said Foy.

"This isn't the moment, Dad," warned Bryony.

"I can't believe they sold mortgages to those samurais," said Foy.

"Do you mean ninjas?" asked Nick. "No income, no job or assets?"

"Whatever," said Foy, his argument weakened by his misuse of the terminology. "Knowing that after two years they'd be paying ten percent interest. And I can't believe that you turned these into securities that were meant to be as low-risk as government bonds and that my pension fund has bloody well bought them."

"If house prices had kept rising there wouldn't have been a problem," said Nick. "People could have kept taking out equity to pay their mortgage."

"To be fair, Nick has been trying to raise this issue for more than a year," interrupted Bryony. "He's really put his head above the parapet."

"Your shares in Lehman's must be worth half what they were a year ago," said Foy. "You should have got out then. It's knowing when to call the market that sorts the men from the boys."

"Just as well Mum works, too, then," said Izzy, who had become almost as good at dissipating tension as she was at heightening it. Bryony smiled gratefully at her.

"Well, I hope this party is paid for with real money," said Foy. "Now there's a credit crunch, organic food is going the way of the dodo and farmed smoked salmon is about as popular as a pedophile at a children's party, so I can't help out."

"Enough, Foy," said Tita firmly. He fell silent. Not a good idea to be rude to someone who will be making a speech about you in eight hours' time, thought Ali. She looked at Nick's face, but it revealed nothing. It struck her that she might have worked in his home for the best part of two years, but she knew little more about him than when she first walked through the door.

19

Sitting at the dinner table later that night with Alfie and Hector, Hester's younger daughter Ella, and an assortment of other children in the center of the tent made Ali both conspicuous and inconspicuous. She was highly visible as the only adult at the table, yet no one at the party wanted to talk to her apart from the children. They were drunk on forbidden fizzy drinks begged from waitresses who weren't accustomed to refusing requests from demanding guests. And there were too many children to interrupt the supply chain. One of them had eaten the decorative rose petals scattered on the table and choked so much she had been sick. Another had stuck a chip so far up his nostril that he had a nosebleed.

This was the only part of Bryony's plan that had failed. Katya was meant to be here to help Ali. After yesterday's news, however, she was persona non grata, although as Ali wandered around the garden with the twins before dinner it seemed every other conversation involved her name. "Thomas hasn't stopped crying since she left . . ." "Did you know she pretended to be pregnant . . . ?" "She used to be a prostitute . . ." "Apparently she's done this kind of thing before."

It was inaccurate to say the battle lines were quickly drawn over Katya and Ned's affair, because that would suggest some people allied themselves with the twenty-seven-year-old Ukrainian who had been foolish enough to believe she was the object of a man's love. Katya was portrayed as a scheming siren who had beguiled a good man by stealing his wife's place in the kitchen and then the bedroom. Ned was viewed as a weak man, unable to resist the advances of a femme fatale. No one knew where Katya had gone. Not even Mira. Katya had given her mobile phone back to Sophia and left no forwarding address. Ali had received one message from her.

"I am expendable," it read.

"So am I," Ali wrote back. Mira was right. It was a mistake to view her job working for the Skinners as anything more than a straightforward business transaction. All it would take was one lapse of judgment and Ali would share the same fate as Katya. Why was there any reason to believe that her messy arrival into their life wouldn't be followed by her messy departure? The Skinners were careless with people, even those they called their friends. Ali's thoughts were rambling and incoherent, like the contradictory currents of a tide turning.

Twice during the meal, Hector accidentally spilled his Coca-Cola over the black dress that Bryony had pressed into her hands the previous evening, insisting it would suit Ali better than it suited her, and suggesting that if she didn't like it she could sell it on eBay. Ali left the tent to go to the bathroom in the house to wipe down the dress. Each time she considered not returning. Once she got as far as the first-floor library and stared out across the countryside, wondering where the nearest town was. It was dusk, and instead of finding the soft pastel sun setting behind the hills uplifting and bucolic, she felt claustrophobic.

"Landlocked," she muttered as she forced herself back into the tent. No one heard, and if they had, no one would have been interested. The only person who had greeted her by name so far was Felix Naylor, who had made a point of coming over to the dinner table to say hello and to ask whether she could recommend him a good book. Julian Peterson had walked straight past her.

Although the stain on her dress was invisible, the sugar made it stick unpleasantly against her thigh and ensured that Leicester wouldn't leave her alone. Ali slouched on her chair behind the bowl of flowers in the middle of the table, grateful for the pole supporting the roof of the tent that stood beside her. Her table was called Cromer Crab in her honor, the only one not named after an Indian province.

Her feelings of alienation were magnified by the fact that Bryony had forgotten to warn the catering staff that there was an adult at the table. So Ali found herself eating tiny burgers made of organic steak with chips as thin as matchsticks and drinking Coca-Cola while everyone else tucked into kumquat lamb tagine and spiced poussins with salt lemon and drank Domaine de Sahari.

"We need to pee," said Hector, pulling at her dress.

"You can go together," said Ali, pushing his glass into the middle of the table again.

"What happens if the ghost of the woman who threw herself out of the window lands on us just as we're going through the door?" Hector asked.

"Ghosts don't weigh anything," smiled Ali, stroking his cheek. "You'll be fine. Your brother will look after you."

After pudding was served, Nick stood up and announced that he wanted to make a toast to Foy, who would then respond with "a few words of his own." As Nick hoped, everyone roared at the absurdity of Foy limiting himself to a few words. He efficiently raised the microphone by a couple of inches, telling the audience that he would lower it again for his father-in-law, prompting another wave of laughter. Despite her mood, Ali smiled. She saw Rick roll his eyes. Nick's two inches of superior height had always been a ridiculous bone of contention between him and Foy. Nick took a conventional approach to speech making. At least at the beginning. He delivered a witty and concise round of thank-yous that, to her embarrassment, included Ali, "the linchpin of the Skinner family."

"Enough of the pretense that I'm part of the family," she wanted to shout. "I'm not a saint. I'm paid to be helpful." He remembered to say thank you to both Bryony and Hester for organizing the party, even though Hester had done little apart from shuffling the seating plan to her advantage at the last minute. On cue, Maud and Izzy presented their mothers with bunches of flowers that were bigger than they were.

Ali stopped listening for a few minutes. Everyone knew that Nick and Foy disliked each other, or at least Nick disliked Foy, because most of Foy's opinions were short-lived, and it seemed an absurd charade to hear him extolling his virtues like this. Then it occurred to her that perhaps other people didn't realize because they weren't exposed to the same conversations that she was.

When she looked up again, the mood in the tent had shifted slightly. People were sitting up a little too straight in their seats. They were a little too attentive. Their smiles with a touch of rictus. Ali caught sight of Julian Peterson. His hard mouth was tighter than usual, a single line of disapproval.

Nick was praising his father-in-law's spirit, his restless energy, his childlike enthusiasm, and his focus. He described how Foy did everything in pairs. "He reads two books at the same time, he buys two cars at once, and he buys his beloved wife two birthday presents." At this, Foy leaned over to Tita and kissed her once on each cheek, his lips barely brushing her skin. It was a well-choreographed performance that Ali remembered well because they rarely showed any physical affection. Tita smiled, and with dramatic flourish, blew two kisses back at him.

There was a smart quip about two presents being the least Foy could do for Tita, a woman who had endured almost fifty years of marriage to a man who considered it a big sacrifice not to be allowed to have two wives. A nervous ripple of laughter wound its way round the tent, and at that moment Ali realized there wasn't a person in the room who didn't know that Foy Chesterton had spent the best part of his married life sleeping with the wife of his best friend. Then, having proved a point to himself and Bryony, Nick backtracked.

He told his favorite story about Foy. This time it highlighted his qualities.

There were two empty cottages on the piece of land owned by Freithshire Fisheries. A Vietnamese family had moved to the village, and they wanted to work at the fish-processing plant. Foy found them all jobs and gave them a house to live in. It had a couple of outhouses that they agreed to rebuild in lieu of rent. They bought a car. They paid him back the rent they owed. They gave up their jobs. They even gave Foy and Tita round-trip first-class tickets to Phnom Penh. At the end of the year they disappeared overnight. The police arrived the following day and discovered both houses had been turned into hydroponic marijuana-growing factories. Nick told this story because he said it showed Foy's generosity of spirit, his lack of prejudice, and the way he supported the small man. Ali thought it also showed his poor judgment, but she clapped anyway.

Then Foy stood up. He thanked Nick for his kind words. He said his audience would be relieved to hear that he wasn't going to make two speeches. He folded the two pieces of paper he was holding in half, and put them down on the table. He faced his guests for a moment and began to speak movingly about his family and friends being the tide that had carried him through the past seventy years, and how pleased he was that so many of them were here to help get him through tonight. His comment prompted more laughter than it should, because his audience was looking for release after Nick's discomforting remarks. He talked of the early days at Freithshire Fisheries, when he had slept in his office to save money on hotels and eaten nothing but smoked salmon for lunch and dinner for weeks at a time.

"I am a self-made man," he said proudly. "I have worked hard, and I have played hard." Then he turned to Tita. "I have not always been a good husband. I am not an easy person. But let no one say I haven't loved this woman for a lifetime." He described the first time he saw Tita standing on a Scottish moor, standing "in a sea of heather, like a harbor in a storm." He added something about how Tita was forever associated with the subtle beauty of the moor in all its wild, untamed freedom, an image that Ali found totally at odds with the reality of the constraints of her life. He praised Tita for being her own person,

for allowing herself to love him, against her own better instincts (neither of which Ali was sure was true), and for the gift of his two beautiful daughters. He continued in this vein and Ali noticed several
people wiping their eyes. Then he looked down at the papers in his
hand and asked everyone if they would allow a seventy-year-old man
a surprise indulgence.

Bryony and Fi Seldon-Kent exchanged concerned looks at this
point, because Foy was deviating from the plan. He took the microphone from its stand, stepped back a couple of paces, and signaled to
the pianist in the corner. He played a couple of chords. The pianist at
least was in on the secret.

"I want to sing you the song that was playing on the radio the first
time I met Tita," he said, his voice choked with emotion.

Then Foy started singing "American Pie." At first he was a little
hesitant, trying too hard for a Don McLean–style American accent.
His voice was uncertain, rough round the edges, but he could hold a
tune. He urged people to join in, and to Ali's surprise many people
in the room began singing the chorus with him, even Jake's and
Izzy's friends. As he gained confidence his voice became smoother.
By verse three he was the only person in the tent who knew the
words. He sang all six verses. And then he went over to Tita, embraced
her, and gave her a small box containing a necklace. "Seventy is the
beginning of something, not the end," he told the crowd. Everyone
broke into spontaneous applause. Some gave a standing ovation. At
the head table only Eleanor Peterson remained seated. Her face was
ashen. Julian stiffly put his hand on top of his wife's, but she savagely
shook him off.

After this, Ali handed over the other children to their parents and
left to put the twins to bed. Their room was on the first floor of the
house, directly below Ali's. They made her push the two single beds
together and search the cupboards for monsters. They said it was too
dark, so Ali put on the bedside lamps and opened the curtains. They

worried about the way the breeze blew the curtains into the room and about the shadows cast by the lamps, so Ali shut the curtains, closed the window, and switched off the lights. Then they started talking about how the wooden paneling might hide secret passageways and made Ali tap every corner of every panel to see if any of them opened. In the end Ali promised to sit with them until they had fallen asleep in the same bed and to come and sleep in the one beside them later.

"Why can't we just have one house and stick with it?" Alfie sobbed into his pillow.

"Why do we have to be on the move all the time?" Hector began to cry.

They were interesting questions. Ali came up with a few hypotheses in her head. Because unhappy people are restless. Because if you earn shitloads of money you have to find a way to spend it. Because if you measure success by what you earn, then the only way to impress other people is to show off what you can buy. Because you are never satisfied with what you've got because someone else always has more than you.

"Because you are lucky," she said. "Imagine yourselves as the wildebeest that we saw in the David Attenborough program, migrating from one place to the other across the African plains. You lead a really exciting life compared to most children."

They sensed the lack of conviction in her voice.

"Think how many of the wildebeest die during the journey," whispered Hector.

Ali started to recite from their favorite Dr. Seuss book. "'Just tell yourself, Duckie, you're really quite lucky! Some people are much more . . . oh, ever so much more . . . oh, muchly much-much more unlucky than you!'"

"We could be like the Crumple-horn, Web-footed, Green-bearded Schlottz," said Hector, "with a tail that's tied in knots that can't ever be undone."

"Or the man who mows the lawn but the faster he mows the faster it grows," said Alfie. Their eyes finally started to close.

Above her, Ali could hear the dull thud of music coming from the Long Room. Razorlight, Black Eyed Peas, Kaiser Chiefs. All the same music that she used to listen to with Rosa, Maia, and Tom. She felt lonely. Jake and Izzy were dancing with their friends. She would have liked to be there with her own friends, or maybe even to join them. After all, they were only four years younger than her. But it wouldn't be appropriate, or at least it wouldn't feel appropriate.

Instead she decided to head upstairs to her own bedroom to collect her belongings. Outside her room, she noticed that the trapdoor that led to the roof was completely open. She craned her neck and saw a perfect square canvas of stars and moon in the sky above. The collapsible ladder was half folded but just within reach. She stretched up to pull it down and climbed up the rungs until she found herself on the lead-tiled roof. It was surprisingly flat. She stood up slowly, tried to get her bearings, and tentatively walked forward a couple of paces, worried about the irresistible pull toward the edge. She guessed she was close to the front of the house on the south side, behind the tip of the gabled window of the twins' room beneath.

"What are you doing here?" a languid voice inquired. As her eyes grew used to the dark, Ali could make out Jake nestled in a narrow lead gap between the window and a chimney pot, where he had the best view of the party. Ali stopped abruptly, unsure whether to retreat or go forward, scanning the area for Lucy.

"She's not here." Ali could detect the sweet smell of grass hanging in the still night air. There was an open bottle of champagne beside him.

"Smoke?" Jake offered. He held out a small, carved clay object to her. "Pipe of peace."

"No. Thanks."

"Come and sit down, at least," said Jake. "We've got the bird's-eye view."

Jake removed his dinner jacket and created a makeshift cushion in the space beside him. He motioned her toward it. Music coiled up from the room below to fill the silence between them. She stared at the jacket.

"Come on, Ali," he said. "I could do with the benefit of your wisdom. The four years of experience that you have on me. Tell me, what is the kindest way that a man can dump a girl?"

"You're stoned," said Ali. It was less recrimination than statement of fact.

She thought for a moment. Jake looked down at the party, as though disinterested in whether she stayed or went. His ambivalence gave her confidence, and she carefully made her way forward, removing her shoes because it was easier to grip the lead roof with bare feet. She sat down beside him and peered over the edge.

The ground was farther away than she expected. There was a small, decorative balustrade that ran across the front of the roof. It was only a couple of feet high. Ali pressed her feet against it, wondering what would happen if a piece gave way.

She might not fall, but she could kill someone standing below. She told herself that she should tell Jake to come down now. But Jake was no longer her responsibility. And besides, she could see the appeal of watching the party from this vantage point. So instead she found herself taking a deep slug from the bottle of champagne he was pushing toward her, and overlooking the pipe.

"I think you need to be completely honest and tell her it's over. Don't give her any hope. It's kinder in the long term. Don't be personal about the things that bother you about her. Keep it simple and say that it was a fantastic relationship while it lasted but it's time for both of you to move on, that you're both too young to be involved in something so serious."

Jake put his hand in the pocket of his trousers and pulled out a chewed pencil and his train ticket. He started writing on the back of the ticket.

"What are you doing?" Ali asked.

"Taking notes," he said. "What you said was word perfect."

"If you learn it by rote, it won't sound sincere." Ali laughed.

They fell silent for a moment. But it was a comfortable silence. They both leaned forward toward the balustrade to gaze once more at the crowd down below. Their shoulders were touching. She could feel the warmth of the top of Jake's arm through his shirt.

The lighting around the garden highlighted the area below like a stage. Everyone on the terrace was visible. Even the darker shapes that had graduated to the Sundial Garden could be seen in the flicker of candles that lit the pathways. They saw Izzy draped over one of Jake's university friends. She was wearing a black dress that she had found in Camden Market. She had taken up the hem, removed the sleeves, and created an off-the-shoulder look that made her look much older than seventeen.

"Don't worry. He's gay," said Jake, as Izzy and the boy disappeared together.

"Did I tell you that the last time Lucy came to Oxford to stay the weekend, she brought a vacuum cleaner with her?" Jake said. "Can you imagine the relentless piss-taking?"

"You got too domestic too quick," said Ali. "It's a good lesson to learn."

"Not something you've experienced?" asked Jake.

"No, my relationships have been a little less conventional," Ali said, deliberately vague.

"I like the sound of 'unconventional,'" said Jake. He pondered for a moment. "Don't tell me, you slept with your tutor? That's the oldest one in the book. Up there with sleeping with your nanny."

"Maybe it's good to get a few clichés out of your system early on in life," said Ali. "Then you avoid them later."

"So if Ned Wilbraham had shagged his nanny when he was younger, then he wouldn't have done it later on in life?" Jake asked.

There was an awkward silence as they considered the content of their banter.

"What do you think of the view?" asked Jake.

"Fantastic," said Ali, "although a long horizon without any sea always makes me feel landlocked and homesick."

"I feel like that at home in London," said Jake. "Not homesick. More claustrophobic. As if I can't breathe because everyone is watching everything I do all the time. Every cricket score, every Latin test, every friendship, every detail of my life held up to scrutiny and found wanting. I don't know how you can tolerate living with my family. Ambitious perfectionists aren't a bundle of laughs."

"Because it's not my family." They both laughed.

"Did you have a happy childhood?" asked Jake.

"You sound like a therapist."

"Don't be evasive. You know so much about me and I know nothing about you. It's a lopsided arrangement."

"I had a childhood of two extremes," conceded Ali. "The first half was all buckets and spades and picnics on the beach. Sometimes, if the weather was good and it wasn't blowing up rough, I went out with my Dad in his boat to work the crab pots."

"He's a fisherman?"

"Seventh generation," Ali confirmed. "There are tombstones with carvings of fishing boats belonging to my ancestors in the churchyard in Cromer. I'd get up with him early in the morning, get in his truck, head for the prom, and load up boxes of bait onto the boat. You go out after high water and come back on the ebb tide. We'd leave Cromer in the dark, with the lights twinkling behind us, and head toward the horizon as dawn was breaking. It's really beautiful. You should do it someday."

"Did you ever get seasick?"

"Never. We'd spend hours at sea, winching up pots, taking out crabs, rebaiting them, and chucking them back overboard. The boat has GPS, but Dad knows where all the potting grounds are just by lining up landmarks."

"Sounds idyllic," Jake agreed. "So when did the skies darken?"

"When I was twelve my sister began smoking lots of dope. She got really heavily into drugs. Heroin, mostly. A couple of years later she moved to a squat in Norwich and stopped going to school. My parents imploded. My mother became someone who struggled to get through each day. My father escaped by spending more and more time on his boat. Sometimes my sister would come home and try to clean up. Then she'd disappear for months. Bad times. Last year I paid for her to go into rehab. She's still there, so we might get a happy ending yet."

"That's a lot to deal with," said Jake.

"All families are frayed round the edges. Most don't completely unravel. We're all stronger than we think."

"Sounds like a good life philosophy," said Jake.

Lucy came out of the house, pale and floaty in her cream dress, and steered a steady course toward the tent, where she stopped at the entrance by an arch draped in pale pink roses and peonies and turned toward the terrace, scanning the crowd for Jake.

"Like a bride abandoned at church on her wedding day," Ali observed, as Lucy nervously flicked her hair back from her face.

"Don't," Jake said with a groan.

"You need to confront the situation head-on," said Ali, this time taking a toke from the pipe. Most definitely a sackable offense, she thought to herself. It occurred to Ali that perhaps she wanted to be sacked. She could feel herself starting to distance herself from her job with the Skinners. Disturbed by these thoughts, she drank some more champagne, a little too quickly, as though, having decided that she wanted to lose herself, she needed to apply herself to the job in hand.

Down below on the terrace in front of the house, small groups were milling about. A stream of waiters and waitresses carrying trays of drinks flowed between them. Bryony was talking to Felix. Their heads were bowed as though neither wanted to catch the other's eye. Foy was talking to Eleanor Peterson, looking hopefully over her shoulder for some diversion. Occasionally someone stopped to shake his hand or kiss him on the cheek, but Eleanor's possessive body language was easily interpreted, and they quickly peeled away.

Eleanor was wearing a floor-length gold taffeta dress that suggested her style was irreversibly forged in the 1980s. She was tanned from an early-summer trip to Corfu and her hair was dyed an odd shade of honey blond.

"She looks like an Oscar," Ali said, and giggled.

"Talking to a Toby Jug," said Jake. They saw Leicester, head tilted toward them, barking furiously, and slid back into the shadows in case he gave them away. "My grandfather had a relationship with her. Years ago. I discovered it . . ."

"I know," Ali interrupted him.

"There isn't a lot that you don't know about my family, is there?" Jake asked.

They watched as Eleanor leaned toward Foy and spoke into his left ear.

"His good ear," observed Jake, passing her the bottle again.

The bubbles burned her throat, and she choked. Jake thumped her on the back, and the third time she felt the tip of his finger linger somewhere in the middle of her spine. She edged forward away from him. Imperceptibly, so that he didn't think it was an accusatory gesture, but enough that she couldn't feel the heat from his hand burning through her dress. Something in their relationship had shifted, but Ali wasn't sure that this new ground was any less treacherous than the old.

"I should go," said Ali.

She looked back over her shoulder at Jake, and he leaned toward her. This time Ali didn't move away. There was a noise from the terrace below. The cord was broken, and they leaned over the edge of the balustrade to see Eleanor shouting at Foy. They watched in riveted silence. Jake put his arm around her. Sublime, thought Ali, exquisitely aware of the current between them through the fog of dope and champagne. Foy stared at the ground, nodding vigorously so that his chins wobbled. He fiddled with the knot in his bow tie and undid the button beneath. His mouth looked odd, as though the lower lip was trying to get as far away from the upper lip as possible. There was a moment when Foy and Eleanor stared at each other with the hot flash of former lovers, and then she lifted the glass of champagne in her hand, threw it in his face, and smashed the glass on the terrace.

"I'm going to tell Tita everything," she shouted, as Tita came over to see what was going on. One look at Foy's face told Tita everything she needed to know. She stood openmouthed as Foy lurched toward Eleanor, hand in the air, as though about to embark on a complicated Scottish dance. Was he going to strike her? wondered Ali. Instead he toppled over and lay at her feet in a crumpled heap. Eleanor knelt down beside him and began screaming.

"I've killed the man I loved," she cried, pulling Foy to her chest. The sleeve of her dress had slipped down so that her well-engineered bra was visible. Her words hung in the warm evening air, and anyone who was outside could hear them. Tita stood immobile, so dizzy she couldn't bend down to touch her husband. Julian Peterson came over and managed to peel his wife off Foy.

It was difficult to work out the exact order of events, because apart from Tita and Foy everyone was in motion. It was as though everything was happening in fast-forward, thought Ali. Bryony raced into the house to phone for an ambulance. Hester ran over to Tita and put an arm around her. Rick laid Foy on his side in the recovery position. Felix Naylor found himself propping up Eleanor, pulling up her bra strap, and trying to get the sleeve of her dress to stay in place while Julian ran to fetch a chair.

"Shit," said Jake. "We'd better go down."

They stood up, and from the terrace below Ali saw Lucy looking back up at them on the roof.

20

∷∷∷∷∷∷∷

Foy moved in with Bryony and Nick to convalesce after he was discharged from hospital in Oxford at the end of June, two weeks after the party. Nick reluctantly conceded that it was impossible for him to go home, principally because Tita refused to have him. Tita argued that Foy couldn't climb the stairs of their house unaided, that he needed help to wash and get dressed, and that he shouldn't be left alone. Having told Bryony and Hester she had been captive to her marriage for more than forty-five years, she calmly explained that she didn't want to become a prisoner in her own home.

In the days after the party, Ali heard Bryony and Hester speak together more than she could ever remember as they tried to broker peace between their parents.

"It's difficult enough to forgive an affair in the middle of a marriage but impossible when you uncover it at the end," Ali heard Hester say to Bryony. "I wish I'd told her before."

"You knew about this?" Bryony had asked.

"Of course I did," Hester had impatiently replied. "You knew, too. You just couldn't admit it to yourself. Don't you remember how Dad and Eleanor always used to go on those evening walks together in Corfu when we were children? You chose to ignore the evidence because you didn't want to knock Dad off his pedestal. The eyes of the favorite child were blinkered."

When Bryony offered to pay someone to come six hours each day to help, Tita gently but firmly told her she was leaving for Corfu midweek, as planned, to prepare the house for the summer, and no one could persuade her to change her mind. A new air-conditioning system was being installed, and it was "imperative" she be there to oversee the work. Nothing was discussed. Eleanor wasn't mentioned. And as far as Ali could remember, her name was never spoken again in front of Tita.

"I'm not having a fucking stranger wipe my arse," Foy protested when Bryony proposed finding live-in help for him while Tita was away. Hester was adamant that her father should stay at home. It was less conviction than negotiating position, because Rick refused to have Foy living with them. So Malea was summoned to the drawing room and doubled her salary overnight by accepting a job as Foy's part-time carer until he was fully recovered and Tita had come home.

It was meant to be a temporary solution to the problem of Foy's limited mobility and Tita's impending absence. Foy approved of the arrangement. So Ali was dispatched to his house to retrieve clothes and essential possessions from a list headed "Foy's Paraphernalia" that he had dictated to Izzy because his hand was still too shaky to write. Its length and precision suggested Foy didn't expect to be going home very soon. The list included tomato plants that wouldn't ripen until the end of July, golf clubs, his favorite jacket, and the wedding photograph from the mantelpiece in the sitting room. Tita offered to drive everything to Holland Park Crescent later that day. She explained that she would also be delivering three unopened boxes containing copies of Foy's self-published autobiography that should have been given to guests at the end of the party.

"They'll make good kindling," she suggested archly. She then kissed Ali good-bye in a way that had a certain finality.

"I have spent most of my life pleasing other people rather than pleasing myself," she told Ali. "Make sure you don't do the same."

Nick's office on the ground floor of Holland Park Crescent was hastily cleared out, and a single bed installed. A chest of drawers was found for Foy's clothes. Ali helped arrange Foy's belongings in his new bedroom. When she pointed out that Eleanor was one of the guests on the far side of the family lineup outside the Oxfordshire church where they had got married almost half a century earlier, Foy asked Ali to remove her from the photograph.

"I need to excise her from my life," he said dramatically, as he watched Ali cut a careful line until Eleanor floated to the floor. Ali picked up the narrow strip of black-and-white photo and wiped Eleanor's face, as if searching for clues that might indicate whether the affair had started before or after the wedding. He instructed Ali to chop Eleanor into tiny pieces and to burn them in an ashtray. Ali found a matchbox, but inside was a small pile of SIM cards, so she fetched her lighter instead. Foy held the ashtray with trembling hands until Eleanor turned to ash. The smoke alarm had gone off, but Foy didn't appear to notice.

"This isn't going to resolve your problem," Ali advised him.

"Why did she wait all those years?" Foy asked, shaking his head in wonder.

"Guilt?" suggested Ali.

"How could she expect Tita to forgive her?"

"Then revenge," Ali said. "Perhaps she wanted to make you as unhappy as she is."

Tita was right. Instead of taking responsibility for his actions, Foy was already looking for other people to blame. A nurse came to the house with what she called "disability aids," which Foy quickly named his "lack-of-sex toys." A grab rail was put in the bathroom next door, and a stool placed in the shower. He was encouraged to wear an alarm round his neck in case he fell over and couldn't get up on his own.

The nurse explained that his mobility would improve, the tiredness would fade, and his speech might come and go for a while, but there was no reason to believe there would be any permanent side effects. The chances of having a more serious stroke over the next three months were high, and as well as taking blood-thinning medicine and aspirin every day, she urged Foy to make immediate changes to his lifestyle.

"No alcohol, fatty food, or salt," Bryony instructed Malea in front of Foy, the day after he was permanently installed at Holland Park Crescent. Bottles of whiskey and other spirits were removed from the drawing room, where he would spend most of the day. Cigarettes were hidden. "Brown rice and chicken for lunch, and a short walk to Holland Park in the afternoon. No other excitement. Ali will read to you from the newspapers in the morning and evening. It's important to rest after a stroke."

"I haven't had a bloody stroke," said Foy petulantly. "It was a transient ischemic attack." His speech was slurred and his mouth drooped to one side, but he seemed to have no problem expressing himself. He still pulled up the twins when they made grammatical errors and managed to persuade Malea to hide a saltcellar in the Chippendale chest of drawers in the dining room where he ate all his meals because he couldn't get downstairs.

"That's just a fancy way of saying 'mild stroke,' Grandpa," Izzy chided him, as she wrapped a rug around his legs. Since the stroke his legs were always cold. "And if you don't look after yourself, you'll have another one, and then Granny will never have you back."

Sometimes, as Ali was reading to him, Foy would fall asleep in the sitting room chair and call out for Tita in his sleep.

"She's gone," Ali would whisper.

"I feel like someone who's had his leg amputated but still feels as though he's got the limb," said Foy. "I'm at forties and fifties."

Ali thought of the days that followed as the calm after the storm. Much later, she would realize they were more akin to the eerie interlude of quiet found as the eye of a hurricane passed over. Bryony was optimistic that the changes made at the top of Lehman's would see the bank through the credit crunch, with Nick's position enhanced. It looked as though the Korea Development Bank might be interested in a deal. The new regime had asked him to investigate the real value of collateralized debt obligations that had originated in Europe, to get a more accurate idea of the scale of losses facing the bank. Bryony saw this as a positive sign of Nick's rising currency in New York. She allowed herself to imagine them all moving there for a couple of years and asked Ali if she would consider coming with them. Her enthusiasm was so convincing that even Ali began to imagine vliving on the Upper East Side and maybe enrolling in a graduate program at Columbia.

The twins made a new friend, a girl called Storm, who came to the house and invented a game called triplets that involved her dressing up in exactly the same clothes as Hector and Alfie. Jake stayed in Oxford to work in a wine bar. Bryony worried that it did nothing to enhance his CV, but Nick seemed unconcerned. Ali got a text message from him. "Come and visit." She didn't respond, and erased his number from her phone in case she was tempted to call.

Sophia Wilbraham got a new, much older nanny and found a top marriage guidance counselor who prescribed weekends in country hotels and less focus on her children. Ali's parents stopped calling to give updates about her sister. Eventually, Jo came out of her clinic and claimed to be cured. She wanted to come and stay with Ali. Ali refused. Jo wrote a letter saying that she understood Ali's reticence and respected her boundaries. She also said that she had found a part-time job in Cromer and would start paying back the money Ali had spent on rehab. A week later a check for the first thirty pounds arrived in the post.

Nick went to work early and came back very late. Bryony came home earlier. There were no deals for her to work on. She spent her days firefighting negative stories in the press on behalf of clients whose share prices were tanking because of the credit crunch. In the evening, everyone now headed to the drawing room to keep Foy company. It added a cozy dimension previously lacking from life in Holland Park Crescent.

Then, at the beginning of July, Nick came back from another trip to New York with even gloomier news about the scale of bank debt. They were sitting in the drawing room with Foy. Ali was reading a newspaper piece to Foy about Gordon Brown's first year in office.

"Two-thirds of Britons think Gordon Brown is an electoral liability," Ali began.

"Just shows how sensible the British public is," grunted Foy. When he was tired he spoke without really moving his lips so that he sounded like a second-rate ventriloquist. Ali couldn't remember a day when she had managed to read an entire article from beginning to end without Foy interrupting. Being sedentary made him even more belligerent, especially if Nick was in the room.

"How did your presentation go?" Bryony asked Nick.

"I told them that the Product Control Group hasn't checked the price of around a quarter of CDOs. Then I had to explain that they seemed to have used the same mathematical models as the traders to value the rest, which means they are worth even less than we thought. Some of them are probably worth a thirtieth of the value they ascribed. With CEAGO, they actually used a lower rate for the high-risk tranches than they did for the low-risk senior debt. Mad." Nick looked exhausted.

"What's CEAGO?"

"It's the biggest CDO position held by the bank at the moment. Lehman's has around one-point-two billion dollars in CDOs and CEAGO accounts for five hundred twenty million dollars. It's difficult to know how much it's really worth but I reckon we still hold ninety-seven percent of it."

"So how did they take it?" Bryony asked.

"Beside the real-estate losses, it didn't look so bad." Nick gave the quick half-smile that had become shorthand for further bad news. "We're a hundred twenty billion down there."

"If you hadn't tried to make a fast buck selling mortgages to poor people who couldn't pay them back when interest rates went up, then you wouldn't be in this position," said Foy. He had developed an unfortunate habit of dribbling if he spoke too fast. Malea had tied a colorful blue-spotted scarf around his neck to mop up the spit. Behind his back, Nick referred to him as the Milky Bar Kid.

"Home ownership was one of Mrs. Thatcher's most fundamental beliefs," pointed out Nick.

"You've been too greedy. You've corrupted yourselves, and you've corrupted the political system. All those bloody Labour politicians are in thrall to the City." Foy ignored Nick's comment.

"I didn't see you complain when Nick bought you *The Menace*," muttered Bryony.

"You bastards are going to bring down the whole financial system," said Foy. Then, mercifully, he fell asleep.

"At least they see you as a steady hand on the tiller," said Bryony quietly.

"There is no tiller," said Nick.

"Why do people always use nautical metaphors to describe the crisis?" Ali had asked one evening, after yet another conversation in the drawing room about when Lehman's might hit the iceberg. Nick had looked at Ali as though he wasn't sure how she fitted into his life. He was so tired that he wasn't even sure how he fitted into his own life. Instead he had given Ali a blank look and turned back to Bryony to tell her that the numbers were unreal and it was difficult to find the right adjectives to describe how bad it all was.

He then described the atmosphere of barely suppressed panic at the New York office. He told Bryony how Dick Fuld had come down from the top floor to address everyone through the internal communications system and had then attended a meeting with senior management in which he kept telling people to stop talking about losses and to fight back.

"He's losing it," said Nick.

"No, I'm not," shouted Foy, suddenly waking up.

. . .

Shortly after this, Felix came to the house unannounced one Friday evening while Nick was still at work.

"Ali," he said distractedly, looking over her shoulder for Bryony. "How are you?"

"She's with Foy in the drawing room," said Ali.

Felix had put on weight. Ali could see his paunch challenging the buttons on the front of his shirt. He was wearing a jacket and tie, but everything was lopsided. Ali followed him into the drawing room, where she was in the middle of a game of cards with Foy. He wanted to teach her to play poker, but they had compromised with rummy to avoid excitement. Felix stood by the mantelpiece, speaking breathlessly. He picked up invitations, glanced over them, and then unthinkingly put them back without noticing whether they were upside down or on their side. He took off his jacket, and Ali saw big fat circles of sweat under his arms.

At first Ali put his behavior down to nerves. He was never completely relaxed around Bryony. Then, as she listened to what he was saying, she realized he was punch-drunk with news from the City. He explained that he had come straight from his office, later than anticipated, because a bank in Pasadena had collapsed, causing the oil price to spike, the Dow to plunge, and Lehman's shares to sink to an all-time low. He wore the happy fatigue of someone for whom the crisis meant front-page stories and a nice fat byline.

"The idea that the crisis in the banking system is somehow isolated from the rest of the economy is bullshit," Felix told Bryony excitedly as he entered the room. "It's like a Russian doll. Everything is connected. CDOs, mutual funds, structured investment vehicles, monolines, credit derivatives . . . The market isn't self-healing. It's fucking self-harming."

"Which must be gratifying to you," Bryony said calmly, as she leaned forward and kissed him on each cheek.

"Hello, Felix," said Foy, peering round from the side of the chair. "I've been saying it for ages. Paying these people too much money made them believe too much in their own mythology. Most of them are mediocre, but giving them these bonuses makes them think they're fucking gods."

"Totally agree, Foy," said Felix. "Why should some fixed income trader get a million-pound bonus while a cancer surgeon on the NHS gets none?"

"Nick called the market last summer," said Bryony protectively.

"I bet he still took his bonus in January, though," said Felix.

"Nick has never been completely motivated by money," said Bryony.

"Come on, Bryony, don't be naïve. Nick would be the first one to storm into Jeremy Isaacs's office if he didn't think his bonus reflected his value to the company. Don't tell me he approved billions of pounds of bonds backed by subprime out of social duty because he felt sorry for poor people who didn't own their own house? He did it because he made money from it."

"Nick never set out to be so rich," said Bryony. "He's been lucky to ride a bull market the past few years, and he's one of the smartest brains in fixed income. He was one of the people who invented credit default swaps. They've called him to New York to try and help sort things out," said Bryony.

"So the mess at Lehman's is as bad as it looks, then?" asked Felix. Bryony fell silent, aware that she had fallen into a trap. Felix saw her face and relented.

"It's just that for so long Lehman's looked as though it was immune to the subprime contagion. And then, suddenly, their figures look way off."

"Well, you guys printed the story they told you pretty unquestion-ingly," said Bryony. She offered him a drink and then called down on the intercom to ask Malea for a vodka and tonic. "So what brings you here?"

Ali and Foy settled back into their game of cards. They were sitting by the window. Outside, Ali could see a taxi with its meter running. It was waiting for Felix. Ali found this disturbing, because it underlined the sense of urgency surrounding this visit. Bryony and Felix now sat facing each other on the sofa. Their knees were almost touching, in a way that suggested previous intimacy rather than renewed attraction. The late-evening sun poured through the window, highlighting their faces in profile.

"There are rumors," began Felix. His face was curiously malleable and always revealed the emotion of what he was about to say before the words came out of his mouth. Ali wondered whether this was a skill honed during his career as a journalist or whether it was something innate. Ali saw Bryony's cheek muscles tighten and the familiar twirl of her tongue around the inside of her mouth. She wasn't reading his signals correctly.

"If this is about my Ukrainian client, I've got nothing to say," said Bryony. "Present us with proof, and then his lawyers will know exactly what it is that you think he has done instead of all this insinuation and gossip. Lots of East Europeans did unsavory business deals when the wall came down. But whatever he's done, there is no way that he was involved in trafficking women. No way."

"It's closer to home, I'm afraid, Bryony," said Felix. "I've had a tip-off about Nick." His voice grew quieter until Ali couldn't hear any more.

The next day, at exactly five-thirty in the morning, there was a persistent ringing on the front doorbell followed by loud banging. No one usually bothered with the chrome door knocker apart from Malea, who loyally polished it once a week, and Izzy, who used it as the mirror of last resort when she was leaving the house. Most people stood patiently by the video intercom system, waiting to be buzzed in.

Although Ali was asleep on the fifth floor, the dull thud was enough to make her stir. She sat up in bed, wondering in sleepy confusion whether it was Bryony's personal trainer or Nick's driver, but they usually came in through the entrance in the basement. She looked at her clock, saw the time, and got out of bed as the noise intensified.

She assumed Bryony was now awake, although to judge from the empty bottle of wine left on the kitchen table last night, Bryony's head must feel as thick as goulash. Perhaps it was even Nick arriving home, having lost his keys. He worked so late at the moment that it wasn't inconceivable his day was just ending as everyone else's was beginning. His waking hours were spent trying to encourage the great Lehman sell-off to reduce the bank's debt.

For a moment she allowed herself to hope it might be Jake, coming home unannounced after a late-night party in London to celebrate the end of his first-year exams at university, except they had finished a month ago. Then, just as quickly, she banished the thought.

Leicester barked and growled. He was on full intruder alert, hurling himself at the letterbox, waiting for someone to put his hand through, knowing this was the only circumstance where he could legitimately sink his teeth into human flesh.

Ali would later discover that the Financial Services Authority had spent almost six months planning its dawn raid on 97 Holland Park Crescent. Thanks to the architects that had overseen renovations, each member of the eight-person team had an up-to-date floor plan of the interior. They also had a blown-up image of the outside of the house taken from Google Earth.

They knew how many mobile phones needed to be collected and how many iPod Touches needed to be checked; they had a rough idea of where computers might be located and Nick's briefcase might be found. They knew that the driver, Mr. Artouche, would be arriving in half an hour with Nick's car, and that this should be searched as quickly as possible and the SIM card removed from the car phone. You could tell a lot about a man's life from what you found in his glove compartment, Ali heard the man running the team tell a junior police officer.

The only detail they had overlooked was the presence of Nick's father-in-law, Mr. Foy Chesterton. No one involved in intelligence gathering had noticed that the most critical room for the purposes of their investigation had been turned from an office into a bedroom over the past week. All the computer equipment had been removed and the filing cabinet relocated upstairs in Bryony's office.

Ali pulled on her dressing gown and went out onto the landing to look out the window at the front of the house. There was a large white van outside with its back doors wide open. There were people wearing plastic overshoes, carrying large transparent polyethylene bags toward the front door. No one was wearing a uniform, but most were dressed in cheap-looking suits in drab colors. In the house on the other side of the street, Ali could see the neighbors observing the same scene from behind the curtains of the first-floor window.

The Darkes were standing in dressing gowns by the van, asking the driver exactly what was going on. The twins came out of the bedroom next door and came over to Ali, sleepily rubbing their eyes. They jostled for space at the window.

"Has Grandpa died?" asked Hector as he observed the scene. Foy was such a large figure in their life that she could understand the logic that his death would result in such fanfare.

"No," Ali said, and smiled. "Can't you hear him shouting downstairs?" They listened for a moment.

"Will someone tell me what the bloody hell is going on?" Foy's voice snaked upstairs. It quivered with the effort of maintaining enough breath to say everything in one sentence.

"Open the door, please, Mr. Skinner," cried a voice from the other side of the front door. "We have a search warrant from Westminster Magistrates' Court."

"It's Mr. Chesterton," Foy shouted back at them.

There was the sound of voices discussing this unexpected development.

"Can you please find Mr. Skinner and ask him to open the door, Mr. Chesterton?"

"Who is it?" said Foy, trying to summon strength he no longer possessed.

"It's the police," the same voice shouted back though the letterbox. "If you don't open, we'll have to make a forced entry."

"Has this got something to do with selling fake organic salmon?" Foy shouted back as best he could. "Because I've got nothing to do with Freithshire Fisheries anymore."

It was typical of Foy that he assumed whatever was happening was related to him and not to anyone else in the house. Then Ali felt guilty because of course he was still confused following his stroke. The recent scandal at his old company had dented both his confidence and his bank balance. The knocking on the door started up again.

Ali heard the door of Bryony and Nick's bedroom open and slam shut. Nick ran downstairs, two steps at a time, so fast that his paisley dressing gown floated behind him in the slipstream. Bryony followed, already dressed in her gym kit. The twins and Ali tiptoed down to the landing on the first floor, where they could observe what was happening in the hall without being seen. Nick opened the door, and a detective from the City of London Police handed over an envelope containing the search warrant.

"Is it something to do with the bank?" Bryony asked as Nick skimmed the letter. "I said you shouldn't rock the boat."

"We have permission to search the premises, Mr. Skinner," the policeman said.

"What's going on, Nick?" Bryony asked sharply.

"I've got no idea."

"Has it got something to do with Lehman's?" Bryony persisted.

"Bryony, the only person I want to speak to right now is a lawyer," Nick said calmly as he glanced over the warrant and put it neatly back in the envelope. "Could you call Hannah and ask her to come over right away? Otherwise, please don't say anything."

"Why do we need a lawyer?" Bryony asked in confusion.

Malea had come up from the basement. When she saw the group of people standing in the hall, she turned tail.

"Malea Cojuangco?" the policeman asked, referring to the notes in his hand. "Please come into the drawing room."

Malea froze by the staircase.

"Malea Cojuangco?" the policeman repeated. Malea nodded to confirm her name.

"Leave her alone," barked Foy. "She's completely legal."

"You want me to get my papers?" Malea asked nervously.

"We're not interested in you or your papers," the policeman abruptly replied. He turned to Nick again and calmly informed him that they were arresting him on charges of insider trading. Malea disappeared back downstairs.

"What the hell are you talking about?" asked Nick. Bryony was pulling at his sleeve, hysterically asking what was happening over and over again until Nick lost patience and shook her off.

Ali listened from the landing. She couldn't quite believe what she was seeing or hearing. She had no idea what insider trading was, but she understood that Nick was in trouble. Izzy had come out of her bedroom and was standing beside her. Her Goth attire didn't stretch to nightwear, and she was dressed in a curious ensemble of men's pajama bottoms and a pale pink sleeveless T-shirt that made her look more childlike and vulnerable than usual. Her face was pale, but this time it wasn't due to layers of foundation.

"I feel as though I've got a walk-on part in *The Wire*." Izzy laughed nervously, hoping that someone would suddenly tell them this was all an elaborate practical joke dreamed up by her father to wind up Foy. She clung on to Ali's arm. Hearing the voices from the landing, a policewoman craned her neck upstairs and suggested that they all come down into the drawing room.

"Look here," said Nick, "it's for me to tell my family what to do. You've got this completely wrong. Let me make a couple of calls and you'll understand you've made a big mistake. Heads will roll."

"If you don't let us start this search, then you will be obstructing the rule of law," the policeman said calmly.

"Do you know who I am?" Nick asked.

"Yes," said the policeman.

He explained that a similar "discreet" search was taking place at the same time in his office at Lehman's. A couple of women came through the door, and the policeman said that they were from the digital forensics team and would be responsible for examining computer equipment to decide what exactly should be confiscated.

"They can download a lot of information from your hard drive onto memory sticks, so the children don't lose their computers. It's less traumatic that way.

"Do you mind if we get started?" said the policeman. "We'll be here for the best part of a day. If we kick off now, we'll have taken most of the evidence to the van before your neighbors get up and start asking awkward questions."

It was a line that might have held meaning if it wasn't for the fact that most neighbors had already left their houses to come and see what was going on.

"Burglary," Nick shouted across to the Darkes, who relayed the message to other people farther down the street. "None of us woke up. Definitely premeditated."

"Let us know if there's anything we can do," said Desmond Darke earnestly. "Glad to see the police are taking it seriously. When we had a break-in last year it took them two days to come and take fingerprints."

"I'll let you know the upshot," said Nick, in a tone that suggested he could be counted on to represent their interests in matters relating to neighborhood security but would appreciate it if they left him to deal with the problem right now.

"Of course. Thanks, Nick. I'm sure you'll get through to them." Then he reluctantly returned home. Nick's tactic worked, and other onlookers dribbled back inside their houses, muttering about how much money they paid to the private security agency to patrol the street, precisely to avoid this kind of unfortunate event.

"Hand over your telephone right away, please, Mr. Skinner," said the policeman, "then we'll give you ten minutes to get everyone in the drawing room. It can be unsettling for your wife and children to see their belongings searched by strangers. We'll locate the exhibit officer discreetly in the dining room opposite."

"The exhibit officer?" questioned Nick impatiently.

"He'll be logging exactly what evidence is found and where, as well as the exact time. We'll be looking for notebooks, checkbooks, and paperwork relating to deals. We've already got bank statements. Can he use the dining room table?"

"Look, I need to get to work," said Nick. "I'm sure you're aware that Lehman's has a huge liquidity crisis."

"I don't think you'll be going to work for a very long time," said the policeman quietly.

"Are they going to search our room?" asked Hector, as they trooped downstairs into the drawing room. "Will they take Laurel and Hardy?"

"They're not interested in guinea pigs," said Ali gently.

A policewoman Ali hadn't seen before was sitting on the sofa. She stood up and offered to go and make them all a cup of tea.

"Can I have hot chocolate. Please?" asked Hector, sensing an opportunity.

"Can someone please explain to me what is going on?" asked Bryony, nervously twisting strands of hair around her fingers.

"Your husband is suspected of being involved in insider dealing," the policewoman explained. "Do you understand what that means?" She didn't wait for an answer.

"We have reason to believe that he has illicitly gathered price-sensitive information to make a profit trading shares."

"Don't be ridiculous," Bryony retorted. "He earns a fortune. Why would he bother doing insider dealing? It's not worth taking the risk. My husband is a very cautious man." Ali was relieved by Bryony's tone, although she wasn't convinced by her description of Nick.

"We recommend that you are honest with the children about the fact their house is being searched and reassure them that anything that is taken away will be returned at a later date," the policewoman said sotto voce to Bryony. "We'll be taking your husband to Bishopsgate police station for a preliminary interview under caution. We'll hold him in a cell until his lawyer arrives."

The policeman came in and told Nick that a press release with skeletal details about the raid had just been released and that an application to freeze all his assets had been approved.

"What does he mean?" Bryony sounded panicked.

"It means that we can't access any money from our bank accounts," said Nick.

"For how long?" Bryony asked.

"Until this is resolved," said the policewoman gently.

21

· · · · · · ·
· · · · · · ·

When Ali got up with the twins the following morning, there was no sign of Malea. For the first time since she had moved into Holland Park Crescent, breakfast wasn't waiting on the table when she came into the kitchen at seven o'clock in the morning. The sink was full of unwashed saucepans, there were crumbs and dog hairs underfoot, and the door of the dishwasher was wide open. Leicester was taking full advantage and had managed to climb right inside to ensure there wasn't a plate or piece of cutlery that could escape his tongue. Hector pulled him out. There was chocolate soufflé on his nose and pasta sauce on his back. Ali opened the door into the garden and watched as Leicester immediately dumped the contents of last night's meal on the grass. She didn't go out to pick it up.

"Where's Malea?" asked Hector.

"Maybe the police confiscated her, too," suggested Alfie. He looked toward Ali for approval for remembering the correct terminology. They seemed remarkably unruffled by yesterday's events, perhaps because they were the only members of the family to retain all their gadgetry and their father's sudden disappearance was nothing unusual. But also because the very insularity that Bryony found so disturbing protected Hector and Alfie from life's squalls.

"When will they bring Daddy's computer back?" Alfie asked as he sat down, waiting for breakfast to appear.

"They're just borrowing it," Hector reminded him. Ali wasn't sure what to say to them about anything.

"They'll bring it back when they've finished playing with it," said Bryony brightly, as she emerged from the larder carrying four packets of unopened cereal, accordion style, between her hands. She had no idea what anyone usually ate for breakfast, so she had chosen the healthiest options. These she put down on the table in front of Hector and Alfie. The twins explained in unison that Malea usually made them eggy bread.

"I don't know how to do that," said Bryony, sounding defeated.

"We'll show you," said Hector. Alfie took her by the hand and led her over to the cooker. Hector lined up eggs, a frying pan, and two pieces of bread, and issued instructions. Bryony managed a small, quick smile that made her face look a little less drawn. She was always pale. But this morning her skin had taken on an almost translucent quality. Her eyes were a shade lighter than usual, and her hair was a briary, unkempt tangle. She was wearing a skirt, a silk shirt, and high-heeled summer sandals that suggested she might go to work at some point. Whether it was out of habit or intent was unclear to Ali.

"You're only as good as your last meal," said Alfie, cracking eggs into a bowl. "Now beat, please."

"What are you talking about?" asked Bryony, as she whisked the eggs together with a fork. A dollop slopped over the edge of the bowl onto her shirt, but either she didn't mind or she didn't notice.

"It's a line from *MasterChef*," explained Hector.

"When do you watch that?" Bryony asked.

"I thought it fell under the auspices of educational TV," Ali nervously interjected, although since she had never seen Bryony or Nick prepare a meal, perhaps they didn't consider cookery an essential life skill. It was one of those things you could outsource.

"Can we have breakfast in front of the television?" asked Alfie. Ali kept quiet, waiting for Bryony's lead.

"What do you think, Ali?" she eventually asked.

"Maybe as a special treat," Ali agreed, not wanting to appear either too strict or too indulgent.

No wonder nannies that worked for stay-at-home mums said it was the worst of all worlds. Hector and Alfie headed to the other end of the room and immediately put on a DVD of *The Great Escape*. Ali could tell because they were whistling the theme tune and arguing over the names of the three tunnels.

"Where's Malea?" Ali asked, as Bryony dipped the bread in the egg and failed to cover the edges.

There were so many unanswered questions, but at least this one was relatively innocuous. Bryony pointed to a note pinned on the fridge. Ali read a sentence formally announcing Malea's decision to resign as housekeeper. Her signature was bigger than the resignation letter. No reason was given. Perhaps the police raid brought back memories of something bad that had happened to her in the Philippines? Maybe her work permit was out of date? Or the Philippine bush wire had gone into overdrive after yesterday's raid and Malea understood how the land lay better than anyone else? Bryony shrugged to indicate she had no idea and still less desire to discuss.

"Do you know how the washing machine works?" she asked Ali.

"I think so," said Ali. "At least, I'm pretty sure I can work it out."

"Thank God. I thought I might have to take the clothes to a laundrette." Bryony smiled weakly. "Then someone can take a picture of me washing our dirty laundry in public." It was a brave rather than a funny joke, and Ali did her best to laugh, but she couldn't help worrying that Bryony was expecting her to fill the domestic void.

"Do you want me to show you how it works now or after breakfast?" Ali blurted out. The rules of engagement had subtly altered. Bryony looked flummoxed.

"After breakfast is fine," she said eventually, acknowledging this shift in the balance of power. "Thanks very much."

Their normal routine dissolved, Ali started to review her options for the day. It would be better for Hector and Alfie to go and play with friends. Given the situation, she imagined the separate-playdate rule wouldn't be a deal-breaker for Bryony. She went to the notice board where the class list was usually pinned, intending to call Storm's nanny to see if they could go play at her house. Storm's mother wouldn't pick up the phone, because she didn't get out of bed until after midday, and she took so many pills to sleep that she wouldn't be woken by the sound of children coming over to play so early in the morning. The list, however, had disappeared, although four drawing pins were still stuck in the board where it had once hung.

"I think it's been removed as part of this investigation," Bryony explained. "Can you believe it? They took a couple of photo albums and all the invitations from the mantelpiece in the drawing room as well. They even took the photograph of Izzy's netball team from her bedroom wall. Probably because it's full of girls in short skirts."

"What exactly do you think they are looking for?" Ali asked, sensing a softening of Bryony's tone.

"They're searching for evidence to prove these ridiculous charges against Nick, I guess." Bryony sighed deeply, and the arm of the silk shirt slipped from her shoulder, revealing a small area of pale flesh. She started massaging it in tiny circles. "We didn't get much sleep last night. Nick got home after midnight."

"Where did they take him?" Ali asked.

"They kept him in a cell at Bishopsgate police station until his lawyer arrived. Then they questioned him for four hours and released him on bail. He could hardly speak when he came in."

"What is he accused of?" Ali asked. "I was just wondering what I should say . . . in case the children ask . . . or other nannies."

"Insider dealing," said Bryony, putting overcooked slices of eggy bread onto plates. Ali sprinkled sugar on top. Bryony chose to ignore the lapse, but Ali could see from the way she chewed her lower lip that it bothered her. "He's accused of using information from someone inside a company to buy shares in it before it was about to be sold or taken over. It's just the FSA trying to flex its muscles because of the banking crisis. And a managing director at Lehman's is a perfect target."

Her manner reminded Ali of the way she spoke to journalists when she was trying to kill a rumor.

"Why would someone do insider dealing?"

"To make money. It happens all the time. That's why I'm so careful about what I say to people about my clients and never buy shares in any of their companies. It's a very dodgy but very simple way of making lots of extra pocket money: if a company is being sold, its value increases and its share price goes up once the deal is announced," explained Bryony.

She stopped and looked Ali directly in the eye. Ali could see a hint of steel. "Nick didn't do this. They've got the wrong man."

"But if someone was to do this, how would they actually make any money?" Ali persisted.

"If you know a deal is happening before anyone else, then you can buy shares in the company before the price goes up and sell them once the announcement has gone out and the share price rockets. You pocket the difference."

"I still don't understand why the police would take the names and addresses of parents at school and photos of your wedding and all that other stuff?" Ali asked.

"Your guess is as good as mine," said Bryony. "Thanks for staying, by the way. When all this is over, we'll remember your loyalty."

Ali's phone beeped to indicate she had a message. She looked down to see who had called but didn't recognize the number. While Bryony took the plates of eggy bread over to the twins, Ali dialed her voice mail to hear a message from Felix Naylor asking her to get in touch urgently.

"We can't talk on the phone," Felix said. "We need to meet. Just name the date and place and I'll be there."

Nick came downstairs. Ali hadn't seen him since he had left in a police car the previous afternoon, and wasn't sure whether to acknowledge what was euphemistically dubbed "the situation." She was taken aback to see him dressed in jeans and T-shirt on a weekday. He hadn't shaved, and his eyes were as puffy and wrinkled as Leicester's.

She stood up suddenly, in case he hadn't noticed she was in the room. Her chair went flying.

"Steady, Ali," he said. "My nerves are shot already."

"Do you want me to make you a coffee?" Ali offered.

"Where's Malea?" Nick asked.

"She's gone," said Bryony flatly.

"What do you mean?" he asked, his brow furrowing. Bryony gave him the note. He read it and tore it up. "Coffee would be great, thanks. So I'm in good fettle for my lawyer."

According to Bryony, Nick had hired the best corporate-fraud defense lawyer in London. She knew the woman charged £750 an hour because Foy was paying and yesterday afternoon it was all he could talk about. Since his collapse, he had a tendency to relentlessly fixate on a single issue until he had exhausted himself and anyone else unfortunate enough to be in the drawing room at the same time.

Nick was carrying all the newspapers under his arm, and a copy of yesterday's press release from the FSA. This he handed to Bryony while he began scanning the newspapers for stories. Despite the fact that a couple of journalists and at least four photographers had arrived outside the house yesterday before the investigators had even left, the FSA had been true to their word and given only a skeletal account of the dawn raid.

"'The Financial Services Authority (FSA) today arrested two senior City professionals at leading City institutions and executed two search warrants in two premises in connection with a significant insider-dealing ring.'" Bryony read the top paragraph out loud twice, the second time a little slower than the first. She stared at it in confusion and then repeated it again.

"It says that two people were arrested and two premises were searched. What are they talking about, Nick? Do they mean because your office was searched, too?"

"Just what it says: they arrested someone else at the same time," said Nick, as he spread out the first newspaper on the table in front of him. "There is an alleged co-conspirator." He didn't look up. His smooth tone was reassuring to Ali, as if underlining the absurdity of his situation, but it seemed to agitate Bryony.

"Do you know who it is? Were they at the police station, too? Did they raid their home at the same time?"

"Yes, yes, and yes." He still didn't look up from the paper.

"So who is it?"

"Ned Wilbraham."

"Ned Wilbraham?"

"Ned Wilbraham," Nick confirmed.

"You hardly know him."

"That's what I told them. It's ridiculous."

"What did they say?"

"They suggested that we were in cahoots. They say that I got the information, passed it on to Ned, he bought the shares, and then we split the difference. I told them they should reconsider a career writing fiction."

"It explains why they've taken the school list, though, doesn't it?" said Bryony, jangly nerved. "And the photo albums. Because they'll find pictures of you and Ned together, won't they? At our party, for example, or at the Petersons' house in Corfu. Isn't Martha on the same netball team as Izzy?"

"You can't build a case around such spurious evidence," said Nick dismissively. "Insider dealing is notoriously difficult to prove. I buy stocks and shares all the time."

"They obviously think they've got something, otherwise they wouldn't pursue it, would they?"

"Sometimes the FSA indiscriminately sticks a net in the sea and pulls out whatever fish they can catch in the hope of scaring off others. It's banker-bashing season, after all," commented Nick.

Ali sat at the table throughout this exchange, wondering whether Nick had forgotten she was in the room. She debated whether to go but felt too self-conscious to suddenly get up and leave when they were in the middle of such a heated debate. His reaction niggled Ali. He should be protesting his innocence rather than finding reasons why he couldn't be prosecuted.

"Why didn't you tell me about this last night?" It was difficult to work out whether Bryony was more annoyed that Nick had withheld information or that Ned Wilbraham was involved.

"It didn't seem relevant." Nick sighed, as though the whole affair was a ridiculous rigmarole. "Still, if we both go down, at least you and Sophia can share lifts for prison visits." He lifted up his espresso to his lips and drank the whole cup without pausing.

"Stop being so flippant," Bryony said angrily.

"Sorry," said Nick. "I just can't take this very seriously. I was underwhelmed by their evidence, and my lawyer says it's going to be very difficult for them to prove any connection between us."

"But in the meantime our bank accounts are frozen, your passport is confiscated, which rather messes up our holiday in Corfu next week, and you can't go to work," said Bryony, her voice rising. "Correct me if I'm wrong, but I would say that all in all, that seems like a pretty shit situation to me."

"My lawyer will get it sorted, Bryony. Please try and stay calm. They haven't charged me with anything yet. They've got to build a case against me to press charges."

"There could be a lot of media interest in this, and it's not sub judice unless you're charged," Bryony worried. "Stories about greedy bankers with their greedy bonuses netting even more money through grubby little backroom deals sell newspapers. No one is more reviled at the moment. Not even pedophiles. They'll be digging around for stories about us."

"The point is, Bryony, that I didn't do it," said Nick firmly.

He still didn't seem perturbed. Instead he insisted they focus their attention on what the papers were saying, so that they could try to build some kind of coherent response. Perhaps Bryony was right, perhaps the antidepressants were numbing his reactions.

"Get our side of the story out first, isn't that always your advice?" he asked Bryony.

He started with one of the tabloids, knowing that their coverage would be the most lacerating. He opened up the *Daily Mail* and folded the paper back on itself to concentrate on the first page.

Bryony sat down beside him. Ali took her plate to the dishwasher and then came back to the table to collect the rest of the dirty dishes. She caught sight of the first headline and stopped to read it over Nick's shoulder. "Banker at Troubled Lehman Brothers Arrested for Insider Dealing." There was a small fact box with bullet points: insider trading was suspected in thirty-two percent of City takeovers; people rarely acted alone; the usual modus operandi was for the person providing the information to get someone else to make the trade with a broker and then split the proceeds; insider trading had become rife in the City during the boom years. There was a photograph of Nick and Ned, "the alleged co-conspirator," taken together at the Christmas drinks party the previous year.

"It's really bad news the way the media is linking this with the banking crisis," said Bryony. "Even if the charges aren't proven, you could end up being the scapegoat for a whole industry. Especially because you were involved in subprime securities and Lehman's has been so greedy and reckless. It has all the ingredients of a perfect scandal."

"I hope you offer more comfort to your clients in times of crisis," observed Nick, who, in Ali's opinion, seemed unnaturally unbothered at the way his life was being unpicked so publicly in a newspaper. He turned the paper over to the next page.

There was a picture of Jake, sprawled on the grass outside his Oxford college, smoking dope from the same pipe that he shared with Ali at the party. His head was resting on the bare stomach of a girl wearing a bikini top and a pair of cutoff denim shorts. Most definitely not Lucy. His arm was pointing toward the camera, his palm flat, in an effort to block the lens. But his reactions were evidently slowed by the dope, and instead he was captured with a leery half-smile in a cloud of smoke, obviously stoned.

"Oh my God," said Bryony. "He's on drugs."

"How could he do this to us?" groaned Nick. "We told him to lie low."

Ali glanced at Nick. She wanted to tell him that he was being unfair, because if he hadn't been arrested then no one would have been interested in a photograph of his son smoking dope at university. The newspaper story was all about the wild lifestyle of the son of disgraced City banker Nick Skinner. It didn't mention that Jake had just got a first in his end-of-year exams.

"It's an old photo," Ali pointed out. "His new flat doesn't have any outside space. He was probably just relaxing after exams. He wouldn't have got a first if he had a big drug problem, and he wouldn't turn up to work at the right time every day."

"Everyone is going to see this," said Bryony, starting to cry.

"Do you think he realizes?" Nick asked. He instinctively reached out for his BlackBerry, but of course, with the exception of Ali, all their mobile phones had been taken.

"I'm lost without my bloody phone," he said. "Can I borrow yours, please, Ali?"

She handed over her BlackBerry, and Nick scrolled down her contacts list, looking for Jake's name.

"Jake isn't in there," said Ali.

"Why not?" asked Bryony.

"I deleted him when he went to university," Ali mumbled.

"What's his number?" Nick asked Bryony.

"Don't you know your son's number?" Bryony asked, as she tapped it in. Her hand was shaking as she gave the phone to Nick. Poor Jake, thought Ali, as he picked up the phone expecting to hear Ali's voice and instead was woken by his father delivering a scathing indictment of his behavior. She could hear him protesting to Nick that one of his friends must have sold the photograph to the newspaper and that it was taken almost two months ago. Jake sounded confused, as well he might, because from Nick's reaction it was as if his conduct had eclipsed the insider-dealing charges.

"How did it go at the police station?" Jake kept asking. "What exactly is going on?"

"Don't try and change the subject," Nick persisted. There was a pause. "Your mother is very upset about this."

He's going to exploit this to take the pressure off him, realized Ali. Bryony was nervously flicking through the *Financial Times*. Her body was taut with tension and her movements quick and abrupt. She found a small piece, more concise and better sourced, largely based on the FSA press release on the front of the Companies and Markets section of the newspaper. She ran her finger over the story, nervously picking apart each sentence. Her hand stopped in the middle and she rubbed the same line over and over again with her finger until the tip was stained with ink.

"It says here that your wife is a senior partner at a City financial PR company and that some of her clients are reconsidering their position in light of the accusations. What do they mean?"

Before Nick could answer, the phone on the desk by the bookshelf started ringing. Bryony got up to get it, half running to the other side of the room. Ali understood from the swift exchange that it was one of the partners at work letting Bryony know that her Ukrainian energy company had called up to say that given the circumstances they would be looking for a new financial PR agency to represent them.

"Did you say someone else could head up the account?" Bryony said.

Her business partner said that she had made the same suggestion, but they were adamant. Bryony said that she would get in touch with them and at least put their case across.

There was a lull in conversation. Bryony's colleague hesitantly suggested that perhaps it was better if Bryony stayed at home and lay low until the initial interest had died down. It wasn't good for a PR company to be the subject of news. Bryony reluctantly agreed. She put down the phone, stared at it for a moment, as if collecting her thoughts, and then came back to the kitchen table.

"Is my Ukrainian client one of the companies that you're accused of buying shares in?" she asked. "No bullshit, Nick."

"It might have been one of them," said Nick, his brow knitted as he tried to recall details. "They mentioned so many in the interview."

"You know that I worked on that takeover deal?"

"Of course," said Nick.

"Why didn't you tell me this last night?" she asked, banging her fist on the table.

"I didn't want to worry you until it's clear what evidence they have against me. My lawyer says they'll say a lot of stuff in the hope of catching me out."

"Even if you're proven innocent, this 'stuff' will have an impact on me," said Bryony. "I can't believe you didn't tell me. You know they've fired us."

"I didn't know that someone would leak it to a newspaper," said Nick apologetically.

"So did you do it?"

"Did I do what?"

"Did you buy shares in my company just before they were sold?"

"No."

"Did you know about this deal from me?"

"What was it called?"

"The codename was Project Odysseus."

"Rings no bells at all."

Ali studied his face as he took Bryony by the hand. Everyone had tics that revealed when they were lying. Will MacDonald's nostrils flared; the twins couldn't look her in the eye; Katya whistled; her sister pulled her lower lip with a finger; her mother couldn't blink. Apart from a slightly plaintive concertina of his forehead, a gesture aimed at provoking sympathy, Nick's features remained passive. His blue eyes were a little watery, his face perhaps more flushed than usual, but that could have been due to the shot of caffeine. His smile was genuine. But Ali remembered the papers she had seen in the drawing room two years earlier when Jake had stumbled upon them sitting on the sofa, and knew that Nick was lying.

"I'd better call the office again," said Bryony, getting up from the table.

"Careful what you say on the phone," warned Nick.

Before Bryony could get to the phone it started ringing, and for the next hour it didn't stop. The first call was from the Darkes next door, offering help and support and suggesting that if the children wanted to avoid the photographers already lined up on the other side of Holland Park Crescent, they were welcome to climb over the fence into their garden and go out through the basement of their house to get onto the street. Perhaps this was how the burglar escaped, Desmond Darke said sarcastically.

"That's kind," said Bryony, "especially since we lied to them about what was going on." She had no sooner put down the phone than it rang again. This time it was Ali's parents. Her mother apologetically explained to Bryony that they had tried and failed to get hold of Ali on her mobile. Ali signaled from the other side of the kitchen that she didn't want to speak to her. Shortly after this, Hester called to say that she would be coming round as soon as possible to help out. Bryony tried to put her off.

"A dawn raid by my sister," Bryony said, and sighed. "I'm not sure I can endure."

Tita called from Corfu to let them know she would catch the next flight home. Bryony said she would be grateful to have some help with Foy. Tita agreed but said nothing about his moving back into their house. Lucy's father phoned to let them know that his daughter was going on a round-the-world trip, and they would be grateful if Jake would avoid contacting her before she left, especially given his drug problem. Bryony put the phone on voice mail and it rang again. This time it was Sophia Wilbraham.

"Bryony, Bryony, are you there?" Sophia's panicky voice echoed round the kitchen. "Ned's been arrested. Something to do with Nick. Call me if you know what's going on. He won't tell me a thing."

"On no account speak to her," Nick called from the bottom of the stairs. "I'm going to call my lawyer again."

"Do you have any money?" Bryony shouted to him.

"Forty pounds," he confirmed.

"How are we going to pay for anything?" she asked.

"We'll be given three hundred fifty pounds a week living expenses until they decide whether to charge me. We're going to appeal to try and persuade them to allow us access to more funds. If I can convince them I have enough assets to cover all the proceeds from the trades they've accused me of making, they might easily award us more."

"How much are they accusing you of making?" asked Bryony.

"Not much," said Nick. "Five million, tops."

"That's a fuck of a lot of money, and they'll make you pay back more," Bryony exploded, "and how can we live off three hundred fifty pounds a week? The mortgage on both houses is about ten thousand pounds a month. Maybe we should just sell Thornberry Manor?"

"You can't sell anything if your assets are frozen," Nick calmly explained. "The only way I can raise any money is perhaps by selling off a couple of paintings or some jewelry through a friendly antiques dealer who will pay us in cash. Totally verboten, but it might be worth doing that before they come and do the inventory of our belongings. Perhaps Ali could help you pick out a few things?"

"This is a nightmare," said Bryony. Nick came over to her and put his arms around her. She remained seated, head bowed, arms folded in front of her. "Why is this happening to us?"

"Someone with a grudge, perhaps," said Nick. "Someone who wants to create a hate figure to atone for the banking crisis?"

Surely the FSA and the police wouldn't raid the house of a prominent City banker without good evidence to prove their allegations? Ali wanted to ask. But Bryony wasn't looking for logic. She just wanted comfort. Ali got up from the table and went in search of an old class list. She found a number for Storm's nanny, but when she managed to get through a couple of hours later the nanny apologetically explained that the girl's mother had said that she couldn't play with the twins.

"Why?" said Ali, furious on their behalf.

"In case there are any drugs in the house," the nanny said.

"But Storm's mum is completely addicted to sleeping pills," said Ali, who had heard numerous stories from this nanny about the mother's erratic behavior, including her seduction of a Polish plumber, her penchant for saying good night to her children on the intercom, and the fact she didn't believe in de-nitting the children because it involved killing animals.

"I know," she whispered. "Maybe we could meet in the park one day. Storm will really miss them. I don't know what else to suggest. These people are all crazy. I'd leave if it wasn't for the little girl."

Ali put the phone down and it rang almost immediately. Perhaps the nanny had relented. But it was the internal phone.

"Ali, is that you?" Foy's voice shouted. "Is anyone going to come and help me get out of bed? You know I can't stand up on my own in the morning. Bloody legs! Where's Malea? Where's my breakfast? And where's that bloody lawyer? If I'm paying for her, then at least I'm entitled to meet her."

"I'll come and help you," Ali offered.

Jake arrived from Oxford a couple of days later, looking chastened. He had been fired from his job at the wine bar because the owner had seen his photograph in the newspaper. He went into the drawing room for what he described as a "ritual bollocking" and then went down to find Ali and the twins in the basement.

"What the fuck's going on?" he asked as he slumped into a sofa. "Dad's the one who's been arrested and everyone's behaving as though I'm the criminal."

Ali gave a whispered chronology of events out of earshot of Hector and Alfie, who were building a Lego city on the playroom floor.

"Your dad seems fairly confident that he'll be proven innocent," said Ali.

"Mum's a mess, though," Jake said.

"Her house has been taken apart by detectives, her husband has been arrested, her housekeeper has left, she's lost one of her biggest clients," said Ali. "She's got a lot to be stressed about. And she's just discovered her son's a drug addict." The last she said in a teasing tone, hoping to illicit a smile.

"Did you know she called The Priory?" Jake gave a hollow laugh. "Can you imagine how embarrassing it would be to end up there and try to contribute to a group-therapy discussion on addiction when you're a very casual dope smoker?"

"It would be surreal," agreed Ali.

"Anyway, she can't pay for me to go there, because all their bank accounts are frozen," said Jake. "I think she's using the drug thing as a diversion."

He stood up and accidentally trod on an intersection. Hector yelled at him.

"You've killed a policeman."

"Doing a raid," added Alfie.

"Why don't you send an ambulance?" suggested Jake.

"We can build a hospital," said Alfie excitedly. To Ali's relief, Hector acquiesced.

"Where's Izzy?" Jake asked. "Mum and Dad didn't seem to know."

"She went to stay at a friend's last night, and she hasn't come home," said Ali.

"Look, shall we take these guys to the park?" Jake suggested. I need to get out."

"You've only just got here."

"I can't stand it here at the best of times, and this is the worst of times," said Jake.

Ali called the Darkes, who agreed to help spirit them away from the house through their back garden and out the basement door, well away from the lenses of prying photographers. Having just seen *The Great Escape* again, Hector and Alfie embraced the subterfuge.

"Bad business, bad business," Desmond Darke muttered after putting a ladder against his garden fence to help them over. It was obvious he was more concerned about the twins' flattening his peonies than he was about their well-being. Ali noticed his wife staring down at them with disapproving pursed lips from their sitting room on the first floor. She was a tall, big-boned woman with large feet and hands. She was wearing a floral dress with a high collar and a bow tied around the waist that made her look like Grayson Perry.

"He's let the side down," Desmond told Ali, as he led them across the lawn, into the house, and up the stairs to the front door.

"What side?" Ali asked in confusion.

"We were more discreet with our money," he said, touching his nose with his finger. "I blame Bryony. If she hadn't worked, she might have stayed at home and looked after him more, so that he didn't feel the need to buy a new Aston Martin every time his bonus came through. Conspicuous greed. Never a good thing."

"What about inconspicuous greed?" Ali asked. He looked at her as though she was being facetious and barked at the twins to hurry up the stairs from the basement and to avoid touching the wallpaper.

"How's Foy?" Desmond asked. "He was always suspicious of Nick. Always said he wasn't one of us. And Tita must be reeling. Absolutely reeling." He looked at Ali expectantly.

As they walked past the kitchen table, Ali could see the *Daily Mail* open on the photograph of Jake in his cloud of smoke.

"That's put an end to your career in investment banking," whispered Ali.

"Well at least some good has come out of this, then," Jake said.

"I tell you what, if it looks as though they need to sell their house, tell them that I'd give them a good price," Desmond said suddenly, as though he was bestowing a great favor. He nudged Ali in the ribs.

"Maybe you could tell them," Ali suggested. "I'm sure they would like to see some old friends."

"Can't have them here with that rabble outside," said Desmond, as he opened the front door to let them out. Ali turned to thank him, but he had already shut the door in their face. In two years, this was the longest conversation she had ever had with him.

They arrived at Holland Park when the sun was at its highest, and sought refuge down one of the tree-lined paths. The twins left Ali and Jake trailing behind. The heat made their voices sound louder and hang in the air longer than they should, which made them both feel self-conscious. Jake kept both hands in the side pockets of his jeans and kicked the path as though there were leaves on the ground, but there was only dust, which sent tiny clouds billowing around their ankles. Hector and Alfie wanted to go to the Japanese garden so they could race backward and forward across the little bridge.

"Sure," said Ali agreeably, grateful for their sense of purpose. "Anything to avoid the adventure playground. It will be hell on a day like this. And full of people who know what's going on."

"You can't control other people's response to what's happened," said Jake. "The most we can do is behave with integrity until it resolves. Mum should forget trying to spin and counterspin. The truth will out eventually. So let's go to the Japanese garden because we want to go there, not because we're afraid of who we might bump into on the monkey bars."

He's right, thought Ali, taken aback by the sophistication of his logic. Jake called out to the twins, pointing out a peacock on the path ahead. His tenderness and sense of responsibility all the more poignant in the circumstances.

"It's because that's what she does for a living," said Ali. "Her instinct is to get out her side of the story and deny everything."

"I've been studying *Beowulf* this year, and I've come to the conclusion that public relations is nothing more than a modern way of wreaking revenge on your enemies. Basically, you pay other people to go to war and maintain feuds on your behalf."

Ali giggled. "Anyway, she should resist the urge to fight, particularly since she hasn't got all the facts straight yet."

"She's convinced your father is innocent."

Jake raised a cynical eyebrow. Ali was taken aback. Until that moment she hadn't really considered the possibility that Nick might be guilty.

"Dad has never been completely comfortable in his own skin," said Jake. "He comes from a very different background to Mum, and instead of embracing their differences, he's tried to reinvent himself as a member of the upper middle classes, using Foy as a role model. So before you ask me if he's innocent, I'll tell you that there's a strong chance I think he isn't. I don't blame him. He's spent a long time trying to reconcile all the contradictory strands in his life, and he's bound to fuck up one day."

Ali looked at him. A curtain of jet-black fringe obscured his eyes so it was difficult to read the emotion behind the analysis. She wanted to reach out and touch his arm, because sometimes a physical gesture was more reassuring than words, but Ali was inhibited by the new equality in their relationship.

"All parents are fallible," she finally agreed, wishing that she could respond more eloquently.

"How's your sister?" Jake asked.

Ali had forgotten the conversation on the roof at the party.

"She's finished the treatment. She wants to do her A-levels again, but my parents think she should stay at home for another year. She thinks she's strong enough to deal with it."

"What do you think?" asked Jake.

"I think she might get bored."

"If she's feeling better about herself, then she might be fine. I mean, Izzy is the only person I know who calculates the calories in her multivitamin, but I think she's got more confidence now and is at least doing it with a sense of irony."

"How many calories does a multivitamin have?" asked Ali.

"Fifteen, apparently." Jake laughed. "And what about you?"

"What about me?"

"When are you leaving?"

"I'll weather the storm." Ali smiled. "I can't leave Hector and Alfie after what's happened."

"Well, let's weather it together," said Jake.

They walked beside each other, intimate enough to suggest they were together but careful not to stray too close. They looked either at the ground or directly ahead at the twins. They agreed that the squirrels were like overweight beggars as they waddled toward them and waited to be fed. They decided that the peacocks looked arrogant and that their tails made a sound like a drum when they fanned them out. They agreed that if the females were human they would wear Vivienne Westwood.

Occasionally, if another couple passed or a boisterous dog lunged toward them, they were forced into closer proximity. At one point their elbows bumped and they lurched away from each other like repelling magnets. This common intent was good, decided Ali.

"Malea left," said Ali.

"Mum told me," said Jake.

"I think she was scared," they both said at once.

"Are you pretending to be twins?" asked Hector, eyeing them with curiosity as he waited for them to catch up.

Ali and Jake fell into self-conscious silence again. Then they both began speaking at the same time.

"How have you been?" they said together.

"Our timing is off," Ali said, and laughed.

"Or on," said Jake.

"Do you know who sold the photograph of you?" Ali asked as they fell into a more comfortable rhythm down a wider path where there was no need for proximity.

"I have an idea," said Jake, "but she denies it."

"Lucy?" Ali guessed.

"She found it in my room the last time she came to stay, when I finally managed to end it," he said. "She was jealous of the girl and incandescent with me for being on the roof with you at my grandfather's party."

"Hell hath no fury and all that," said Ali.

They walked into the Japanese garden together. Hector and Alfie insisted they should all cross the bridge together the first time.

"If one dies, then we all die," declared Alfie.

"There might be explosives underneath," said Hector seriously.

"Like *The Bridge on the River Kwai*," said Alfie.

"It's a Japanese garden," said Hector.

"It was the British who planted the explosives," argued Alfie.

"They've been watching a lot of war films with your grandfather," Ali told Jake.

They started out on the circular path around the garden. The twins insisted on holding hands between Jake and Ali. As they got closer to the stream, they all let go and picked up speed so that by the time they reached the bridge they were racing to get to the other side.

"Quick, quick, before they get us," shouted Hector, who was in front.

"Who gets us?" Ali shouted behind.

"The prison guards," he yelled.

"And the sharks," said Alfie, pointing at the giant carp in the pond.

"And the FSA," said Hector.

"And Storm's mummy," said Alfie.

"We're being pursued by the FSA." Ali giggled as she and Jake hurtled across to the other side. When they were all safe they lay on the ground, laughing breathlessly at themselves. A couple passed them and remarked on what a happy family group they made.

"Your parents must be very proud," one of them said to Ali. They all cackled even louder at the absurdity of the idea.

Hector and Alfie said they wanted to go round once more and asked Jake and Ali to wait for them on a bench beneath a huge acer on the other side of the stream.

"Sure," said Jake, plonking himself down in the middle. Ali sat down beside him.

"They need to let off steam, they've been cooped up for two days."

They both leaned forward, hands gripping the edge of the bench. Ali was grateful they could focus on the twins, who had reached the beginning of the path again. She began to tell Jake about Storm's mother refusing to have them to play.

"She was wild about them before this happened," Ali complained.

"It will be interesting to see who sticks by us," said Jake. "The people who are with you on the way up aren't always the same as the ones who stay with you on the way down."

"Your parents have hundreds of friends. Even if fifty percent desert them, they'll still have more than my parents have ever had."

"They have hundreds of acquaintances. It's not the same thing. The first hint of failure and the invitations will dry up. Just you watch."

The silence between them was filled by the sound of the water rushing over a series of stone waterfalls into the pond beneath.

"It reminds me of the swimming pool in Corfu," said Ali.

"God, do you remember when you came down to the pool with the twins and Lucy got so angry?" said Jake.

"You were the one that was angry," Ali pointed out.

"It was because she was always jealous of you," said Jake.

"Why would she be jealous of me?" asked Ali.

"She always thought you were more integrated in our family than her," Jake said with a shrug.

"I'm paid to be integrated," said Ali.

"You're grounded, and she's insecure," said Jake. "Some people find that threatening. I find it attractive."

"Don't you find it strange that so many Japanese tourists come here?" asked Ali, trying to nudge the conversation toward more neutral territory. "If I went to Japan I wouldn't go in search of an English garden. It's like someone from China coming to London to visit Chinatown, or Americans eating in McDonald's."

"Maybe they're homesick. My grandfather always eats smoked salmon when he's in Greece."

They kept talking. Jake discussed which author he should choose to study in depth at the end of his second year—Seamus Heaney or Thomas Hardy. Ali asked whether studying Heaney meant he couldn't answer questions on *Beowulf* in his finals. Jake suggested he should opt for Hardy because he liked the idea of people being held prisoner to fate. When Ali asked him why, he said that sometimes having too many opportunities was inhibiting, and it let you off the hook to think life was preordained. Ali said she wasn't sure that she would ever be able to write an essay again, but Jake said it was like riding a bicycle. The twins came over to ask for water and something to eat, and then returned to their game on the bridge.

She could feel Jake's hand beside her own and wondered how long it had been there, and whether he was aware that the tip of his little finger was touching the tip of her little finger. Her whole body was focused on this tiny connection. She hardly dared to breathe in case it was broken. This can only end badly, Ali thought, as she felt the surge of energy between them, as though their fingers were conducting electricity. The sun edged around the top of the tree, and Ali squinted against the glare and the heat.

She didn't look down. They both stared ahead. Then she felt Jake's finger creep closer until it was on top of her own, and any ambiguity disappeared. He stroked her hand slowly from top to bottom with the tip of his thumb. Much later, she would look back at this moment and consider how such a tiny gesture could change things in ways that you couldn't possibly imagine at the time. She would wonder if she knew what was to come, whether she would have pulled away and insisted it was time to go home, and how that would have changed the course of events. At the time, however, she was too filled with desire to speak or move. She felt nauseous with longing and, apart from that, nothing except the rapturous "nowness" of being lost in the moment.

"This is clearly a really bad idea from many different points of view," Jake said slowly, without looking at her. Ali nodded in agreement. His hand was now completely on top of hers. He had made the first move, but she hadn't resisted. Their fingers curled together, and for a few minutes they sat without speaking, staring vacantly ahead at the Japanese bridge, even though the twins were now on the other side of the garden.

They came out of the park through the little-used gate on the west side because there was less chance of bumping into anyone they knew. It was a cut-through that led them almost opposite Foy and Tita's house. As they passed the carefully tended containers outside the front door, Ali looked up and saw a light on in the upstairs sitting room. Through the window she could see Tita sitting at a desk reading the newspaper. She had on bifocal glasses that she used only when she was sure she was alone.

Ali was almost certain that Tita had told Nick and Bryony she wouldn't be home until tomorrow. She wondered whether they should ring on the doorbell and go in for an impromptu cup of tea, then decided Tita might not approve of such spontaneity. Ali didn't particularly trust any of her instincts right now. Besides, Alfie and Hector were fighting over whose turn it was to go on Jake's shoulders, and after what had just happened it was a relief to be arguing with them and to physically separate herself from Jake.

"I'll time you," she heard herself say. "Five minutes each."

"Then I need a rest," said Jake.

Ali felt breathless. Her senses were heightened, so that she could smell the Chinese jasmine growing up the side of Tita and Foy's house all the way up the street, she could feel the beat of music from the house opposite in her stomach, and when Jake bumped into her and put his arm on her shoulder to steady himself, she was sure Hector could feel the charge between them.

It doesn't matter what you know about the illusionary or transitory nature of lust, it's a higher force, decided Ali. It reminded her of being caught in a rip current, of being dragged from shore in a narrow channel of water, unable to swim against the tide. She remembered her dad's advice: Don't try to get back. Stay calm. Eventually the rip will lose strength and you can swim diagonally back to shore. Aim for locations where waves are breaking. Applying the theory in a threatening situation was the biggest psychological challenge, he used to say, but if you didn't you could drown.

Ali didn't dare catch Jake's eye, in case he suddenly decided he had hit a false note.

"Do you want to go and see Granny?" Jake asked the twins. They nodded enthusiastically. A few minutes later, Ali and Jake found themselves heading home alone.

22

. . . .

Apart from the Darkes, who were more interested in discussing the new surge of journalists in the street than in the twins' movements, no one else noticed Jake and Ali come back into the house. Leicester was sunning himself on one of the areas of the lawn that wasn't strewn with dog shit. He lifted his head sleepily and then dropped it back onto the grass in disgust at the hand that life had dealt him since Malea left.

The television in the kitchen was switched on to CNBC, but there was no one watching it. An American commentator was talking about the crisis at Lehman's and interviewing a British banking expert. Jake and Ali stood for a moment in front of the screen, careful not to touch each other.

"There are fears Lehman will have to take further asset write-downs and could face funding problems if the U.S. Federal Reserve removes the emergency borrowing window for investment banks that it opened after Bear Stearns collapsed," said a voice that Ali recognized as belonging to Felix Naylor. He had become ubiquitous.

"It's your godfather," said Ali, turning the screen toward them.

"The stock is coming down at the rate it's coming down because a number of people believe strongly that the company is headed for bankruptcy." A banking analyst explained that the bank's share price had dropped to $9, its lowest since 1998, and there were rumors that a buyer was sought to prevent it from being the next domino to fall after the collapse of Bear Stearns earlier in the year.

"What has caused the credit crunch?" the reporter asked Felix.

"Low interest rates, cheap credit, bank deregulation, too much faith in mathematical models, subprime, hubris, greed . . ."

"I've heard it all before," said Jake.

"It's like learning a new language, isn't it? Every time the same words are repeated, you understand a little bit more."

"Shall we discuss this in my bedroom?" asked Jake suddenly.

"What about Hector and Alfie?"

Jake ran a finger down the side of Ali's face. "They're not here. Did you know you are at your most endearing when you're worried?"

He took her by the hand. As they crept past the door of the drawing room on their way upstairs, they could hear Foy snoring. Ali wondered if Bryony had remembered to bring him his tea at four o'clock. They climbed the first couple of flights slowly. Once they had got past Bryony and Nick's bedroom, their pace sped up so that by the time they reached the final flight up to Jake's room they were bounding up two steps at a time. Then they were in his room. Ali locked the door behind them.

The main light wasn't working, and the curtains were closed. So the only light in the room came from a purple-and-red lava lamp on a desk in the corner. Both of them were out of breath. Ali tried to speak, to say something that would take some of the intensity out of the moment, but when the sound came out she didn't recognize her own voice. Maybe lust affected the brain in the same way as a stroke, she thought, reminded of the way Foy described himself as an actor who could find the right lines but was unable to deliver them.

Instead she leaned back against the door and found her head cushioned by a purple dressing gown that once belonged to Lucy. She recognized the perfume. Floral with a hint of something fruity. Jake leaned over her, his forehead tenderly touching the top of her head so that she could breathe in his familiar smell. Her familiarity with the rest of his family made him seem like a known quantity, although she had hardly ever spent any time with him. His hair was longer than ever, a wild tangle, like his mother's. His coloring, the exotic combination of dark hair and blue eyes, connected him to his father and Izzy. His lips, plump and slightly cherubic, belonged to the twins.

Reminded of Hector and Alfie, Ali wondered whether she should try to pull back from the brink. Jake was right, this was obviously a bad idea. His breath against her neck made her shiver with longing. That was the wonderful thing about the alchemy of passion, thought Ali, the slightest gesture became something beautiful.

Jake said something, which could have been either "It's so hot" or "You're so hot." When she replayed the scene afterward, Ali tried both versions and then opted for silence because it meant she could focus better on remembering the lazy watchfulness of his eyes, or the way he chewed his lower lip.

It gave her time to recall the exact sensation as he doodled small circles down the side of her neck with the same finger that had touched her in the park, and she pulled him toward her. They kissed almost chastely on the lips and then looked at each other, as if confirming the reciprocity of the situation. They were on the brink of something. It reminded Ali of when she jumped off Cromer pier.

They kissed again for what seemed like ages, but was probably a couple of minutes. Kissing sometimes seemed more intimate than sex, thought Ali. He tasted salty. This time, Ali could feel the intent in Jake's body. He pressed himself against her, one hand in her hair, stroking the back of her head, the other roaming over her buttocks through the soft cotton fabric of her skirt. She could feel his erection hard through his jeans.

Without letting go of each other they made their way to the bed, tripping over shoes, books, and dirty clothes. Jake fell back on the bed and pulled Ali on top of him. She straddled him and leaned toward his face so that she could see the way his mouth opened slightly wider and his eyes clouded over with pleasure. It was both exhilarating and terrifying to discover that someone needed you as much as you needed them.

"I've imagined fucking you at least a couple of times a day since the party," Jake whispered.

"Me, too," said Ali, leaning over to undo the buttons of his shirt. His skin was dark and smooth. There were thin wisps of chest hair, more than last summer, thought Ali, as she languorously stroked him with the fingers of her right hand and watched his eyes half shut in pleasure. His hands tugged down the straps of her top and her bra until her breasts were exposed. He pulled her toward him and took a nipple in his mouth. Ali felt more waves of pleasure surge through her body.

She couldn't remember afterward exactly how she found herself underneath him with her knickers halfway down her legs and Jake inside her. That first afternoon they had sex so many times that later, it was difficult to distinguish between each entanglement. When they tried to map out the genesis of their sexual relationship months later, they argued over the exact order of events. His fingers inside her, her mouth moving down his body, his mouth between her legs, her hand around his cock. Ali had previously considered herself a person capable of restraint, but Jake made her feel completely untethered.

They probably wouldn't have emerged that night, but at about seven-thirty in the evening the internal phone rang. It was Bryony asking Jake if he knew where Ali was. Ali looked shocked, less by the question than by the fact that another world coexisted alongside the one inside his bedroom.

"They're all at Granny's," he said sleepily, as he looked at Ali sliding down his body.

"Granny is down here with Hector and Alfie," said Bryony.

"Well, she was most definitely there when we left them," he said, trying to keep his voice even.

"Who is we?"

"I mean me. I think Ali went somewhere else."

"Are you all right? You sound strange."

"Just a little worried about things." Jake groaned.

"Will you come and join us? Hester and Rick are coming over."

"Sure, just give me five minutes," said Jake, closing his eyes in pleasure as Ali took him in her mouth. The phone dropped to the floor.

Ali hastily pulled her skirt and top back on and found her knickers tangled in the duvet. She came out of Jake's room tentatively, trying to work out a plausible excuse for being there, in case someone was outside on the landing. As she went downstairs, reason seeped back. She worked out how long she had been in his room and calculated she had been gone for almost three hours. She started to worry about Hector and Alfie, and whether anyone would have bothered to give them tea. She considered what had just taken place and was surprised to find that she didn't feel guilty. For the first time in two years she wasn't concerned with what Bryony thought.

She went down into the drawing room and apologized for falling asleep in her room. Bryony gave a sweep of her hand to indicate that it didn't matter, although just three days earlier the same infraction would have met with a round of tongue twirling and possibly a few words of disapproval.

The room looked different. It took a moment for Ali to realize that the Jupe table had been moved from the dining room and now sat beneath the window at the far side of the room. Izzy was carefully examining various objects on the table, trying to find the jauntiest angle to show off a sculpture or the best arrangement for the set of tiny painted enamel boxes that usually sat on the mantelpiece in the dining room. It was an incongruous sight. The teenage Goth handling these delicate antiques. She looked up at Ali as she came into the room and gave a small smile.

Ali curled her toes in the carpet as she decided where to sit down, but the pile between her toes was sensory overload after what had just happened. She felt almost nauseated. Everything seemed to suggest sex: the curve of the mantelpiece, the sylphs on the side of a vase, the glimpse of Izzy's thigh, the peonies Tita had picked from her garden.

"Do you want me to put Alfie and Hector to bed?" Ali asked, hoping she could extricate herself from another evening in this room with the extended Skinner family.

"Later," said Bryony vaguely.

"You forgot to bring me tea," Foy admonished her. He spoke slowly, and his words were slightly garbled, but there was no mistaking his tone.

"I was out with the twins," Ali apologized.

"Well, the sunshine has obviously done you good," said Foy, looking her up and down appreciatively. "I think your legs have grown." Then he returned to the pile of newspapers on the table beside him. The newspaper in his hands trembled.

Ali sat down next to Tita, who was reading yet another historical biography. She slumped back into the sofa, hugged a cushion to her chest, and curled her legs beneath her, trying to make herself as small as possible. She noticed a scratch that started above her knee and stretched up toward her thigh, and the idea that it was Jake's nail that had made this mark made her want to leave the room and go back upstairs to his room again. She absentmindedly touched the beginning of the blemish with her finger and immediately missed him so much that when he came through the door into the drawing room she heard herself emit a low moan of desire. "Was it a good book you were reading?" Tita asked Jake as he came over to kiss her on the cheek. Jake glanced at Ali, wondering what she had told them.

"Very good," said Jake. "*Tom Jones* by Henry Fielding. It's one of my set texts. I've got a copy of the original edition with all his drawings."

"I had a walk-on part in the film," said Foy. "With Susannah." No one reacted.

"Wonderful," said Tita, her eyes narrowing as she glanced from

Jake to Ali and then back to Jake. "Didn't Fielding end up marrying his wife's maid because she was pregnant?"

"After his wife died," Ali confirmed.

Ali flushed and put a hand to her cheek. Her features had softened. She felt immobile with torpor, so that even if Bryony asked her to get up to check on the twins, she wasn't sure that her body would cooperate. Jake sat on the floor between her and Tita, so that his shoulder touched the ball of Ali's foot. The proximity was exquisite and unbearable at the same time. She was relieved that Nick was somewhere else, because he would surely have noticed.

"I hope you'll show some self-restraint from now on, Jake," said Tita, pointing at the *Daily Mail*. "We've been dragged through the mud enough. Even that ridiculous woman from next door refused a cigarette from me as though I might be a drug hustler."

"'Pusher' is the right term," Jake corrected her. From the other side of the room, Ali saw Izzy smile.

Ali was relieved when the telephone rang and everyone switched their attention to the imminent arrival of Hester and Rick. Bryony instructed her sister to avoid the press by coming through the ground floor of the Darkes' house, but she ignored her advice and even paused on the top step for a few photos.

Hester gave a round of extravagant hugs to everyone as soon as she came into the room. She was wearing a black dress, which added to the general feeling that she was treating what had happened as a kind of death. Perhaps Hester was right, thought Ali. To judge from the behavior of people around them over the past forty-eight hours, it was certainly a kind of social suicide.

"Dad, you look terrible," said Hester as she bent down to kiss her father on the top of his head. "I hope they're trying to protect you from the worst of the stress."

There was a delay as Foy summoned an appropriate response.

"Women in black dresses always send me into a decline," said Foy, "but I'm not dead yet."

"It's because someone gave him a bottle of Tenuta dell'Ornellaia last night," said Tita. "I found the evidence in his bedroom. He'd drunk the whole bottle."

When Hester came to Ali she offered sympathy for the situation she found herself in.

"So dreadful for you," Hester said, clutching onto her, so that Ali's top started to slide down her shoulder. "It must be so difficult dealing with the emotional fallout. The poor children." She turned her attention to Jake, who looked so relaxed that Ali kicked him with the tip of her foot. "Where are Hector and Alfie?"

"They're watching television downstairs," said Bryony.

"I imagine in the circumstances that regulating screen time isn't a priority," said Hester.

"Correct," said Bryony.

"I saw shares in Nick's bank took another hammering today," said Rick. "We live in incredible times." He then handed over a basket of vegetables from his allotment. "Every little bit helps, I know. You can send Jake and Izzy over whenever you like to dig up vegetables. There's a lot of pleasure to be gained from the simple things in life. That's a lesson you'll all have to learn now."

"Thank you," said Bryony, with barely concealed fury.

"I can think of better examples," Jake muttered to Ali.

"Now, have you thought what to do about schools? What are your local options?" Rick asked.

Bryony explained that an antiques dealer who Nick had known for years was going to come round in the next few days to value some of their possessions so that they could pay the school fees next term.

"This should all be sorted within the next month," she said breezily.

"Oh," said Hester, sounding almost disappointed. "What happens if they decide to charge him?"

"They won't. He's innocent," said Bryony.

"Where is the protagonist of this great drama?" asked Rick, in full English-teacher mode, searching around the room as though Nick might be hiding behind a piece of furniture.

"Nick has gone to ground," said Bryony, walking toward the mantelpiece to busy herself, stacking up invitations to events that they now wouldn't attend. She had her back to them, but Ali could see her face in the reflection of the mirror. She looked more worried than she had even on the day of the raid. Even her lips were pallid.

"Probably a good idea to keep a low profile," said Rick.

"He won't be coming home for a little while," said Bryony, shuffling the invitations in her hand like a deck of cards. "It's a tactic to try and divert press attention." She took a deep breath and turned round to face them.

"Do you mean Dad has moved out?" asked Jake slowly.

"For the moment," said Bryony.

"When is he coming back?" asked Izzy.

"Once the media attention has died down," said Bryony. "The story about Dad is dovetailing with the news about Lehman's. They're trying to sell the bank, but they can't find a buyer. It's their only lifeline now."

"You mean Daddy's bank might collapse?" asked Izzy.

"There's still a couple of possibilities, but it'll probably be a take-under rather than a takeover," said Bryony, sounding more composed.

"What does that mean?" Jake asked.

"It means it will be bought at a price below where the shares are trading. It's catastrophic but less catastrophic than the alternative."

"So where is Dad right now?" asked Izzy.

"He's staying with a friend," Bryony said, so vaguely that Ali wondered if she really knew. "We just need to sit this out for a couple of months until we hear if he's going to be charged. If they decide to prosecute, then everything becomes sub judice, so journalists can't write about us anymore. If they don't, we can go back to life as normal."

"When did he go?" asked Foy. "He didn't bother saying good-bye to me."

"Nor me," said Bryony quietly. "Sometimes it's better that way."

23

August 2008

These were the things Ali didn't tell Felix Naylor the second time she met him in the café in Bloomsbury. She didn't explain how an old friend of Nick's had come round the day after he disappeared and paid £150,000 in cash for the frog with the emerald eyes and the jewel-encrusted warts, the two Caffieri bronzes, and the small picture by Augustus John that hung in the dining room. Apparently it was less than Bryony should have gotten, because of the problems with provenance. The antiques dealer had explained that he couldn't sell them on the open market, so they would probably find their way to Russia at a slightly lower price. He had counted out the money in £1,000 piles, which Bryony hid in the piano. A temporary measure until a better hiding place could be found, she told Ali, as she pressed six weeks' wages into her hand and told her to suspend the twins' piano practice routine.

Nor did she tell Felix that Nick had disappeared (if you believed Foy) or taken refuge with a friend (if you believed Bryony). This omission was an act of charity. She didn't want to give Felix the idea there was a vacuum waiting to be filled. It was obvious to Ali since she had first come across Felix that he cared for Bryony more than he should.

And she didn't tell Felix that every night since the trip to the park six weeks earlier, she put the twins to bed and then went up to Jake's room, because she understood that as long as their relationship was secret, it remained viable.

Since the beginning of the crisis, the children and Ali had taken over the top two floors of Holland Park Crescent. Bryony was too busy to come up and had made her office on the kitchen table in the basement, because she wanted to be in what she described as "the bowels" of the house.

"So this time she can see the shit before it happens," Foy had wryly observed from the chair in the drawing room where he spent most of the day. Tita visited him every morning to help him in and out of bed, but she never mooted the possibility of his returning home. Once Ali had caught Tita hiding a bottle of whiskey down the side of Foy's chair.

"She's trying to do away with me," Foy had joked.

From that table, Bryony spent her hours on the phone to lawyers, colleagues at work, and the few friends who still bothered to stay in touch. She spent a lot of time dealing with debts, pleading clemency with banks, trying to prioritize payments, canceling direct debits, and learning the art of living off £350 a week. An enterprising tabloid photographer had managed to snatch a photograph of her pushing an amateurishly packed shopping cart in the Costco parking lot. Someone else had told a newspaper that she was selling clothes on eBay. It was just as well the long lenses couldn't reach the basement kitchen, where they would have found the double sink permanently piled with dirty dishes, the chrome cooker smeared with cooking oil and caked with food, and a floor that was cleaned up mainly by Leicester. Bryony and Ali periodically tackled the laundry pile and filled the dishwasher in an irrational way that would have made Malea tut with disapproval.

Since Malea had left, the whole house had descended into disarray, but nowhere more than on the top two floors, which had developed a particular flavor of their own. The curtains at the front of the house were kept shut in case a vigilant photographer spotted an opportunity, adding to the dark, murky atmosphere. Beds were no longer made. Sheets were unchanged. The carpet was never vacuumed. The guinea pigs roamed freely, eating the remains of food raided from the larder by Hector and Alfie. Or perhaps the tiny droppings that Ali found belonged to mice. Books, football cards, remote-controlled cars, DS games were strewn from inside the twins' bedroom to the landing outside. They watched television and played computer games whenever the urge seized them.

The landing had become a communal area where they all played together: Old Maid (the twins' favorite) and Monopoly (Izzy's favorite) to while away time. Sometimes they watched television in Ali's room. Since the Darkes had removed the ladder from their side of the garden fence, no one wanted to leave the house in case there were photographers stationed outside, although Nick's departure seemed to have dampened the enthusiasm for pictures.

Izzy's room looked as though it had been ransacked. You had to wade through clothes to reach her on the bed in the middle of the room. She spent her days reading or watching films. She stayed away from Facebook and e-mail, where everyone was talking about what was happening to her family as though it was a reality TV show, and she assiduously avoided newspapers.

The top floor, however, belonged to Jake and Ali. The air in the room was a musky mix of pheromones and the faint smell of sex. Any adult sensitive to the signs of uninhibited sexual abandonment would have taken one look at the twisted sheets, the stains on the duvet, and the paraphernalia of last-minute contraception to know that its inhabitants were in the throws of a passionate affair. But Foy couldn't get up there, and Bryony didn't bother.

At first they had locked the door, but as the days turned into weeks and everyone seemed impervious, they got more blasé. Only Izzy noticed a certain thawing in their relations, commenting on how Ali and Jake argued less than they used to and spent more time with each other than they did with anyone else.

"I know Ali won't shop me to the press," Jake told his sister.

They spent hours in his bed. Jake said the red-and-purple lava lamp reminded him of the gentle undulations of Ali's body, especially her breasts and her arse. Ali said that it reminded her of the inside of her head and the sensation she was floating away from reality in a bubble of pleasure.

Sometimes, they would lie beside each other and see how long they could talk before desire took over. Jake would tell her how he loved the way she climbed on top of him and fucked him slowly without looking away. Ali would tell him how she loved falling asleep with her thigh glued to his after they had sex. Jake would describe how, when he buried his head between her legs and made her come, her nails scratched at the sheets so hard the cotton had worn through. Then they would have sex again. Sated for a while, they might discuss their situation in general terms. They agreed they were out of control and there was little point in talking about specifics.

Ali read a piece in the paper that said that in the early stages of romance the chemical makeup of men's and women's brains was no different from those suffering from obsessive-compulsive disorder. Jake said that he thought about her all the time and kept pieces of her clothing hidden in his room, so that he could smell her even if she wasn't there. Ali said he sounded like Leicester dragging his bedding round the house.

They were in that state where every detail of each other's life was fascinating to the other and everything was imbued with significance. So when they discovered that they could both hold their breath underwater for more than a minute and they had the same nightmare about drowning as children, it cemented their sense of destiny.

Sometimes Ali drew up a list in her head of all the reasons she shouldn't be having a relationship with Jake: she was the family nanny; he was only nineteen; she was abusing Bryony's trust; it was the kind of story the tabloids could exploit; it would only end badly. She would resolve to end it or at least try to avoid him for a couple of hours. But then Bryony would ask her to go upstairs and check whether Jake wanted something to eat, or Foy would request a book that was in his bedroom, or the twins would ask Ali to persuade him to play poker, and the whole cycle of desire would begin again.

"How long do you think this thing with your dad will go on?"

"Forever, hopefully," Jake had answered. A response, from Ali's perspective, that had the merit of being both right and wrong.

"Aren't you worried about him?"

"All I think about is you," Jake said, and shrugged. "Dad will either be proven guilty or innocent, and although I think he's guilty, he's got a good lawyer, which means he'll probably be found innocent."

They laughed a lot and then felt guilty when they went downstairs and found Bryony sitting tensely at the kitchen table in exactly the same position as when they had left her a couple of hours earlier. She was nearly always on the phone. Sometimes she would be talking to clients. She would tell each of them the same thing.

"My work is completely separate from my husband's . . . He isn't living with us . . . He hasn't been charged with any offense . . . The accusations against him have no impact on my ability to do the best possible job for you . . . This isn't the time to be test-driving a new financial PR company . . . You need someone who knows your company inside out . . ."

Aside from the Ukrainians, at least two other clients had fired Bryony from their accounts and another three were considering their position. One said they needed "a fresh pair of eyes to look at their relations with the media in these challenging economic times." Ali knew this because Bryony had asked for the e-mail to be forwarded to her BlackBerry. Once Ali heard Bryony speaking to Nick.

"Can't you at least come and see the children?" she whispered into the phone. "Or maybe we could come and meet you somewhere? Where are you?"

"You'll be trailed by reporters," Ali heard Nick reply.

"I don't understand why you can't come home," Bryony said. "There's even more people camped on the doorstep since you left."

"It would be worse if I was there," Nick said. "And you've got more chance of keeping your clients if I'm out of the picture."

"It couldn't be worse. And I could bear it more," Bryony said flatly. "Ned Wilbraham's still at home."

"Throw the press a couple of bits of bait about him to get them off your back," said Nick. "No one's dished the dirt on his affair with the nanny. You know he still sees her?"

"How do you know that if you never see him?" Bryony asked.

Two days after this exchange, Ali, Jake, Izzy, and Foy were sitting on the sofa in the drawing room with the curtains closed when the doorbell rang. It sounded throaty, exhausted like the rest of them, although actually this was probably due to lack of use. Ali couldn't remember the last time that someone had dared come to the door without calling first. Everyone, from Bryony's colleagues to the personal trainer who came to get the money Bryony owed her, knew to call to say exactly when they would be arriving.

They had all seen the picture in the newspaper of the unwitting pizza delivery man who arrived at the house at the end of a long, fruitless day for the photographers gathered outside. In his nervousness at the long lenses trained on him as he rang the doorbell with one hand and held three Margheritas aloft in the other, he had tripped and dropped all of them on the ground. The following day he found himself on the cover of a tabloid newspaper below a headline that read something like "Fat Cat Pizza Delivery Falls Flat." So when the bell rang, the four of them glanced at one another, shared worried looks, and then did nothing.

"Photographer?" suggested Ali.

At the beginning of the scandal, an occasional enterprising tabloid photographer might have rung on the doorbell, hoping for an early-morning snatch shot of Bryony without makeup, looking harassed. The early birds sometimes caught Foy collecting the newspapers from the front doorstep, and the first week he obligingly helped them fill column space by making pompous declarations of his son-in-law's innocence. "My daughter will stand by her husband," he told them one day. "My daughter is not the kind of woman to walk away from a man at the first sniff of trouble," he said on another. Both sparked news stories. It caused profound irritation to Bryony, who felt as though she not only sounded guilty by association but was being presented as a latter-day Tammy Wynette, standing by her man. Foy was apologetic and gave in to her pleas to exchange nothing more than pleasantries with journalists, who sensed a man who couldn't resist giving an opinion when asked.

Now everything was more streamlined. After complaints to the police by the Darkes, when photographers congregated they mostly remained stationed behind an invisible cordon on the opposite side of the road. Their presence provided a useful barometer of unfolding events. If the Financial Services Authority was about to release more information or "someone close to the family" had sold a story, their numbers would mysteriously swell hours before anything was officially announced. They were like sharks. More intuitive than sharks, decided Ali, because they seemed to anticipate the bloodletting before it happened.

Today there were so many that the photographers had once again resorted to stepladders. There was even a television crew. All of which made the unexpected visitor in their midst even more worrying. The bell started to ring in a long, continuous drone. Leicester threw himself at the front door, barking furiously. Without the table, the flowers, and the piles of newspapers in the hallway, there was nothing to absorb the noise of his high-pitched yelp. The dog scratched and pawed at the door, skidding on the piles of unopened post. He hadn't been out for a proper walk in almost three days. Since Malea had left, no one took responsibility for him.

Finally Foy got up and edged slowly toward the drawing room window. He tentatively pulled the outer edge of the heavy curtain to one side and craned his neck to try to identify who was standing at the top of the stairs. His hand trembled. Ali saw him shaking his head in disbelief at this new betrayal by the body that had been his ally for so many decades.

"Where are Hector and Alfie?" Foy asked breathlessly, half turning toward Ali. "Could it be them?"

"Downstairs. Watching TV," Ali said. Foy returned to his position of watchfulness.

"It's an adult," he said after a long silence.

"Well, that narrows it down," said Ali, trying but failing to rouse a smile.

"Could it be Dad?" Jake asked, his tone neutral. "Maybe he's in disguise?"

No one laughed. Jake and Izzy often discussed the possibility of their father making a clandestine visit to the house to explain to his family what was going on. His absence increasingly felt more like betrayal. They didn't entertain the possibility that Nick might never come back.

"Could you be a bit more descriptive?" Jake suggested without moving from the sofa. He was going through the file of newspaper cuttings amassed by Foy. He was in the middle of a piece from *The Sun* describing how Nick Skinner's guard dog had set upon the newspaper's photographer. There was a picture of a leg with stitches and a large photograph of Leicester, looking quizzical and distinctly unmenacing. He was wearing a white diamante collar that Nick had bought Bryony as a joke to celebrate Leicester's birthday. "White-collar criminal," read the caption beneath the picture. Jake laughed, pushed the piece into Ali's hands, and kissed her on the inside of her wrist. Ali anxiously looked round to see if Foy or Izzy had noticed. They hadn't.

"She looks familiar," rasped Foy, in a voice as throaty as the doorbell.

"Do you recognize her?" asked Jake hopefully.

"I don't recognize her, but she looks familiar," Foy muttered. "That's the best I can do."

"Maybe it's one of Izzy's friends?" suggested Ali, pulling away from Jake.

"Who would dare to arrive unannounced here?" Foy asked. "It's like one of those houses with the mark of the plague on the door."

"Some of Izzy's friends are stupid enough," said Jake, hoping to get a rise out of his sister.

"Fuck off, Jake," shouted Izzy without looking up from her book at the other end of the room. No one admonished her. She had become so withdrawn that any response was gratifying. A couple of weeks after the photo of Jake had appeared, she had been photographed leaving one of those Kensington nightclubs favored by public-school types, wearing a tiny silver minidress and draped over the shoulder of a male friend who, it transpired, was the son of a hedge-fund manager who had been shorting Lehman's shares. "Consorting with the Enemy," screamed the headlines. It was the only time since he had disappeared that Nick had contacted Ali. He sent a text from a phone number that she didn't recognize, saying simply, "Protect them." She didn't tell anyone, and quickly deleted the message.

"I've got it," said Foy excitedly. He stepped abruptly backward and bumped into the arm of a chair. Ali darted forward to catch him in the small of his back. He felt frail and bony as she gently pushed him upright. "It's that nanny who slept with Cupcake's husband."

Ali looked out the window, tracing Foy's finger to the top doorstep. But she knew it was Katya even before she saw the long legs and the lean, gymnastic body. Katya stood by the intercom, head bowed, shoulders slouched, trying to make herself as insignificant as possible.

"Ali, are you there?" Katya called through the letterbox. "Please let me in." Sensing a story in their midst, the photographers on the other side of the road stirred and idly began attaching lenses to their cameras. Someone asked Katya about her relationship with the Skinners.

"How do you know them?" a voice shouted. Katya ignored them.

"Do you know where Nick Skinner is?" someone shouted. "Has he tried to contact you?"

Foy leaned back against Ali. She didn't resist. He needed the ballast, and his closeness was comforting. The sleeve of his jacket tickled her nose. It smelled musty. His breath was short and uneven. Tita really should take him to the doctor, thought Ali. But Tita was too busy worrying about her daughter and her grandchildren to bother with her husband. Uxorial detachment was the price of infidelity. He breathed out and Ali could smell stale alcohol from the night before on his breath. She caught Jake's eye.

"Have you met Nick Skinner?" someone shouted at Katya from the huddle on the other side of the road.

"Shall I let her in?" Ali asked.

"Why not?" asked Jake.

"Where have you been?" Ali asked Katya gently. They sat together on the sofa in the drawing room. Leicester was asleep between them, snoring contentedly. Katya stroked him, and he growled in his sleep. She pulled her hand away.

"He's the most misanthropic dog I've ever met," said Ali, pleased to have space between her and Katya so that she could escape the smell of cheap perfume. Katya frowned in confusion.

"He hates people," explained Ali. "So don't be offended."

"I saw this in the paper," said Katya, pulling her leather wallet from her handbag. This time, instead of the fifty-dollar bills, she pulled out a neatly folded copy of the photograph that Ali had taken for Foy's olive oil label and pressed it into Ali's hand. Someone had circled Ali's name in pencil at the top of the photo. Katya pulled out a packet of cigarettes and offered one to Jake and Izzy.

"You can't smoke in here," said Foy, sounding alarmed. He peered around the side of the armchair to underline his disapproval. "It's bad enough that you're wearing shoes. I'm the only person allowed to wear shoes in this room." His petulant tone made Katya laugh.

"If you saw the state of my feet, you'd want me to keep them on," said Katya, fiddling with rows of bangles on her left wrist.

"I thought you'd gone back to Ukraine," Ali questioned her.

"I got another job in London," said Katya.

"As a nanny?" Ali asked.

"In a bar." Katya shrugged. She paused for a moment. "They play music. It's called Whispers."

"Is it fun?" Ali asked.

"I can't believe you're still here," said Katya, her voice lowered, "when this is all about to come tumbling down around you. Everyone says the same thing. Why don't you get out while you can? Go and finish your degree. You were always the one with all the plans. What are you doing here with these people? They are bad news."

Alfie and Hector burst into the room and ran over to Ali. They landed upon her body with such force that she was pushed back on to the sofa. They giggled and pulled at her, their voices muffled as they each buried their faces into her armpit. They breathed in her smell and she stroked them on the back with small circular movements until they gradually calmed.

"These are my two reasons." Ali smiled.

"We missed you," they said, turning in her arms to face the rest of the room.

"I've been here all the time," said Ali. "Do you remember Katya?"

"Where's Thomas?" Alfie asked, immediately making the association.

"He's at home with his parents," said Katya in an even tone.

The door handle turned, and Bryony came into the room.

"What's she doing here?" Bryony asked, pointing at Katya. The way Bryony nervously darted across the room toward them reminded Ali of an animal that couldn't decide whether it was in flight or fight mode. "Don't you understand the authorities are looking for even the most tenuous evidence to connect Nick and Ned? You need to leave."

"I'm sorry," Katya apologized, getting up from the sofa. "I wanted to see Ali."

"They'll start digging for information about you," said Bryony, pointing at the window. "Anyone who comes here is of interest. And given your history, I would have thought you'd want to keep a low profile at the moment."

"Calm down, Mum," said Jake. "They'll hear you outside."

"I'll go right now," said Katya. She pressed a piece of paper into Ali's hands. "The address where I work," she whispered.

"Why haven't you got the television on?" Bryony demanded. She waved the controls at Foy and Jake. "They've got a new angle. Felix called to warn me. I think they're going to call someone else in for questioning." Katya called out good-bye to them all, but only Ali responded.

"What's going on?" rasped Foy in confusion. He pushed down his hands on the arms of the chair to lift himself out for the second time in less than half an hour. His hands were so withered that you could see the tendons stretching beneath the loose skin. Foy closed his eyes and bit down on his lower lip to focus all his strength into his enfeebled biceps. His upper body shook with the effort as he lifted his body above the seat of the chair. For a moment he was suspended, trembling in the air, like a heavy object on the end of a crane. Then his arms collapsed and he fell down into the cushion again. No one said anything.

"I'll let myself out," said Katya, as Sky News came on. Foy craned his neck round the side of the armchair to watch. He wasn't going to make another attempt to get up on his own, but Bryony, Jake, Ali, and Izzy stood too close to the screen for him to see. A business reporter stood outside the Lehman's building in New York. The bank had just announced third-quarter losses of $3.9 billion. Shares were trading at just $7 a piece and it looked as though a last-ditch deal with Korea to buy the bank had fallen through. The female reporter's eyebrows arched as though she was wincing.

"What does it all mean?" Jake asked Bryony.

"It means, short of a miracle, Lehman's is going to the wall," she said. "Which means your father has lost a fortune in stock options."

As they struggled to absorb this information, the report switched to the Lehman's building in Canary Wharf, "the center of a major insider-dealing ring."

"God, they're making it sound as though these two events are connected," said Bryony.

"We went there," shouted Hector and Alfie excitedly.

A picture of Nick fleetingly appeared on the screen.

"Daddy, Daddy," the twins shouted at the television. Hector started crying as though it had suddenly dawned on him that his father was someone he could now find only on the pages of newspapers and on television screens. It was a close-up of Nick wearing black tie at the Mansion House dinner. Ali recognized it from the photo that used to sit on the table beside the drawing room door. She looked over to the table. The photo had disappeared.

Ali glanced over at Foy and saw a small tear of self-pity roll down the side of his cheek. Jake saw, too, and went over to his grandfather and put a hand on his shoulder while turning toward the television screen in the corner of the room.

"Fugitive Banker May Have Another Accomplice," the headline flashed.

"He's not a fugitive," Bryony shouted at the television screen. "He's given a statement and gone to ground to get you bastards off his back."

"Do you know where he is, Mum?" Jake asked.

"He's safe and well. That's all you need to know," snapped Bryony without looking away from the screen.

Bryony turned up the volume so loud that the twins stuck their fingers in their ears and started chanting.

"Make them be quiet, Ali," Bryony pleaded.

"Shut up," Foy shouted unhelpfully.

Ali went and sat back down with them on the sofa. She picked up Hector and sat him on her knee.

"Why can't we go and play at someone's house?" he sobbed into her shoulder. "It's so boring being here all the time."

"No one wants us," said Alfie, kneeling beside Ali to pat his brother on the back.

"Why not?" asked Hector in between sobs.

"They liked us rich, but now we're poor," explained Alfie, "and they think it could be infectious."

"Only Ali wants to play with us," said Hector. "Don't leave us, Ali." He clung onto her, limpetlike.

Jake came over and joined them. He picked up Alfie and put him on his knee. Alfie and Hector held on to each other. They sat in silence as the report about Nick began in earnest. There were rumors that disgraced City bankers Nick Skinner and Ned Wilbraham may not have been acting alone when they bought shares in stock-market-listed companies that were about to be bought or sold. The reporter gave a brief explanation of how insider trading worked. "Insider dealing carries a maximum sentence of seven years in prison."

He turned again to the charges leveled against Nick. Ali and Jake leaned forward toward the television. Nick was accused of making a series of transactions over a period of three years, using information believed to have come from the same source.

"It is believed that the FSA has made significant inroads into iden-tifying where Skinner was getting his information," said the reporter in an annoying tone that indicated he knew full well who fell under suspicion, but was unable to reveal their identity because it might prejudice the investigation.

"I'm going to ask Felix if he knows who it is," said Bryony, tapping a message into her BlackBerry.

"Careful, they'll be monitoring your messages, Bryony," Foy pointed out.

"I know what I'm doing," said Bryony. Her phone rang immedi-ately. She listened without saying anything for a minute and then put down the phone and slumped onto the sofa. She lay there for a moment, staring up at the chandelier.

"What did Felix say, Mum?" asked Jake.

"He said that they think it is me," said Bryony simply. "They think that I am the person who fed Dad information. I am their main suspect."

For the second time that day, the front doorbell rang. Bryony went to answer it. Ali knew before she opened the door that it would be the police with a warrant for Bryony's arrest.

24

· · · · · · ·
· · · · · · ·

September 2008

There was awful symmetry that when Bryony called Foy, Ali, Jake, and Izzy into the drawing room later that day to reveal that the accusations of insider trading against Nick all involved her clients, CNBC flashed the news that Lehman's stock was trading at $3.71 a share, its lowest level ever. Less than a year ago it was worth $86.18 a share. The boats are all sinking at once, thought Ali, remembering Nick's comment in Corfu.

"I don't understand. What does it all mean?" asked Foy in confusion, glancing from Bryony to the television screen and then back again. He was in the middle of eating lunch, a ham-and-mustard sandwich, hastily prepared by Ali. There were crumbs stuck to the mustard around his mouth, crumbs in the trench where his sweater wrinkled over his stomach, and crumbs all over the floor. Leicester sat openmouthed at his feet, hoping for a piece of ham to drop. Foy's grip on the sandwich was so feeble it was a race to eat it before it disintegrated. But at least he could manage unaided. He could no longer guide a fork to his mouth without asking Ali for help.

"It means that the FSA thinks that I was passing on information about deals involving my clients to Nick," said Bryony, her voice shaky. "They assume I'm the deep throat."

"Nick used information about your clients to buy shares?" Foy confirmed.

Bryony nodded her head.

"It's too much coincidence for him to be innocent," she told them.

On the television screen Lehman's shares fell again, as if there was some magical connection between Bryony's loss of faith in her husband and the world's loss of faith in the banking system.

Bryony was paler than ever, and Ali noticed that her hands shook in her lap. She half considered walking to the stiff, upright chair where Bryony was perched to steady those hands in the way Bryony had steadied hers the first time she had driven the car to school almost two years ago to the day. It remained one of the most intimate moments they had shared.

But she suspected Bryony was too proud for sympathy. And it would have meant moving away from Jake. Being physically apart from him increasingly felt like more loss than she could bear. For the first time, the previous night, Ali and Jake had a conversation where they dared to imagine a future for themselves outside the confines of 97 Holland Park Crescent. Jake suggested Ali should see if she could transfer to Oxford and do her final year at university with him. They could live together. She could meet his friends. They could rent a cottage in the countryside. It sounded like a song by an indie band, thought Ali, enjoying the daydream.

They had lain naked on the bed beside each other, holding hands, having just had sex for the third time that night, imagining themselves shopping in Sainsbury's, sitting in a Cotswold pub drinking cider, painting the walls of their bedroom. It was a bittersweet image. Because Ali understood, even if Jake didn't, that the moment their relationship came out of the shadows it was probably doomed.

"I can't believe he's done this to me." Bryony's voice was almost a whisper.

"Maybe the FSA is trying to exert maximum psychological pressure by getting to you, to make Dad cave in and admit to something he hasn't done?" Jake suggested. If nothing else gave them away to Bryony, it would be Jake's optimism in the face of the disaster that had befallen his family. He had the drunken happiness of someone in the early stages of a love affair. Even Izzy now turned to him and told him to "get real."

Jake's arm was resting across the back of the sofa, and he casually stroked the back of Ali's neck, letting his finger come to rest on her shoulder. Ali shifted away, worried that someone might notice. She glanced round the room and saw Foy was focused on his sandwich, Izzy was shredding the skin around her fingernails until they bled, and Bryony was staring at her hands, flummoxed at her inability to control them.

"Over the past five years I've worked on six big deals for clients, and in every case Ned Wilbraham bought shares in those companies. The FSA says that all the information came from your father," said Bryony quietly.

"How do they know?" asked Izzy.

"I don't think they have any evidence, but I think they're probably right," said Bryony. "He had a bank account where money was transferred to him from Ned every couple of months."

"Dad hardly even knows Ned Wilbraham," said Jake.

"Or likes him," observed Izzy.

"And Mum hates his wife," said Jake.

"I kept trying to tell them that we have nothing to do with the Wilbrahams. They showed me a photograph of Nick and Ned together in Corfu and another of the three of us at school sports day. They wanted me to admit that we were part of a crime syndicate. It would be laughable if it wasn't so serious."

"Maybe there's a simple explanation?" suggested Foy.

"As far as the FSA is concerned, it's very straightforward: I passed Nick information about the deals I was working on, he passed it on to Ned Wilbraham, who bought the shares, and then they split the profits when they were sold," explained Bryony. "It's very neat."

"So you definitely didn't give Nick this information about your companies?" asked Foy. "Not even inadvertently?"

"Of course not," Bryony said impatiently. "Why would I do that? It would destroy the business that I have spent years building and ruin my reputation. As it is, I've already lost five clients, and everyone agrees it's best if I don't show my face in the office."

"So why would Dad do it?" asked Jake. "It's not as though he needed the money."

Bryony pointed at the television screen. The CNBC reporter was pointing at a graph showing the decline of Lehman's shares, explaining that they had lost ninety-three percent of their value since January 31.

"I don't know, because I can't get hold of him," said Bryony, staring at Jake and Izzy as though she wasn't sure how much truth they could endure. "But I think it might have something to do with the crisis at Lehman's."

"Go on, Mum," said Jake. "If you don't tell us, we'll just read it in a newspaper."

"Lehman's always paid out most of its bonuses in stock," said Bryony. "Two years ago your father's share of the company was worth fifteen million pounds, now it's worth less than one million. I think he saw the storm clouds gathering and thought that doing a bit of insider dealing was a good insurance policy against losses at the bank."

"Well, if that's the case, he's a fucking fool!" Foy exploded with some of his old bravado. "And even more of a fucking fool to get caught. This kind of thing goes on all the time, but it's only the amateurs who show up on the radar." He was warming to his theme, rubbing his hands up and down his trousers, sending a confetti of crumbs onto Leicester's head.

"You're not being helpful," Jake warned his grandfather.

"I'm paying for his bloody lawyer," said Foy, "so I can say what I like. I built my business brick by brick, from the foundations up. Nick always had it too easy. He's never had to really work for a living. Selling bundles of debt isn't a real living. Bloody snake-oil salesman." He slumped back in his armchair.

"Actually, Dad has always worked really hard," protested Izzy. "That's why he was never around."

"His great risk-minimizing formulas don't look very clever now, do they?" Foy continued.

Hector and Alfie were downstairs in the kitchen, fiddling with the music system. The sound of Cat Stevens singing "Wild World" at full volume suddenly filled the house. Everyone jumped. Then it switched to "Two Little Boys," the original version that Foy had bought for them. No one moved, momentarily shocked into silence by the noise, and relieved that it drowned out Foy.

"Turn that racket off," rasped Foy, leaning forward as if he was going to try to get up out of his armchair. His sandwich fell from his hand, and Leicester greedily gobbled it up.

"I need to find a good lawyer who specializes in corporate crime, Dad," said Bryony. She didn't have the strength to argue with her father. "Otherwise I'm going to go down for something I didn't do."

"Won't Daddy tell them that you're innocent?" asked Izzy.

"I'm sure he will, but that doesn't mean they'll believe him," said Bryony flatly.

"We should phone Julian," said Foy emphatically. It was a line he had obviously used in the past when stuck in a tight corner.

"Why?" asked Jake incredulously.

"He might be able to help us," said Foy.

"How can he possibly help?" asked Izzy. "And why would he?"

"Eleanor has just sold a story about her fifty-year relationship with you to a tabloid newspaper," said Bryony bitterly. "That's not the sort of help we need right now."

"Eleanor has lost the plot." Foy sighed. "She's not in her right mind."

"So how did Nick find out about which of your clients were buying or merging with other companies if you didn't tell him, Bryony?"

asked Ali. It was the first time she had spoken. Bryony looked at Ali as if surprised to find her in the room with them.

"I don't know. The police asked me the same question, and I couldn't give them an answer. Do you have any ideas?"

On Sunday night, after she had read the twins four chapters from *Alice's Adventures in Wonderland*, an appropriate choice in the current circumstances, Ali went to her bedroom and began tidying it. She started with the wardrobe, haphazardly pulling out everything until she was left holding a handful of clothes that belonged to her when she first moved in with the Skinners.

She put together on the bed an outfit that she once wore at university, trying to imagine herself wearing it for a lecture on eighteenth-century writers. She smoothed down the wrinkled purple T-shirt and the jeans. "John Locke, Daniel Defoe, Jonathan Swift, Alexander Pope, Samuel Richardson, Henry Fielding, Laurence Sterne." Ali did a roll call of authors she had studied, pleased with the way she could remember not just their names but the order in which the lectures had taken place.

She closed her eyes for a moment and saw herself dressed in this pair of jeans and this T-shirt, lying on her back in the grass, dreaming about Will MacDonald as he quoted, "'Words are but wind; and learning is nothing but words.'" She tried to remember the subject of her last essay: Was it the exploration of solitude in the fiction of Richardson, Defoe, and Sterne, or the relations between castration, clocks, midwives, and the military in *Tristram Shandy*?

Then she remembered a rucksack of books that she had stuffed at the back of a cupboard at the top of the wardrobe, and impulsively dragged over a chair so that she could pull it down. There was one on the rise of the City of London as the financial and commercial capital of the world in the eighteenth century; another on the dominance of political power by mercantile interests; a book by Carole Pateman about patriarchal society and the sexual subordination of women; and *The Birth of a Consumer Society* by John Brewer.

She carefully took each one out of the rucksack, cleaned off the dust with the purple T-shirt, and put them in an orderly pile on her bedside table, resolving that she would take advantage of her incarceration to do some background reading to prepare for her return to university. Whatever Nick had done and whatever Bryony's role in his crime, it was obvious to Ali that she was living in a house of cards. "We're nearing the end game," she had told Jake. It was one of her few certainties.

For a moment, she allowed herself to imagine studying at Oxford with Jake. When he was with her it seemed almost possible. When they were apart it became a prospect as absurd as the Mad Hatter's tea party. She turned her attention back to the pile of clothes. Most of them had been given to her by Bryony: some were castoffs that she no longer wore, others ill-advised purchases made during one of Bryony's snatched forays with a personal shopper to Selfridges or Harvey Nichols. Ali remembered a conversation with Mira and the other nannies about the inverse relationship between wealth and generosity. "She makes me pay for my own milk . . ." "They buy children's portions for me in restaurants . . ." "I have to show receipts even if I've only bought a packet of M&M's after school." None of their complaints resonated with her.

Ali counted at least ten pairs of shoes that Bryony had given her. She put on a pair of jeans that Bryony had bought for her in New York, some Belstaff boots that Bryony had never used, and a Sass & Bide top. She looked at herself critically in the mirror.

Many of the clothes were too formal. These she put in a bag for her friends. Her old clothes from Norfolk went in the Oxfam pile. Then Ali turned her attention to the chest of drawers. She removed all four drawers and tipped everything onto the floor: knickers, socks, scarves, belts, notebooks, booklists sent in the early days by her tutor, hoping to lure her back to university, letters from her mother, toys that belonged to the twins.

Then she pulled out the Francis Bacon poster from the back of the wardrobe and decided she would hang it in the drawing room where the original used to be, in the hope of raising a laugh from Foy. She attributed this flurry of energy to a desire to impose order on the creeping chaos that had enveloped the Skinners. It was the same mentality that took hold among civilian populations in war zones or among aid organizations delivering relief in the aftermath of natural disasters. Bryony was right. Routine and order were the best antidote to anxiety and uncertainty.

In the midst of this disarray, at the point where everything looked much worse than it had before she began, she heard her phone beep. She glanced down and saw a message from Jake.

"Can't sleep, want company?" it read. She frowned at Jake's punctuation. Was he trying to say that he couldn't sleep or was he asking her whether she couldn't sleep? Ali tapped in "yes and yes" into her BlackBerry. Even before she had sent the message, the door handle started turning and Jake poked his head around the bedroom door, holding a couple of bottles of beer.

"They're warm," he apologized, "and I don't have an opener."

Ali saw him glance around the room, checking past her shoulder to the wardrobe, taking in the plastic bags of clothes lined up by the dressing table and the piles on the floor. He came over to the bedside table and picked up one of the books that Ali had piled up.

"I read this last term," he said, leafing through the pages of John Brewer's *Consumer Society*, trying to decipher the tiny notes that Ali had made in the margin.

"What conclusions did you draw?" Ali asked.

"That everything that is happening now is the logical end to what began in the eighteenth century," Jake said. He put down the book and glanced at Ali's phone with her unsent message to him. "We'd make a great essay-writing team."

"I should check on Hector and Alfie," said Ali, busily stuffing clothes back into the wardrobe.

"They're asleep in Alfie's bed with Leicester," said Jake.

"It makes them feel secure," said Ali. "Were they underneath their duvets?"

Jake put his arms around Ali from behind. His hand strayed beneath her T-shirt, and she leaned back into him.

"How come you are so responsible?" asked Jake.

"I was forced to grow up quickly," said Ali simply. "And I'm paid to be." The last was inaccurate. Despite the money hidden in the piano, she hadn't been paid for weeks and she didn't feel very responsible anymore.

"Why don't you sit down for a moment?" Jake suggested, gently pushing her toward the bed.

"I feel too agitated," said Ali, allowing him to nuzzle her neck. "I keep thinking about things I've seen, to do with your dad, wondering whether they're relevant or whether I've misinterpreted them." She paused for a moment. "I've heard him talking to Ned Wilbraham on the phone. I've seen him with papers belonging to your mum. Sorry I'm not being very articulate."

"You think that Dad is guilty?"

"There are things that don't add up."

"Dad has always kept his cards close to his chest." Jake had stopped in the middle of the room. He leaned against her.

"What do you mean?"

"Did you know his parents are still alive and live somewhere up north? I found out when I was looking through some papers unearthed by the FSA during the search."

"Do you think your mum knew?"

"No," said Jake flatly.

"Why don't we go out?" Jake suddenly suggested. He went over to the window and looked outside. There was no one there. Bryony's arrest and Eleanor's exposé had the benefit of satisfying the insatiable media hunger for a new angle about the Skinners at least for today.

"Your Mum doesn't want you to go out at night."

"If you're with me, that's different." He pulled Ali toward him.

"It would make me complicit."

"I know a bar on Ken High Street which might be open."

"It will be full of your friends."

"We could just walk? When was the last time you left this house?"

Ali tried to remember. It was when she went to see Felix Naylor, two weeks earlier.

"What about money?"

Jake pulled out a wodge of cash from his pocket.

"Where did you get that?" asked Ali.

"From the piano," he said, and laughed.

Years later, when she was coming to the end of her first tenure as a university lecturer, Ali wondered whether the way that Jake and she happened upon the Whispers club that night was by accident or design. She had retraced their steps a thousand times, searching for new clues, and reviewing old evidence. Sometimes she tripped over double negatives trying to imagine what would have not happened if she hadn't gone there.

The facts were these: They had left the house, wandered around the dark sidewalks that hugged the edges of Holland Park, listening to peacocks shriek through the night air. They had crossed Kensington High Street and headed south through Warwick Gardens. A radio was on in the basement of one of the houses.

"Russian oligarch," said Jake, as strange guttural voices drifted through the window.

"Ukrainian nanny," Ali corrected him. Over the past couple of years she had developed a good ear for the different nuances of the languages spoken around her. "I know the nanny who works there. She's from a village outside Kiev."

They continued toward Earls Court. They walked with a sense of purpose, enjoying the freedom. Neither questioned the other's decision to take a left turn or cross a busy road and head for a side street. They held hands in public for the first time. There were no photographers to worry about. Hector and Alfie weren't there to slow them down. And Jake's presence made her feel more secure than she should, wandering the streets of London at one o'clock in the morning.

"Aren't you cold?" she asked Jake, suddenly noticing that he was wearing only a black T-shirt and jeans.

"Stop trying to look after me, Ali," he said, but she could hear the smile in his tone. "If you look after people too much, you undermine their capacity for looking after themselves. That's what you said about your sister."

Ali wrapped the jacket she had grabbed from the Izzy pile tightly around her. It was black velvet with silver studs around the wrists and collar. It made her feel feminine and strong all at once. It was beautiful but totally inappropriate.

"Great jacket."

"Your mum gave it to me."

"My parents were always good at presents."

"Very generous," agreed Ali, careful not to endorse his use of the past tense.

They continued to walk in comfortable silence for a while. A group of teenage kids riding BMX bikes cycled by on the sidewalk, and Jake bumped into Ali's shoulder as he jumped out of their way.

"London at night is something I've almost always experienced from the back of an Addison Lee cab," said Jake.

"You used to take the Tube to school," Ali reminded him.

"I mostly hitched a lift with Dad's driver," Jake confessed. "I wonder what's happened to him."

Ali recalled the driver who used to arrive at the house at seven forty-five every morning. He was so short that all you could see of him was a tweed cap hovering above the steering wheel. The cap looked out of place in central London, but he told Ali that it reminded him of the village where he was born in Armenia. Ali said that it reminded her of home, too, and he smiled and she saw that he had at least three gold teeth. Nick used to tease him that he looked like an extra from a Merchant Ivory film, possibly *The Remains of the Day*, but

Mr. Artouche had never been to the cinema in England and the joke was lost on him.

"Did you know that his wife cleaned offices all night so that they could pay for their eldest son to go to private school?" Ali asked.

"I didn't," said Jake. "And now I'll never have the chance to ask him because he's gone, too. I wonder when all this is over what will actually be left? I mean, how many of Mum and Dad's friends have stuck around? Dad's gone. Malea's gone. And my grandfather is slowly drowning at the bottom of a wine bottle, vengefully supplied by my grandmother."

"It's best not to think about the future too much," said Ali gently. "Take each day as it comes."

"Or each meal as it comes, like Izzy," said Jake. "You know, sometimes I wish that I had a borderline eating disorder, just to have something to focus on that didn't have anything to do with all this. I wish I had the luxury of spending two hours deliberating whether to eat a plate of smoked mackerel and half a Ryvita."

They were in a side street, just off the Earls Court Road. They stopped as a small group of disheveled-looking men poured out of an imposing double door in the narrow pedestrian walkway. They were wearing crumpled suits, their shirts flapped around their hips in the breeze, and their ties, the kind with tiny elephant motifs, were askew.

"Where next? Might as well party while Rome burns," slurred one of the men.

"Have you calculated your net worth recently?" asked another. "Because our stock's worth fuck—in fact, it's worth less than fuck."

"Closed off seven percent today, and Monday's going to be a bloodbath," said the drunker one of the group.

"What I really don't get, I really don't fucking get, is why Fuld said the bank had plenty of capital and then reported a two-point-eight-billion-pound loss. It makes us look as though we don't know what the fuck we're doing."

"Skinner's fucked us all up the arse. Made us look like a bunch of fucking criminals as well as a bunch of fucking incompetents."

"He was right, though. He saw this one coming. Can't take that away from him. He was just trying to hedge." The others laughed uproariously.

"Who do you think he had on the inside?"

"I heard it was his wife."

"Let's get a drink," said Ali, anxiously pushing Jake toward the door of the club. She looked at his face and could tell from the tightened jaw and curl of his upper lip that he had heard. They both looked up to see where they were heading.

"Whispers," read the huge flashing neon sign above the door.

A naked neon woman with flashing pink nipples lay on her side on top of the W.

One of the men turned to Jake.

"Go for the Catholic girls, the guilt gives them a different taste." He leered, pressing a finger into Jake's chest.

A bouncer asked them both for ID. He led them downstairs into a cavernous underground room and asked them if they wanted to sit at the bar or whether they wanted a booth.

"What's the difference?" asked Ali.

"Booth is more private." The bouncer winked.

"Booth, then," shouted Ali above the noise. As their eyes adjusted to the dark, Ali saw the room was full of young women in varying states of undress. On a stage behind the bar, five or six girls were pole-dancing. Men, it was mostly men, although Ali counted five other women among the audience, looked up at the dancers as they performed for them. Occasionally one waved a note at a particular girl who then bent down to allow the man to tuck it in her knickers.

"I think this is a lap-dancing club," Jake shouted in her ear.

"Great detective work, Watson," said Ali.

It was too difficult to be heard over the music. They followed the bouncer to the other side of the room to a crescent-shaped booth flanked with a comfortable leather-look banquette. There were two small tables at each end of the crescent. Jake headed for the middle ground, leaving a space for Ali to his right. The bouncer handed them a thick leather-bound menu, and Ali was mildly surprised to hear Jake ordering lobster Thermidor and a bottle of champagne.

"Have you ever done this before?" she shouted over a song by the Black Eyed Peas.

"Absolutely not," Jake shouted back in her ear. "I just think it would be helpful to have something to do with our hands." He pointed across the room. There was a man at the bar, fingers magnetically hovering in front of a pair of breasts as a woman bent over to put her arms around him. Round the corner of the booth beside them, a woman straddled a middle-aged man who feverishly kneaded her buttocks, despite the signs hanging at the bar warning that men shouldn't touch the dancers.

"I think we should go," said Ali, her eyes glancing back and forth along the bar that dominated the center of the room. She couldn't pick out Katya, but she was sure this was the place where she worked. It hadn't yet occurred to her that Katya might be one of the dancers.

"You know," said Jake, leaning back against the faux leather banquette, "in some ways, we couldn't have chosen a better place. There's no way those stooges are going to let a photographer in here, and it's so dark I can hardly even see your face. No one will notice us. They're too busy having a good time."

He closed his eyes in mock blindness and searched for Ali's face with his hand. He slowly ran three fingers from the top of her forehead down over her brow and nose and onto her chin. A woman, dressed in a G-string and tiny bikini top, interrupted them.

"Do you want me to dance for you both?" she asked in an Eastern European accent. "I like to do couples. I can do half a dance each."

"No, thanks," said Jake politely.

"I'll give you a discount," said the girl, leaning toward Jake so that her breasts rested perilously close to his gaze, "it would be a pleasure to dance for such an attractive couple. Say, twenty pounds each?"

"Maybe another time," said Jake. "Try us a bit later."

"Why did you say that?" asked Ali, as the girl curled away on precariously high heels to the booth next door.

"I didn't want her to feel rejected," he said.

"I think you're injecting too much emotion into the relationship," said Ali. "This is a purely mercantile arrangement."

Jake was looking at the woman dancing on the pole behind the bar, her legs slowly scissoring in the air until she was doing the splits. Her breasts somehow managed to defy gravity by remaining at right angles. It was a skilled performance, although the middle-aged men watching from tables around the bar were more interested in her body than her technique. A few cheered; one asked her to take off her knickers and do the same thing again naked. When she refused, he laughed and waved a wad of twenty-pound notes in her face. Every time she said no, he added another twenty-pound note. When he reached a hundred pounds, she took the money and gave it to one of the bouncers to look after. She peeled off her knickers, catching the heel of her shoe in the elastic, and began again. Ali noticed that the girl behind the bar discreetly removed them and neatly folded them up as you might with a child.

"I could have done this instead of becoming a nanny," mused Ali. "Plenty of students do."

"Selling your body is the logical culmination of the capitalist dream," said Jake. "The globalization of the East European sex industry began with the fall of the Berlin Wall and the end of communism. Everything has its price. That book on your bedside table is all about how the social contract turned into the sexual contract."

"It's not freedom," said Ali.

"It's freedom for some but not for others," argued Jake.

The bouncer who showed them to the booth came across and asked if they were looking for a particular kind of girl. Since they had rejected the petite Eastern European brunette, he wondered if they might prefer an Oriental girl. "We have some lovely exotic Thai girls," he explained, "and a couple of spicy Latinos. They're very good with beginners. Very warm. There's a few English girls, too, if you want someone who speaks the vernacular."

He was like a kindly and patient waiter, relaying news of today's specials.

"Can you explain how it all works?" asked Jake. "We're novices here."

"Absolute beginners," reiterated Ali.

"A topless dance costs twenty pounds, and it's ten quid more if the girl is naked," he explained. "There's a no-touching rule. You have to keep your hands on the bench. She can touch you, but you can't touch her."

"Do you have to pay to talk?" asked Jake.

"Time is money." The man smiled. "Twenty minutes of hospitality costs two hundred pounds. If you want to talk, phone a friend."

"Are there any tall, blond, long-legged Ukrainian girls with large, firm breasts?" Ali asked him.

"Ali," Jake said, laughing, "we're not going there."

The bouncer pulled out a tiny flashlight from one pocket and a handwritten list from another and searched for names.

"How about Lara?" he asked, pointing to a bored-looking woman sitting at a table beside the bar.

"Bigger breasts and longer legs," Ali requested.

"Are you doing this for me?" Jake asked. "Because big-breasted blondes aren't really my thing."

"Or the girl dancing at the moment?" the bouncer suggested. "She's more expensive than some of the others."

"Why?" asked Ali.

"Watch her dance and you'll understand," he said.

Ali stood up and took a couple of paces toward the bar out of Jake's line of vision. The girl on stage wound herself around the pole like a snake. She moved languidly, almost lazily, without looking at the men gathered below. Ali turned to the bouncer and beamed.

"Great," she said. "We'll have her."

"I'll get her after she's finished. Tonya's on for fifteen minutes, then she's all yours," said the man. "If you're interested we have even more private facilities upstairs."

"Just one more thing," Ali asked. "Are they all named after characters in *Doctor Zhivago*?"

"I can't believe you've done that," said Jake, shaking his head so vigorously that his dark curls bounced from side to side. He poured himself another glass of champagne. It spilled over the edge of the glass. "What are you going to do when she comes over?"

"We'll negotiate a price, and then we'll get her to dance for us," said Ali. "You can't go to a lap-dancing club and leave without a lap dance. It's like going to Corfu without tasting the honey, or going to Cromer without eating a crab, or going to Australia without stroking a koala . . ."

"I get the picture," interrupted Jake, "although I doubt many other people would see it that way."

"How would they see it?" asked Ali.

"They would find it seriously dodgy that the family nanny took me to a lap-dancing club and then chose a girl to dance for me," said Jake. "Can you imagine the headlines?"

"Don't be so tabloid about it, Jake," said Ali. "Fathers used to take their sons to prostitutes for their first sexual experience."

"You're not my dad, and this is not my first sexual experience," Jake pointed out.

"But I do have authority over you." Ali smiled, leaning toward him to kiss him on the lips.

"And where will you be while all this is going on?" Jake asked.

"Right here beside you," said Ali. "In case anything goes wrong."

"What could go wrong?" Jake asked.

"You might be tempted to touch her," Ali suggested. "Or you might finish early. Or you might get a cricked neck from staring up at her breasts."

"I can't have a lap dance with you sitting beside me," said Jake. "What will you do while I'm having it?"

"I'll eat the lobster Thermidor," said Ali.

"It just wouldn't feel right doing it in front of you eating a lobster, Ali," pleaded Jake.

"Then I'll have the prawn and avocado instead," said Ali.

"It's got nothing to do with the food, it's to do with you," said Jake.

"These men are all doing it in front of their friends," said Ali, pointing at three men on the adjacent table.

"It just doesn't feel right," said Jake, nervously eyeing the woman coming toward them. She was wearing a tiny miniskirt, gold shoes, and a red sequined top. Except, as she sashayed into the booth, Jake realized that he knew her.

"Katya?" said Jake, the expression on his face alternating between astonishment and relief. Ali nodded.

"I got you good." Ali laughed.

"Did you know she'd be here?" Jake asked.

"Curtain open or closed?" Katya smiled.

"Closed," said Ali.

"I took a punt," said Ali. "I want to ask her some questions. I think she might be helpful to your mum."

"Hello, Jake." Katya ran a hand through Jake's curls, saying something in Ukrainian.

"He has grown into a handsome man," she said admiringly before sitting down between them.

Katya's clothes were garish, and the heavy makeup drew too much attention to her eyes and lips. She had lost weight, which accentuated her long legs and broad shoulders.

"Welcome to the land that feminism forgot." She smiled. Her breasts were precariously tethered in the well-engineered red top, somewhere between a bra and a bikini.

"I am truly sorry for everything that has happened to your family," said Katya apologetically, turning toward Jake.

"It's no worse than what happened to you," said Jake.

She leaned over and took a drink from Ali's untouched glass of champagne. The bouncer poked his head through the curtain.

"Give them a special hospitality rate," she instructed him. She turned to Ali. "Otherwise you'll end up spending two hundred pounds for twenty minutes of my time."

"So what's it like working here?" Ali asked.

"I'm going to tell you the only three facts about lap dancing that you need to know," said Katya, taking another sip of Ali's champagne. Jake offered to pour her a glass, but she said she didn't drink on the job. "One, it's ideal for English men, because they can't dance. Two, it makes it difficult to like men. And three, you double your tips when you're ovulating."

"How do you know that?" asked Jake.

"Some American scientists did a study," said Katya.

"Couldn't you do something else?" asked Ali.

"I earn good money." Katya shrugged. "I'm the best dancer, so they look after me well. The other girls are great. Most of them are students, but there are a couple of nurses and a prison warden, and a couple of nannies. It's a good club. But I miss Thomas, and some of the men are awful."

"Have you seen him since you left?" Ali asked.

"Ned has brought him to see me a couple of times," Katya said.

"Have you seen Ned since this scandal broke?" Jake asked. Katya eyed Ali.

"We won't say anything," she promised. Katya nodded.

Ali explained to Katya that Bryony had been arrested and accused of passing on information about her clients to Nick. Katya shook her head.

"She didn't do it," she said. She paused for a moment. "But Ned and Nick did. Nick spied on Bryony to get the information for Ned."

"Would you tell the FSA what you know?" asked Jake.

"Sure," agreed Katya.

It was the early hours of Monday morning when Jake and Ali arrived back at Holland Park Crescent. They found the twins asleep, lying in exactly the same position on their sides, facing each other, thumbs in mouths. Perfectly symmetrical. They were wearing pajama bottoms but had removed their tops, and Ali could see their torsos glistened with sweat. She opened the window. The long, hot summer had sucked the energy out of the night air, and the breeze barely stirred the curtains. The duvet was lying on the floor, and both guinea pigs were asleep on top of it. All the lights were on. Ali kissed them both on the cheek, gently closed the door, and headed up to Jake's room.

Ali smiled as she came in and saw the signed Arsenal shirt and the White Stripes poster. She went over to the photos of Jake hanging on the wall and touched them tenderly. Her hand drifted to the chest of drawers. There was such an array of objects scattered over its surface that the wood beneath was barely visible. An out-of-charge iPod, hair ties belonging to Ali, an empty box of condoms, loose cigarettes, a couple of tampons, a silver bangle of Ali's that Jake liked wearing, an eyeliner. Ali's hand hovered above them. She was about to remove her stuff from the pile, then changed her mind. She liked this casual entanglement of their lives. It suggested a permanence that was comforting.

The room was like an old and familiar friend. She loved the way it smelled of them. She loved the deep red walls. She loved the way that no one else came in here, not even Leicester, who had taken to roaming the length and breadth of the house with his blanket in his mouth in search of a secure berth. Mostly Ali loved the way it belonged to them. It was the only place they could be completely uninhibited together.

Her ears were still ringing from the noise of the music at the lap-dancing club. Whispers had been an assault on the senses. It was too loud, too dark, and too airless.

This must be intentional, so that no one could think clearly about what they were doing there, decided Ali. Otherwise they might notice that the dancer who collected the £20 notes had an ugly bruise on her right buttock, that her bikini top was old and frayed, and that her smile stopped as soon as the money was paid.

"What are you doing?" asked Jake, who was already lying on the bed, hands behind his head, legs splayed, with an erection so big that it made Ali smile at the comedy of the human body. "I've got a lot of pent-up frustration that needs releasing."

Ali laughed. She began slowly undressing in front of him, tantalizingly removing her clothes, rolling them into a ball, and throwing them at his head. Jake pleaded for mercy. She felt pleasantly drunk. Tomorrow they would tell Bryony what they had learned from Katya. Perhaps, later, they could even tell her about their relationship.

"There wasn't a dancer in that club more gorgeous than you." Jake sighed as Ali sauntered naked toward the bed.

"Do you want a lap dance?" she teased.

"As long as it lasts longer than two minutes," he said, and groaned.

"I think those clubs encourage premature ejaculation," said Ali as she slid along his body.

On the other side of the Atlantic, a lonely figure was also making his way home, after a long weekend at the office. Dick Fuld, guest of honor at the Skinners' Christmas party two years earlier, was being driven to his New York apartment from Lehman's office at 745 Seventh Avenue. He looked impassively ahead, as if paralyzed, as the car sped through the empty streets. The usual arrogance and bluster had disappeared as he absorbed the news that the last-minute deal with Barclays had fallen apart and his bank was to file for Chapter 11 bankruptcy, in what would be the biggest bankruptcy in U.S. history. Downstairs in the kitchen at Holland Park Crescent, Bryony was watching these scenes on television.

"The ships have all sunk at once," she muttered to herself. The screen was now showing the front page of *The Wall Street Journal*: "Crisis on Wall Street As Lehman Totters, Merrill Is Sold and AIG Seeks to Raise Cash."

A panel of experts began discussing the repercussions of this new catastrophe. One of them described it as a "financial tsunami." Felix Naylor pointed out that Lehman's employees were unusual in that they owned a third of the company through share options that were now worthless. Someone mentioned greedy bankers and cited the example of the insider-trading charges against Nick Skinner and Ned Wilbraham, "two of the highest-paid bankers in the City."

Bryony glanced at the clock on the wall and saw that it was seven o'clock in the morning. She checked her new pay-as-you-go mobile phone to see if there were any messages from Nick. There were none. She went up into the drawing room and peeked through the curtains to find a crowd of photographers waiting outside. She needed to get everyone downstairs to face this day together.

Ablaze with nervous energy and pent-up anxiety, Bryony ran upstairs, two at a time, until she reached Jake's room. She didn't bother to knock on his door. Instead she clumsily turned the handle, immediately waking up Ali, the lighter sleeper of the two. Ali watched as Bryony stood in the doorway, squinting to adjust to the poor light in the room. She calculated that she had a couple of seconds until Bryony absorbed the scene before her.

Ali forced herself to take shallow breaths. She remained completely still, lying on her side, naked, on top of the duvet, beside Jake. They were facing each other and holding hands. Ali tried to disentangle her fingers, but Jake resisted and instead gripped hers tighter in his sleep, pulling Ali toward him, nuzzling her neck. Bryony took a half-step back toward the door, as though she had been winded.

For a moment Ali wondered whether Bryony had seen them and decided that this was a problem she was going to confront later, when she had dealt with other more pressing issues. Or perhaps she didn't mind that her son and her nanny were sleeping with each other, as long as they didn't advertise their relationship in public. The truth was, for a couple of seconds, Bryony was frozen.

Ali closed her eyes, remembering how Hector and Alfie used to think that no one could see them if their eyes were shut, and wishing it were true. There were a couple of seconds of respite, and then the sound of Bryony screaming pierced the silence. Ali couldn't remember what she did first. Did she try to pull the duvet around her? Or was the weight of Jake's body too heavy to gain any purchase? Maybe she grabbed Jake's arm to wake him up? Probably the latter, she decided, because the noise Bryony made was so animal that she could hear the twins stir in her bedroom below. Ali saw the look of revulsion on Bryony's face and knew her relationship with Jake was over.

"What's going on?" Jake asked sleepily as he sat up, rubbing his eyes.

Bryony wasn't looking at him. In a storm of anger, she rushed to Ali's side of the bed and began picking up clothes randomly from the floor and throwing them at her. Knickers, bras, trousers, T-shirts. Many of them belonged to Ali. Some of them had even once belonged to Bryony, a fact that seemed to enflame her further. She noticed Ali's things on the chest of drawers and swept them all onto the floor with her arm. Her eyes were flashing, and her hair was wild. Ali imagined she might physically attack her.

"Get out, get out," Bryony screamed over and over, her body quivering with anger. "We've done everything we could for you, and this is how you repay us."

Ali had always envisaged that one day she might be able to have a rational conversation with Bryony about her relationship with Jake. Imbued with the optimism of those in love, she had even allowed herself to dare to think that Bryony might share their happiness.

She imagined telling Bryony that it had begun only recently, that nothing had happened before Jake went to university, and that they were properly in love. She would have agreed that it was unorthodox, and imagined Bryony telling her the best relationships always were.

She would have explained to Bryony that she could understand if she didn't want anyone to know in the current circumstances. She would have told her that her feelings for Jake were genuine and that she was planning to move to Oxford so that they could be at university together. In the event, it was all a hideous muddle of ugly words and accusations.

"You've let me down, just like the rest of them," Bryony howled. Ali curled into Jake's arms, and he wrapped himself around her, trying to protect her from the flying clothes and the occasional book. Apart from Nick, who else had let her down? Ali wondered. Was she talking about Foy? Or Izzy? Or nannies gone by?

Bryony accused her of everything from selling stories about their family to the newspapers to stealing the photographs missing from the drawing room. She even suggested that Ali had slept with Nick. She called her lots of names that Ali later tried to forget. Slut, tart, whore were the ones she remembered. "I really thought I could count on you. I want you out of here before the end of the day."

It was like poisoning a beautiful garden, Ali had told her friends later.

"You can't do this, Mum," Jake had shouted. "It's as much my fault as Ali's."

Ali felt hurt by his reaction. He should have been defending their relationship rather than conceding culpability. Later, she understood it was an attempt to be emollient to someone who was out of her mind with stress. At the time, however, it had seemed more like surrender.

25

December 2009

Ali saw the Skinners one last time. Just before Christmas the following year, she happened to pick up a crumpled newspaper from the table in a café where she had gone to crack the introduction of her final essay of the term. She was completing the final year of her degree in London, and the café was a haven away from the noisy flat she shared with other students in Mile End Road. She turned to the favorite destination of procrastinating students, the obituaries section, and beside the two main pieces, found a short sidebar dedicated to Foy Chesterton, "entrepreneur who introduced smoked salmon to the masses."

It was exactly twelve paragraphs long. Ali searched beneath the facts, to see if there was any hint of the scandal that had enveloped the family seventeen months earlier, and was pleased to find none, unless you included a passing reference to Foy being a *bon viveur*. Otherwise it was a straightforward chronology of his life.

Ali remembered how often he had threatened to regale her with the history of Freithshire Fisheries, and how everyone had always shouted him down. Now, as she read, she felt regretful that she had never bothered to hear him out, because it was a predictably colorful story.

It described how he had left school at sixteen, spent a year in Greece, and started a business importing olive oil to the UK, at a time when it could be bought only in pharmacies that recommended it to soften earwax. "Like using Meursault on carpet stains," Foy had apparently said. When he was twenty, he took a three-month sabbatical from his business to walk around the British coast. But he never got beyond Sutherland in northern Scotland, because he was distracted by a small smoked-salmon farm that he found there, and by Tita Marshall, the daughter of its owner. They were married the same year, 1959, and their first child, Bryony, was born three years later.

It went on to detail other key moments in his life: how Foy was among the first to talk about the health benefits of eating fish, and made it his personal crusade to introduce smoked salmon to every household in Britain; how he had a walk-on part in the 1963 film *Tom Jones*, because he was friendly with Susannah York, who played the main female part. Did he sleep with her, too? Ali marveled. How he was the centerpiece of a BBC documentary about the Hebridean islands, directed by his oldest friend, Julian Peterson.

In his later years it said he had returned to his roots, producing olive oil from his small holding in Corfu. The penultimate paragraph described how he stunned guests at his seventieth-birthday party by singing all six verses of "American Pie." Finally, it mentioned that he lived in Holland Park and was survived by his wife, Tita, and their two daughters, Bryony and Hester. Both names were of Greek origin, reflecting the family's long love affair with Corfu.

Foy Peterson, entrepreneur, was born on June 9, 1938. He died on December 5, 2009, aged 71.

It didn't mention how he died. Ali imagined it was another stroke. What was the point of sucking all the fun out of life just to live a couple of years longer? he used to say to Ali. *Carpe diem* was the motto he wanted written on his gravestone. So Foy continued to smoke cigars and drink red wine smuggled into the drawing room at Holland Park Crescent by complicit visitors, including his wife and sometimes his two eldest grandchildren. "A life well lived," the obituary writer concluded, and Ali couldn't argue with that. The problem with people who live life to the fullest is that they don't recognize their capacity to cause pain to those around them. They're too busy having a good time to notice that others might not be.

She tore the page out of the newspaper and put it in her bag, not sure exactly why she was keeping it. Perhaps she would send it to her parents. They would be interested in Foy's story, and since she had left her job and gone back to university, they could talk about the Skinners without the resentment that existed in the past.

She flicked through to the death notices and saw that his funeral would take place the following weekend in a local church, close to the village where he was born. It was a few miles from where the Skinners used to have their second home. Thornberry Manor had been sold. Katya had shown her the page advertising its sale in a copy of *Country Life* left at her flat by Ned.

Ali stood at the back of the church, just in front of the vestry. It provided the best vantage point to watch mourners arrive, and meant that she could hide behind the font when the family came in. The church was packed, and there were people standing outside. Four loudspeakers had been erected in the graveyard to broadcast the service. It was a windswept, rainy day, and through the open door Ali could see a brightly colored landscape of open umbrellas. She looked down at her watch and noted that it was already five minutes behind schedule. Timing never had been Foy's good point. She smiled to herself and turned to the order of service.

There were two readings. Jake would recite a passage from *The Tempest* ("We are such stuff as dreams are made on"), a decision, Ali liked to think, that might have been inspired by her pointing out the play's connection with Corfu. Bryony's reading was a poem by Dylan Thomas, "Do Not Go Gentle into That Good Night." An inspired choice, thought Ali, muttering the second line to herself: "Old age should burn and rave at close of day." That's what they should inscribe on Foy's gravestone.

She felt suddenly sorry that she hadn't seen him before he died. He was one of the few adults during her two years at Holland Park Crescent who never treated her as though she were invisible. It might have been because his need for approval meant he required affirmation from everyone around him, but nevertheless his attention had mostly felt like a blessing. And the very traits that made him impossible to his family were also those that made him so entertaining to others. He had also leapt in at the very end to defend her from Bryony's accusations.

She felt tears well up and turned to the rest of the order of service. She was crying for herself, not for him. There were no surprises with the hymns. "All Things Bright and Beautiful" was, perhaps, a little feminine for Foy's taste. "Jerusalem" and "Dear Lord and Father of Mankind" were more robust choices.

It would be an event characterized more by what wouldn't happen rather than what would happen, Ali decided. Nick Skinner wouldn't be making an appearance; Julian Peterson wouldn't be giving the address; Hester wouldn't be reading the lesson, because she had argued with her mother about biodegradable coffins.

Ali craned her neck over the people standing in front of her to see who she could recognize. Desmond Darke and his wife were in a pew toward the back of the church. Ali could see the profile of his angular face. He gazed into the distance, his features set hard, probably engaged in an internal debate about whether Foy really deserved his presence here. He was studiously avoiding the small, dark figure beside him, who Ali immediately recognized as Malea. The church was full, and she was pressed uncomfortably close to his left flank, her face impassive as always.

She could see Sophia Wilbraham's parents a few pews in front. Neither Sophia nor Ned was present. It had caused a huge row, but inevitably Sophia had prevailed. Ali knew this because after seeing the notice about Foy's death she had immediately gone round to

Katya's flat. Ned had sheepishly emerged from the bedroom and asked Ali's advice on whether he should ignore his wife and just turn up at the funeral. He was still promising to leave Sophia and have a baby with Katya. He had even brought Thomas to Whispers during the day a couple of times to see her. But it was an act of desperation, because he could sense Katya was in retreat.

Toward the front of the left-hand row of pews, Ali recognized Julian and Eleanor Peterson. She was clutching a handkerchief and dabbed at her eyes every few minutes. She stood out from the crowd because she was wearing a 1950s-style lemon-colored dress. It was the one Foy had described her wearing in his dream. Ali had recently learned from Katya that Eleanor had been diagnosed with an inoperable brain tumor that made her behavior unpredictable and sometimes aggressive. It explained her extraordinary outburst at Foy's birthday party but didn't soften Tita's attitude to Foy, who was never allowed back home. Fi Seldon-Kent sat in a chair at the back, looking down at her notebook. After a few minutes Ali realized that she must be organizing the funeral.

Nick was probably footing the bill. Ali knew from Ned that Nick was very busy with his "fantastic new job" at another investment bank. He had been guaranteed a first-year bonus, double his last one at Lehman's. Those who played a part in creating the crisis would be the last ones to pay for it, thought Ali.

At quarter past twelve the church fell silent as the coffin was brought in. The family walked slowly behind in pairs. Tita came in first, holding Izzy's arm. She looked straight ahead, tall enough to see over the single wreath on the oak lid to the end of the nave. She was wearing a tailored gray jacket and skirt that matched her eyes. Izzy was wearing a black minidress and short coat that showed off her long legs to best effect. Ali thought she saw a purple streak in her dark hair, but the heavy makeup and black nail varnish had been replaced by a softer, more feminine look. She sat down beside a boy waiting in the pew for her. He put his arm around her, and Izzy leaned in to him. Her eyes were puffy from crying. Izzy was closer to her grandfather than any of the other children. Tita sat erectly beside her. She didn't look round once. Both hands rested on the front of the pew, holding the order of service.

Jake came in with Bryony. Ali forced herself to look at Bryony to avoid staring at him, although she could feel his presence in her stomach. Bryony's hair was longer than Ali remembered. The contrast with her black suit was dazzling—like looking into the sun, thought Ali. Behind her were Hester and Rick and the other grandchildren.

The twins wore identical black suits.

Ali hadn't seen Hector and Alfie since the day Bryony had discovered her and Jake in bed. She had said good-bye to them in the drawing room a couple of hours later. She could still remember every detail of that terrible scene. For the first time since she moved into Holland Park Crescent, she had worn shoes in the room. Her hastily packed bags were stacked in the hall. There was the old rucksack that she had brought with her the day she moved in, and another bag that Jake had found for her. Jake pleaded with her not to leave, but it was impossible for her to stay.

"How can I?" Ali told him. Finally he acquiesced. He never offered to go with her.

Ali remembered how the twins had clung on to her bare arms and legs until they were stuck together with sweat and tears. Bryony had tried to peel them off, but each time she managed to get one of them to detach, the other clung back on with ever more determination. The next day, Ali's legs and arms were black and blue with bruises and there were so many scratches from their fingernails that she had to wear long sleeves for the next couple of weeks. They had screamed so loudly that Desmond Darke had rung on the doorbell to make sure everything was all right. Alfie and Hector had fought harder for her than Jake, thought Ali. Perhaps he realized that a relationship forged in the shadows would shrivel in the glare of daylight.

"Just wanted to check everything was in order," Desmond said gruffly when Izzy answered the door. "You've put the people in this street through enough shame." He craned his neck to try and see what was going on.

"You're a pompous old fart," said Izzy, slamming the door in his face.

Bryony had pleaded with Foy, Jake, and Izzy to help her with Hector and Alfie, but they had all refused.

"I don't disapprove of their relationship," Foy had shouted over the twins' screams. "You're being completely irrational."

"That's because your moral compass is so wildly out of synch," Bryony had screamed back at him. "You're no example of how to behave."

"Your mother and I have managed to stay together for almost fifty years—that's a kind of achievement," Foy said with some of his old bluster.

"At what cost?" Bryony shouted at him. "You're not even living together."

"Don't take out your frustrations over my behavior on Ali and Jake," said Foy. "It's not fair."

"She's the nanny," Bryony had yelled. "She's meant to be looking after his interests. God knows when it started."

"She's four years older than him," Foy pointed out. "Hardly makes her a kiddie fiddler. And I told you when she moved in that it was asking for trouble employing an attractive girl with a hormonal teenager in the house."

"She's one of our employees," shouted Bryony. "We pay her to be loyal."

"Right now, she's our only employee," said Izzy. "And when was the last time you paid her? It might be a good idea to keep her. What does it matter if Ali and Jake are in love? She's a big improvement on Lucy."

"Imagine if those tabloid journalists find out," said Bryony. "I can see the headlines now. Don't you think they've raked over our lives enough?"

"Who's going to tell them?" challenged Foy. "The only people who know are the people in this room, and we'll take the *omertà*, won't we?"

For a brief moment Ali thought she might still be in with a chance. But Bryony's chin was set in that way that indicated her mind was made up.

"She doesn't belong here," Bryony said.

"Where will you go?" Jake asked when the taxi arrived to collect Ali.

"Katya's," she whispered. "I'll give you a call when I get there." The last noise she heard was the sound of Hector and Alfie crying and Foy trying to soothe them. She didn't look back.

Instead of phoning Jake, however, Ali called Felix Naylor and told him that she needed to meet with him urgently. Felix started to explain that he was up to his neck covering the Lehman's crisis. In the background Ali could hear televisions blaring and raised voices. He sounded distracted. He must be at work already, she decided, looking at her watch. It was quarter to nine in the morning.

"It's about Bryony," Ali said. "And Nick. You told me to call if I found out anything significant."

"Can't it wait?" Felix asked, unable to mask his impatience. Ali thought for a moment. She could meet him the following day. But she knew that if she didn't unburden herself immediately, her resolve might fade. She needed to tell him now, before the hurt and the resentment set in her body and she decided Bryony wasn't worth saving.

"I have some information that might help Bryony. I'm not working for the Skinners anymore, and I'm planning to go away." Ali knew he would come. In the same way that she knew, if she called Jake to ask him the same question, he wouldn't.

They met in the café in Bloomsbury. The music was turned off this time in favor of a television loudly reporting that America's fourth-biggest investment bank, Lehman Brothers, had filed for Chapter 11 bankruptcy protection in New York in the early hours of Monday morning.

They sat companionably beside each other opposite the screen. Occasionally, Felix's hand drifted toward the television to indicate some new angle on the unfolding drama, and Ali read another breaking news alert. "Merrill Lynch Sold to Bank of America," "Fed Bails Out AIG."

Each time, Felix swore under his breath. When the iconic images of Lehman's employees carrying cardboard boxes from their offices in Canary Wharf flashed across the screen, a couple of students on the table beside them cheered.

"Greedy bastards," one of them said.

"This is the banking sector's Nine-Eleven," Felix told Ali. "It's financial Armageddon."

Felix was so excited that even the tips of his ears burned red. Ali was unsure how to win his attention. So she came up with a headline of her own.

"I've been having a relationship with Jake," she announced, as she saw the footage of Dick Fuld, the guest of honor at the Christmas party two years earlier, being driven away from the Lehman's office in New York in the dead of night. For the first time, Felix looked away from the screen. "Bryony has found out."

"You've been sleeping with Jake?" he asked incredulously, his eyebrows raised in perfect arcs of surprise. Ali nodded.

"She's thrown me out." She waited for a few words of sympathy or a comforting pat on the arm. But none came.

"Are you going to sell your story?" Felix asked, giving her a deep, penetrating look that Ali imagined he used when trying to gauge whether an interviewee was about to answer a question truthfully.

"Of course not," said Ali, affronted. Felix looked relieved. He thought for a moment.

"Do you want money?" he asked, as though suddenly understanding why she wanted to see him. "I know that Bryony has some in reserve."

"I'm not going to do anything to hurt Jake," said Ali defensively. "Not everyone is motivated by money. You're not."

"Sorry, I just assumed . . ." said Felix.

"Assume nothing," said Ali. "Isn't that what a good journalist does?"

"What is it you want to tell me?" Felix asked.

Ali urged him to open his notebook and gave him a pencil from her pocket. It was one that Jake had chewed. She felt the first wave of loss sweep through her body.

"Write it down so you don't forget the details." He smiled at her persistence.

Ali outlined everything that she had learned from Katya. She spoke slowly and precisely, trying to recall the exact order of their conversation. She explained how Nick Skinner and Ned Wilbraham hatched their insider-trading plan five years ago as a way of making easy pocket money. The first year or so they kept their transactions simple, buying small quantities of shares using information Nick had purloined from Bryony. Nick always provided the information, and Ned always bought the shares through his broker. It was a modus operandi that never seemed to fail.

"Are you telling me that Nick spied on Bryony to buy shares in deals that she was working on for clients?" Felix asked incredulously. Ali nodded.

"He looked through documents Bryony brought home. He knew the password to her BlackBerry. Sometimes they bought shares in companies they knew were about to lose value to cover their tracks. The money went into a bank account in Katya's name. They shared the profits later."

"Has Katya told anyone else about this?" Felix asked, chewing the end of Ali's pencil thoughtfully.

"She thought she would be implicated because the bank account was in her name," said Ali. "I'm the only person who knows, apart from Jake."

Ali continued. She said that as time went by and no one seemed to notice what they were doing, they became more reckless. When Nick realized that Lehman's was in trouble, he started raising the stakes, as a way of compensating for the disaster he saw ahead. This must have been when the FSA noticed.

"Nick wanted to know where Bryony was traveling to and who she was meeting, to try and work out what companies might be involved in takeover deals," said Ali.

She told him how Nick and Ned communicated using pay-as-you-go mobile phones, replacing the SIM card every couple of weeks. She explained how Nick described Bryony to Ned as "the golden goose," because she had information that they could use to buy shares just before companies announced new deals.

"Do you have any evidence to prove any of this?" Felix asked. His tone was interested, not suspicious.

Ali started from the beginning. She told him how she had caught Nick using Jake's computer early one morning, a few months after she started working at Holland Park Crescent, and explained that this was the only computer that the FSA hadn't seized in the raid because Jake had it in Oxford.

"Why do you think this is significant?" Felix asked, leaning toward Ali.

"I think he was using Jake's computer to look at documents that he sent to himself from Bryony's BlackBerry," said Ali. "He had her phone with him, and he knew her password, because I saw him accessing her e-mails when we were in Corfu."

Ali put her bag on the table and brought out the leather-bound daybook. She gave it to Felix.

"This has all the dates in it and details of where Bryony was traveling," she said, pressing it into Felix's hands. "I think Nick used this to try and work out what deals she was working on so that he could gauge which shares to buy."

She pulled out a matchbox from the bag. "These are SIM cards that were hidden in Nick's office at home. The FSA didn't find them because Foy had moved in there. They'll show that Nick and Ned only communicated with each other. Do you think this might help Bryony clear her name?"

"I think it might," said Felix, clasping her hand. "You've done a very good thing. You don't deserve to be treated the way she has treated you."

Six months later, the FSA's charges against Nick had been thrown out on a technicality. Nick's lawyer managed to prove that in each of the eight charges of insider trading, rumors of takeovers had been published on the Internet, either in online chat rooms or in esoteric online financial bulletins. Since the information was already publicly available, technically it was no longer inside information. Nick was off the hook.

From the evidence supplied by Ali, Bryony, however, knew that Nick was guilty and that she could never trust him again. Moreover, his actions had jeopardized her business and career. She had gone back to her company after the charges were dropped but had to build up her client base from scratch. It was only after news of their separation that people stopped viewing her with suspicion. No one thought Bryony complicit in her husband's activities, but many thought she had been careless. Now, of course, as she thought about this in the church, it struck Ali that in trying to save Bryony, she had destroyed their marriage.

Ali looked up again and saw that the twins had stopped in the middle of the aisle and turned toward each other, like a mirror image, their arms dropping to their sides. Everyone watched with rapt attention. From this distance even Ali couldn't tell them apart. She felt herself step forward. She wanted to go and kiss them, to stroke their hair and reassure them that everything would be fine. But then Jake turned around to persuade them to keep walking, holding out his own hand for them to take. It hovered in the air, and its familiarity was like a blow to Ali's solar plexus.

Jake saw her. For a moment, their eyes locked. Ali felt a familiar stab of desire and knew he felt it, too. She was relieved that amid the general chaos of the scandal, no one apart from his immediate family had ever known about their relationship.

Hector and Alfie took each other by the hand again and continued up the aisle. Jake turned away, chewing his lower lip. The twins went to sit in the pew behind Bryony with a woman Ali assumed was their new nanny. She was in her early forties. Hector sat in the middle, and the woman reached around them with a soft, comforting arm. Ali was pleased to find her reactions toward her replacement were uncomplicated. She was relieved at her warmth and felt no twinge of jealousy.

Just before the end of the service Ali slipped out, back into the shadows, before anyone noticed she had ever been there.

ACKNOWLEDGMENTS

I am very grateful to my editors, Sarah McGrath in New York and Mari Evans in London, for all their encouragement and enthusiasm, and to the rest of the team at Michael Joseph in the UK and Riverhead in the United States. Heartfelt thanks to my agent, Simon Trewin, and to Ariella Feiner.

Big debt to Ed Orlebar for putting up with it all. Thanks also to Mark Astaire, Aubrey Simpson-Orlebar, and Rupert Pitt for demystifying the world of finance, and to Tom Jones for his expertise on collateralized debt obligations. Elizabeth Robertson is a font of knowledge on insider trading. Thanks to all the nannies I spoke to, particularly Joanna Clark.

To gain insight into the collapse of Lehman's, I read the following excellent and entertaining books: *Too Big to Fail* by Andrew Ross Sorkin, *A Colossal Failure of Common Sense* by Larry McDonald, and *The Devil's Casino* by Vicky Ward.

I gathered lots of helpful background from *Whoops!* by John Lanchester and *Fool's Gold* by Gillian Tett.

As always, thanks to my first readers, Helen Townshend and Henry Tricks, and to Rosa Chavez and Isis Calderon. The following people have given vital encouragement at difficult moments: Becky Crichton-Miller, Charlotte Simpson-Orlebar, Hatty Skeet, and Roland Watson.

Some of the most helpful and insightful people have asked not to be identified, but you know who you are, and I am very grateful for your time and sharing your stories.